LP
JOHNST **Firestick**
FIREST
1 **Firestick ; 1**

Johnsto

FIRESTICK

FIRESTICK

WILLIAM W. JOHNSTONE AND J. A. JOHNSTONE

THORNDIKE PRESS
A part of Gale, a Cengage Company

LIBRARY OF CONGRESS CIP DATA ON FILE.
CATALOGUING IN PUBLICATION FOR THIS BOOK
IS AVAILABLE FROM THE LIBRARY OF CONGRESS

ISBN-13: 978-1-4328-8102-3 (hardcover alk. paper)

Published in 2021 by arrangement with Pinnacle Books, an imprint of Kensington Publishing Corp

Printed in Mexico
Print Number: 01   Print Year: 2021

FIRESTICK

CHAPTER 1

There was a time when Elwood McQueen considered wading into a good brawl with fists, feet, and elbows flying to be about as much fun as a fella could have with his britches still on. But those days were mostly past . . . Mostly.

And so it was, on a sunny afternoon in April when he got word of a ruckus breaking out in the Silver Spur Saloon, McQueen went there with the intention of taming things down, not joining in the ruckus. After all, as the duly appointed marshal of the little West Texas town of Buffalo Peak, that's what folks expected from him as part of his duties — to tame things down.

But no sooner had he stepped through the batwings of the Silver Spur than the strict performance of his duties was put to the test. For starters, the first thing he laid eyes on was the homely, angrily snarling face of Greely Dunlap. That alone was enough to sour the good intentions of practically anybody. And then the whiskey bottle came sailing through the air and nearly ended its flight against McQueen's forehead. He managed to duck at the last second, the bottle only skimming off his hat instead of splitting his skull.

"Now you made me waste a whole bottle of good whiskey, you duded-up son of a sidewinder," bellowed a tall, lanky cowpoke, addressing the man he had viciously swung the whiskey bottle at, missing his mark, and then losing his grip on the bottle when the man ducked. "That earns you more of an ass-whuppin' than you already had comin' to begin with!"

"You tell him, Grady," Greely Dunlap said, shouting encouragement to his younger and even homelier little brother. "A *double* ass-whuppin' is what's called for, says I, and there's no sense wastin' any more time about it."

"Make it a triple," added a third man, one Newt Woolsey by name, a short, stocky redhead who regularly hung around with — and got in trouble with — the Dunlap brothers. "I want me a piece of that slippery-fingered skunk, too, and I ain't about to be left out!"

The object of all this anger was a middle-aged man of average height and build who stood on the back side of a round-topped gaming table, where he and the trio now converging on him had apparently been playing cards. The individual being threatened was a stranger to McQueen. He had wavy yellow hair, with a smooth-shaven face made up of rather delicate features, and he was clad in a gray frock coat and black string tie, attire qualifying him for the "duded-up" assessment from Grady Dunlap.

But anyone bothering to look a little closer would have noted something more: There was a hard-edged wariness in the stranger's eyes that conveyed no hint of fear or delicate intentions when it came to what he was faced with.

"Be careful, Firestick," advised Art Farrelly, the balding fireplug of a bartender on duty at the Silver Spur that afternoon, as McQueen came out of his crouch and took a long stride forward. "Those Dunlaps are spoiling for a fight, and you know what mean drunks they can be."

"Yeah, well, gettin' damn near scalped by a flyin' whiskey bottle don't exactly put me in a friendly mood neither," McQueen muttered out the side of his mouth as he proceeded straight for the knot of men clustered around the card table.

There was only a handful of other customers in the place at that hour, a mixture of cowpokes and shiftless townies bellied up to the bar and shifted down a ways from where the trouble was getting ready to boil over. The sight of McQueen continuing to advance with fire in his eyes caused the bunch to collectively shift down a bit farther.

The way the four men at the table were positioned, only one of them — the yellow-haired stranger — was facing toward McQueen. This made him the only one with any awareness of the marshal's approach. Woolsey had his back turned completely, and the Dunlap brothers, closing in on the stranger from either side, were focused solely on him, their intended target.

The stranger's eyes widened hopefully for a moment, but then, having no way to be certain on whose side the big, wide-shouldered new arrival would turn out to be, they once again took on their wary appraisal.

"All right," McQueen said in a loud, clear voice as he stepped up close behind Woolsey. "Everybody smooth down your hackles and just stand easy. Whatever this is about, there ain't gonna be no lettin' it get out of hand."

"The hell there ain't," Greely barked a quick reply. The sudden intervention of McQueen's voice had caused him only the slightest start and wasn't enough to make him take his eyes off the stranger as he continued talking. "We caught this slick varmint cheatin' at cards and we're about to teach him how that don't go around here. But we ain't fixin' to gut him or shoot him — we ain't even heeled, just like you warned us when we come to town. So it ain't no never-mind of yours, Marshal. We're just gonna give him a good thumpin' to drive home the point of bein' more careful who he tries to cheat in the future."

"Yeah. Comes down to it, we'll practically be doin' a public service," added his brother, Grady.

"Nobody was being cheated, Marshal — if, in fact, that is your calling," said the stranger, addressing McQueen's lack of a badge, which he often neglected to pin on. "The truth of the matter is that the poor attitude these gentlemen display toward losing is matched only by the poor skill they display when it comes to playing poker."

"Now he's callin' us liars," said Woolsey, his words intentionally adding more fuel to the fire.

"That's a name I'll stand from no man!"

11

roared Grady in response. And before McQueen could say or do anything more to try and stop him, the older Dunlap brother accompanied this exclamation by unleashing a clubbing backhand aimed straight at the face of the yellow-haired man.

The stranger, somewhat distracted by the arrival of McQueen, was caught partially off guard. But his reflexes were sharp enough that he still managed to jerk his face back in time to avoid the full impact of the blow. Nevertheless, it landed hard enough to knock him staggering away from the table.

McQueen lunged forward, reaching to grab Woolsey by the shoulders, with the intent of flinging the smaller man out of his way so he could get at the brothers before they closed in on the stranger and inflicted more damage. In his haste, however, the marshal forgot what a wily scrapper the redhead was in his own right. Although he'd never turned to look directly back at McQueen, Woolsey had been very aware of how close he'd moved up behind him. So when the lawman's hands started to clamp onto his shoulders, Woolsey bent his knees just enough to drop below the closing fingers and at the same time twisted sharply at the waist, whipping around with the point of his elbow and driving it full-force into McQueen's stomach.

A great gust of air exploded from the marshal as he doubled forward. Anticipating this, Woolsey suddenly straightened his legs and simultaneously jerked his head straight back, hard, slamming it into McQueen's lowering face.

Now it was McQueen's knees that buckled, though not purposefully. He lurched to one side, stunned by the head butt. He could taste blood filling his mouth and feel the sticky warmth of it dribbling down over his chin.

On the other side of the table, the yellow-haired stranger struggled to regain his balance as the Dunlap brothers rushed him, angling in from either side. Wanting badly to land a blow of his own, Grady allowed his eagerness to outweigh his caution and ended up paying for it when he stepped into a lightning-fast right jab the stranger threw even as he was still leaning back. The fist-to-chin collision popped solidly, stalling Grady's forward momentum.

Landing the punch seemed to somehow reset the stranger's balance, enabling him to get his feet planted as he turned to face the oncoming Greely. Once again, his fists lashed out in a blur of speed, leading with another jab, a left this time, followed instantly by a right hook that snapped Greely's head to one side and caused him to do a stutter-step off in that direction rather than continue his straight-ahead charge.

Meanwhile, McQueen was still dealing with the unexpected burst of aggression from the scrappy Newt Woolsey. Momentarily staggered by the smaller man's initial attack, the marshal fought to right himself and get braced for whatever the redhead tried in the way of a follow-up. When it came, it was another example of Woolsey's shrewdness and the fighting skills he'd honed to compensate for his lack of size. He went for McQueen's legs, aiming a piston-like kick meant to crush the bigger man's kneecap and either dislocate it or possibly break the leg.

But McQueen's history of being in ruckuses had taught him a thing or three about fighting, as well — including a host of defensive moves, both orthodox and the kind a body sometimes made up on the spot. His reaction to Woolsey's attempted kick fell in the latter category. Seeing the foot cock back and then start to hurtle toward his knee before he was properly balanced for a quick sidestep, the marshal instead leaned forward and swung his fist in a downward chop that struck hard just above Woolsey's ankle. The impact resulted in a loud *crack* of gristle and bone as the redhead's foot and leg were knocked violently away, suddenly making him the one off balance. He pitched to the floor, reaching frantically for his damaged foot with both hands while howling in pain.

Pausing only long enough to backhand some of the blood from his mouth, McQueen pounced on Woolsey. He resorted to a variation of what he'd originally meant to do when he'd first reached for the redhead. Leaning over, he seized the fallen man by the scruff of his neck and the waistband of his trousers. Straightening up, shoulders and thick arms bulging under his homespun shirt, the marshal lifted the still-howling Woolsey and whirled him around as if he were no more than a toddler. When he'd turned to where he was facing the three other combatants, McQueen hoisted his burden to chest height and then thrust his powerful arms outward, releasing Woolsey and sending him airborne until he crashed across the lower backs of the Dunlap brothers as they were bunching together in their renewed attempt to gang up on the stranger.

Woolsey yipped like a kicked dog, the sounds he emitted mixing with the grunts

15

of surprise that escaped Greely and Grady as they were slammed forward and knocked off their feet. All three of the troublemakers tumbled down, tangled together in a kicking, arm-thrashing, cursing pile.

Shoving away the table and swatting aside tipped-over chairs, McQueen barged forward, following the missile he had launched. On the other side of the flailing pile, the yellow-haired stranger stood poised with raised fists, the expression on his face once again wary, but also touched with a hint of amusement.

"Hope you don't mind me hornin' in," McQueen said to him as he leaned over to yank the limp form of Woolsey off the pile and toss it to one side, "but I figure you'll be okay with sharin' the finishin'-up of these last two with me."

Grinning as he reached down to pull Grady back to his feet, the stranger said, "Always been a big believer in sharing, Marshal. One apiece works out about as even as a fella could ask for."

And so it went that, for the next handful of minutes — after getting both Grady and Greely upright and finding they still had the hankering for a fight left in them — the stranger and the marshal stood back-to-back and obliged that hankering with a flurry of traded punches. The stranger continued to demonstrate a measure of finesse and boxing skill — ducking, sticking, jabbing, cutting Grady down steadily but unhurriedly. Greely and McQueen — and Grady, too, for what little offense he was able to muster — relied more on hooks and sweeping roundhouses mixed with a few elbow smashes, the occasional uppercut, and lashing kicks from time to time.

Greely was big and strong, but he also was flabby around the gut and soaked inside with too much alcohol. And although McQueen was a good twenty years older and not as spry as he'd been in his heyday, he was still powerfully built through the chest and shoulders and relatively trim at the waist. So his whittling down of Greely was not as clean or precise as the methods being employed by the stranger, but he was nevertheless getting the job done.

None of which was to say the Dunlaps were willing to go down easy. They were tough and durable and damned stubborn about hitting the floor. Even after they were clearly bested, they refused to quit.

This, then, was the scene presented to Jim Hendricks, a mountain of a man who happened to be one of McQueen's two deputies, as he barged through the Silver Spur's batwings. All four combatants, bloody and battered, were still on their feet throwing increasingly arm-weary punches.

Hendricks took one look and didn't hesitate to react in a way he'd found to be always effective for such situations. Almost lazily, he drew the revolver from the holster on his hip, pointed it ceilingward, and fired off a shot. The whole room shook from the blast. Farrelly, the bartender, and the men lining the bar — even though they were watching Hendricks the whole time — jumped at the sound. More importantly, though, the brawlers froze in what they were doing and let their fists fall loosely to their sides, bruised faces turning to look at Hendricks.

"Whatever this was about, it is now over," the deputy proclaimed. Then, aiming a scowl at McQueen, he added, "Thunderation, Firestick, how did you let yourself get involved in this? You oughta know better."

"Aw, take it easy, Moosejaw," McQueen replied wearily. "Like you never jumped in the middle of a fracas before."

"That was the old days. We're supposed to be older and wiser now. What's more, we wear badges. That means we're supposed to be *breakin' up* fights, not joinin' in."

McQueen raised one hand and patted his

chest. "Well, I forgot to put on my badge today. Reckon that must be why I slipped and allowed myself to be tempted into joinin' this scuffle." He looked around, glaring at the Dunlap brothers, both of whom remained standing, though weaving somewhat unsteadily. "But badge or no badge," he added, "I still got the authority to charge these varmints with disturbin' the peace and strikin' an officer of the law. They know damn well who and what I am, and they decided to tangle with me anyway. So they're gonna get what they got comin'."

"You want to throw 'em in the hoosegow?" Hendricks said.

"That's exactly what I want." McQueen gestured offhandedly toward the sprawled form of Woolsey. "Have 'em drag their pet red-haired rat along for the trip and and throw him behind bars with 'em."

"For how long?"

"I'll let you know after I think on it some. I might decide to pile on a few more charges."

Hendricks frowned. "You know Tolsvord ain't gonna like that much."

"That's too bad," McQueen said. "For his sake, we've gone easy on these no-accounts way too often. I figure it's time we clamped down on 'em a little harder for a change —

and past time for Tolsvord to recognize they're a lost cause for him and everybody else."

"If you say so, Firestick." Hendricks waggled his gun at Greely and Grady. "You heard the man. Grab hold of your pet red-haired rat and bring him along. You're all invited for a stay in the exclusive little hotel we run."

Wordlessly, the brothers grabbed the sagging Woolsey — one by the feet, the other under his arms — and headed for the front door ahead of Hendricks. Before following them out, the big deputy looked over his shoulder and said, "I'll send Moorehouse over to see about patchin' you two up. Then I'll have him take a look at these three."

McQueen shrugged. "I suppose. No particular hurry, though . . . especially not for them."

CHAPTER 2

Once Hendricks was out the door with his charges, McQueen turned to the yellow-haired stranger who'd been standing quietly by with a bemused expression on his face. "Now then," said the marshal. "I gave you the benefit of the doubt, because I know those three jackasses to be liars and trouble-makers. Thing is, that don't necessarily prove you *ain't* a card cheat. I hope you're not gonna disappoint me by turnin' out to actually be one."

"Trust me, Marshal, I very sincerely do not want to disappoint you," said the stranger. "Like I told you before, those men were such terrible players there would be no need for me or anybody else to cheat in order to beat them."

McQueen regarded him for a moment before making a gesture to indicate the paper bills that, along with the cards, ashtrays, and drinks, had been spilled from the table. "Reckon these winnin's are yours, then."

The stranger returned his gaze, the bemused expression remaining in place. He said, "If that's intended to be some kind of trick to test my honesty, Marshal, then that would make me the one disappointed in you . . . I hadn't yet had time to clean those gentlemen out entirely, you see. So not all of the money scattered there is mine. However, since I do know the amount I had in front of me before the trouble broke out, I'd like to claim what is. The rest can be returned to the men your deputy hauled away."

"Minus the amount owed for damages, that is — from their part, not yours," McQueen said.

"Sounds reasonable," the stranger allowed.

"Reasonable, maybe. But not really necessary," said Farrelly, the barkeep, who'd come out from his station to start righting chairs and putting things back in order. "The boss learned a long time ago to furnish this joint with sturdy trimmings that wouldn't bust up so easy every time a fracas broke out. Looks like it paid off once again. I don't see nothing that suffered much damage."

He paused in what he was doing to glance upward. "Except for the ceiling, that is. Doggone it, Firestick, does Moosejaw have to fire off a blast into the ceiling *every* time he shows up to tame down a spot of trouble? Lookit up there. That's three times in the past six months, and last time it was with a doggone shotgun!"

"Moosejaw don't like wastin' words," McQueen said.

"Well, he oughta try not liking to waste bullets for a change. He's gonna have that ceiling peppered with so many doggone holes that the next time we get a frog-strangler of a rain, it'll leak in here like one of those Swedish shower baths I've heard tell about."

"Art," McQueen said, "when's the last time we had a frog-strangler of a rain around these parts?"

Farrelly frowned. "Well . . . I don't know exactly."

"You don't know because you can't remember. *Nobody* can remember. Because it never happens."

"We get some doozies now and then," Farrelly said stubbornly. "But that ain't the point. The point is, if Moosejaw keeps shooting holes in the ceiling, it's just a matter of time before it'll start to leak from even only —"

"Okay, okay. I'll talk to him about it."

"I mean, it ain't like he ain't big enough to just march in and give a loud snort if he wants to —"

"You made your point. I *said* I'll talk to him about it," the marshal interrupted for a second time, his tone growing a mite testy.

While McQueen and Farrelly were talking, the stranger had quietly gathered up the cards and money scattered across the floor. He placed the deck of cards on top of the table Farrelly had pushed back into place, and alongside it a thin stack of bills — minus a thicker bundle, his winnings, that he kept for himself. Brandishing the latter, he announced, "Gentlemen. Since I was a participant — albeit a reluctant one — in the disturbance that disrupted everyone's afternoon, I'd like to make amends by offering to step over to the bar and buy a round of drinks."

One of the onlookers already at the bar responded by saying, "Heck, mister, that wasn't no disturbance to us. It was a right entertainin' show you put on."

One of the other patrons leaning on the bar next to the speaker gave him a quick elbow to the ribs, then was equally quick to add, "But that don't mean we won't still accept your offer to stand a round of drinks."

"Reckon I'd better get back in place to do some pouring, then," said Farrelly as he headed once again for the bar.

The stranger pointed to the money he'd placed on the table and said to McQueen, "That rightfully belongs to those other players. I presume you'll see that it's returned to them?"

The marshal hesitated for a moment, making a sour face, before finally reaching for the bills. "I ain't done bein' mad at those boobs yet, so I hate to do anything in their favor," he said. "But, yeah, I'll see to it this gets back to 'em."

The stranger smiled. "I trust also that you will be accepting my drink offer? Or are you not allowed to imbibe since you're on duty?"

McQueen's sour expression suddenly turned into a wide grin, accompanied by a hearty chuckle. "Mister, I wouldn't *have* a job that didn't allow for a little imbibin'. Which ain't to say I go around half-pickled or anything like that. But I do enjoy a few nips on occasion, and I reckon this measures up as one of those occasions. So lead on, I surely do accept your offer."

By the time they took their places at the bar, Farrelly had already served the other men farther down the line. Moving back to stand before McQueen and the stranger, the first thing he did was place a couple of damp bar towels in front of them. "The laundry lady will likely raise hell with me about the bloodstains, but here, you fellas might want to take a swipe at some of your cuts and scrapes before you get down to drinking."

The long mirror behind the bar was the pride of the otherwise rather austere establishment. The Silver Spur's owner, Irish Dan Coswick, liked to boast how he'd had it shipped special all the way from New Orleans, and he took great offense at any mention of the few distortions and blurry spots to be found across its surface. It nevertheless *did* give the place a nice added touch and proved quite helpful at the moment for the marshal and the stranger to see their reflections in order to take some "swipes" at their wounds. The latter, upon closer examination, proved numerous though mostly superficial.

"I guess," said the stranger as he dabbed at the raw, reddened swelling under one eye, "we can take a certain amount of satisfaction in the fact that those men your deputy took out of here looked considerably worse than us."

Wiping his chin clean of the partially dried

blood smeared across it, McQueen grinned. "Like the old joke that goes, 'You oughta see the other fella, eh?" Then his grin stretched even wider. "Of course, when you take into account those ugly-assed Dunlaps and stack 'em up against a couple of handsome gents like us, you'd be quick to conclude they looked considerably worse even before we did any poundin' on 'em."

Now it was the stranger's turn to chuckle. "If you say so."

As he continued to utilize the mirror's reflection to dab at the damage done his face, the stranger also used it to discreetly make a closer appraisal of the man standing next to him. He saw a solid six-footer in his middle fifties with a full head of gray-flecked hair, a broad face anchored by a strong jaw, ice-blue eyes separated by a blunt, moderately large nose. His attire was simple — homespun shirt and denim trousers, the latter tucked into a pair of high-topped buckskin boots with fringes around the top cuffs. He wore a walnut-handled Frontier Colt in a well-worn holster on his right hip, and moved like he knew how to use it. And although the stranger had seen the marshal's wide grin and the laugh crinkles at the corners of his ice-blue eyes, he'd also noted those eyes narrowing and deepening to a much darker blue during flashes of anger. In summation, the stranger made McQueen for a self-assured, generally easygoing individual, but one with a dangerous edge that marked him as no one to be trifled with.

Setting aside his bar towel and raising the shot of red-eye Farrelly had placed before him, the marshal said, "I thank you for this, mister. Could thank you more properly if I knew your name, which, it occurs to me, I never got around to hearin'."

The stranger raised his own glass. "It's Lofton. Henry Lofton."

"And I'm Elwood McQueen . . . Here's to you."

Both men tossed down their shots.

Returning his glass to the bar top, Lofton said, "Now you've got me curious. You say your name is McQueen. But your deputy — the big fellow you referred to as Moosejaw — kept calling you 'Firestick.' It may not be polite to probe too much since we've only just met, but I'm thinking there's got to be an interesting story or two behind such colorful names. Care to enlighten me?"

CHAPTER 3

Without waiting to be asked, Farrelly had already begun pouring refills. As he did so, one side of his mouth pulled into a wry smile. "Oh, there's stories behind those names right enough," he said. "Don't keep the poor fella in suspense, Firestick. Go ahead and tell him."

"Now, Art. Don't go makin' more of it than there is."

"Aw, come on," the barkeep protested. "I've heard you tell plenty of tales about your mountain-man days. No need to be shy about it now."

"Mountain-man days?" echoed Lofton. "Now I'm really intrigued. You must tell me more."

McQueen tossed back his second shot, then pushed the emptied glass toward Farrelly, saying, "Okay. But enough panther juice. Pour me a beer to keep my tongue oiled for the tellin'. That'll be strong

29

enough."

After downing his own drink, Lofton said, "Same for me on the beer."

Once a tall brew was in front of him, McQueen began. "I was born and raised a farm lad back on the flatlands of Iowa. One of my pa's brothers, Uncle Eugene, ran a little country inn on the main road that bordered the south end of our land. Most of the travelers who stopped by his place were headed out West, some were comin' back. The yarns he heard from those returnin' and then passed along at family gatherin's were wondrous tales to the ears of this restless farm boy. I knew at an early age I wasn't cut out to be chained to a plot of land or a backbreakin' plow or any of the rest that went with it. Hearin' those tales of the West pretty much set the course I knew I'd be followin' the first chance I got."

McQueen paused for a moment, a trace of sadness passing briefly over his face. "Reckon I'll always feel a mite guilty about leavin' my pa with one less set of hands to work the farm," he continued. "But I think he knew early on, just like I did, that it wasn't something I was cut out for. So I tell myself I sorta balanced it out by also leavin' him one less mouth to feed. I remain hopeful he didn't think poorly of me for the rest of his days."

"At any rate, light out is what I did at about seventeen or so. Headed straight for the Colorado Rockies." The glory days of mountain-mannin' — the beaver-trappin' and such — had mostly run out by the time I got on the scene. But there was still a livin' to be made in pelts and hides and huntin' meat for the minin' camps. I lucked out by fallin' in with some fellas here and there who showed me the ropes and didn't leave a greenhorn to starve or freeze to death those first couple winters. In the end, I had some pretty good years there in the Rockies.

"But then" — the marshal sighed after taking a pull of his beer — "I got a fresh dose of wanderlust, and knew the only way to scratch the itch was to roam farther west. So that's what I did. Spent some time in and around Yellowstone. Moved on to the Cascades. Looked out on the Pacific Ocean . . . Eventually, though, the Rockies beckoned me back. It was on the way there, at a rendezvous in Wyoming, that I met a couple of rascals who I wasn't able to shake — and never really wanted to, truth be known. The three of us have stuck together from that point on."

"Let me guess," Lofton interjected. "I'm

31

betting I just met one of them, sort of, in Deputy Moosejaw."

"That'd be another bet you'd win," McQueen allowed. "His real name is Hendricks, by the way. Jim Hendricks. I'll get to how he came to be called Moosejaw in a minute, but while we're at it, you might as well know that the second rascal I ran into at that rendezvous can be found hangin' around these parts also. He's my other deputy, in fact. His name is Malachi Skinner."

"No nickname for him?"

"I'll get to that in a minute, too." McQueen took another drink of his beer. "After the three of us throwed in together there in Jackson Hole, we spent the next several years in the high country." Meager years, from a money-earnin' standpoint, through much of it. But some mighty good times all the same. We were wild and free, and we always had meat to eat and a tight shelter from the cold and rain.

"When the Civil War came along and tore hell out of most of the rest of the country, it never really touched us up there where we were. Hell, the two armies had been fightin' for months before we ever even heard anything about it. When we did, on account of all three of us livin' away from so-called civilization for as long as we had . . . well, we never really understood what the fuss was about and we weren't rightly sure which side we belonged on if we would've decided to go off and fight."

"Too bad more didn't feel that way," Lofton said bitterly. "It might've saved the senseless slaughter of a lot of innocent young men."

McQueen shrugged. "What it boiled down to, in the end, was that the war never came around us, so we never went lookin' for it. Thinkin' back on that time now, after the passin' of years, I wonder if we did the right thing. We weren't cowards, I'm certain of that much. But that's the only thing I'm certain of. We live in this country, we reap the benefits, such as they are . . . But we never fought for 'em. Maybe we should have."

"But neither did you fight *against* the side that prevailed," Lofton pointed out. "There's always that to consider."

"Reckon that's one way to look at it." McQueen heaved a sigh. "Anyway, we gradually worked our way down out of Colorado and into the southern Rockies and the San Juans in New Mexico." It was there that we ran into some serious trouble with hostile Indians. Oh, we'd had skirmishes before. Plenty of 'em in plenty of different places. But it was usually a hit-and-run kind of thing, never nothing that dragged out for very long.

"Once we got in amongst the Jicarilla and Coyotero Apaches, though, it was a whole different kettle of fish. They got real intense about lettin' us know we wasn't welcome in their mountains, and we took a stubborn — and probably not too smart — stance when it came to lettin' 'em know we wasn't of a mind to be run out. And so it went for the next handful of years. Lots of run-ins, some of 'em pretty bloody. We managed to keep our hair and our lives, but it came powerful close to goin' the other way more times than I care to think about."

McQueen paused for another long pull of his beer. When he lowered his glass, there was a wry smile on his face. "It was from those Injuns, you see, that all three of us got our nicknames. Firestick for me, on account of my skill with a long gun when it came to nailin' anything I shot at — be it a four-legged critter or the two-legged kind. Moosejaw for Hendricks, due to the time he got caught alone and was ambushed by a party of braves; after he ran out of bullets, they closed in on him with war clubs and tomahawks and he fought 'em off with the jawbone of a moose skeleton that happened to be lyin' on the ground of the gully where they had him cornered."

"Samson of the San Juans!" Farrelly cackled. "I never grow tired of hearin' that yarn."

"I can see why," said Lofton in a somewhat awed tone.

"That only leaves Malachi, the fella you ain't met yet," McQueen said. "Him they took to callin' Beartooth on account of the fierce way he handled a knife — one he kept as sharp and deadly as a grizzly fang."

"I take it the Apaches got a firsthand taste of that skill also?"

"Often enough for 'em to come up with the name. Not that Beartooth didn't prefer usin' a gun and bullets as often as he could," McQueen explained, "but somehow he ended up fightin' in close quarters on several occasions and, when he did, well . . . it was his knife that got him out alive."

Lofton wagged his head. "You called Moosejaw the Samson of the San Juans a minute ago," he said to Farrelly. "I'd say the full trio — Firestick, Beartooth, and Moosejaw — sounds more like the Three Musketeers of the Mountains."

The puzzled looks Lofton got in response to that remark made it quickly evident his reference to the popular Dumas novel was lost on this particular audience. Instead of trying to press the point, he simply let it go, saying, "Never mind. Trust me, it was meant as a compliment. Though, on second thought, those mountain adventures might very well have surpassed anything they could be compared to."

"I don't know about that," allowed Mc-Queen. "What I do know is that spinnin' yarns about those days is a sight easier than livin' through some of 'em was — *barely* makin' it through, in some cases. But it was the life we chose, and, by and large, we had some fine times. What's more, we took those names the Injuns hung on us as badges of honor, sort of, and commenced callin' each other by 'em, even amongst ourselves. Got to be such a habit, that when we came down out of the mountains and mixed with other folks, they picked up on usin' 'em, too."

"I guess the only thing that leaves, if you'll indulge my curiosity a bit more," said Lofton, "is how the three of you ended up as lawmen here in the town of Buffalo Peak? What was it that made you finally leave the mountains? I'll venture another wager that it wasn't because the Indians finally ran you off."

McQueen shook his head. "No, our pullin'

out wasn't on account of the Injuns." Hell, we got to a point there toward the end where they quit takin' so much notice of us. Not meanin' there was any love lost between us and them. We mainly learned to sort of steer clear of each other. But the creepin' years were addin' up, and they don't steer clear of nobody. Each season when the mountain winter came around, the cold bit a little deeper into our bones and took a little longer to seep back out. Plus, the game got scarcer and the huntin' trails seemed longer and harder to travel. One spring, the three of us looked around and somehow just seemed to know it was time to come down out of the high country.

"Since we all had a hankerin' to see this Texas we'd been hearin' about on and off for years, here is where we headed. Happened that durin' my years passin' through Wyoming, I spent some time with a horse-wranglin' crew. That was another hankerin' I had — to someday take another turn at tryin' my hand with that. My pards thought it sounded all right, too, so we bought ourselves a little spread west of here and settled in to raise and sell horses. Been at it for a while now, and it's workin' out pretty fair." McQueen's broad shoulders rolled in a shrug. "Along the way, when we started seein' how the town of Buffalo Peak was havin' more and more trouble with rowdies comin' around causin' trouble, we decided we ought to pitch in and help tame things down. For our trouble, we ended up gettin' badges slapped on ourselves. Far as I can tell, the townsfolk seem to think that's workin' out pretty fair, too, and so that's how things stand."

"Quite a tale. Quite a tale, indeed," said Lofton.

"This is the West, mister. Everybody's got a tale to tell," said Firestick. Then he flashed one of his wide grins. "Only, not everybody is so long-winded and as willin' as me when it comes to sharin' theirs. You might want to keep that in mind when that curiosity of yours gets to tuggin' on you around some-body else."

"I'll be sure and do that."

"Okay. But before you take my advice too much to heart, how about allowin' me a turn at some curiosity? You got me wonderin' if you're a gamblin' man by trade who maybe plans on stickin' around these parts for a spell? Or are you just passin' through?"

"I planned on staying over a night or two in your hotel," Lofton answered. "Get some sleep in a warm, soft bed. Have me some decent meals. Then, yes, I'd figured to drift on. It's what I've been doing for some time now, ever since . . . well, let's just say a love affair that didn't go well. What you might call a big gamble I failed to win."

"Sorry to hear that," Firestick said earnestly. "But you *are* a gamblin' man, then?"

Lofton shrugged. "It's how I've been getting by. Earning a few bills here and there, enough to eat and enjoy a few creature comforts now and then. But I'm not what you'd call a high roller by any means. I do okay against other small-stakes players and cowboys with a month's pay burning a hole in their pockets. But that's about it."

"Can't help noticin' that hogleg you got strapped to your hip," said Firestick, gesturing. "Mighty fine-lookin' piece. A .45, ain't it? You wear it like you for sure know which end the bullets come out, yet you made no attempt to pull it against those jackasses when they was backin' you into a corner. Excuse me for sayin', but I find that kinda curious."

Now it was Lofton's turn to smile, a somewhat guarded lifting of the corners of his mouth. "I suppose that does seem a little odd, doesn't it? A gambling man not playing his ace against three-to-one odds? Reaching for the gun crossed my mind, to be sure, but as you saw, none of those men were armed. That crossed my mind, too. A stranger in town drawing against three unarmed locals? There are many places, I'm afraid, where — no matter the odds or anything else — such an act could go very bad for a fellow in my position."

"Reckon I can see how you might look at it like that," allowed Firestick. "I've been in those kind of places, too — where things are stacked right from the get-go against anybody from the outside."

"None of which is to say I *wouldn't* have gone for my gun if the situation had started turning too ugly," Lofton admitted. Then he smiled again, this time more openly. "But then you showed up, and events took a different turn . . . a far more interesting and colorful one."

Firestick worked his jaw from side to side, still feeling the effects from Woolsey's head butt. "Yeah. Interestin' . . . I reckon that's one word for it."

CHAPTER 4

Buffalo Peak straddled a nameless old trail that ran between Presidio and Sierra Blanca. In time, the portion of the trail passing through the settlement's heart came to be called Trail Street. As the town grew, an accumulation of shops and businesses eventually lined this main artery, with individual residences sprinkled behind in a haphazard pattern that defied any attempt to lay out an orderly grid of side streets.

The feature that gave the town its name was a blunt-topped butte jutting up out of the flats to the northeast, like a cast-off chunk that got tossed down from the Vieja Mountains rising high and ragged farther to the north. The story went that someone early on had remarked how the butte resembled a buffalo's hump, and for a long time travelers passing through the territory referred to it as such. When it came time to name the town, however, the consensus of

41

those involved decided that "Hump" sounded unappealing whereas "Peak" somehow did not — and so Buffalo Peak it became.

Firestick had often contemplated this bit of history without ever understanding why one term was favored over the other. After all, the way the butte was rounded off at the top, it more accurately *was* a hump rather than a peak. In the end, though, he was all right with whatever the place was called. That was the way he, Moosejaw, and Beartooth had found it when they'd arrived on the scene, and therefore it was the only way they'd ever known it. And especially now that they'd settled in and signed on as lawmen, they were right-down-to-the-ground loyal to all aspects of their new home. That's just the way things went with them.

Firestick was thinking about those things as he left the Silver Spur and headed toward the jail. Talking with Lofton about the old days had put him in a reflective mood. That wasn't surprising. What was different, though, was how he'd reached a point where he could talk about those past times without feeling a bit melancholy over their passing, the way he used to.

Oh, he still treasured those wild, free days and always would. But he'd also come to realize and accept that he was enjoying this newer phase his life had moved into, as well. And why not? He still had his two good pals by his side, they were getting by as well or better than ever, and they were still managing to find enough challenges and excitement to keep any sign of boredom from creeping in. What more could a body want?

Well, Firestick was reminded as he drew abreast of the Mallory Hotel, there was one thing that had been mighty scarce up in the high, lonely reaches . . . romance. While he was no stranger to lust and had answered its call on a number of occasions over the years with the sporting women who could be found at rendezvous and elsewhere, that wasn't the same thing. Not by a long shot. Nor had he ever taken up with an Indian maid, like a lot of mountain men did. He had nothing against this practice — he'd just never found himself in a position where it had become an option for him.

But now, here in Buffalo Peak, he'd finally run across someone who planted thoughts in his head of the kind of things he figured had long since passed him by. Her name was Kate Mallory. She owned and operated the hotel, having taken it over when both of her parents died in an influenza epidemic. She was smart, tough, stubborn, and sassy.

She was also lovely to look upon in a sultry, dark-haired kind of way, with a throaty voice and a sense of humor displayed frequently by uninhibited, bawdy-sounding laughter. All in all, she made Firestick's heart race faster than any woman he'd ever met. And, to his surprise and delight, she'd let him know in no uncertain terms that she felt the same way about him.

As he passed the hotel, Firestick suppressed the urge to stop in. Just to see Kate, to gaze upon her for a minute. But he resisted. For one thing, he needed to get to the jail and make sure Moosejaw had gotten the prisoners locked up without any more trouble.

For another, freshly bruised and battered the way he was, he knew he'd probably get a chewing out from Kate when she saw him. Not that she wouldn't hear about the fight at the Silver Spur soon enough anyway, and not that Firestick would hold off seeing her for very long regardless, but he just didn't need to be in too big a hurry about it.

The jail, one of the newest buildings in town, had been built near the far west end once it was decided that Buffalo Peak needed a marshal and a place to detain lawbreakers. It was a sturdy, thick-walled adobe structure, very basic yet quite functional.

As he was drawing near, Firestick saw Frank Moorehouse coming out the front door. Moorehouse was the town barber — mainly. That was what was painted on the window of his shop back up the street. But it was generally known that, due to some battlefield training he'd received during the war, he was also the closest thing the town had to a doctor. And, for those desperate enough, he served as a dentist, too, though extraction was about the only remedy he offered.

Spotting the marshal's approach, Moorehouse paused just outside the doorway. Dangling from one hand was the battered leather "doctor's bag" he kept stocked for the good of his fellow citizens. He was a portly, bespectacled man with a walrus mustache and bristly eyebrows that danced animatedly when he spoke, always reminding Firestick of a pair of woolly caterpillars trying to find purchase on the wire rims of the spectacles.

"Having completed my treatment of combatants from both sides of the recent engagement," the multitalented barber announced loftily, referencing his recent visit to the Silver Spur, where he'd patched up

Firestick and Lofton, and now had apparently finished doing the same for the Dunlap brothers and Newt Woolsey, "I will state for the record — basing my conclusion solely on objective evidence in the form of damage inflicted — that you and your blond-haired accomplice appear deserving of being proclaimed the winners of said engagement."

"Tell me something I don't already know. I was there — remember?" Firestick drawled.

"Okay. You want something you don't already know?" Moorehouse said. "Each of the Dunlap brothers suffered a badly cracked and loosened tooth, among other things, as a result of their encounter with you and your new friend. In each case, I had to dig out the damaged tooth. So, my bill to the town for treating the victims will be a bit larger than usual, due to the use of my skills in two separate fields — medical *and* dental — being required."

"Why tell me? You're on the town council that authorizes payment of submitted bills. Pitch your own case."

"Indeed, I will."

Firestick arched a brow. "While you were at it, I'm surprised you didn't decide they all needed haircuts, too."

46

"In my professional opinion, as a matter of fact, they do." Moorehouse shrugged. "But that's a personal choice, and one the Dunlaps, as witnessed by their overall shaggy appearance, not to mention the fact they've never seen fit to visit my shop, obviously don't make with any regularity. So I therefore avoided bringing it up."

Behind him, Moosejaw poked his head out the jail door. "If you'd've took a pair of scissors and a razor to those gamy polecats," he said, "they likely would've howled as loud or louder than when you yanked their teeth."

That made Firestick grin. "They yelp it up pretty good, did they?"

Moosejaw rolled his eyes. "Did they ever. You'd've thought somebody was diggin' arrows out of 'em."

"I'm surprised you didn't hear it all the way back up the street," Moorehouse confirmed.

"I'm sorry I missed that," Firestick said, his grin widening. "You sure there ain't another tooth or two you oughta dig out, now that I'm here to be in on it?"

Chapter 5

"Stick with him, Jesus! Ride him down — show him who's boss!"

These words of encouragement came from Malachi "Beartooth" Skinner as he leaned leisurely on the outside of a small corral, arms folded across the top rail. Inside the corral, the individual to whom he was shouting encouragement was involved in the very *un*-leisurely pursuit of trying to stay on a sleek, black, wildly bucking bronco. The rider, Jesus Marquez by name, was a lean, wiry, brown-skinned vaquero — one of two employed by the Double M (for Mountain Men) Ranch, the outfit Beartooth owned with his pals Moosejaw and Firestick. Jesus was young, barely out of his teens, yet already highly skilled in the ways of breaking and training horses. This was thanks to the tutelage of his uncle, Miguel Santros, also employed by the Double M and presently leaning on the corral rail next to

Beartooth.

As the two men looked on, the bronc continued to leap and whirl and buck, furiously attempting to dislodge its passenger. But despite being jerked from side to side and snapped back and forth, Jesus remained in the saddle as if nailed there. Through the thickening cloud of dust being kicked up, Beartooth thought he actually saw the young man smile from time to time, after the black would make a particularly frantic maneuver that failed to unseat him.

Beartooth glanced over at Miguel, who was focused intently on his nephew. The older man's leathery, deeply seamed face showed no emotion, but Beartooth could tell he was both pleased and proud.

"Kid's a natural," Beartooth suggested.

Miguel's shoulders moved in a faint shrug. "I'd like to think I had a little something to do with his skill," he said. "But it is true that Jesus is a fast learner and arrived possessing a fine set of tools for me to work with."

A moment after those words came out, the black leaped high and twisted its body sharply while still in the air. The combination move caught Jesus by surprise and threw him badly off balance. The horse came down jarringly hard on all fours, first landing stiff-legged, but then instantly twisting the opposite way. Its young rider couldn't react fast enough and was sent flying.

"Oh-oh," muttered Beartooth. "I think the toolbox might've just got a dent in it."

The two men clambered quickly over the fence and hurried into the corral with the aim of making sure the fallen Jesus didn't get trampled before he could regain his footing. The black showed no intention of trying anything like that, however, instead circling away to the far side of the corral and halting there, feet planted wide, blowing hard, watching the humans with suspicion and perhaps a trace of defiance in its gleaming dark eyes.

Beartooth and Miguel knelt beside Jesus and gently helped him rise to a sitting position. The young man looked dazed, momentarily disoriented, and was sucking hard to regain some of the breath that had gotten knocked out of him. Beads of sweat stood out on his forehead and began trickling down the sides of his face, making muddy tracks through the thin layer of dust that had settled there.

"Just take it easy for a minute," said Beartooth. "Nothing's broke, is it?"

Jesus blinked. "I . . . I don't think so."

50

"Move your legs and then your arms. Slowly," instructed Miguel. When his nephew had done this, he said, "Good. You are going to be fine."

Jesus looked around, his eyes taking on some clarity now. "Fine enough," he allowed. "But not until I have the chance to prove so by climbing back on that black *diablo* and then staying there until he knows that I am his master."

Miguel nodded. "I am proud to hear your resolve. And I believe you when you say what you will do. However, that should wait until tomorrow to take place."

"Tomorrow?" echoed Jesus, his expression showing disapproval of the idea.

"Sí," said Miguel firmly. "If you get back on the black now, you will be able to break him, it is true. But if you do that, he will always hold a grudge and never be the completely fine mount he has the makings to be. On the other hand, if you allow him this small victory today, then wait until tomorrow to break him, he will remember and appreciate that, and he will go on to be an even finer mount, one with his pride and spirit still intact."

Jesus looked thoughtful, but at the same time a bit skeptical. "I know well that horses have spirit. But are they also capable of things such as pride and holding a grudge?"

"Indeed so," Miguel assured him. "If you want to be a top horseman, you must always remember that. It will improve your mastery over the animals and will separate you from the so-called bronc stompers employed by too many cattlemen hereabouts."

"Bronc stompers?"

"Men who will ride a horse to death in their hurry to break it, rather than take a little extra time and allow the animal the chance to adjust to what is going on, what is being asked of it."

Jesus scowled. "Breaking a horse by riding it to death accomplishes nothing."

"Least of all for the horse," said Beartooth.

Jesus turned his head and looked at the black. Their eyes locked and held for a long moment — until Jesus said, in a low voice, "Tomorrow."

The black chuffed and dug at the ground with one of its front hooves.

Miguel smiled. "He says he will be waiting and is looking forward to it."

Beartooth straightened back up. "Tomorrow it is, then. I'll go ahead and unsaddle the black, then turn him out with the others. When Jesus's rattled bones have finished settlin' back into place, you two go on to the bunkhouse and get cleaned up for supper. Take it easy for a while, until Miss Victoria rings the bell to come eat."

After he'd seen to the black and put away the saddle and bridle Jesus had been using, Beartooth left the corral area and headed for the main house of the Double M Ranch headquarters. The house was a two-story, wood-frame structure, something a bit uncommon to the area. It was built straight and true and solid, always with a fresh coat of whitewash, trimmed in bright green. When Beartooth and his companions had made the decision to quit being mountain men and settle into more conventional lives, they had agreed that wherever they put down roots, they would build and maintain a fine, substantial home. The main house at the Double M was the result, and each man took pride and worked hard to make sure it always lived up to their goal.

The sinking sun of late afternoon cast a long shadow ahead of Beartooth as he strode along. By his reckoning, he had endured fifty winters in his lifetime, give or take a couple either way. He was a sliver under six feet tall, square-shouldered, lean and solid. Unlike Firestick, there was no gray in his reddish-brown hair. His clean-shaven face was too narrow and his green eyes too intense and probing for him to be considered classically handsome. But he had an easy grin, with a slightly roguish slant to it, that made men want to be pals with him, and certain kinds of women — especially given how the grin came combined with a deeply dimpled chin — want to learn more about what was behind that roguish slant.

As he stepped up onto the front porch, Beartooth was met by a wave of delicious-smelling cooking coming from inside the house. He detected roast pork, cabbage, fresh-baked bread, and some kind of pie. Peach, he thought. He was sure of the first three; the pie might have been more a case of wishful thinking as far as exactly what kind it would turn out to be. In any case, he knew it was sure to taste great thanks to the kitchen talents of Victoria Kingsley, the Double M's cook and housekeeper.

Entering the house and passing through the parlor, Beartooth paused in the kitchen doorway to breathe in more of the delightful aromas and at the same time drink in the equally pleasing sight of Victoria. She wore a short-sleeved brown blouse buttoned at the throat, a full-length flower-patterned skirt, and a white apron tied at the waist. Beartooth preferred seeing her in this kind of apron rather than the bib-style ones, with shoulder straps that muted her mature, all-over-womanly curves. Victoria was nearing thirty and no longer willowy, but to Beartooth's eyes — and to those of any red-blooded male with a lick of sense — she was still a mighty fine-looking gal. Her chestnut hair was thick and rich, her face was unlined and finely sculpted, and she had eyes as blue and sparkling as the deepest, purest mountain pool Beartooth had ever looked into.

Sensing his presence in the doorway after she had placed two loaves of bread in the warmer, she turned her head and glanced back over her shoulder. "Oh," she said. "I didn't hear you come in."

"Sorry. Didn't mean to startle you."

Victoria gave a faint shake of her head. "You didn't. I think I've finally gotten used to how quietly you, Firestick, and Moose-jaw move . . . especially for such large men. Whenever I turn around, I'm prepared to find that one of you has entered the room while I was looking away."

She spoke with an English accent, at times stronger than others, as befitting the land of her birth before coming to America and eventually to the West with a spirited cousin who was a dreamer and a hopeless romantic.

That cousin — her name was Estelle, and she'd been closer than a sister ever since childhood — had convinced Victoria without a great deal of difficulty that the arranged marriage her parents were pushing her into with a man for whom she felt no love would be a tragedy she'd regret for the rest of her life. So the pair had fled together to the hopes and thrills and promises of a new country.

On the way west, to a wildly expanding world of cattle empires and endless opportunities such as Estelle had read about in books, she contracted pneumonia and died. This left Victoria jarringly alone and needing to fend for herself on the Texas frontier. Her pride refused to let her contact her family back in England for aid. She vowed to forge on in pursuit of all that she and Estelle had set out after. With her looks, she could have easily succumbed to any number of marriage proposals, but she wanted something more than to settle for an arrangement of convenience — the very thing she had escaped — as a means to simply be taken care of by someone.

So instead she sought whatever socially acceptable "woman's work" she could find — washing, mending, cleaning, cooking — in order to get by independently. Eventually this led to her hiring on as cook and house-keeper for the men of the Double M. It wasn't the culmination of her dreams, to be sure, but it was a safe, acceptable position, one she often had to remind herself not to become too complacent with.

"Hope you understand we don't move the way we do to unnerve you," Beartooth was explaining. "It's just that, the way we lived out in the wild and up in the mountains for all those years, we learned to move silently or we might sudden-like quit livin' at all."

"I understand," Victoria said. "I can't, for the life of me, figure out why anyone would want to pursue that extreme lifestyle, but I understand how you had to adapt in order to survive."

Beartooth smiled. "Nobody can ever appreciate that lifestyle unless they've felt the urge and gone on to live it. It ain't something you can sit down and reason out as a good idea or a smart way to live. It's something that's either in you or it ain't."

"And to this day it remains in all three of you, doesn't it?" Victoria said with a faint smile of her own. "The love for that life and those times, I mean."

"Yeah, I reckon it does," Beartooth admitted, somewhat surprised to hear himself say so. "But, barrin' something drastic, I don't see any of us ever returnin' to it. There are plenty of old-timers still walkin' the mountain paths and trappin' the streams, but it's really a young man's game. Me and my pards, we decided we were a little long in the tooth to keep after it."

"Nonsense. The passage of years means little to hardy men like you three."

"Maybe not. But there are other ways to prove it." Beartooth shrugged. "You're right, though, about the love for that life — the savorin' of it, I guess you could say — still bein' in all of us. I'm pretty sure Firestick and Moosejaw feel the same way. Only, like I said, barrin' something drastic, I don't see any of us returnin' to it."

"Let's hope not," Victoria said. "Surely you must know there are many in these parts who would hate to see you leave."

Her words left Beartooth at a loss for how to respond. Since settling here in the Buffalo Peak area, Firestick and Moosejaw had each found romantic interests in town. To them, Victoria was a welcome addition to their ranch life — competent and eye-pleasing in her role — but that was as far as it went. Beartooth's feelings toward her, however, had grown into something more. And there'd been indications she might have similar feelings toward him, but as of yet, neither had gotten around to expressing anything with words.

So, Beartooth wondered, when Victoria responded to the possibility of him and his friends returning to the mountains by saying, "Let's hope not," then adding how there were many who would "hate to see you leave" . . . was she speaking only for the "many" — or was she including herself? Or was she perhaps speaking *mainly* for herself?

It was ironic, considering how Beartooth always had a smooth, easy way with women — albeit the *certain kind* he'd mostly come in contact with before — that here he was feeling flummoxed, not sure how to act or what to say, when it came to the first woman who might truly mean something to him. Flummoxation like this was enough to actually drive a man back up into the mountains!

With Beartooth momentarily tongue-tied, Victoria followed up on her own remark by saying, "Before you wash up for supper, would you mind bringing in some fuel for the stove's wood bin? Otherwise I might forget and then run short for tomorrow's breakfast. And I really dread going out to the woodpile in the predawn hour."

"Sure. No problem," Beartooth replied, grateful for the disruption of his awkward silence. "With all the chores you do around here, us fellas ought to do a better job of keepin' that bin full for you — without havin' to be asked."

"I don't mind fetching some for myself, except, like I said, early in the morning. A rat jumped out at me one time when it was still too dark to see well, and I've been skittish ever since. And right now I need to stay here and keep an eye on those pies in the oven."

Beartooth's eyebrows lifted. "*Pies,* as in more than one? I thought that was part of what I smelled. Peach, right?"

"Sorry, but no," Victoria said, knowing how fond he was of peach pie. "They're both blueberry this time. But I promise to make peach next, before the end of the week. All right?"

Picking up the bucket for hauling in the wood for the stove, Beartooth said, "I'll hold you to it. And I aim to make sure you'll have plenty of wood for the baking. In the meantime, though, blueberry ain't exactly a hard sacrifice. So, you stay here and guard 'em good while I commence to fetchin' your fuel."

CHAPTER 6

"The boss sure ain't gonna like it, I can tell you that much. Hell, I can guarantee it. He ain't gonna like it one damn bit!"

Firestick scowled fiercely in response to these words. "Your boss 'don't like it'?" he mimicked. "You think me or anybody else in this town likes those three jackasses showin' up every two, three weeks and startin' some new kind of trouble? Well, here's a guarantee right back at you — nobody does. Least of all me. Tolsvord's had plenty of chances to rein in the Dunlaps and Woolsey, but all he ever does is pay their fines and wag his finger at them and then turn 'em loose to come around and stir something up all over again."

"And that's what he'll do again this time. Pay their fines, I mean. Just tell me how much it is so I can let him know, and he'll send somebody around with the money first thing tomorrow."

Firestick shook his head stubbornly. "Nope. I ain't gonna make it that easy. Not this time. Oh, there'll still be fines, don't worry about that. Stiff ones, too. But they're also gonna serve some time behind bars. If Tolsvord ain't willin' to tie some knots in their tails, by God, I am. Since they go around actin' like what little brains they got is in their asses, maybe a knot down there close will help straighten out their thinkin' a little."

Cleve Boynton was a tall, rawboned individual with bushy, prematurely white sideburns bracketing a weathered face that, more often than not, was gripped by a stern expression. The cause for the latter, at least part of the time, had to do with the fact he was the foreman for Gerald Tolsvord's Box T Ranch and had wranglers like the Dunlaps and Newt Woolsey to deal with.

"Doggone it, Firestick," he lamented now, as he stood before the marshal's desk in the front office area of the jail building, "you know the pickle I'm in with those three. You think I ain't full aware they're a bunch of . . ." He hesitated, eyeing the heavy wooden door that led back to the cell block. The fact that the door was closed gave him reassurance the men back there couldn't hear him, so he continued, "Well, they're jackasses, just like you said. But you also know the rest of the story — how the Dunlaps are kin to Boss Tolsvord's wife. Her brother's boys, I think. Anyway, she rides Tolsvord to keep cuttin' 'em slack, and he rides me to keep tryin' to get something resemblin' work out of 'em."

Firestick sighed. "I can appreciate the fix you're in, Cleve. And, for that part, I'm sorry. But that don't change a dang thing. I aim to send a message to them three, and Tolsvord, as well. You go ahead and tell him that. Put it all on me. That should leave you clear from takin' any blame."

"I don't know about that. I go back to the ranch without 'em, no matter what my story, the boss is bound to be plenty sore," said Boynton. "Plus, I had work lined up for those yahoos tomorrow morning. Not having 'em there to take care of it — even given the half-assed job they usually do — will either leave it undone or force me to pull somebody from some other job."

"Like I said, I'm sorry for how it lands on you, Cleve," Firestick told him. "But my mind's made up. I ain't gonna go easy on 'em, not this time."

"Okay. If your mind's made up, I guess that's all there is to it," said Boynton, his shoulders sagging somewhat in defeat. He started to turn away, then once again hesitated. "The boss is bound to ask, so what do I tell him as far as how long you figure to keep 'em locked up? And you said there'll still be a fine, too?"

Now it was Firestick who seemed to hesitate. His brows puckered for a moment as if in deep thought. Then he said, "Okay. Tell him this. Three days and thirty dollars for each of the Dunlaps; four days and forty dollars for that weasel, Woolsey."

"That seems a mite steep, if you don't mind my sayin'," responded Boynton, frowning. "And why more for Newt than the other two?"

"Because the little bastard sucker-butted me and loosened four of my front teeth, that's why," Firestick snapped back. "Likely be near a week before I can chomp into a good steak again. As far as the fines . . . well, that's what they are, and that's all I got to say on it."

Boynton's frown stayed in place. "You basin' any of that on some kind of legal rules or regulations that are in place? Or are you makin' it up just to suit yourself?"

"Hell, Cleve, you know Buffalo Peak ain't got no legal mumbo jumbo in place on the books. The town council handed me and my pards some badges and hired us to keep a lid on things. So that's what we're doin' to the best of our abilities and, in some cases, yeah, we're makin' it up as we go along." Firestick paused, took a deep breath, and then exhaled through his nose. "Now, I've said what I got to say, and I ain't in the mood for no more explainin'. So, go tell it to Tolsvord. If that don't satisfy him, tell him to haul his ass in here to town and I'll tell him to his face. Otherwise, all he's got to do is send the money and I'll turn his men loose as soon as they've served their time."

Boynton turned and stomped out, clearly not happy with the answer and not looking forward to passing it on to Tolsvord.

After he was gone, Moosejaw, who'd been looking on silently from where he was seated in a chair tilted back against a side wall of the office area, said, "I kinda feel sorry for ol' Cleve, the fix he's in. He ain't really a bad sort."

"Nobody said he was," Firestick replied. "And I don't like seein' him squeezed in the middle, neither. But I can't help it. The whole thing really falls back on Tolsvord not havin' the backbone to stand up to his wife. If he did that, and then backed Cleve to make those three blockheads toe the mark like he does the rest of his crew, everybody'd be better off."

"Yeah, you're right about that. In more ways than one," Moosejaw allowed. "Nothing any good ever comes from a man lettin' a woman run roughshod over him. It plumb ain't natural."

Firestick eyed him under a sharply cocked brow. "You tellin' me you've made those kinds of feelin's clear between you and Daisy?"

Moosejaw's chair dropped down flat with a hollow *thump*. His round, smooth-shaven face went from an expression of bold certainty when he was making his declaration, to abruptly looking not so sure. "Here now. Ain't nobody talkin' about me and Daisy. In the first place, it ain't like we're hitched or anything. In the second place, when it comes to a gal like Daisy, well, there's things you got to keep in mind. I mean, you gotta admit, my Daisy ain't like most regular gals."

"That's true enough," Firestick said, grinning at the way he had his big friend squirming a little. "Most gals can't bend a horseshoe straight or drink their weight in firewater or out–arm wrestle ninety percent of the men in town. Little things like that, you're talkin' about, right?"

"Along those lines, I reckon. Yeah."

"And also maybe along the lines of — if she ever heard you talkin' about how no gal has the right to run roughshod over a fella — she might haul off and throw a punch at you?"

The Daisy in question was Daisy Rawling, who owned and operated the town blacksmith shop, which she had taken over from her late husband. She was a sawed-off slice of femaleness, standing only five-foot-two by standard measurement, but about a foot and a half taller when you factored in attitude and sass. A cap of butter-yellow curls, worn functionally short, framed a face that was actually quite pretty. Pug nose, ready smile, and big, luminous brown eyes. Her build was what could be called chunky but not fat, certainly not in the sense of being soft; it was more like she had a layer of rubbery muscle over womanly curves. Anyone who'd ever seen her handle the tools and tasks of her trade could attest to those muscles being more than just for show.

Nor was Firestick's remark about her throwing a punch merely part of needling Moosejaw — a handful of loudmouths who'd made the mistake of commenting disparagingly about a woman blacksmith within earshot of Daisy had found themselves flattened for their trouble.

The romance that blossomed between Daisy and Moosejaw had stemmed directly from her taking one good look at him not long after his arrival in town and deciding that the six-foot-six walking redwood tree was man enough to handle her. From there, Moosejaw, who'd seldom shown much interest in women before, never had a chance. And as unlikely a pair as Daisy and Moosejaw made visually, Firestick and Beartooth had never known their big comrade to be happier, while those acquainted with Daisy said the same about her.

At the moment, however, this fact wasn't quite enough to assuage Moosejaw's concern about drawing Daisy's ire if she were to hear about his "women running roughshod" statement. "That kind of thing'd never apply to me and Daisy," he protested in a tone that sounded like it was meant to try and convince himself as much as anyone. "It ain't a matter of havin' the right or not. It's just that she'd never ride me to do something that went against my grain, and I'd never put her in a position where she had to."

"If you say so," Firestick allowed, deciding he'd done enough poking with the needle. "But that obviously ain't the case with Tolsvord and his wife. The way she's puttin' the spurs to him where her loser nephews are concerned has *got* to go against his grain. Yet he keeps lettin' her get away with it."

"You think holdin' this bunch behind bars for a spell is gonna change anything?"

"I have my doubts. But that don't change my mind none."

Moosejaw's mouth spread in a sly grin. "Maybe Mrs. Tolsvord will show up and try puttin' the spurs to *you* about her nephews and their buddy, Newt."

"She could try." Firestick scoffed. "All she'll accomplish would be goin' away with some dulled-up spurs if she does."

Further discussion of the matter was interrupted by the entrance of a man who strode in confidently and then pressed the door closed behind him. He was an elderly gent, average-sized, still carrying himself straight and strong. He had a neatly trimmed mustache, bone-white in color, that contrasted with a set of unruly eyebrows, also white. Beneath the brows, a pair of alert, quick-moving dark eyes swept back and forth between the two lawmen.

"Heard talk you'd taken in some some new boarders," he announced. "Expected you'd be wantin' me to babysit, so I figured I'd go ahead and save you the trouble of havin' to come fetch me."

"Well, now. That's right prompt and thoughtful of you, Sam," said Firestick. "Indeed, we'll be needin' your services for tonight and about three more. You available for the duration?"

The elderly gent nodded. "Got nothing better to do. You know my requirements. 'S'long as you hold up your end, I'll hold up mine."

Sam Duvall was a former New York City constable, a widower with a touch of tuberculosis who'd come West for his health after the passing of his wife. He lived alone in a small cabin on the south side of town. When Buffalo Peak first decided it needed a town marshal, Sam had been approached, due to his background in law enforcement. Though grateful for the offer, he'd turned it down, citing his age and health. Once Firestick and his pals signed on, however, they approached him with a different proposition. For occasions when there were prisoners in the lockup overnight, they asked him to serve as jailer. Sam, who admitted to being bored much of the time by the quiet and solitude of his lifestyle, had jumped at the chance.

The "requirements" Sam spoke of for taking the job were pretty simple and had noth-

70

ing to do with monetary payment. He asked only for supper and breakfast to be served from the kitchen of the Mallory Hotel, the makings for plenty of coffee to drink in between, and the allowance for his dog, Shield, to accompany him during his stay.

"Sounds like a done deal to me," said Firestick. "Got Shield with you?"

"As always. He's waiting outside."

"Well, bring him on in whenever you're ready. There's plenty of coffee fixin's, you know where everything is. We'll see to gettin' some supper sent over from the Mallory."

"What about supper for the prisoners?" Sam asked.

"They likely ain't in no mood to eat right away," said Moosejaw. "They're sufferin' the effects of hangovers and from receivin' a well-deserved thumpin'."

"I'm comin' back for the late-duty turn. I'll see to gettin' 'em some vittles if they're up for anything then," Firestick said.

Since the three former mountain men also had a ranch to run in addition to their lawmen obligations, the way they worked it out in the normal course of things was to have at least one of them present in town and at least one at the ranch during the daytime hours. Each evening, they took supper together at the Double M, using that opportunity to bring one another up to date on anything pertinent and discuss it accordingly. Then, after supper, one of them would return to town for a "late duty" tour to make sure everything was in order, that all the shop doors that were supposed to be locked were secure, and that things were suitably quieting down.

"Do you know who it is we've got behind bars?" Moosejaw asked Sam.

"A whole lot of nothing, the way I heard — the Dunlap brothers and that little runt who follows 'em around. Willoughby or some such?"

"Woolsey," Firestick said. "You may have got the name wrong, but the rest of what you said was dead-on — the three of 'em don't amount to a hill of beans. They can be ornery and troublesome, though, so don't take no guff off of 'em."

"That'll be the day," Sam muttered.

Rubbing his ample stomach, Moosejaw said, "I'll tell you something else he got dead-on. All this talk about supper is makin' me hungry. I didn't realize how late it was gettin'. We'd best get headed out to the ranch before long, Firestick, or Miss Victoria will be servin' us a cold supper by the time we get there."

"Like that'd slow you down any from puttin' away a pile of it," said Firestick. "But you ain't wrong, it's time to get headed that way. We'll stop by the hotel and arrange for your supper to be sent over, Sam. Then I'll see you again a little later on."

"Me and Shield will be lookin' for you. I'll have a pot of coffee brewed."

CHAPTER 7

Cleve Boynton was in no hurry to get back to the Box T.

Oh, he was anxious enough to crawl into his bunk and grab himself a stretch of shut-eye at the end of a long day, that much was true. But the part that would have to come beforehand — him telling Boss Tolsvord about how Marshal Firestick had the Dunlaps and Woolsey locked up in jail and wasn't planning on releasing them until he'd kept them for a spell *and* received a stiff fine — that was the part he was in no hurry for. Tolsvord was bound to holler like a scalded dog.

Not that he'd be hollering *at* Boynton, exactly, but the ramrod would have to stand there and listen to it all the same. And the hardest part of all would be acting like he had a shred of sympathy for the three damn fools, when all the while he actually didn't blame the marshal for throwing those bumbling clowns in the clink. He wouldn't even mind too much if Firestick kept them there for good.

Boynton couldn't let on about such feelings, of course. And, while it was true the trio was half-assed, at best, when it came to doing any work around the ranch, they were still three sets of hands he'd have to get by without in the days to come. But Boynton could shift the rest of the crew around in order to manage that. All he really had to get past was breaking the news to Tolsvord.

For the sake of putting off this unenviable yet inevitable task, Boynton had hung around town after leaving the jail, until dusk was starting to settle in. Since the Box T was a couple hours' ride from Buffalo Peak, that meant it would be dark by the time he made it back. But that was no problem; he had a trusty horse under him, and they both knew the way well enough, even in the dark.

For a little while, as he rode along, Boynton toyed with the hope that maybe he'd find Tolsvord turned in early so he could hold off telling him anything until tomorrow. But that was no good, not really. If he stalled and didn't get it off his chest right away, Boynton knew he'd spend a restless night fretting over it, and that would only make things worse when he did have to face the boss in the morning.

These troublesome thoughts, mingled with the more pleasant ones of the cute little barmaid who'd been flirting with him at the Lone Star Palace, Buffalo Peak's other main saloon, where he'd killed some time before riding out, occupied Boynton's mind as he loped southeast toward the Box T. The murkiness of evening was thickening, the air was starting to cool quickly now that the sun had gone down, and the scent of the prairie grasses in late spring filled his nostrils. It wasn't as nice as the perfume of the cute little barmaid had been, but to a man who made his way working cattle out on the range it was still a good smell.

The sky was clear, and as it turned from murky gray to velvety black, a blanket of stars gradually began to glimmer. Lost in his thoughts and mildly awed by the unfolding of this heavenly display, Boynton was slow to notice the group of horsemen who topped the crest of a low hill off to the southeast.

The ramrod's first reaction was to wonder what would bring out so many riders — there appeared to be at least two dozen of them — at an hour when most outfits would be finishing supper and getting ready to turn in. From there, his mind quickly jumped to suspicion. Was he looking at a pack of rustlers on their way to wide-loop somebody's cattle?

None of the surrounding spreads had big enough crews to muster that many men all at once, though. Not that a couple of neighboring outfits couldn't have thrown in together for some reason. But what could that reason be? And why at this odd hour?

His suspicion swelled and a chill ran through him, part anger and part anxiety. If that pack of hombres was up to no good, he could all of a sudden be in a bad predicament. If they decided to swoop down on him . . .

But then, as quickly and unexpectedly as they'd appeared, the whole pack wheeled around and dropped back out of sight behind the crest. One minute they were there, silhouetted motionlessly against a low array of just-emerging stars, then the next minute they were gone.

Boynton reined his horse to a halt and gawked in confusion. Was he seeing things? Had the shifting light and shadows that came at this time of night played some kind of trick on his eyes? Had he really seen what he thought he did — or was it some kind of illusion brought on by snapping too suddenly out of the snarl of thoughts and worries that had been filling his head?

But if it was an illusion, then why could he hear the fading sound of so many hoofbeats carried on the still air? His own horse was at a standstill, and the night all around was otherwise quiet. Except for the low rumble of those departing hooves . . . until they'd faded completely and then there was only the occasional soft blowing of his mount.

Damn it, there *had* been riders up there on that hill! But who were they and what were they up to? And why had they turned tail and taken off at — apparently — the mere sight of *him*?

For an instant, Boynton felt the urge to give chase. Run them down and try to get some answers. After all, if they *were* rustlers or owlhoots of some other stripe, then he owed it to his neighbors and friends to give warning, spread notice that something fishy and possibly dangerous was going on. It didn't take long, however, for him to decide there were better ways to serve that purpose than to go charging off in reckless pursuit and possibly force the confrontation that had only just been avoided. Cleve Boynton didn't lack for grit, but neither was he foolhardy.

Furthermore, while he surely was willing

to sound a warning if there was a genuine threat, at the same time he didn't want to end up looking like a fool by raising a false alarm and maybe stirring up a panic, only to have it turn out there was a logical explanation for those mysterious horsemen.

A frown pulled hard on Boynton's face.

Those mysterious horsemen.

There was something more about them — something more than just their number and the odd hour and the way they'd turned and fled — that gnawed at a corner of the ramrod's brain. Something elusive that bothered him apart from all the rest of his suspicions. He concentrated hard, straining almost physically to try and drag it out. In his mind's eye he could see them again, a lumpy mass skylined so briefly up there on the crest, bunched together though spread out somewhat. Given the distance and the weak wash of stars behind them, individual features had been impossible to discern. Yet he'd been able to make out the distinct outlines — head and shoulder silhouettes thrusting up above the blur of their horses — of several of them.

Head and shoulder silhouettes posed briefly against the stars.

Not tall men. Spare and wiry, he somehow

sensed. The largest of them only average-sized.

No hats.

Something peculiar about the shapes of some of the heads. A hint of bright color at the hairline of one or two? A sense of longish hair reaching down to the shoulders.

No hats . . . A sense of longish hair . . .

Suddenly a new chill streaked through Boynton, this one far deeper and colder than the previous time. The elusive thing that had been nagging at him all at once became clear.

Holy Christ.

He didn't want to believe it, didn't even want to think it. But in his gut, he knew. Knew with sickening clarity what he had just glimpsed.

A man who frowned on the practice of spurring horses too aggressively and was proud of always avoiding it himself, Boynton nevertheless did so now and sent his mount streaking for the Box T as fast as the startled beast could run.

CHAPTER 8

Buffalo Peak had two saloons, the Silver Spur and the Lone Star Palace, plus a nameless Mexican cantina just within the eastern town limits. A small room adjoining the dining hall of the Mallory Hotel also contained a modest bar. Clientele for the latter consisted mainly of hotel guests and town businessmen who stopped in evenings before going home, wanting someplace quiet to relax with a drink or two rather than visiting either of the saloons, where the cowboys looking to let off a little steam frequently got a mite rowdy. The cantina was a quiet, friendly place that attracted mostly Mexican vaqueros from the surrounding ranches.

Firestick's standard routine, whenever he returned to town for late-duty rounds, was to first check each of the saloons to see if any signs of trouble were brewing. From there, he would walk the length of Trail

Street, checking the businesses and shops on either side to make sure they were securely locked and that nothing appeared to have been disturbed. At the far end of the street, he would also look in on the little cantina. His Spanish was pretty limited, but the proprietors, Julio and Lucita Ramirez, were a nice, hardworking couple who always gave him a friendly welcome.

At that point, on most nights, when the jail was empty and there was no reason to stop by there, before finishing his rounds with a final check on the saloons, Firestick would double back to the hotel and pay Kate a call. Most times, when she knew he was scheduled for late duty, she would be waiting for him in her office, where they would visit and have a drink together — wine for Kate, bourbon for Firestick.

Occasionally, Kate would already be retired to her private apartment on the second floor and Firestick would join her there. Although they were two adults unbound by any other commitments and had every right to consort with one another as they saw fit, they nevertheless kept these visits as discreet as possible. Despite the attraction between them being recognized by a number of folks around town, they chose to play the whole thing pretty close to the vest.

This was done mainly as a consideration to Kate, given how hard she'd worked to earn her place as a respected businessperson. Despite that, everybody knew how a woman's reputation was always at greater risk for even a *perceived* lapse in behavior. Otherwise, Firestick was so proud to be linked to such a fine beauty as Kate that he would have liked nothing better than to shout it to the moon!

This night, as he rode back into town from the Double M, Firestick was thinking, as he often did, about these disparities and complications. If it wasn't so annoying, it would almost be amusing — the uncivil behavior to be found in so-called *civilization.*

In the wild, everything was a lot simpler, a lot more clear. It was strictly a matter of survival. There were plenty of things that would kill you, but none were the result of jealousy or of petty, poisonous gossip aimed at harming someone for no particular gain except trying to make the target conform to what the all-powerful "they" deemed to be *right.*

Firestick cautioned himself inwardly not to allow this pondering to get him too worked up. It wouldn't do to mingle among the citizenry with a chip on his shoulder that might make him overreact to a minor slight or remark. The badge he'd remembered to pin on this time before leaving the ranch meant he was supposed to keep a cool head — especially since he'd already slipped up once today by getting into a brawl with the Dunlaps and Woolsey. He didn't want to start out this evening primed for a repeat.

He reined up in front of the hotel and swung down to tie his horse at the hitchrail out front. He always started his late rounds here, since this was where he would be finishing up. Which reminded him of another reason not to sink into a foul mood: In only an hour or so, he'd be in the company of Kate. A smile lifted one corner of Firestick's mouth. Come to think about it, it had been a while since he'd visited her up in her apartment. Maybe tonight would turn out to be one of those . . .

"Elwood. I'm glad you got back to town."

Apart from someone meeting him for the first time, there was only one person who used his given name. On top of that, there was no mistaking her low, throaty voice when she spoke.

Firestick turned from knotting his reins on the rail and looked to see Kate standing in the doorway of the hotel. Backlit by the golden glow of lantern light from within, her face was cast in shadow. But he could still see her expression well enough to be able to tell that something was troubling her.

"What is it? What's wrong, Kate?" he said.

"Inside. In the barroom," she said. "We've got a situation with some cowboys that's starting to turn kinda ugly."

Firestick stepped up on the broad porch that ran across the front of the building. "Who is it? Do I know 'em?"

Kate nodded. "One of them is Gus Wingate."

"Wingate?" Firestick echoed. "Haven't seen him around much since . . . well, since that shooting."

"I'm pretty sure that's the way he's wanted it," said Kate. "Still, he's been showing up here fairly regular. Every two or three nights. He only comes by late in the evening. He's drinking awful heavy. He comes here to pick up a couple bottles to take home with him, usually stays long enough to put away a good deal of bar stock before he leaves."

"As I recall, that trouble with Owen Rockwell left Wingate in a mighty low place," Firestick noted. "Sounds like he's tryin' to drink his way back up out of it . . . or maybe deeper in."

"I agree," said Kate. "But it's the Rockwell thing that's caught up with him tonight, and it's what's got me worried. Rand Wilson and Whitey Chapman, from the Bar 6, are inside, too. Why they chose to come by here instead of one of the cowboy saloons, I have no idea, but whatever the reason, they did. Now they're claiming to have been good friends of Rockwell, and the two of them — Wilson especially — are riding Wingate pretty hard about what happened."

"Sounds like something that needs a lid clamped on it before it gets too far out out of hand."

"That's why I'm glad you got back to town. Thomas has the night off, and I'm afraid Little Al doesn't do well in situations like this."

"That's okay. I do," said Firestick tersely, confidently.

Gus Wingate was a well-liked individual, at least he always had been. He was a widower with a small cattle ranch just south of town. One night, a little more than two months earlier, he'd shown up at the Lone Star Palace with his two hired hands. They were celebrating the fact that their herd had survived the winter in good shape and it looked like they'd have quite a few head ready for market as soon as they got them fattened up on spring grass.

In the saloon, however, Wingate ran afoul of Owen Rockwell, a proddy young man who worked a neighboring farm with his kid brother and mother, a widow woman. Owen fancied himself a bit of a gunhand. He also fancied that Wingate was making unwelcome advances on his mother and he demanded for it to stop. Wingate denied any such thing, claiming his only interest in Margaret Rockwell was as a friendly neighbor. Owen called him a liar. Loud and clear, right in front of everybody.

The whole thing escalated very quickly. And it climaxed before Firestick or any of his deputies could be summoned to intervene.

Owen forced the confrontation into gunplay. And Wingate, who carried a sidearm for rattlesnakes and other varmints that might be encountered out on the range but had never come close to pulling on another man before, surprised himself and everybody else in the Palace that night by outdrawing the would-be gunny and killing him with one shot.

It was all over by the time Firestick and Beartooth got there. And with everyone present testifying it had been a clear-cut case of self-defense, there were no charges to be brought nor anything else required in the way of legal follow-up. Owen's mother was devastated, of course, and even more so when she was told there was no basis for acting on her demand that Wingate be arrested. Ironically, Wingate ended up punishing himself in ways the law never could. Not a day went by that he wasn't tormented by his conscience and sense of guilt over killing a young man, no matter how justified.

And now, tonight, a new pair of bigmouths were dredging up the pain and guilt in him all over again. Having seen Wingate's suffering after the first incident, Firestick had no intention of allowing him to endure more if he could help it.

CHAPTER 9

As soon as the marshal stepped into the barroom, it was clear who the troublemakers were. There were only four men in the room.

One of them was Little Al Seavers, Kate's part-time bartender. He was a diminutive individual, barely topping five feet tall, scrawny and riddled with arthritis that gave him a severe limp and twisted, huge-knuckled hands with which he somehow still managed to serve drinks. He had a pale, pinched face with slicked-back hair and a pencil mustache, and at the moment he was wearing an expression of considerable worry. When he saw Firestick entering, his face quickly relaxed some.

At a round-topped table against one wall, Gus Wingate sat alone. Normally he was a solid six-footer, early forties, trim and quite handsome by most standards. Having not seen him in a while, though, Firestick was mildly shocked by how shabby, unshaven, and hollow-eyed he now appeared. He was hunched protectively over a shot glass and a half-empty bottle of whiskey, like they were the most coveted things in his life.

At the bar, leaning back against it but turned so that they were facing out toward Wingate, were two lean, young cowpokes. Each had a glass of beer in his hand; each wore a cocky, lopsided grin. Firestick recognized them as Rand Wilson and Whitey Chapman, riders for the Bar 6 brand. He didn't know much about Chapman, but in recent months, Wilson had drawn some passing interest from the marshal and his deputies due to the way he'd taken to wearing his sidearm in a tied-down holster and the increasingly bold strut he exhibited whenever he came to town. There was talk of how fast and good he was with a gun and how he'd backed down more than a few of his fellow wranglers at the Bar 6.

In other words, Wilson was cut from the same cloth as too many other young men who developed a level of skill with a six-gun and then unfortunately started to let that define them and their actions. Tonight, it appeared that Wilson was looking to make that definition even more sharp and clear.

"Well now, gents," Firestick drawled easily, "what have we got goin' on here this evenin'? Is it just me, or is there a dose of tension cracklin' in the air?"

His grin continuing to hang lopsided, Wilson said, "Can't say I follow what you're talkin' about, Marshal. The only thing I know of cracklin' around here are the joints in that sawed-off, crippled-up excuse for a bartender. It's pure disgustin' to try and enjoy a drink when you got to listen to the clickin' and creakin' of his every move."

"That's an interesting observation," said Firestick. "Makes me wonder why, if it bothers you so, you don't go elsewhere to do your drinkin'?"

"Because I drink where I damn well please," Wilson responded. "You want to wonder about something, why don't you wonder why that rickety old pile of bones don't crawl off and die somewhere instead of shufflin' around, creakin' and clankin' and disgustin' folks?"

"Okay, that's enough," Firestick said through clenched teeth. "You're insultin' a decent man who works hard to make an honest living. And I already know that, before I came in here, you were harrassin' Wingate over there. On top of that, you've been drinkin'. If I wanted, I could make all that add up to drunk and disorderly conduct and use it as grounds for tossin' your sorry asses in the clink."

"I'd like to see you try it," said Wilson, his body going rigid.

"Don't tempt me, you mouthy pup. I said that's what I *could* do. I'll settle, instead, for you and that grinnin' skunk beside you to hightail it out of town and not come back until your brains and attitudes are workin' a little more sensible."

Wilson's nostrils flared, and his eyes blazed with fire. "To hell with that, Marshal Mountain Man. You ain't up in the high country with a bunch of unwashed beaver chasers no more. We got laws and rules down here that have to be followed, no matter if a bunch of town idiots *did* slap a tin star on your chest. That means you can't go shovin' folks around and threatenin' to lock 'em up just because it suits you."

"I ain't started shovin'. Not yet," said Firestick. "Up to now I've just been *suggestin'*. If you're smart, you won't stick around to find out the difference."

"Maybe we oughta listen to him, Rand. Maybe it ain't worth it to push things no further," said Whitey Chapman.

"You'd be wise to pay attention to your pard," Firestick pressed. "Whether you like it or not, I *am* the law in Buffalo Peak. Gettin' tangleways of me means more of the same when it comes to my deputies, Beartooth and Moosejaw. I can guarantee that ain't something you'd find to your likin'."

"What ridiculous names." Wilson sneered. "Beartooth . . . Moosejaw . . . and Firestick. How can anybody take the law serious when it's being dished out by men who not only lug around handles like those, but who are actually *proud* of them?"

Firestick's eyes narrowed. "A fraction of what we endured to earn those names would have sent you runnin' home to your mama's tit, boy. Don't ever forget it. And no matter how we're called, the badges we wear stand for themselves."

"Yeah? Where were those badges and what were they supposed to stand for on the night this craven coward" — Wilson gestured toward Gus Wingate with his free hand — "goaded Owen Rockwell into a shoot-out and then drilled him dead? How about that?"

"You're right about one thing," Firestick allowed. "Neither me nor my deputies were on hand to try and stop the flare-up between Wingate and Rockwell. Apart from that, though, you got your facts twisted around just exactly backwards. According to more than a dozen witnesses, it was young

Rockwell who did the goading and then paid for it with his life. All Wingate did was act in self-defense."

"That makes for a mighty tidy story. But if it's true, *if* Wingate is so lily-pure innocent and all he did was defend himself, then why is he so racked by guilt? Look at him. He's sittin' there tryin' to crawl into that bottle in order to try and hide from his guilt and shame. He's feelin' so low-down because he knows damn well what he did. Killin' the sole support of a kid brother and a mother — a poor woman who already suffered bein' made a widow — and leavin' 'em alone to try and scratch out a living on that hardscrabble chunk of land."

"Shut up. You don't know what you're talking about," said Wingate, speaking for the first time. His voice was flat, wooden, and his eyes never lifted from the bottle in front of him, as if he were talking to it rather than responding to Wilson. "I tried to make amends . . . offered to help them work their land. Made every overture I knew how . . ."

"My, how noble and generous that was. After you ripped away her son's life, you offered to patch it over by plowin' and seedin' a couple acres of land for Mrs. Rockwell." Wilson snorted derisively. "If I ain't mistaken, that's the very thing that led to the differences between you and Owen in the first place. You was lookin' to do some plowin' and seedin' when it came to his mother, but not the kind that had anything to do with land."

Wingate shot to his feet, sloshing whiskey from his glass and causing the bottle to wobble precariously atop the table. "That's a filthy lie! I'm sick of it and I'll listen to no more!" As he said this, he thrust his right hand down over his hip, fingers splayed wide, reaching, digging. But there was nothing there to grab. He wasn't wearing a gun tonight.

Wilson howled with mocking laughter. "Look at that drunk bastard! He's reachin' for a gun when he ain't even wearin' one."

Whitey Chapman, now encouraged back into the taunting, said, "Hell, we can fix that. I'd be willin' to lend him mine since he's so set on slappin' leather with you, Rand."

"Leave that iron pouched!" Firestick commanded harshly as he stepped forward to insert himself between Wingate and the two cowboys.

Turning toward Wingate, who was weaving unsteadily on his feet, the marshal placed a palm against his chest and pushed, not very hard, saying, "Sit down before you fall down." The slight pressure was enough to drop the rancher back onto his chair. He landed hard and somewhat unevenly so that the chair threatened to topple over before he managed to keep it upright.

Turning back to Wilson and Chapman, Firestick said, "This ends right here and now, you understand? Nobody's slappin' no damn leather — not here, not out in the street, not nowhere. You two are shuttin' your yaps and makin' tracks home to the Bar 6, or you're goin' in the clink. Make up your minds and do it quick."

Wilson shook his head determinedly. "No good, Marshal. I won't hold for either one of those choices. That son of a bitch tried to pull a gun on me! The only thing that stopped him was the fact that he was too drunk to realize he wasn't heeled. But that don't make no difference. It was the same as callin' me out, and I ain't about to walk away without givin' him what he wants."

"You saw him. He's so drunk he can't hardly stand up," said Firestick. "You'd gun him down easy, no matter if he was armed or not."

"That's his problem, not mine. He's the one who called it. All somebody has to do is give him a gun and we'll settle it. And when I blow his brisket clean out to the middle of

Trail Street, it'll be just another case of *self-defense.*"

Now it was Firestick who gave a hard shake of his head. "No. I can't go along with that. I gave you your two choices. That's all there is to it."

"I see there bein' a third choice, Marshal," said Wilson, his voice tight, fighting to stay controlled. "I could slap leather against you first . . . and then still get around to Wingate."

A corner of Firestick's mouth quirked upward ever so slightly. "You *could* do that . . . if you was good enough. Which you ain't, but if you're bound and determined to try, then that'd relieve me of any regret I might have over killin' you. Because it would make you too damn dumb to let live."

Chapman suddenly vacillated back the other way. "Can't say I like the way you're thinkin', Rand. Can't say as I want any part of goin' straight up against the law over something so —"

"Don't, then," Wilson snapped. "Back away, you chicken-livered puke. Ain't like I need you for doin' what I got to do."

Flailing his arms drunkenly, Wingate muttered, "Give me a damn gun. I'll show you who *ain't* chicken-livered." But when his gestures accidentally bumped over the whiskey bottle, he forgot everything else and grabbed desperately to minimize the spillage.

"Don't worry, you pathetic drunk. Your turn's comin'," said Wilson, all the while keeping his eyes trained on Firestick. "But first I've got to teach some manners to an old mossback who thinks havin' a tin star on his shirt gives him the right to meddle wherever and however he sees fit."

"It's the right or wrong of a thing that makes me decide where to meddle," said Firestick. "The way you been actin' and runnin' your mouth here tonight is wrong. But it ain't nothing compared to how wrong it would be for you to try and skin that hogleg on me. That'd be the *wrongest* — and last — thing you ever did."

A wild, reckless light flared in Wilson's eyes. "I don't see it that way. So that takes us to the point of there bein' only one way to find out who's got the straight of it. And I'd say the time for that is right . . . about . . . now!"

The cowboy's right hand streaked downward for the shiny Colt riding loose in the tied-down holster on his hip. He was fast. His hand was a blur as it clamped on the grips of the shiny weapon and jerked it free.

But before the Colt's muzzle could be

raised and leveled, Firestick's gun began to speak. Once, twice, it roared. The sound was deafening in the confines of the small room. Two slugs hammered into Wilson's chest, an inch below his heart. The impact knocked him back against the bar, where he seemed to hang for a long moment, suspended awkwardly, before his loose, limp body started a slow slide down. The shiny Colt slipped from his dead grasp and clattered to the floor ahead of him.

CHAPTER 10

Next morning, over breakfast at the Double M, Firestick was relating to everyone the previous night's events in the Mallory Hotel barroom.

"What about Chapman, the other Bar 6 rider?" Moosejaw wanted to know. "Did you just let him go?"

Firestick shrugged. "Why wouldn't I? True, he was part of givin' Gus Wingate a hard time earlier on. But he didn't join in the shootin'. Matter of fact, he even tried to talk Wilson out of goin' ahead with it."

"Too bad, for his pard's sake, Chapman wasn't more convincing," said Beartooth.

"At least he tried," Firestick allowed.

Around a mouthful of bacon and eggs, Moosejaw said, "How about Wingate? What became of him after the gunsmoke cleared?"

"The whole thing shook him up considerable," Firestick replied. "Sorta jarred him out of his drunkenness. Enough, anyway, so's he was able to climb onto his horse and head for home. Though not without takin' a couple bottles of who-hit-John with him when he went. Accordin' to Kate, that's become a pretty regular thing for him lately."

Moosejaw nodded solemnly. "Poor devil. Still tormentin' himself for shootin' Owen Rockwell, no matter how he got crowded into havin' no choice. That's what caused him to quit packin' a gun, as well as what led to the hard drinkin'."

"Maybe so, but from the way Firestick described it," Beartooth pointed out, "it didn't keep him from *wantin'* to grab a gun — until he remembered, through his drunken fog, that he didn't have one."

"That's a rather unfair assessment, don't you think?" said Victoria, who was seated at the dining room table with the men of the Double M, including the vaqueros, Miguel and Jesus. "You can hardly blame a man for seeking to defend himself upon feeling threatened. Reaching for a gun came from force of habit — from always carrying one in the past. The fact that there was no longer one there to grab came from his greater will to never be put in a position where he'd have to use one again. That remains a commendable measure if you ask me."

"I think Miss Victoria is lookin' at it the right way," Firestick said. "Goin' unheeled was a choice Wingate made when he was sober and clearheaded. Grabbin' for a gun later on, when he was in a drunken fog as you put it yourself, Beartooth, was exactly the kind of reaction he wanted to keep from turnin' into another shooting. Except for the heavy drinkin', I see him as a fella tryin' hard to walk a better path after what happened with Rockwell."

"Maybe so," Beartooth said again. "But I think a man has to stay true to his nature, that's all I'm gettin' at. Somebody who's always had a gun within reach — and I don't mean those who make a livin' at that kind of thing, just regular fellas, ranchers and wranglers and such. Those kind have always *relied* on havin' that backup. You all of a sudden strip it away, either by their own choice or for some other reason, it's apt to leave 'em exposed-like. Their thinkin' is the same in a given situation, but now they don't have all the tools to face it the way they used to. Like what happened to Wingate last night. To me, you go against your own grain that way, you're plain puttin' yourself at risk."

"That only holds true," Victoria countered, "in an environment where guns and violence are such an accepted way of life. If more honest, law-abiding men put away their guns, like Gus Wingate did, and left handling the varmints and owlhoots, as you call them, to duly appointed officers of the law . . . well, I believe the entire frontier would be better off."

Beartooth paused with a piece of heavily buttered bread raised partway to his mouth. He smiled crookedly, enjoying seeing the color rise in Miss Victoria's cheeks when she was on the scrap. "In other words," he said, "what you're suggestin' is that the frontier needs more fellas like Firestick, Moosejaw, and me to make it a better place."

Victoria started to make a quick reply, but then held herself in check. She could see that Beartooth was teasing her to get more of a rise out of her. Pursing her lips somewhat defiantly, all she said was, "Well. You *are* officers of the law, are you not?"

"You darn betcha we are," declared Moosejaw, aiming to lighten things up a little. "Especially Firestick. He's a real rip-snorter. All you gotta do is tally up everything that happened yesterday to see how he's bent on clearin' the bad hombres out of the territory — either by tossin' 'em in the clink or by settlin' their hash permanent-like."

Firestick frowned. "Don't make it sound like I enjoy those kinds of things too much, especially when it comes to takin' a man's life. But if a person crosses a certain line, then they've got to be dealt with. That's all there is to it. If somebody don't hold that line, then decent folks will never have the chance to live in the kind of place like Miss Victoria is hopin' for."

"Well spoken," said Victoria.

Moosejaw cocked an eyebrow. "Yeah, I almost forgot. In addition to bein' a man of action, Firestick can sling words pretty good, too."

"Comes to that," said Beartooth, regarding Firestick as he raised a mug of coffee, getting ready to take a drink, "how is it you're on hand to be slingin' words so early in the day, anyway? After takin' the late turn in town last night and runnin' into all the excitement you did, I expected you'd stay in the sack a little extra this morning."

"Would have liked to," Firestick replied. "But I figured I'd best get back into town before too long. Tolsvord will likely be showin' up to snort and bellyache about me keepin' his men locked up. And I imagine Mick Plummer, the boss of the Bar 6, will

104

be comin' around as well, to get the details on his man Wilson bein' shot. Wouldn't hardly look right if somebody wasn't on hand to deal with 'em."

Looking thoughtful, Moosejaw said, "Occurs to me . . . didn't young Wilson have an older cousin or uncle or some such who also rides for the Bar 6?"

"You know, I think you're right," agreed Beartooth.

Firestick shrugged. "Guess I never heard that. Not that it makes any difference now — or would have, even if I'd known it last night. Kid crowded me into not havin' any choice but to do what I did."

"A kin of Wilson's might not see it that way. You'd best keep that in mind," pointed out Beartooth.

"All the more reason for me to get on into town and face whatever comes of it, then. Wouldn't be fair to stick you or Moosejaw with the chore when I was the one mostly in the thick of things in each case."

"I ain't worried about you bein' fair to me or Moosejaw," Beartooth said as he lowered his cup after taking a drink. "If it comes to trouble, you know the three of us have always done a pretty good job of facin' that kind of thing together."

"Of course I know that," Firestick said.

105

"But I don't see this turnin' into anything like that. I really don't. Everybody knew the Wilson pup was on the prod and that it was sooner or later gonna lead to only one thing. If he had friends or kin who cared much about him at all, they should've spoke up long before this."

"Okay, you stubborn cuss. Have it your way," Beartooth said with a sigh. "Plumb too bad you can't stick around the ranch for a while, though. This is the morning Jesus is gonna finish breakin' that black stallion." He cut his gaze to the young vaquero. "Ain't that right, bronc buster?"

Jesus smiled shyly. "*Sí,* Señor Beartooth. Now that the black has been left with his pride and dignity, it is time for me to finish the job."

Moosejaw looked puzzled. "Whose pride and dignity? The horse's?"

"It's a long story. Miguel will have to explain it to you sometime," Beartooth told him.

"If Miguel says it, then it must be so. Never seen anybody who knows more about horses than him," Firestick remarked. "And as far as stickin' around to watch Jesus finish gentlin' that black, I sure would like to — but I'm afraid I can't."

Victoria, who'd gotten up from the table

106

to fetch a pot of fresh coffee from the stove in the adjoining kitchen, paused on her return to take a long look at something that had caught her eye out the dining room window. Then she said, "You may have not have to go all the way to town to take care of some of that business you mentioned, Marshal."

Firestick turned his head to look at her. "How's that?"

"Outside. There are two riders approaching . . . I recognize one of them as Gerald Tolsvord."

CHAPTER 11

By the time Tolsvord and the second rider, who turned out to be Cleve Boynton, reined up before the Double M's main house, Firestick, Beartooth, and Moosejaw had emerged to stand waiting for them on the front porch.

"Mornin', Tolsvord," Firestick greeted. "You're out and about mighty early."

"Always been my way. It's served me well, and times like these give me no reason to change." Tolsvord was a heavyset man somewhere in his fifties. He had shoulders wide enough to balance out some of his expanded gut; a fleshy, heavy-jowled face piled around a surprisingly dainty nose under bristly brows that always seemed on the verge of scowling — a trait not lacking this morning.

Noting this, along with the man's words, Firestick said, "By 'times like these,' I expect you're tiltin' toward the fact of me havin' three of your men in my jail. Is that what brings you around?"

"It's certainly something I have on my mind," Tolsvord replied. "But right at the moment, I consider it a secondary matter. You know Cleve here, my ramrod." He jerked a thumb toward Boynton. "He came across something that might be a lot bigger and more urgent. We'd like to talk to you and your deputies about it."

The somberness of Tolsvord's tone and the expressions on the faces of both men was enough for Firestick to say, "Light on down, then. Tie your horses and come inside, let's hear what this is all about."

A handful of minutes later, they were in the house, seated once more around the dining room table. Victoria, with the aid of Jesus, had hurriedly cleared away the breakfast dishes and poured cups of fresh coffee for everyone. Miguel and Jesus then excused themselves to go begin the day's chores. Victoria returned to the kitchen to make another pot of coffee and to start washing dishes and pans, telling the men to call if they needed anything.

After stirring a spoonful of sugar into his coffee, Tolsvord wasted little time getting to what he'd come to discuss. "As you quickly will see, this is a bit of a tricky thing. On the one hand, we don't want to overreact and cause undue alarm. On the other, if we're able to confirm what Cleve is convinced he saw, then we surely *will* want to spread the word and sound an alarm."

"I guess the first thing is for one of you to tell us what it was Cleve saw — or thinks he saw," Firestick said.

Tolsvord nodded. "Indeed. Best, of course, for Cleve to tell it himself."

All eyes shifted to Boynton. The ramrod squirmed a bit uneasily in his chair, then leaned forward to rest his elbows on the table as he began to talk. Quickly, concisely, he related his experience the previous evening of spotting the mysterious horsemen who quickly turned and disappeared as soon as they'd been sighted. "The whole thing was strange and unsettling. At first, I didn't quite know what to make of it," he summed up. "But then, after I pondered on it some and played it over in my mind a couple times, everything I'd been able to make out . . . well, I came to the conclusion that I skedaddled home to tell Boss Tolsvord."

"Indians," Tolsvord blurted, as if he was no longer able to hold back. "What Cleve is convinced he saw was a pack of Indians."

"Whoa," said Moosejaw as he and the

other two former mountain men were rocked back in their seats.

"Indians," repeated Firestick, frowning. "That's a troubling and unexpected thing to hear. You're suggestin' a pack of renegades is on the prowl — is that it?"

"That's sure the way it looked," said Boynton. "And they were out and about in a place where they had no business being. You tell me what it means."

"Have there been any reports of Indian trouble anywhere around?" Tolsvord asked. "Any rumblings of trouble brewing on one of the reservations that might have resulted in a pack of young hotbloods busting loose?"

Beartooth shook his head. "Nothing we've heard of. Nothing that's come our way as of yet."

Boynton licked his lips. "I'm thinkin' they were Apaches."

"Now you're goin' from bad to worse," groaned Moosejaw. "But it wouldn't be a first for Apaches to go out raidin'. Last anybody heard they're still chasin' Geronimo somewhere up in New Mexico."

"Why do you say Apaches?" Firestick wanted to know.

"From the look I got at 'em," said Boynton. "I've run across some Comanches in my time. They're bigger built, and I've never seen 'em in a pack where there wasn't some feathers or bright colors or headdresses showin'." He shook his head. "Wasn't any of that with this bunch. They were small, wiry, wearin' all drab colors. No feathers or hats. Long hair and maybe some headbands, but otherwise bareheaded."

"That sounds like Apaches, right enough," agreed Moosejaw. "But except for that bunch runnin' with Geronimo, they're supposed to be contained up in San Carlos . . . unless Geronimo has decided to head down this way."

"No, we would have heard something about that. The soldier boys up north might not be able to catch Geronimo, but he ain't runnin' so far ahead of 'em that he could make a swing in our direction without us gettin' word," said Beartooth. "But don't forget there's still some others that have never been captured down in the mountains of Mexico. Could be there's a pack of them who decided to cross the Rio for some hell-raisin'. The Mex government don't really have 'em contained very well in the Sierra Madres. A renegade pack like Boynton is describin' could squirt across the border and nobody'd notice until they commenced to raidin' and carryin' on."

Boynton's forehead puckered. "Not that

I'm complainin', mind you, but what I can't figure out is — if it *was* a raiding party I saw — why didn't they take out after me when I caught sight of 'em?"

"Could be they weren't ready to tip their hand yet," said Firestick. "Could be they were on their way to raid somewhere else, and attackin' one lone man wasn't worth their while. All that's supposin' you're right about it bein' Injuns at all."

"You don't believe me?"

"I didn't say I didn't believe you. I said, if you're right. You came here with some doubts of your own, didn't you?"

"Maybe doubts . . . Maybe I just don't want to believe what I saw."

"What we came here for," said Tolsvord, "was to seek your help in trying to make certain. Like I said at the start, the last thing we want is to cause undue panic. No, make that the second-to-the-last thing. The very last thing is for this renegade pack, if they're out there, to start killing and raiding without any warning."

"You three are the best trackers in the territory," Boynton quickly added. "We were thinking that, if I take you to where I saw those riders, you could pick up their trail and see where it leads. Or maybe you could tell something simply from the tracks."

113

"Hey, that ain't a half-bad idea," said Moosejaw.

"No, it ain't," agreed Firestick. "You want to take a crack at pickin' up that trail, Moosejaw? In the meantime, I'll get into town and send out some telegrams, see if there've been any other sightings anywhere around. Though I'll have to word 'em careful-like so's not to rile things up until we have a better idea what's goin' on."

"What about me?" said Beartooth.

"In case there *are* some renegade bucks on the prowl," Firestick told him, "don't you think it'd be best for one of us to stick close to the ranch to keep an eye on things?"

"Yeah, I reckon," Beartooth allowed reluctantly.

Tolsvord said, "That's what I intend to do, too — get back to my place, where I can keep a sharp eye out without stirring up the rest of my hands until we know something further." He aimed a scowl at Firestick. "Once we do, one way or another, you and me still have to take up the matter of my men you've got locked up. Especially if there are Indians on the prowl, we'll need every gun we can get."

Firestick met his scowl evenly. "Like you said, once we know something further as far as what Boynton saw, then we can take up that matter."

"As soon as I get a look at those tracks and have a chance to make something out of 'em, me and Boynton will send word," said Moosejaw.

Firestick quickly threw down the last of the coffee in his cup and then stood up. "Okay, sounds like we got us a plan. The quicker we get this pinned down, the better. So, we'd best get to makin' some tracks of our own."

CHAPTER 12

The stern-faced woman on the seat of the small buckboard expertly handled the team of horses pulling the rig as she swung them smoothly in alongside the section of iron fence bordering one side of the cemetery. When she had both team and buckboard aligned parallel to the fence, she reined to a halt so that her rear wheels stopped just ahead of an arched gateway.

Well-crafted cursive lettering, fashioned from iron and welded between the top and bottom frames of the arch, read BUFFALO PEAK CEMETERY. An eighth of a mile to the northeast, the town, only just starting to bustle with activity at this early hour, was crowded in on either side of the old trail. The latter, continuing on toward the west, made a long, gentle northerly curve away from the cemetery, as if in respect to its privacy and sense of isolation.

The woman climbed gracefully down from

her seat and spoke a word to the well-trained team, commanding them to hold in place. Then she walked around to the rear of the buckboard and withdrew from its bed a basket of brightly colored flowers, their different hues brought out nicely by the early morning sun. The woman, by contrast, was dressed rather dully — dark blue bonnet and matching dress, full-length skirt and collar buttoned at the throat. Her form was trim, and her face might have been called handsome not too many years prior; perhaps still would be if not for the stern, chiseled expression that looked as hard as some of the tombstones that dotted the cemetery. Under the bonnet, her hair was reddish brown and pulled back into a severe bun.

Carrying her basket, the woman passed through the gate, under the lettered arch, then angled a short way to her right, where a pair of tombstones stood slightly apart from any others. She stood for a long moment, just gazing down at them. The inscription carved on one read HIRAM ROCKWELL . . . 1835–1879 . . . *Beloved Husband and Father . . . Called by God too* soon; on the other, OWEN ROCKWELL . . . 1859–1881 . . . *Beloved Son and Brother . . . Taken too soon, too tragically.* The ground in front of the latter had been disturbed not all that long ago, and the outline of a rectangular blanket of sod, still taking root, was plainly in evidence.

Folding the front of her skirt down over her knees, the woman sank onto the soft, greening grass between the two stones and began distributing the flowers from her basket. As she did this, she murmured softly to each, and from time to time she would hum strains of the popular hymn "In the Sweet By and By."

After the woman had been thus occupied for some time, a man emerged from behind a tall cottonwood atop a low rise toward the middle of the cemetery and began slowly walking toward her. The man was of average size and build, clad in a gray frock coat, white shirt, black string tie. The hair visible under his wide-brimmed hat was thick and wavy, yellow in color. On his hip rode a .45-caliber Colt revolver in a black leather holster.

As the man walked toward the woman, he did so with no sense of menace and without giving any impression he was stalking her. He simply strode unhurriedly in her direction. When he had drawn within ten yards of where she knelt, he stopped and removed his hat.

At that point the woman turned her head

118

and saw him standing there.

"Mrs. Rockwell? Mrs. Margaret Rockwell?" said the man.

"I am."

"My name's Lofton. You sent for me."

The woman's expression did not change. "I'm relieved to see you made it. Had another week passed, I would have begun to fear that something had either happened to you or . . ." She let the words trail off.

With a faint, disarming smile, Lofton finished for her, saying, "Or that I'd absconded with your advance money and wasn't going to show up at all."

"I suppose my thoughts might have turned that way, yes." Margaret started to rise.

Lofton held out his hand. "Please. Finish what you're in the midst of doing. I didn't mean to interrupt. I just wanted to let you know I was here. If you like, I can wait at a greater distance and let you have your privacy."

Margaret rose the rest of the way to her feet. "No, we should go ahead and conduct our business. As I told you in my letter, I come here every Wednesday. When I do, I usually spend most of the morning. So, I will have plenty of time to complete my private business after you and I have discussed the balance of ours."

"If that's the way you would like it," said Lofton.

"It is. But let us complete our discussion outside of the cemetery grounds."

Lofton nodded agreeably and followed Margaret out through the arched gateway and back to her team and rig. He noted the somber expression on her face and thought to himself that he'd seldom, if ever, seen anyone carrying around a stronger mix of pain and anger.

Proceeding to the front end of the buckboard, Margaret reached up into the boxed area under the seat and withdrew a leather purse with a thong drawstring. Turning back to face Lofton, she opened the purse and withdrew from it a folded-up piece of paper and a roll of paper money tied with string.

Holding out the roll of money, Margaret said, "Here is the balance of the amount we agreed on for your services." When Lofton took the roll, she added, "I'll wait for you to count it, if you like."

Lofton shook his head. "You had faith that I'd respond to your advance. I'll trust that the proper amount for the balance is here."

Margaret next held out the piece of paper. "Here are the names of the two men I wish for you to . . . render your services against," she said.

A corner of his mouth lifting, Lofton said, "Never heard it put quite that way. But it's clear enough, I reckon, since we both already know what it is you're talking about."

He unfolded the piece of paper and looked at the writing on it.

Also gazing down at the paper, from the opposite side, as if she could read through it, Margaret said, "The top name, Gus Wingate, is the black-hearted murderer who killed my son. The second name, Elwood McQueen, is the marshal of the town yonder — the coldhearted coward who refused to take any action against Wingate for his evil deed. It therefore falls to me — through your services, as stated — to see that they are held to account in order for justice and decency to prevail."

Lofton didn't say anything right away, continuing to study the names. When he lifted his eyes, he said, "Happens I saw Marshal McQueen in action yesterday shortly after I hit town. He was dealing with some rowdies in one of the saloons. So, him I'll be able to find again with no trouble. But what about this Wingate? Where can I locate him and how will I recognize him?"

"Three miles due south from here you will find a small creek running off to the west.

Follow it to where it bends southward and passes between two large hills. To the east is my farm. From the top of the westernmost hill, you will be able to see Wingate's ranch. He has a small cattle spread. I am told his herd and his operation have good promise of growing, though at the moment, appearance-wise, it is hardly impressive. The main house is a soddy, and the outbuildings are rudimentary at best. He currently has two hired hands who share the soddy with him. I bear them no ill will."

"I'll keep that in mind," said Lofton. "But if they try to interfere in some way that poses a threat to me or to the success of completing my job, I can't make any promises."

"As you see fit," Margaret said coolly.

"The marshal, of course, will be a little tricky. But I'll figure something out in regard to him."

"I trust you will."

Studying her more closely, Lofton decided he'd been wrong in his earlier assessment. It wasn't pain and anger etched on her face — it was pain and *hatred.* "Do you have any particular requirements you'd like to see carried out in either case?" he asked.

Margaret blinked. "I'm not sure I understand."

"Well, I don't want to be too graphic or indelicate," Lofton said, abruptly seeming somewhat uncomfortable about going into more detail, "but sometimes I'm asked to ply my trade in a particular way. Generally, I do gun work. As opposed to stabbing or strangling or some such. Do you see what I mean?"

Margaret considered silently for a moment. Then she said, "Ideally, I would like for each of them to know the pain and suffering I've had to endure from the loss of my son. But I don't see how that's possible. So dealing with them in whatever manner best suits you will have to suffice."

"That's good," Lofton said, nodding. "Keeping it basic and simple is always best."

"In your line of work — delivering death — that may very well be," said Margaret. "Going on living, unfortunately, is never simple."

Lofton didn't know what to say to that. He passed the roll of bills from one hand to the other. Then, regarding Margaret closely once again, he said, "Just as a matter of curiosity, can I ask you another question?"

"If you wish. It remains to be seen whether or not I can — or will — answer."

"How is it someone like you came to know about contacting someone like me?"

Without balking, Margaret replied, "A little over two years ago, when we were desperately fighting the illness that soon after claimed my husband, we made a trip to El Paso to see a doctor there. A specialist, he was supposed to be, though he was of little to no use. At any rate, in the El Paso train station, as we were leaving, you passed through. A man talking with my husband pointed you out and, in hushed whispers, told how you were a notorious gun-for-hire. For whatever reason, that stuck with me. So when I was struggling with the dilemma of how to make Wingate and McQueen pay for their egregious actions — or lack thereof — regarding my son's death, I thought of you. That led to my placing the blind ad in the El Paso newspaper, that resulted in our exchange of letters and, ultimately, your presence here."

"Very enterprising of you," said Lofton. Once more he switched the roll of bills from one hand to the other. "And, in the end, lucrative for me."

"So it would seem."

Lofton finally shoved the roll of bills into the pocket of his frock coat, saying, "Very well. I guess that concludes the remaining issues between us. I'll leave you once again to your private time, and I'll be about taking care of what you've hired me to do. You will know, of course, when the job is done."

"Yes, I shall."

Lofton started to turn away, but then paused. He was moved to say something he'd never said to anyone before with any job. "I'm sorry for the losses you've suffered, Mrs. Rockwell. I hope, when I'm done, you find a measure of . . . well, peace and comfort."

Margaret held his eyes, made no reply.

With that, Lofton took his leave. He circled the near end of the cemetery and began walking unhurriedly back toward town. Behind him, as Margaret passed through the arched gate one more time, he could vaguely hear her humming. It took him all the way to the edge of town before he could place the tune . . . "In the Sweet By and By."

CHAPTER 13

Saetta stood with wiry arms crossed over his chest, eyes locked with the man before him. Both were dressed similarly, in coarse cloth leggings tucked into moccasin boots and loose-fitting calico shirts belted at the waist. Unadorned headbands contained shoulder-length spills of glossy, coal-black hair.

In addition to the similarity of their attire, there was a definite resemblance in the bronzed, flat facial features of the two, though Saetta's carried the mark of more years. He was also taller and wider through the shoulders than the younger man. The latter, however, was nevertheless straight and solid of frame, and his expression conveyed nothing if not youthful confidence and determination.

They were positioned some distance away from the rest of the men in the secluded mountain camp. The others were busy carving and curing the meat and scraping hides from the near-skeletal remains of a half-dozen cow carcasses sprawled near the edge of the camp. As they worked, all of the men seemed to be concentrating intently on their tasks, yet every once in a while, one of them would cast a brief, furtive glance in the direction of the two who stood apart.

"Your face is clouded with anger, Taluma. Anger toward me," Saetta was saying to the young man before him. "This is not good. Because you are my nephew, my blood, I have allowed you to voice your complaints and to brood. But now you have said your piece and I have said mine. That must be the end of it. I will not allow you to continue showing your displeasure with my decisions, especially not in front of the other men. It undermines my role as leader of this undertaking."

"I have nothing but great respect for you, my uncle. I do not seek to cause you trouble in any way," replied Taluma. "But what one feels strongly and deeply in his heart is not easy to mask on the outside."

"I understand the deep passion that stirs your feelings. It runs in our bloodline, and I am proud to see you continuing this trait. But there is a time to allow your passions to control you, and there are times when you must control them. This is such a time. That means following my lead and not wearing your personal feelings so openly." Saetta's gaze bored intently into the face of his nephew. "One day, you may very well lead a raiding party of your own. If and when you do, you must lead with strength and conviction. Until then, you must follow, listen, and learn."

For the first time, Taluma looked away, unable to continue meeting his uncle's penetrating gaze. "I understand, my uncle," he said. "It is just that I thought this raid would include more than only hunting and gathering. Especially when we saw that lone rider last night, I could not understand —"

"You wanted blood and revenge for all that the White Eyes and their brown brothers to the south, the Rurales, have done to our people," Saetta finished for him. "You think I do not have those same feelings? But a good warrior must always strike wisely as well as bravely. To have attacked that lone rider would have gained us what? The life of one White Eyes — and from that a warning sent to all the others in this area so that they can band together and come hunting us."

"But he must have seen us, as we did him. Will he not report the sighting and cause the other White Eyes to come looking for us anyway?"

"Maybe. Maybe not. We slipped away quickly and silently. He will have doubts about exactly *what* he saw. He will wonder who we were and why we did not hail him or give chase. With luck, since he was returning to one of the surrounding ranches from town, he may have been under the influence of too much drink and when he awoke this morning he will not be clear if he truly saw anything at all."

"That seems a great deal to hope for," said Taluma.

"Perhaps. But it is better than the certainty of the attention we would have drawn by attacking him."

"*Let* us draw attention. *Let* more White Eyes come after us," said Taluma stubbornly. "Then we will be able to kill many more!"

"And what of *this* effort, then?" Saetta gestured to the work the other men were performing. "The meat to feed our women and children and old ones." The hides for blankets and shelter. The other supplies we plan to load our pack ponies with before we return to our homes . . . Fighting the White Eyes who swarm here to hunt us will not leave us time for any of that. And, yes, we may kill many of those who come after us — but they will kill many of us, too. And what good will that do for our families waiting in the mountains across the border?

"Geronimo has been chased by the White Eyes and has been fighting their soldiers for many moons now. He is feared and very brave and much talked about . . . But what *good* is he doing our people?"

Taluma's eyes blazed. "He is sending a message that our people will never be defeated by the White Dogs who would have us grovel before them and be sent to live on the desolate, disease-ridden wastelands they call reservations."

"That may be true," Saetta said evenly. "But I repeat . . . what *good* is that doing the people of our mountain village? Does it help protect them while he is away? Did it feed or shelter them during the harsh months of this past winter?"

Again, Taluma had to look away, unable to hold his uncle's steady gaze.

"It is fine for you to admire Geronimo. I do, as well, for who he is, what he does," Saetta went on. "Though it would sadden me and your mother, my sister, maybe one day you will ride away to join him. But in the meantime, I am asking you to recognize that there is also worth in what we are about here. You will know this when we are welcomed and see the people rejoice upon our return home, our pack ponies laden heavily with life-sustaining essentials."

"I know these things, my uncle," Taluma replied. "But I would join in the rejoicing more eagerly if I returned with White Eyes' blood on my knife blade or arrow tips. Or knowing that a bullet from my rifle had stopped a hated white heart."

Saetta showed his teeth in a smile that had no humor. "Be patient, my nephew. Once our pack ponies are loaded and we are ready to return home . . . it then should not be difficult to find opportunities for the spilling of white blood, even as we take our leave."

In response to this, Taluma's eyes widened and his mouth spread very wide.

CHAPTER 14

"So, do you believe Cleve Boynton?" Kate asked.

Firestick shrugged. "I don't *dis*believe him. I don't think he's flat-out lyin', if that's what you mean. It's more a matter of whether or not the riders he spotted were what he's convinced they were."

"Will Moosejaw really be able to determine very much if Boynton takes him to where he saw those riders?"

"You bet he will," Firestick assured her. "He'll be able to read their sign as plain as . . . well, as plain as you can read the guest register here at your hotel."

Kate smiled. "You haven't seen the handwriting of some of my guests. Sometimes what they scribble is far from plain."

They were seated over coffee at a rear table in the dining room of the Mallory Hotel. In the lull time between breakfast and lunch, they had the place to themselves except for a pair of elderly ladies who were chatting and drinking tea before the wide front window, enjoying the view of the comings and goings up and down Trail Street. Fine for them, Firestick thought, but as far as he was concerned, he had the best view in town sitting right across from him.

Hell, for that matter, just about the best view anywhere. He'd seen the sun rise and set from high mountain reaches, he'd gazed up at a star-studded sky reaching forever above vast stretches of silver-blue desert, and he'd looked out on the dimpled blue Pacific Ocean. But he'd never seen anything prettier than the smiling face of Kate Mallory.

She was almost pretty enough to make him forget the more serious matters the day had presented, but he knew he couldn't allow that.

"One thing for sure," he said with a sigh, "is that whatever Moosejaw finds when he gets to where Boynton is takin' him — unless there are no tracks at all and the whole thing turns out to be some kind of hoax or hallucination — it's likely gonna require an investigation. That many riders out there at that time of night just appearin' and then disappearin' smells mighty fishy, no two ways about it."

"Are you thinking rustlers?" Kate asked.

"That'd be one explanation for it."

She regarded him with dark, smoldering eyes. "But you don't believe it's as simple as that, do you?"

Firestick took a drink of his coffee. "No, I'm afraid I don't. Ridin' in from the ranch, I couldn't shake the feelin' that . . . well, that Boynton saw exactly what it was he thought he saw."

"Indians? Apaches?"

"If it's Injuns at all, it'd most likely be Apaches. A band of renegades crossin' over from down in Mexico."

"But there hasn't been any Indian trouble around here for years," Kate said, her face nevertheless showing concern.

"I know that," Firestick said. "But what's happened around here in the past ten, twelve years?" Without waiting for an answer, he went on, "A lot of growth, right? Not only in the town, but also in the number of farms and ranches surroundin' it on all sides. Some have growed into pretty good-sized operations."

"Tempting targets, in other words."

"One way of sayin' it. Everybody knows that most of the Apaches — except for Geronimo and his pack runnin' loose again — are on the reservation at San Carlos. But what folks tend to forget, mostly because they want to, is that there are still pockets of Chiricahua holed up down in the Sierra Madres. That may be across the border, but it ain't that far away. Not from us. But it *is* a good long way from Mexico's central government. So as long as the Apaches stay mostly in the mountains and don't raise too much hell down in the villages — where the pickin's are mighty slim to begin with — it ain't worth it to build up a Rurales force big enough to hunt them down and flush 'em out."

"How many do you think are down there?"

Firestick shrugged. "I couldn't make a good guess. If they massed together, it might be sizable. But Apaches tend not to fight or raid in very large numbers. If Boynton saw a couple dozen like he claims, that'd be a pretty big raidin' party."

"So you're thinking they may have decided to raid up this way because, as you put it, the 'pickings' are better?"

"Could be reason enough. We got plenty of cattle for meat and hides, not to mention plenty more in the way of goods that most likely are mighty scarce where they're at."

"So they'd be raiding to steal things they can take back to their people? Not necessarily to . . ." Kate let the words trail off, her expression showing a trace of hope that the things she'd named might be all there was to it, yet at the same time knowing it really wasn't.

Firestick hated clarifying it more bluntly. But he wouldn't lie to her. "If and when Apaches raid, Kate," he said, trying to make his tone gentle even if the truth wasn't, "they ain't likely to stop at makin' off with a few things and not doin' some killin', too."

Kate gazed down into her coffee for a long moment. Then, lifting her face, she said, "What about the telegrams you sent off? When do you expect to hear something back from them?"

"I'm hopin' by later this afternoon. I didn't want to make 'em sound too urgent, in order to keep from causin' undue alarm." Firestick reached across the table and placed his hand over hers. "Same with you, gal. This hunch I got could be off by a mile. We can't be sure of anything until Moose-jaw gets back. *Then* we'll know what we're dealin' with. In the meantime, I sure didn't mean to upset you. I was only sharin' my honest feelin's with you."

Kate found her smile again, albeit a rather faint one. She turned her hand over inside his and curled her fingers upward, squeezing. "I know you could never be anything but honest with me. I wouldn't want you to be," she said. "And after all, I'm a big girl. I've lived on the frontier a long time. I can face reality."

"If there *are* Apache raiders in our valley, then Boynton has given us a pretty good early warning. And if it comes down to it, we've got plenty of good men we can round up quick-like to deal with 'em," Firestick assured her. "Until then, I reckon I don't have to say that what I've shared with you here stays only between us until we know something more."

"Of course. I understand."

Further talk was halted as their attention was drawn by the sight of Henry Lofton entering the dining room. He stepped in from the front lobby. He held his hat in one hand and was smoothing his wavy hair with the other as he looked around. He beamed a pleasant smile at the two elderly ladies by the window, and then his eyes swept to Firestick and Kate.

"Morning, Miss Mallory . . . Marshal," he greeted as he came over to their table.

"And good morning to you, Mr. Lofton," Kate replied.

Firestick merely nodded.

"Pardon the interruption. But I saw you

two through the front window as I was passing by, thought I'd step in and say hello," Lofton explained.

"It's not an interruption. You're a guest in my establishment — you have every right to approach me," said Kate.

Firestick smiled wryly. "Well, since you're a visitor to our town and I'm the marshal hereabouts, I guess that puts me in a position to say you have every right to approach me, too."

Marilu Rivers, whose duties included cooking and overseeing housekeeping for the hotel, appeared from the kitchen. "Hello again, Mr. Lofton," she said, a bright smile splitting her round ebony face. "Come back for more breakfast, or are you ready for an early lunch?"

Putting a hand to his stomach, Lofton said, "Heavens no, even after a brisk walk around the town to try and work some of it off, I'm still stuffed from the breakfast feast you put before me earlier."

"You sure? Not even room for a cup of coffee? Or maybe some tea?"

Lofton looked like he was wavering. Until Kate decided for him by saying, "By all means sit down and join us, Mr. Lofton, and let Marilu fix you something. If you

138

didn't try any earlier, she brews an excellent tea."

"How can I resist the invitation of two such lovely ladies?" Lofton said, holding up his hands in a sign of surrender. "Tea it is, then, Marilu."

"I think I'd like some as well, please," said Kate.

"How about you, Mr. Firestick?" Marilu asked. "I ain't never known you to drink tea, but do you want more coffee?"

"No thanks, Marilu, I've had my fill for the time bein'," the marshal told her. "Besides, I've got to head on out shortly."

"I hope I'm not chasing you away," said Lofton as he pulled out a chair and sat down.

"No. I've just got things to tend to."

Lofton smiled. "On second thought, why should I be questioning your departure? That would put me in the most enviable position of being left alone in the company of our lovely hostess."

"Or," said Firestick, cocking one eyebrow, "since you're such a tea fancier, maybe you oughta join those two fine ladies over by the window who already have a pot of tea served up to them."

"My goodness. Am I about to be fought over by two such manly specimens? What *is* a girl to do?" Kate said sarcastically.

"You could wail for us to stop . . . or maybe faint," suggested Lofton.

"Either that, or just sit back and enjoy the show," Firestick said.

Now it was Kate who arched an eyebrow. "You know, all of this might be more amusing if you two hadn't demonstrated only yesterday how you're capable of breaking into fisticuffs over the slightest provocation."

"Oh-oh. I was hopin' I was gonna be spared this lecture," said Firestick.

"You're just lucky other things have kept popping up. But I had no intention of sparing you a lecture indefinitely," Kate told him.

"If I had any sense, I would take this opportunity to follow Firestick's advice and slink away to join those ladies over by the window," said Lofton. "But in fairness to the marshal, ma'am — not to mention myself — the fisticuffs we became involved in yesterday were hardly the result of a 'slight' provocation. I was set upon by three thugs who showed every intention of doing me considerable physical harm. Luckily, the marshal showed up and prevented that from happening."

"Oh? From the cuts and bruises on each of your faces, it looks to me like physical harm still took place," Kate pointed out. "And, from what I understand, those three poor men currently occupying the jail suffered even worse."

" 'Three poor men'?" Firestick echoed. "Kate, you're talking about the Dunlap brothers and and their little rat buddy, Newt Woolsey. You know as well as anybody they're about as worthless as three coyote turds. For all the trouble they've caused around town over the past year and more, they deserved to have their heads knocked together a long time ago — and harder, even, than what they got yesterday."

"I suppose you're right," Kate said, looking suddenly somber. "After all, I'm the one who got you involved in another provocation last night and a young man ended up dead. What gives me the right to lecture anybody about throwing a few punches?"

"Now, doggone it, don't even think about blamin' yourself for that," Firestick said, his tone gently scolding. "All you did was point me in the direction of a situation that was headed for gunplay anyhow. Would it have been better if you hadn't asked me to get involved, and Gus Wingate would have got shot by that young proddy Wilson instead of the way it went? I'm the one who had to shoot the kid. I can live with that, so don't

141

you dare whipsaw yourself over the small part you played."

Marilu reappeared with a pot of tea and two cups. Sensing that the conversation going on now had turned very serious, she merely set down the tray and left without her usual friendly banter, saying only to let her know if anyone wanted anything more.

After she left, Lofton reached to pour tea for himself and Kate. "I heard about the trouble in the barroom here last night," he said. "It's always regrettable when a situation ends with a shooting. Even more so when a young life is lost. Yet all too often it's a still-wet-behind-the-ears proddy under the false belief that the gun makes the man who brings it all on, and then that proddy has to pay for it."

Kate regarded him. "You sound like you've encountered that kind of thing fairly often, Mr. Lofton."

Lofton lifted his cup and blew across the top. "I'm a drifter, Miss Kate. You don't roam this part of the world for very long without running into men who make their way . . . and, ultimately, meet their fate . . . with a gun in their hand."

CHAPTER 15

The black stallion had been gentled.

When all was said and done, the effort it took Jesus to ride him down on this second day was somewhat anticlimactic. It was almost as if the stallion had had time to think it over — just like Miguel had predicted — had decided he'd made his statement on the first try, and was now ready to give in to the inevitable.

Not that he was completely docile about it, as Jesus could testify better than anybody, due to the wild ride he'd been treated to. But in the end, the black settled to a smooth trot around the corral, blowing heavily, with the rider still in place on his back.

Beartooth and Miguel once again watched the whole thing from outside the corral fence, and when the black finally quit bucking and went into his trot, their smiles were outdone only by the one Jesus was wearing.

"Good work, my nephew," Miguel called

approvingly.

"Top-notch ridin', boy," agreed Beartooth.

Even as he said this, out of the corner of his eye the former mountain man caught sight of another rider approaching the Double M. Inasmuch as he'd been on alert all morning after the visit from Boynton and Tolsvord, Beartooth cussed himself inwardly for not having spotted the newcomer sooner. With the potential for Indians in the area, he never should have let anyone get that close without him noticing.

Fortunately, the approaching horseman wasn't an Apache. What was more, he was someone Beartooth recognized. As Miguel slipped through the corral fence to help Jesus finish soothing the black and get him rubbed down, Beartooth moved to greet the visitor.

"G'morning, Mr. Beartooth," said the young man as he reined up.

" 'Mornin' to you, Brody," Beartooth responded.

"Boy, that's a good-looking horse they're working there in the corral. I could see just the tail end of Jesus's ride as I was coming across the flats. I wish I would've come along earlier to have seen all of it. I bet it was really something."

"Yeah, it was," Beartooth allowed. "Jesus is turnin' into a top bronc buster, and that black sure enough put him to the test."

Abruptly, earnestly, the young man said, "You got any more broncs need busting?"

Beartooth looked up at him, squinting. "Is that what brought you around this way? You lookin' for work, Brody?"

"Matter of fact I am, sir. I need to earn some money real bad, and I'm willing to work plenty hard for it."

Beartooth studied him more closely. He didn't know the Rockwell family well, not on a personal level, but he was quite familiar with their situation. Brody, not yet out of his teens, was the youngest son to Margaret Rockwell, a widow woman who was trying to make a go of a small farm off to the south and a bit east of the Double M. Following the death of the father a few years back, before Beartooth and his pals had come to the area, the widow and her sons had been making a valiant effort, though they were just barely scraping by. And then, only a couple months ago, the oldest son, Owen, had gone and gotten himself killed in a saloon shoot-out in town.

Running all this through his mind, Beartooth didn't doubt that the young man before him now had need of money and would likely work hard to earn it. But what troubled him was the thought of where that would leave Mrs. Rockwell, as far as trying to maintain their farm all on her own while Brody was employed elsewhere.

"Well, seein's how this is a horse ranch, we almost always have some horses comin' and goin'. And, yeah, a good share of 'em need to have the bark rode off when we first get 'em," said Beartooth. "You got some experience as a buster, boy?"

Brody frowned. "Well, not exactly. But I'm a pretty good rider. Everybody says so. With Jesus and his uncle to teach me, I reckon I could catch on to bustin' fairly quick." He paused a moment, then quickly added, "But I'll do any kind of work you got. Mucking stalls, feeding the stock, grooming horses . . . Anything."

Beartooth continued to regard the boy. He was a tall one, going to go over six feet by the time he was done growing. Had a good set of shoulders, too, that he'd fill out once he muscled up some. For the time being, though, he was almighty lean, damn near scrawny. The gun belted around his waist and riding low in a fancy holster — his late brother's rig, if Beartooth had to guess — looked like almost more than he could lug around. Yet his smooth, handsome face showed signs of sun and wind, meaning he was used to outdoor work. And farming was no picnic, not by anybody's standards.

"Your ma know where you're at?" Beartooth asked.

Brody's eyes darted, like he was going to tell a lie. But then he decided against it and gave a short shake of his head instead. "Nossir. Not rightly. She goes into town every Wednesday to visit my pa and brother at the cemetery. She'll be gone most of the day, won't have no way of knowing I left, too, unless she beats me back."

"Are you shirkin' your home chores by comin' here?"

Another head shake accompanied by another "Nossir." Then the boy elaborated. "That's part of the trouble. Since Owen died, Ma don't seem to give much of a hang whether the farm keeps going or not. Me and her did some plantin', but you could tell her heart wasn't really in it. I take care of feeding what few animals we got left. A handful of hogs, a few chickens, couple of milk cows. We've got enough grain stored up to take care of 'em for a while. After that, I don't rightly know what Ma's got in mind."

"Sounds like she's still lost in her grief,"

Beartooth said. "Over the death of your brother, I reckon, since that was most recent. Probably still some over your pa, too. But I expect she'll snap out of it by and by. She's a tough frontier woman. She must be, or she wouldn't have lasted this long after losing your pa."

"I hope you're right. But even if she does snap out of it, I'm afraid it might be too late," Brody said.

"How so?"

"Seems like the taxes we owe on the farm are considerable overdue. I don't rightly know how that kind of stuff works, but some fella from the bank in town came out a week or so back and told Ma it was a serious situation. That was his words — a 'serious situation.' Said if he didn't get a payment mighty quick, the bank was gonna have to . . . some fancy-sounding word. I forget what it was . . ."

"Foreclose," said Beartooth.

"Yeah, that's the one. A fancy way of saying they'd take the farm away from us, right?"

"That's what it amounts to. Money-grubbin' skunks," Beartooth said bitterly. "How much are they wantin', do you know?"

"I never heard the number. I got the

impression it's considerable."

"And your ma's got nothing?"

"Appears not. She was always mighty frugal with a penny, and I thought she had some put away. But not no more, she says."

Beartooth rubbed his jaw. "Well, here's the thing, son. First off, me and my pards, with the help of Miguel and Jesus, who we've already got workin' for us, have got what needs doin' around here pretty well covered. We really don't have work for an extra hand. Secondly, even if I could offer you some work I'm afraid it wouldn't pay all that good. Part of what keeps Miguel and Jesus on is that we provide meals and a roof over their heads. But you've already got that. Far as flat-out money pay, especially to stack up against a tax bill you reckon is considerable, I don't see how we can —"

"Any amount would help. It'd be a start," Brody insisted. He swung down from his saddle and moved to stand directly before Beartooth, looking him straight in the eye. "At least I could turn over to Ma *something* she could offer as part of a payment toward those doggone taxes. It might hold that banker rascal off for a little while longer. And it might even be enough to nudge Ma into acting like she cared again so's we

149

could work together toward settling the rest."

Beartooth felt himself wavering. Normally, he was the least sentimental of the three former mountain men, a firm believer in getting tougher when the going got rough and always finding a way to pull himself up by his own bootstraps. He wasn't easily moved by hard-luck stories, and he couldn't abide a whiner. But that was hardly what the kid was doing, was it? He wasn't looking for a handout, and he sure as hell wasn't whining. All he wanted was a chance to *earn* a way out from under for him and his ma.

Beartooth rubbed his jaw some more. "Now, look here, I can't make no promises as far as steady work. I need to ponder on it some and see if I can come up with an odd-job list you could tie into. I'd also have to hash it over with my partners. We get past that, maybe I can keep you busy for a while after all."

Brody's face split into a wide grin. "You won't be sorry, Mr. Beartooth. I'll work hard for you."

"I won't tolerate nothing less. For starters, can you sling a whitewash brush?"

"You bet I can."

"Okay. There's dang sure some of that needs doin' around here. But that leads to another question, something you need to get square on your end . . . How's your ma gonna take to you workin' for the Double M?"

Brody appeared momentarily puzzled. Then he said, "Why, I reckon she'd be glad for the money I'd be bringing in. Leastways that's what I'm counting on — don't see why she'd feel otherwise."

"Maybe you and me remember different," Beartooth said. "But the way I recollect, after your brother got himself . . . After what happened to your brother, that is, your ma was naturally pretty tore up. Sad, not surprisingly, but also angry. Angry at havin' her son took away from her, and angry at everybody who was anywhere close around when the shootin' happened. Gus Wingate took the brunt of her blame, of course. But she also had plenty to aim at my pal Firestick, the marshal, for not arrestin' Wingate for murder. She had trouble acceptin' that it was a fair fight and your brother lost, makin' it self-defense on Wingate's part . . . Do you see where I'm goin' with this, boy?"

Brody looked sullen. "Sort of."

"What I'm thinkin' is," Beartooth went on, "Firestick bein' a partner in the Double M and me even bein' one of the town deputies who she probably looks at as bein' in on not arrestin' Wingate . . . Well, I can't help but wonder how open she'd be to you workin' for us."

Brody dropped his eyes for a minute and dug the toe of one of his boots into the dirt. Then, abruptly, he lifted his face and met Beartooth's gaze. "You're right about how Ma feels. She plumb hates Gus Wingate. When he sent one of his hired hands over with an offer to help with our plantin' and such, she pointed a gun at him and ran him off. She told me afterwards that if it had been Wingate himself, she would've pulled the trigger on him . . . And you're right, too, about how she feels when it comes to Marshal Firestick. I don't think she hates him as bad as Wingate, but there ain't no love lost toward him, that's for sure. But I ain't ever heard her mention you or Mr. Moosejaw, the other deputy."

"All the same, you can see why I'm wonderin' how she'd feel about you workin' here."

"Maybe she *wouldn't* like it, but doggone it," Brody said, his face flushing, "I'm near a man grown. I got a right to have some say of my own when it comes to what I do and where I go. Especially since it seems like she's gone and given up on everything. I miss Owen, too, but there's still life left in *me.* And her. And the farm — the place our whole family put years of work and sweat into — still has a chance of makin' it, if the bank gives us some breathing room and I can get Ma to start pullin' together with me again."

"You got grit, son, I'll give you that," Beartooth said with an admiring smile. "I'm thinkin' we can find some work around here for you, but I gotta say I ain't comfortable seein' you tangle with your ma over it. You're all each other has right now. Keep that in mind."

"I'd never forget that. You think I ain't seen her go through enough pain so's I'd be in a hurry to cause her more?" Brody's expression grew even more intense, almost anguished. "The thing is, Mr. Beartooth, I recognize the truth about Owen. How he took to spendin' too much time in those Buffalo Peak saloons, drinkin' and playing cards and carousing with the girls. And how he came to think he was mighty big stuff — but not big enough, not for his own good, the way it turned out — with *this* dang thing." He slapped the gun riding on his hip.

Brody took a deep breath, let it out slowly through his nose, then continued. "Ma saw it building up, too. At first she tried to talk to him about it, but he'd always argue her down. After a while, she quit trying. She just looked the other way. And then, after Owen got himself killed — even though she knows he was on the prod for trouble, she's *got* to know — she won't accept the truth. She's still looking the other way and blaming others for what Owen brought on mostly on himself. And, I'm thinking, down deep maybe she's also trying to keep from blaming herself for not being able to turn him away from the path he went down."

"If you work half as hard as you ponder things out," Beartooth said, "it might be worth keepin' you around for the long haul."

"I'll take that as a compliment," said Brody, his expression finally relaxing some.

"That's how it was meant."

"So are you ready for me to start in on that whitewashing now?"

"Reckon there's time to mix up a batch and get a few hours in," Beartooth allowed. "But after lunch, I think you owe it to your ma to let her know what you're about. You don't want to have her get back from town and go to frettin' because you ain't around, do you? Even if it comes to a spat, she deserves to hear the straight of what you got in mind."

"Yeah. I guess that'd be only right."

"But like I said, there's time for some whitewashin' and lunch before you have to deal with that."

Beartooth was thinking once again about the potential Indian trouble. He was hoping to get word by later that afternoon on what Moosejaw was able to tell from the tracks of those horsemen Cleve Boynton had seen. If it turned out there *were* Apaches on the prowl, then that would change the whole matter of sending young Brody off alone to return to his farm. It would bring into question Margaret Rockwell returning from town alone, as well — not to mention concerns for the safety of all the other settlers and ranchers in the valley.

For the time being, though, there was nothing to do but wait and see what conclusions Moosejaw was able to reach. For Beartooth, the best way to handle waiting was to keep busy in order to help the time pass.

As he led the way toward one of the sheds he intended for Brody to start whitewashing, he pointed at the gun riding on the young man's hip. "You gonna commence your whitewashin' with that thing on?" he asked.

Brody blinked. "Well, I . . . I guess I ain't rightly decided. I mean . . . The thing is, I've only just lately started going around heeled. Truth to tell, I sorta forgot I even had it on."

"You said that's your brother's rig?"

"Uh-huh. Used to be."

"Mighty nice-lookin' one, I'll say that."

"The undertaker handed it over along with the rest of Owen's things. Ma said she never wanted to lay eyes on it again, so I've been keeping it mostly out of sight in my room. At one point I thought about taking it into town and seeing what I could get for it. You know, as money toward that tax bill. But I hate to part with it. It meant an awful lot to Owen, even if it did lead to . . . well, you know."

"A gun is just a tool, Brody," Beartooth told him. "It can be useful, or it can be *mis*used. It's all up to the person handlin' it. If you decide to hang on to that one and keep wearin' it, I hope you learned from your brother about the wrong things it can lead you to."

"Yeah, I've seen that clear enough," Brody said solemnly. "The only reason I strapped it on today was . . . well, I thought it might make me look older, more of a man, since I was coming to ask for work."

"A man makes himself from the inside, son. No gun can do it for you," Beartooth replied, just as solemnly. "Remember that."

"I will, sir."

Beartooth grinned. "Here's another thing to remember. You don't need to wear a gun for doin' whitewashin'."

Chapter 16

Firestick had left the Mallory Hotel dining room and was on his way to relieve Sam Duvall at the jail, when the *kraack!* of a rifle shot cut through the other sounds along Trail Street. The accompanying bullet sizzled through the air a fraction of an inch behind his head, singeing the small hairs on the back of his neck, and smacked into the outside wall of Moorehouse's barbershop.

The marshal's reflexes kicked in instantly. He hurled himself forward, diving to the ground and then scrambling frantically to gain cover behind a watering trough on one side of the street — the opposite side from where the shot had originated. As he squirmed in behind the trough, two more shots chased him. One chewed dirt just short of where he was crawling; the other skimmed the heel of his moccasin boot.

All up and down the street, people scurried to get clear of any errant gunfire —

158

ducking into the doorways of shops and businesses, jumping back away from windows. A teamster at the reins of a freight wagon leaped from his seat and rolled under the elevated loading dock at the far corner of Greeble's General Store; two riders who'd just pulled up in front of the Silver Spur Saloon sprang from their saddles and pounded across the strip of boardwalk before lunging through the batwing doors to make it inside.

Behind the watering trough, Firestick was gripping his drawn Colt, but he dared not poke his head up to return fire for fear of getting it blown off. As best he'd been able to tell, the shots had come from the vicinity of a currently empty building that had once housed a photography business — either from a window in the building itself, or from an alley that ran beside it.

Two more shots slammed into the trough, jarring its contents so that some water sloshed over the edge onto Firestick. He cussed in anger and frustration at being pinned down the way he was. Determined to somehow *un*pin himself, the marshal used his elbows to drag his body forward, aiming to wriggle to the end of the tank, where he reckoned he might be able to lean out and get off some shots of his own.

Another slug hammered the trough. Following it, a voice called out, "Crawl on your belly like the low-down worm you are, Marshal. Damn you! You're gonna find out you can't go around murderin' innocent young lads and just get away with it! Not when it's a nephew of mine, you black-hearted bastard!"

So, that was it. *A nephew of mine . . .* Firestick recalled Moosejaw and Beartooth saying at the breakfast table that morning something about Rand Wilson having a relative who also worked at the Bar 6. An uncle or a cousin, they'd thought. Well, it seemed pretty clear now that it was an uncle. And he'd shown up hell-bent on getting some revenge.

Firestick had a sinking feeling that trying to talk sense to the man wasn't likely to do much good. But he had to try. If at all possible he wanted to avoid more killing — especially his own.

"If this is about Rand Wilson," he hollered back, "that wasn't my call. I tried every way I could to give him another out. But he wouldn't have any. When he went for his gun, I had no choice but to shoot back."

"You didn't have to kill him!"

"There wasn't time not to. He was too fast and too good for me to play around

160

with target practice."

"You're right about one thing — he was too good. If you hadn't shaded him somehow, you'd've never been able to beat him."

"I'm tellin' it to you straight, mister. Go ahead and mourn the loss of your nephew, but don't make what happened to him worse with more bloodshed."

"Long as it's your blood that gets spilled, it'll only be better. That will make it a settlin' of accounts."

As this exchange was taking place, Firestick continued to belly forward, careful to keep his head and shoulders pressed down low. His hat had been jarred from his head when he initially hit the dirt, so there was no danger of it poking up to reveal his movement. Reaching the end of the trough, the marshal began to curl around the narrow face, positioning himself so he could reach out at ground level and return fire. Keeping the rifleman talking was helping to pinpoint more closely where he was.

"My deputies will be showin' up any second, you damn fool," Firestick bluffed. "When they do, you'll be outnumbered and outgunned, and the only thing you'll likely accomplish is gettin' yourself shot to hell."

"If I was dumb enough to fall for that, you stinkin' liar," the vengeful uncle called back, "then I'd be gettin' what I deserved. But I happen to know for a fact that your deputies ain't showed up in town yet today. So that makes *you* the one who's outnumbered and outgunned and prime for gettin' shot to hell!"

Two more slugs chewed into the water trough.

Firestick swore under his breath. Just as he feared, there was no talking sense to this damn fool — not any more than there had been with his nephew. What was more, Firestick had another fear: There were plenty of good, honest men in town who weren't likely to stay ducked down out of the line of fire much longer if this continued to drag on. Some of them were bound to try and come to their marshal's aid. And while Firestick might welcome — and maybe even *need* — their help on the one hand, on the other he hated the thought of a well-meaning citizen possibly catching a bullet due to his predicament.

Then, belatedly, another thought struck him. What had the rifleman meant when he'd said, "So that makes you the one who's outnumbered and outgunned"? Up to that point, Firestick had understandably been focused only on the man pouring lead his way. Could it be he'd brought an accomplice

162

with him?

Firestick's field of vision from where he was burrowed behind cover was mighty limited. Nevertheless, he now looked around, cutting his eyes high and low over as much range of sight as he had. It was this action — ironically, as the result of the rifleman's careless remark — that probably saved his life. The abrupt visual sweep revealed none other than Whitey Chapman, Rand Wilson's pard from last night in the barroom, drawing a bead on the marshal from half a block up the street. The grim-faced young cowboy was leaning out from behind the corner of the Lone Star Palace, on this same side of the street, a revolver fisted menacingly at the end of his extended arm.

Firestick didn't have time to think. He just reacted. Twisting his body out from the way it was half-curled around the end of the trough, he squared his shoulders in the direction of Chapman and raised his Colt. He rapid-fired three shots just as Chapman was getting off one. The latter plowed down into the water sloshing around in the trough, kicking up a harmless geyser. Firestick's rounds hammered the corner of the saloon, splattering away wood chips and dust. Chapman jerked back out of sight without the marshal being able to tell whether or not he'd been hit.

Attempting to take advantage of this distraction, seeing that Firestick's attention had not only been diverted, but also that he'd fired off half the rounds in his gun, a heavyset, Winchester-wielding man came rushing out of the abandoned photographer's building. Into the middle of the street he ran, angling toward the watering trough behind which Firestick lay, repeatedly firing the rifle as he advanced.

"I've got you now, you son of a bitch!" he bellowed, continuing to alternately lever and trigger the Winchester, riddling the trough relentlessly.

But then, between rifle blasts, two different-sounding shots sliced down through the haze of powder smoke curling in the middle of the street. The rifleman stopped moving forward. His arms dropped heavily to his sides and he lurched to his left as if buffeted by a strong wind. Ragged blossoms of blood appeared on the side of his head. The Winchester slipped from his grasp and, continuing his sideways lurch, he toppled limp and lifeless onto the dusty street.

A shockingly sudden silence gripped the scene.

After a few tense seconds, Firestick raised his head to peer over the rim of the water trough. His eyes fell on the rifleman lying motionless on the ground. Unmistakably dead. Then he swung his gaze farther down the street. Walking slowly toward him, reloading his Colt .45 in stride, came Henry Lofton, looking calm and quite unflappable in his spotless frock coat and string tie.

CHAPTER 17

Firestick clambered to his feet and began to move quickly but cautiously toward where he'd last seen Chapman. He held his Colt at waist level, extended slightly forward. Edging around the corner of the Lone Star Palace, he came in sight of Chapman once more. The young cowboy was sitting splay-legged on the ground, leaning back against the side of the building. His gun lay in the dirt between his legs, and he held his left hand clamped to his right shoulder. Worms of blood crawling out from between his fingers signaled that the marshal had, indeed, scored a hit with one of his rounds.

Chapman rolled his head and looked up at Firestick with pain-dulled eyes. "Don't shoot, Marshal. I'm done."

"You're not as done as your rifle-happy partner out in the street," Firestick grated. "Who the hell was he, anyway?"

"Name's Oscar Mantel. He was Rand Wilson's uncle."

"I gathered that much. What made him so hell-bent on gunnin' for me the way he did? What kind of line did you feed him about the shoot-out between me and Wilson?"

"It wasn't like that. I swear. I told it to him straight, but all he heard was how Rand was dead. After that, he went into a rage and swore he was gonna get even."

"And you were all too eager to help him. Is that it?"

"No. No, I didn't want nothing to do with it. B-but he threatened me. Called me yellow for not backin' Rand's play better in the first place . . . Said if I didn't go along with settlin' the score when it came to you, then he'd be lookin' to square things with me next."

Firestick's lips curled back, baring his teeth in a snarl. "I let you walk away last night, and what did it get me? You show up today as part of an ambush attempt. Give me one good reason why I shouldn't put another bullet in you to make damn sure you never come back around again."

"Because," said a voice at Firestick's shoulder, "that's not the way it works for somebody who wears a badge like the one you got on. I understand the urge, believe me, but you're better than that. There are laws and proper procedures to follow, and you're one of the ones who has to set the example for sticking to them."

Firestick turned his head and met the gaze of Frank Moorehouse, his eyes magnified through the lenses of his spectacles. The portly barber/doctor/dentist stood there somewhat gingerly holding a long-barreled Schofield revolver. "You're not injured, are you?" he asked.

"No. But not for lack of tryin'," Firestick replied, his expression relaxing a bit. He jerked his thumb toward Chapman. "This skunk is, though. Not as bad as he deserves, but I reckon we'll leave it go at that."

Moorehouse said, "I haven't had a chance to examine the one in the street yet, but it looks like he's —"

"Dead," Firestick finished for him. He stepped off the end of the boardwalk, leaned over, and picked up Chapman's discarded gun. Straightening up, he used it to gesture toward Moorehouse's Schofield. "You might want to put that away," he said, "and trade it for that doctor's bag you haul out from time to time. I'm guessin' there's a slug in the shoulder of this one who's still alive. Since you're so bent on keepin' him that way, you'd best get it out of there and then patch him up so's he don't bleed to death."

Moorehouse nodded. "Sounds like that's what's in order."

He turned and started to return to his shop. Until Firestick stopped him, saying, "Frank." When Moorehouse looked back, the marshal gestured once more to indicate the gun he was still holding. "Reckon you were on your way with that to lend me a hand when I was pinned down. Thanks."

Under his drooping mustache, Moorehouse's mouth twitched with a brief smile. "Think nothing of it. I'm just glad I didn't have to use the old relic, it might've blown up in my hand."

All up and down the street, people were starting to emerge from doorways. Some were doing so rather timidly still, others were exhibiting an eager curiosity now that the shooting was over.

A knot of men milled at the mouth of the alley where Chapman lay. Firestick motioned to a couple of them he knew by name. "Smith. Hill . . . Keep an eye on this jasper for me. Make sure he don't try any funny business and that he behaves while Moorehouse is tendin' to his wound. I'll be back to take him into custody."

"We'll do that, Marshal."

"You damn betcha we'll see to it he don't try anything more."

With that assurance, Firestick turned and stepped out into the street, heading toward where the fallen rifleman lay. More people were gathering there, drifting closer from all sides. Apparently the sight of a dead man held more attraction than one who was only wounded. Nevertheless, they parted to make way for Firestick as he strode up.

Lofton stood directly over the body, gazing down with no emotion showing on his face. His gun was back in its holster.

Leathering his own hogleg, Firestick said, "That was some mighty prime shootin', mister. And don't think I ain't grateful for it."

A faint smile touched Lofton's mouth. "Just returning the favor, Marshal. You stepped in yesterday when those three men had me cornered. I owed you one."

Kate came pushing through the crowd at that point. "Thank God you're all right," she said breathlessly, moving closer and slipping her arms around Firestick's waist.

The marshal was somewhat surprised by this public display, though he hardly minded it. Still, he said, "Careful, you'll get all smudged. Rollin' around in the mud alongside a water trough ain't a bad idea when you're duckin' bullets, but it don't exactly make a body good huggin' material."

"I don't give a darn," said Kate. "As long as you're standin' upright so I *can* hug you."

"Like I was just sayin', that's mainly thanks to Lofton here."

"And like I was saying, I was just returning a favor."

Sam Duvall appeared, coming from the jail. The sawed-off shotgun he was wielding made it easy for him to forge a path through the crowd. "Sorry I didn't make it quicker, but the old bones don't move as fast as they used to," he said, his breath coming in gasps. After turning his head to bark a couple short coughs, he added, "What the hell happened here anyway?"

"This hombre," said Firestick, pointing down at the dead man, "is a relative to the fella I had to shoot last night in Kate's place. The fact that the young fool didn't give me no other choice didn't seem to matter — Uncle here was lookin' to even the score by bushwhackin' me."

"That's the way it is sometimes with certain folks. They're like weeds," remarked Lofton, a trace of bitterness in his tone. "You chop one down, more out of the same cluster pop up and you have to chop some of them, too."

"Well, I hope to hell that ain't the case here. I want this to be over with," said

Firestick. He raked the surrounding crowd with his eyes. "How about it? Anybody else kin to Rand Wilson or Oscar Mantel? If so, speak up now. I don't want it to be that way, but anybody else who comes gunnin' for me over this will get the same damn treatment."

The marshal's words hung in the air like a raised fist. Nobody responded.

A bald, gangly man edged forward. He wore an ill-fitting striped suit and was holding in his hands a silk top hat with fraying around the brim. "With your permission, Marshal," said Clem Worden, the town undertaker, "I think it would be proper to get the body out of the street now. Or at least cover his face. Dreadful as his actions were, I feel we should show that much decency. Do you want me to go ahead and take care of that?"

"Yeah, you're right, Clem," said Firestick, exhaling a deep breath. "Go ahead and bring your wagon around. Do what you need to."

"I'll hold him with his . . . . nephew. Until someone from the Bar 6 shows up to hopefully advise on burial preferences. I expect to be hearing something soon."

Firestick made a sour face. "I wasn't looking forward to facin' Mick Plummer after

I'd shot just one of his men. This sure ain't gonna make it any more pleasant."

"Assuming this Mr. Plummer is the boss of the brand these men rode for," Lofton said coolly, "maybe he needs to shoulder the responsibility of keeping them better in line."

CHAPTER 18

The noon hour came and went.

Once all the mid-morning excitement had died down, activity around town seemed to turn sluggish, but with an undercurrent of tension.

Firestick walked down to the telegraph twice to see if any responses to his inquiries had come in. Nothing. When he returned to the jail, he paced back and forth in front of his desk.

Lunch was sent over from the Mallory Hotel dining room — a slab of fried beef, a scoop of beans, and some corn bread for the prisoners. The Dunlaps and Woolsey shared one cell; Whitey Chapman was in the other. For Firestick and Sam Duvall, the fare was enhanced with an additional slab of beef and some buttered potatoes. Firestick picked distractedly at his plate. In his cell, the wounded Chapman did the same until the Dunlaps coerced him into handing his meat and corn bread through the bars to them since he had no appetite.

And then, at half past one, the sluggish period came to an abrupt end.

That was when Mick Plummer, boss of the Bar 6, came galloping down Trail Street at the head of four other horsemen. They rode straight up to the jail, scattering other traffic on the street ahead of them and kicking up a rolling cloud of dust in their wake.

In the jail, Firestick and Sam heard the stamping hooves outside. The marshal moved to the front door to see what it heralded. He was hoping it was Moosejaw returning with a report on what he'd been able to determine from the tracks of those mysterious riders Cleve Boynton had seen. Instead, he pushed open the door to find himself gazing at Plummer, reined up at the hitchrail astride a pawing, broad-chested Appaloosa gelding.

Plummer was a beefy, thick-shouldered man of fifty with a neatly trimmed mustache spiked by gray. He had a deep, rough-edged voice that came out as a bit of a growl even when he was in the best of moods. Which wasn't today.

"For the love of Christ, Marshal," that growl sounded now, "are you bent on putting me out of business by gunning down my whole damn crew? Ain't I got enough stacked against me what with the elements and cow thieves and everything else — do I need you out to get me, too?"

"I ain't out to get nobody, Plummer. Less'n they go against the law or show their hand as bein' out to get me first," Firestick drawled easily. "Seems to me you'd best calm down some before you blow a gasket and put your own self out of business."

The dust cloud that had been boiling behind the Bar 6 bunch now caught up and came rolling forward over them and Firestick as well. Squinting against this, Plummer said, "Calm down? How in blazes is a body supposed to calm down after a morning like I've had? First having to chase rustlers from hell to breakfast, and then getting back to the ranch only to find out —"

"Wait a minute," Firestick said, holding up a hand. "That's twice now in just a handful of words you've mentioned cow thieves and rustlers. What's goin' on with that?"

"Just what it sounds like. One of my herds got hit last night. A pair of nighthawks heard 'em bawling and fussing, and when they went to check, they saw where it appeared a couple dozen or so had been thinned out. It was too dark for just the two of 'em to take out after the rustling skunks right away. It would have meant leaving the balance of the herd, and they might have ended up riding into a trap. But first thing this morning, me and these boys" — Plummer jerked a thumb over his shoulder — "headed out to try and track the thieves. We lost 'em in rocky ground. Don't change the fact, though, that cattle got took. Like I said, it was only a couple dozen head. But that kind of thing, if it keeps up, can bleed an outfit dry."

"Has it been happenin' regular?"

Plummer shook his head. "No. We've been lucky. Went through all of last year without hardly a sign of such trouble. All the more reason to nip it in the bud."

"Any other outfits been hit lately?" Firestick wanted to know.

"None I've heard of." Plummer paused, his thick brows pulling into a scowl. "But hold on now. I appreciate you showing interest and all, but number one, that ain't what I came here to talk to you about. And, number two, ain't rustling out on the open range kinda out of your jurisdiction to be worrying about?"

"It might be stretchin' my jurisdiction in a strict legal sense," Firestick allowed. "But stock stealin' in our valley ought to be a concern to everybody, oughtn't it? Remember, me and my partners got a small ranch of our own."

"That's true. And I already said I appreciated you takin' an interest. But that still don't . . ."

Plummer let his words trail off as a new commotion arose in the street behind him. He cranked his head to look around, and all eyes followed his as two more riders came thundering up in a fresh cloud of dust.

It was Moosejaw and Cleve Boynton. They'd clearly been riding hard, and the grim expression on each of their faces pretty much gave the answer to what Firestick immediately wanted to know.

"Well?"

The big deputy crowded his horse up alongside Plummer's. Jutting out his chin and first cutting his eyes to the Bar 6 men gathered on either side, he brought his gaze back to Firestick but kept his words guarded. "Boynton wasn't wrong," he said.

Firestick spat a curse, not quite under his breath. Then he said, "All right. We need to talk about it inside." Pinning Plummer with a hard look, he added, "You, too. This is gonna concern you, in more ways than one. But while we're chewin' it over, how about givin' your boys some leeway to go wet their whistles, maybe grab a bite to eat, since they probably ain't had no lunch yet?"

Reading the intensity in the marshal's eyes, Plummer was quick to answer with a nod. "You heard the marshal," he said to his men. "You're free to go have a bite and a couple beers. But don't scatter, and don't by God get drunk! I'll be rounding you up to head back to the ranch before long."

As Moosejaw swung down from his saddle, he also addressed the Bar 6 men, saying, "We got a couple hard-rode horses here, fellas. Could I get one or two of you to take care of 'em for us — cool 'em down and then let 'em have a good drink? I'll stand you all a drink in turn next time you're in town."

The fact that whatever was needing to be discussed inside appeared to be mighty important wasn't lost on the cowboys. Nor was the fact that, although the words of the big deputy were spoken politely, they amounted to an order as much as a request. Plus, the proper treatment of a good horse was something they all recognized as having its own importance. So, there was no hesitation in a positive response from the four.

CHAPTER 19

Moosejaw wasted no time going into his report once everybody was gathered in the jail office. Present were him, Boynton, Plummer, Sam Duvall, and Firestick. Sam's dog, Shield, lay quietly and obediently at his master's feet. The heavy door leading back to the cell block was closed. Coffee had been poured and handed out all around.

"Twenty-five, twenty-six ponies," Moosejaw was saying. "Found their tracks right where Boynton led me. They came in out of the south and a bit east, veered sharp north after he spotted 'em. We followed their sign as far as the foothills of the Viejas before I turned us back. I figured it wouldn't be long before the tracks got mighty hard to follow, and I didn't want to risk ridin' into an ambush."

"That was smart. Right now bringin' word back so's we can start gettin' folks warned is the most important thing," said Firestick.

"Warning folks about what?" Plummer was quick to say. Then, even as the question was tumbling out of his mouth, the realization of what the answer might be hit him. "Hey now! He's not talking about the rustlers who hit my herd, is he? A force of twenty-six men?"

"I think they're one and the same, yeah," Firestick told him. "But we ain't necessarily talkin' rustlers in the way you're thinkin'."

Plummer cocked his head back. "What's that supposed to mean? This is hardly the time for riddles, Marshal."

"Both of you hold on a minute and let me finish my tellin'," Moosejaw interjected somewhat testily. "I said I made it out to be about twenty-six ponies. The thing is, though, close to half of 'em was leavin' prints that showed way too light. I figure they wasn't carryin' riders."

"Any of the ponies shod?" asked Firestick.

"Nary a one."

"Packhorses, then. They're figurin' on raidin' and makin' off with a big haul."

"Only way to read it, I'd say," agreed Moosejaw.

Firestick's expression took on an added grimness as he asked his next question. "Apaches?"

"Couldn't see anything to say it *wasn't* Apaches," Moosejaw replied. "And it's really the only thing that fits . . . We know there's some of 'em not that far away, holed up down in the mountains of Mexico. Exactly the direction they came from. They've adapted to the Sierra Madres down there, so high-tailin' it straight into the Viejas for however long they plan to be around here, makin' a camp they can stage their raids out of and use as a hideout in between . . . Like I said, it all fits."

Plummer removed his hat and ran the meaty fingers of one hand back through his hair, saying, "Holy Christ. I feel like my head is about to explode. I came here thinking I had one set of problems, but what I'm hearing now . . . Holy Christ!"

"What's this about you bein' hit by rustlers?" Boynton asked him.

"Last night. Somebody drove off twenty or so head," Plummer said, still looking a little stunned. "Whoever it was led 'em into the Vieja foothills. Me and some of my boys tried following 'em this morning but lost their tracks in the rocky ground, same as you."

"I never said I lost their tracks, I said they would have got mighty hard to follow," Moosejaw quickly corrected him. "But as for the rest of it, like I keep sayin', it all f —"

"Okay, okay. We get the picture," Firestick cut him off. "From this point on there ain't no other way to look at it but as havin' an Apache raidin' party in our valley, and we've got to move fast in order to deal with 'em."

"Just how do we go about that?" Sam Duvall asked.

"We start out by warnin' the outlying farmers and ranchers of the danger they may be in," replied Firestick. "The bigger outfits, like Plummer's Bar 6 and Tolsvord's Box T, have got enough men who can be armed and pulled in close around the main buildings to hold off any direct attacks there. That don't mean the fringes of their cattle herds won't still be at risk to get thinned some more, though, as Plummer here has already experienced. But the smaller ranches and farms, where there's just a family and maybe one or two hired hands, at most, are in worse danger. They're the ones we've got to get word to pronto and, in some cases, maybe bring 'em into town for safety."

"What about the town itself?" said Boynton. "Any chance those savages might be showin' up here?"

Firestick shook his head. "Not a full-on

attack, no. We're only talkin' about a dozen or so braves, remember. Although that's actually quite a few for an Apache raid, especially Chiricahuas like these are bound to be if they came up from across the border. Apaches don't mass big forces like the Sioux or Cheyennes up north."

"Cherry-cows like to hit fast and savage in small groups of only three or four. If this bunch decides to go kill-raidin'," Moosejaw said, "they could split into two or three smaller bunches. Like a grapeshot bomb explodin' in all different directions at once. Keeps anybody chasin' 'em practically runnin' in circles."

"But the marshal said they brought all those pack ponies to load up and make off with a haul," said Plummer. "If they're mainly after supplies, will they still take time to go kill-raiding?"

"Can't see a bunch of Apache broncos ridin' into an area and *not* doin' some killin'," said Firestick. "Yeah, the pack ponies mean they're after supplies — meat and hides, blankets, tools, guns, cartridges, whatever else they can sneak away with or plunder. But that don't mean they'll stop there. Cherry-cows plumb love killin' White Eyes. Once those pack ponies are loaded, two or three bucks could be chosen to peel off from the rest and start leadin' those ponies back across the border while the remainder split into a couple smaller bunches, just the way Moosejaw told it, and start raidin' not only for the killin', but also to divert attention away from the departin' pack train."

"Diabolical devils," Sam Duvall muttered.

Moosejaw said, "Don't rightly know what diablolly — dobolili . . . whatever the hell that word you just used *means* — but Apaches can damn sure act like devils. That's for certain."

"But we ain't gonna stop at just sending out warnings and putting everybody on guard, are we?" said Boynton. "I mean, somebody's also gonna be going *after* those red devils, right?"

Firestick gave him a look. "How long you lived in these parts, Boynton?" he said. Then, not waiting for an answer, he added, "Goin' after maraudin' Apaches is like goin' after a prairie fire. You gotta be mighty careful the wind don't shift sudden-like and you find yourself caught by the flames curling back on you."

"Just ask anybody from any of the dozens of cavalry patrols that've gone out after 'em over the years," Moosejaw chimed in. "Think of those bombs I mentioned before.

By the time you get to a place where the grapeshot hit, the damage has usually been done. All the while you got to be careful the next flyin' chunk of hate don't hit *you,* and pretty soon you start to wonder just who's after who."

"Nevertheless, somebody has to go after the savages," insisted Plummer. "You'll be sending for the army, won't you, Marshal?"

"I'll notify both Fort Davis and Fort Leaton," Firestick answered. "They're about equal distances from us. I'll leave it up to them to argue about who sends some soldiers. Then it'll be a matter of how long it takes for a patrol to show up. But in the meantime, we got plenty we need to be doin' ourselves."

"Does that mean you're going to take charge of things until the soldiers get here?" Plummer asked. There was no objection or challenge in his voice, just curiosity.

Firestick said, "Unless you got somebody better in mind. I figure me, Moosejaw, and Beartooth know as much or more about fightin' Injuns than anybody else around. Maybe even the soldier boys who make it here, dependin' on who they send."

"And we *are* the law hereabouts," Moosejaw pointed out.

"Ain't necessarily a matter of that," said

Firestick. "Like Plummer questioned a while ago, our jurisdiction as lawmen technically ends at the city limits. But I figure this is bigger than that — this is a matter of survival for some folks out there. As men and as neighbors, that means it falls within the jurisdiction of all of us."

"You'll get no argument out of me, Marshal," Plummer responded. "I'm glad to hear you and your partners are *willing* to take the lead, that's all I was asking. Just tell us what you want us to do."

"For starters," said Firestick, "I want everybody here to scatter and round up all the able-bodied men in town. Try to do it without scarin' hell out of the womenfolk. Have 'em gather in the Lone Star Palace, there's enough room there to fit everybody. Soon as I get telegrams off to the forts, I'll meet y'all there and we can start layin' down some further plans."

Turning to Cleve Boynton, the marshal added, "That's gonna include the Dunlaps and Woolsey. Much as I mean to teach those jackasses a lesson, there's bound to be a better time for it, and I full expect they'll get around to givin' me another chance to do so. In the meantime, I'm gonna release 'em to you. Like Tolsvord said earlier this morning, the Box T may need all the guns it can muster. If there's an ounce of worth-while sand in that trio of lunkheads, now is the time for 'em to shake it loose."

"I'll do my best to try and get it out of 'em," Boynton said.

Turning next to Duvall, Firestick said, "Go ahead and let those three out, will you, Sam? After that, I'm hopin' you're willin' to continue stickin' close for a while. I know you didn't sign on to be a full-time jailer, but that'll still leave the wounded Chapman kid back there, and I'd just as soon not leave him on his own."

The old constable bobbed his head. "If that's the way you want it, Marshal. I live in this valley, too. Me and Shield are willin' to pitch in and do whatever we can to help."

Chapter 20

Gus Wingate leaned on his posthole digger and felt his guts once again roll and then clench with the threat of voiding their contents. Trouble was, there was nothing left to bring up. He'd already gotten rid of everything the three previous times he'd puked. Or was it four? Hell, he couldn't remember. Not that it mattered. Each time it had felt like he was heaving out everything short of his toenails. And each time what came up had been disgusting and foul-smelling and left him weak-kneed, feeling like he was going to pass out . . . or die.

Hanging on the wooden handles of the digger, with rivulets of cold sweat pouring off his face, he felt that way again now. Even before he threw up.

Maybe that was the answer. To die. Maybe that was the only thing that was ever going to end his misery and the grinding weight of guilt that caused him to keep drinking to excess and ending up in this sorry, low-down condition.

Gus didn't particularly want to die. Yet, of late, he'd got to thinking that death was something swirling around him in an ever-tightening circle, drawing steadily closer. First his daughter, his precious little Polly, had caught the fever and died in her crib in the middle of the night four years ago. Then, less than a year later — out of grief, many said — his wife, Betty, had succumbed. He'd endured that, tough as it was. He had to go on, he kept telling himself; he had to make something of this ranch, for their sake, in order to prove that settling here on the frontier had been more than a foolish whim, that it meant something, that it had real substance even though it had cost the lives of his loved ones.

Yeah, Gus had gotten over those hurdles and through the lonely, empty-feeling times that came with them. But then, just when it looked like things were finally going to pan out and he could maybe feel satisfied and whole again, that damn Owen Rockwell had started getting in his face. Repeatedly. Making snide, lying remarks and throwing dirty hints about Gus lusting after the Widow Rockwell, Owen's mother.

Finally, in a smoky, stinking saloon, it

came rushing to an explosive climax. Gus carried a sidearm, the way almost all ranchers did, against the threat of running across rattlesnakes or other varmints out in the open places, but he'd never in his life thought about drawing it against another man or, in his wildest dreams, envisioned himself a "gunny" of any sort.

Yet that was what it came down to. Owen pushed and pushed . . . until that night, in front of too many other people and at a time when Gus had had just enough to drink that he no longer quite had control over his better sense, his hands streaked to pull holstered iron. And, amazingly, Gus's weapon had cleared and fired first . . . leaving a young man dead on the floor.

The whole thing left Gus feeling wretched, disgusted with himself. It somehow hit him as bad or worse than the passing of his loved ones. No amount of assurances that he'd been backed into a corner and that he'd only acted in self-defense — a conclusion even supported by the law — made him feel any better. He kept feeling the buck of that Colt in his hand, and in his mind's eye he kept seeing Owen Rockwell jerking backward and then falling in that horribly loose, lifeless way that meant he was never going to get up again.

The one thing that *might* have helped drag him out of the hole his guilt was pulling him down into, would have been a sliver of forgiveness, or at least understanding, from Margaret Rockwell. But it was made very clear that his loathing for himself was but a grain of sand compared to her mountain of raging blame and hatred for him.

So, Gus put away his gun and started picking up bottles of whiskey instead. The only thing that erased the images of that night and the feel of the Colt bucking in his hand was the feel of a whiskey bottle tipped up often enough until the images blurred.

With the help of his two faithful hired hands — Lyle Marsh and Sylvester Krause, who carried the load of running the ranch more like partners than mere employees these days — Gus struggled from day to day, frequently backsliding at night, maintaining hope, albeit slim, that he could yet get a handhold on the rim of his pit and start to drag himself out.

And then last night happened.

The shattering blast of gunfire, the acrid stink of powder smoke. Again. A young man sliding loose and limp and dead to the floor of a barroom. Again.

No, Gus hadn't drawn a gun this time, hadn't squeezed a trigger. But he'd wanted to. He would have — or would have tried — if a gun had been within his reach. But that was a moot point, really. He'd been in the thick of it all the same. Hell, he *was* the trigger. The shooting and killing all due to him.

Death. Swirling around him, closer and tighter.

At last Gus was able to lift his head and straighten up. The cramping in his gut had subsided, though he still felt a little weak in the knees and remained glad he had the digger to lean on. Sweat continued to pour down his face. He wiped some of it away with the back of his forearm, shirtsleeve already soaked from previous swipes. Cautiously, he took a deep breath, hoping it wouldn't trigger another stomach convulsion. When it didn't, he gulped more air, and it seemed to make him feel a bit better.

God, he had to quit doing this. Had to get hold of himself.

His gaze drifted and came to rest on a low ridge that rose up a short distance beyond the sod house that stood in the middle of a flat, grassy expanse. The sod house that he'd promised Betty would only be temporary, their home only until the ranch started paying off and he had the time and money to build her a nice wood-frame dwelling. Well, the ranch was finally starting to do fairly well these days . . . if he didn't piss it all away with his drinking and wallowing in self-pity. But the wood-frame house still wasn't built, had never even been started.

With Betty and Polly occupying plots of ground up there on that ridge, it had never seemed all that important anymore. Yet sometimes, like he did now, Gus wondered if Betty was looking down — maybe from the ridge, maybe from a higher place — and feeling disappointed in him for not following through. That led to more wondering about the whole "looking down" thing. Was there truly a hereafter, a heaven from which dead loved ones could gaze down and see what those left behind were doing or not doing? If that was the case, then lately Betty had a lot more than the unbuilt house to be disappointed in where he was concerned.

Gus pulled his gaze away from the ridge.

Damn! He had to get hold of himself, his life . . . for so many reasons.

Turning away from the ridge, squinting in the late-afternoon sun, Gus next looked to the east across the rolling, grassy plain dotted with clumps of grazing cattle. His cattle. Far in the distance, rising above the smudge of a tree line, was a curl of blackish smoke. That would be Lyle and Sylvester burning brush that they'd cleared from alongside the creek that bordered Gus's property, thinning it so the younger, weaker cattle didn't get caught in it and bogged down when they went to drink.

Good men, Lyle and Sylvester. They, too, deserved a hell of a lot better than they'd been getting from him lately.

Under his breath, Gus once again cursed his weakness, his wretchedness.

It was as he started to return his attention to the postholes he was supposed to be digging that Gus spotted a lone rider approaching from the general direction of Buffalo Peak. The gait of the horse was steady, unhurried, and the rider sat his saddle well. Shading his eyes for a better look, Gus was pretty sure he didn't recognize the visitor, who was wearing a gray frock coat and a black string tie that stood out starkly against his bright white shirt. Yet there was something so calm about his posture and the measured speed with which he was approaching that Gus felt no sense of alarm, only curiosity about what might be bringing him out this way.

When he got closer, the rider called out, "Good afternoon to you, sir."

"And to you," Gus replied.

"I've been staying over in town for the

past couple of days," the stranger explained. "My horse had a muscle strain in one of his legs and the liveryman there has been nursing him. He wanted me to take him for a little test ride this afternoon and see how it's acting now."

"Judging by the way you rode up, horse appears to be stepping just fine."

"Yes, he does."

"Pete Roeback's got a mighty fine hand when it comes to horses. You took him to the right place for some healing."

"Speaking of places," said the stranger, "this is the Wingate spread, is that correct?"

"Why, yes it is."

"And you'd be Mr. Gus Wingate?"

"That's right." Gus frowned a little. "Do I know you?"

The stranger smiled a thin, somewhat pitying smile. "Everybody knows me, Mr. Wingate . . . sooner or later."

"Not sure what that's supposed to mean," said Gus.

"It means," said the stranger, sweeping back the front of his coat and in the same smooth motion drawing the Colt .45 from the holster on his hip, "that I am Death, and it's time for you to become fully acquainted with me."

The Colt roared once, spitting flame and

lead and drilling a slug straight into the center of Gus Wingate's forehead. Somehow, in the split second before the bullet entered and blew apart his brain, Gus had time for a flash of final thoughts: *God, I never* really *meant I was ready to die . . . I hope I see you again soon, Betty and Polly.*

CHAPTER 21

A lean-to attached to the rear of the Double M's main house served as a washroom where the men scrubbed up for mealtime and after a hard day's work. Lathered and rinsed of the whitewash splatter that had streaked his face and forearms, Brody Rockwell emerged from there now, squinting into the slanted afternoon sunlight. While his exposed body parts were clean, the same could hardly be said for his clothes. A generous collection of white splotches decorated his shirt and trousers.

Leaning against the side of the house, waiting, Beartooth wagged his head at the sight of the lad. "I could've swore I gave you a brush to use on that ol' shed," he drawled. "Did you decide you'd rather pour the whitewash all over yourself and rub it on with your body instead?"

Brody grinned. "Reckon I might've been swinging that brush a mite too strong," he admitted. "I wanted to be sure and get the shed finished so's I'd make a good impression and you'd have me back for more work."

"Well, you accomplished part," Beartooth told him. "You impressed me with a good job, and I'm willin' to have you back . . . *if* your ma will allow it, that is. Considerin' the shape of your clothes, in addition to worryin' about her not wantin' you here on account of her dislike for me and Firestick, now we got to figure she might not want you to come back for fear of you gettin' drowned in a tub of whitewash."

"Aw, she'll understand that part okay," Brody assured him. "One of her favorite sayings is: 'Honest work is sometimes dirty work, and it'll all come out in the wash.' "

Arching a brow skeptically, Beartooth said, "That's a real charitable outlook. Reckon we'll find out soon enough how she really feels when I get you back home."

Brody looked puzzled. "Not sure what you mean when you say *you* are gonna get me back home, sir. I know the way well enough. After all, I got here okay. And if I leave out now, I've got plenty of time before it gets dark."

"That's all true enough," Beartooth allowed. "But I got to ponderin' that, in case

199

your ma gets a bee in her bonnet about you workin' for the Double M — and now with your whitewash-splattered clothes to boot — well, maybe you could use some reinforcements when you talk to her. I'm one for standin' by the men I hire and who stand by me."

"That's real square of you, Mr. Beartooth," said Brody. "But really, it's not necessary. Like I said before, I'm near a man growed. I figure it's time I started standin' my own ground. A fella ought to mind his ma, sure — up to a certain point. After that, he's got the right to say for himself."

"I admire an independent streak in a man. Lord knows, I had one of my own about your age. Matter of fact, I never outgrew it." Beartooth's forehead creased. "How about this . . . I been cooped up on this ol' ranch for the past three or four days straight. Much as anything, I was lookin' for an excuse to take myself a good ride. I ain't been out your way in quite a spell — what if I was to tag along with you for just a ways and then I'll veer off and leave you to deal with your ma on your own?"

What Beartooth was really looking to accomplish, of course, was finding an excuse to accompany the lad due the possibility of there being Indians in the area. He hadn't heard any word on Moosejaw's findings yet, so he didn't know one way or the other. He was thinking in terms of *just in case.* He cringed at the thought of young Brody running into a raiding party on his way back home, yet he didn't want to rattle him if it was unwarranted. Also, no matter their differences, it would ease Beartooth's mind to check on Mrs. Rockwell, too.

After considering Beartooth's proposal, Brody said, "Well, since you put it that way, I got no objection. It is kind of a lonely stretch back to the farm. And, hey, on the way I can show you what a good rider I am, in case you want to try me at bronc-bustin' sometime."

"If you ride a horse with all the energy you put into whitewashin', ain't much doubt you *could* be a bronc-buster." Beartooth chuckled. "Long as you don't get overeager and try to pick the horse up and carry it for a while, that is."

Brody gave a little laugh, but for just an instant, a trace of something that had absolutely no humor in it came and went in his eyes.

"Well, best we saddle up and get on our way, then," said Beartooth.

Brody took a step to follow him, but then

stopped abruptly, patting the pockets of his whitewash-streaked britches. "Whoops. Wait a second, I left something in the washroom. Go ahead, I'll catch up with you." With that, he spun on his heel and trotted back toward the lean-to.

Beartooth chuckled again and continued in the direction of the corral.

CHAPTER 22

Close to forty men were gathered in the Lone Star Palace saloon by the time Firestick got there after finishing his business at the telegraph office. Somewhat to the chagrin of owner Earl Sterling, only a handful were drinking. Still, even the dandified Sterling, who made a habit of seldom taking interest in anything that had no money-making potential, recognized the current situation as something bigger than a matter of mere dollars and cents.

The buzz of anxious conversation that had been filling the room suddenly died down when Firestick came in. Without saying anything right away, he proceeded back to where there was a raised stage, upon which Frenchy Fontaine — the Palace's main attraction, other than what got dispensed over the bar — performed nightly song-and-dance numbers. None of the usual piano music or catcalls accompanied the marshal

203

when it was he who climbed up, however. The deep concern etched on the faces turned to him made it plain how seriously every man present was taking this matter.

"All right," Firestick started in. "I reckon the word has already spread what this is about. Appears we've got an Apache raidin' party in our valley. About a dozen bucks leadin' ten or so packhorses. Means they're here to stock up on meat and other supplies to take back to their mountain village, somewhere down across the border."

"We need to see to it the only thing they get their fill of is hot lead!" somebody shouted. "Let's see 'em try and take *that* back across the border!"

A murmur of assent swelled from several others.

"That sounds real good," said Firestick. "But meanin' no offense, it also sounds like the talk of somebody who ain't ever fought Apaches before. Reckoning it's gonna be easy to run down this bunch and shoot it out with 'em like a gang of outlaws or some such, is all wrong."

"You just said there's only about a dozen of the red devils. Look around, we'd have 'em outnumbered near four to one."

"More than that by the time we gather in wranglers off some of the ranches," somebody added.

Firestick shook his head. "You ain't gettin' the picture. In order to fight anybody or anything, you first got to be able to see 'em. By the time you see an Apache — if you *ever* see him — there's a good chance you're already dyin' from havin' one of his arrows or bullets in you."

"You make it sound like they're ghosts instead of flesh-and-blood humans. But they *are* flesh and blood. So if they bleed, they can be killed."

"I never said they couldn't be killed," Firestick argued. "I'm just tryin' to tell you they're damn awful hard to corner into any kind of position where you *can* kill 'em."

Moosejaw moved up to stand alongside Firestick. The big deputy didn't mount the stage, but he towered high enough above most of the men in the room to be easily seen and heard. Facing outward, he said, "What you got to remember is, Apaches are masters at strikin' from concealment. They can hide behind not much more than a cactus needle or under a pebble. I've heard former cavalry troopers tell stories of havin' been out huntin' Apaches for weeks on end without layin' nary an eye on one . . . even after a soldier ridin' right beside 'em might've got picked off deader than a beaver hat."

"What's the point of gathering us here?" a voice called out from the crowd. "Just to tell us what fierce fighters the Apaches are?"

Standing beside Moosejaw, Mick Plummer now turned to face out at the others. He wasn't as tall, but his booming growl of a voice ensured he got heard. "Gawddammit! If you'll all shut up long enough, the marshal and his deputy are trying to tell you what the point of this is. They know what they're talking about when it comes to Injuns. So, if you got the brains to be quiet and pay attention, what they have to say will help us deal with the red devils and maybe save some white lives in the process!"

When things quieted down again, Firestick went on. "I just came from sendin' wires to Fort Davis and Fort Leaton. One of 'em, I ain't heard which one yet, will be sendin' troops to give us a hand with our problem, but at best, it's gonna take a few days before any get here. In the meantime, we got to decide on how best to look out for ourselves. Way I see it, that means three steps we need to take . . . Warn. Guard. Fight back."

The marshal paused a couple minutes to let his words sink in, then continued. "By

206

'warn,' I mean we got to get word out pronto to the outlyin' ranches and farms so they can arm themselves, fort up if necessary, prepare however they need to for the danger that might be comin' their way. I'm thinkin' three pairs of riders — good horsemen, well-armed, on fast mounts. The fewest ranches are to the north, short of the mountains. The heaviest concentration of smaller places is to the southwest. So, I suggest two sets of riders head out to the southwest. One of 'em curls west and north, the other curls to the east. The third pair of riders goes due east and curls north . . . That should sweep the area fairly fast and put the fewest men at risk." Firestick's eyes hardened. "Should be obvious that this *will* involve risk for the riders. I'll be askin' for six volunteers when we wrap up here, so some of you young, lean jaspers with strong horses be thinkin' about it."

Pete Roeback, who ran the town livery, spoke up. "That sounds pretty good, Marshal. But some of those small farms to the southwest, like the one run by my cousin Carl, have only got a ma and pa and one or two small kids. Even if they're warned and try to fort up, they won't be able to mount much resistance if they get singled out by the Apaches."

Firestick's expression tightened. "I know, Pete. I thought about your cousin . . . and the Millers, the Widow Rockwell and her boy, maybe a couple more out that way. The riders will need to move fast and won't be able to spend much time after they give their warnin'. The only thing I can come up with is sendin' out a couple wagons with crews of heavily armed men to round up those families and bring 'em into town . . . if they'll come. It'd mean leavin' their homes and most of their possessions totally unprotected."

"Man, that'd be a tough decision to make," somebody muttered.

"But a helluva lot better than riskin' your wife and kids to the Apaches," another voice countered.

"If I can get a couple men to go with me," Roeback said somberly, "reckon that's what I'll be doing — going out after Carl and his clan. Maybe I can bring in one of his neighboring families, too."

"That's your choice to make, Pete. One I can't fault," said Firestick.

From behind the bar, Earl Sterling, who'd been listening to the discussion with an air of indifference, abruptly appeared to take a greater interest. "If I may raise a point, Marshal," he said. "First, you're talking about sending out six men to warn the outliers. Now you're considering a wagon-load of two of more men going out — say, eight to ten in total. Simple math makes that as many as sixteen men that would be subtracted from the force we have here now. Not quite half, but uncomfortably close. That would considerably shave the four-to-one odds we were talking about having against the savages only a few minutes ago . . . Is that really wise?"

His question stirred an uneasy rumbling.

Roeback, a tall, deceptively slow-moving sort with work-gnarled hands, a weather-leathered face, and pale blue eyes that carried the faraway look of a man who's ridden the river up one side and down the other, turned his head and fixed those pale blues on Sterling. "You saying those women and kids out there ain't worth the effort of trying to save?"

The stare-down was no contest. Primped, pampered, and immaculately groomed Sterling, with his square-jawed good looks, muddy brown eyes, and a history of showing no spine for confrontation, wilted like a delicate flower in a hailstorm. "Good Lord, no. No, that's not what I meant at all, Pete. I was just . . . just pointing out how important it is to take everyone's safety into consideration."

"If anybody's worried about the town bein' attacked by these raiders," Firestick cut in, "I don't see that as bein' very likely." Leastways, not a full-on charge of any kind. But that don't mean the Apaches might not try sneakin' in under cover of dark — either at dusk or in the murky predawn — to do some nibblin' around the edges. That's what I meant by we have to 'guard.'

"The heart of town here along Trail Street I figure is about as safe as anywhere in the valley. But the outermost houses of the residential area, the Mexican cantina down at the east end, the corrals out behind Pete's livery . . . those kind of spots, and there are a few others, might offer targets for the cherry-cows if they get to feelin' frisky. Overall, the town ain't at too much risk, but until this is over, everybody needs to be on full alert, and especially for the overnight hours, we'll need to post guards at key places."

Pastor Bartholomew Rich of the First Baptist Church — "Pastor Bart," as he was affectionately called by most everyone — raised a hand to get Firestick's attention. When the marshal's gaze cut to him, he said, "Our church is very securely located. Anyone seeking refuge — no matter if they're regular attendees of my services or not, and especially the families who may be coming in from out of town — will be welcome to stay under our roof for the duration of this dreadful circumstance. We'll move things around, do whatever's necessary to make room and provide as much comfort as possible."

"That's mighty generous, Pastor Bart," Firestick responded. "When we break up from here and go about the other plans still to be finalized, we'll make sure word gets spread about your kind offer."

Firestick paused, licking his lips. In spite of Moosejaw's frequent ribbing about him being an accomplished word slinger, this was the most jabbering he'd done all in one stretch for a long time. He eyed the rows of bottles on the shelves behind the bar and thought how good a shot of red-eye would taste right about now. But, of course, that would have to wait.

"All right," he said, looking out over the crowd again. "That leaves the 'fight back' part."

This drew heightened interest and stirred an eager rumble. Firestick was glad the willingness for a fight was there — that was always good — but at the same time he realized most of those expressing it had no firsthand experience when it came to going up against Apaches. If they did, they wouldn't be so damn eager for more.

"Plummer here lost cattle to the raiders last night," Firestick said. "It's a certainty they'll pick off some more tonight, from somebody. We don't have time to warn all the ranches beforehand, and even if we did, their cattle are scattered too wide for any hope of protectin' all the herds. If it was just a matter of losin' more beef, I'd almost recommend swallowin' that loss and holdin' on with only the steps I've already talked about. Let the Apaches take some meat and go on their way."

"Here now," said Plummer, scowling. "You might recommend such a thing, but I hardly think —"

"Save your breath, it ain't gonna be that way," Firestick interrupted. "It ain't gonna be that way, because I don't figure those cherry-cows are aimin' to stop at stockin' up on just meat. They came after more supplies than that, and you can bet they're ready to kill to get 'em."

"You can double-down on that bet," Moosejaw added, "by countin' on 'em, at some point, to start killin' for the sake of killin'. They'll raid for meat and other supplies only so long — then at least part of 'em will concentrate on raidin' strictly to kill White Eyes."

"That's why we can't stop at merely settlin' in to protect ourselves and then waitin' for the cavalry to get here," Firestick explained. "Lives are gonna be lost one way or the other. So, we might as well spend those lives — and hope we can keep that spendin' to a minimum — by settin' out after those cherry-cows and drivin' 'em off before they get the chance to have it all their way."

"Most of us here are all for that," said Frank Moorehouse. "But most of your spiel up to now has been about how savage and tricky the Apaches are to fight."

"And I ain't changin' that tune, not a lick," Firestick told him. "Above all else, I want every man here to get this through your heads — goin' up against Apaches is a gruelin', blood-spillin', life-takin' thing like you ain't ever experienced before." Tryin' to chase 'em down out in the open would be next to suicide.

"But every indication is that they've gone into the Vieja Mountains to the north and are likely settin' up a camp there out of which to make their raids. Now, that ain't sayin' goin' after 'em there is gonna be no picnic, either. They've adapted to mountains as a means to survive and keep away from soldiers on both sides of the border. That makes 'em damn near as fierce and slippery as the Yaquis in other parts of Mexico — *el tigres de rocas,* the tigers of the rocks."

"If you're trying to instill confidence and recruit a force to go after the red devils," Sterling commented dryly, "you might want to consider honing your technique a bit."

Ignoring him, Firestick said, "But the thing we got goin' for us, the ace in the hole that might give us an edge by way of a surprise those cherry-cows won't be lookin' for . . . is the fact that, as most of you are aware, me and my two deputies also happen to know a thing or three about mountains and mountain fighting."

Another anxious rumble went through the crowd.

"What, exactly, have you got in mind, Marshal?" somebody asked.

Setting his jaw, sweeping his eyes over the faces looking up at him, Firestick said, "What I'm proposin' is to strike back at the Apaches and bust up their raidin' plans by hittin' 'em where they'd least expect — right smack in their own camp." He paused, watching a few heads bob, hearing some cautiously approving murmurs, then continued. "Apaches don't like to fight at night."

They'll do it, but they don't like it. They'll maneuver and put themselves in position during the dark hours, sometimes lead off livestock like they did last night, but they'd rather do their fightin' and killin' in the day. They're especially deadly and effective at dusk or in the predawn hours.

"What I've got in mind is to circle wide with a team of about half a dozen men, then work our way back through the Viejas until we find their camp. We wait for night to spring on 'em, killin' off their pony herd and as many of the braves as we can. Any who survive will be on foot, with their plans blasted to hell and their spirits shattered from believin' their medicine went bad. They won't bother us no more."

"But any who are left on foot you'll try to hunt down, won't you?" asked Plummer.

Firestick shook his head. "Big difference between a defeated Injun and one who has reason to come back lookin' for vengeance."

While the rancher was trying to digest that, Frank Moorehouse, with a concerned look on his face, said, "Who'll be leading that team into the mountains? You, Moose-jaw, and Beartooth won't all three leave the town, will you?"

"No, at least one of us will stay behind," Firestick told him. He tossed a glance

215

Moosejaw's way, then added, "We'll have to hash out amongst us who that will be."

"But before we get to hashin' on that, there's other things to set in motion without wastin' any more time," Moosejaw said. "We need to get those riders sent out to start warnin' the outlyin' ranches and farms. And some escort wagons, too, if that's what's been decided, to bring in the smaller families who don't have much hope of protectin' themselves."

The marshal nodded. "You ain't wrong, old friend. There's also those vulnerable spots around town we need to fortify a bit." He swept his gaze over the crowd and lifted his voice. "Okay, I need volunteers who are willin' to ride out with warnings for —"

His words were cut off by a wild-eyed, harried-looking man bursting in through the Palace's batwing doors. It was Sylvester Krause, one of Gus Wingate's hired hands. "Good God, Marshal," he blurted breathlessly. "You gotta come quick — Mr. Gus has been murdered dead out at our ranch!"

CHAPTER 23

When they'd gotten a little more than three miles away from the Double M, Brody Rockwell drew back on his reins and brought his bay gelding to a halt.

"What's the matter?" asked Beartooth, reining up beside him.

"My horse," Brody answered. "It feels like he's starting to step kinda light on his left front foot. I think he may have picked up a stone or something."

Beartooth frowned. "I didn't notice anything in his stride."

"Maybe not. But I can feel there's something bothering him," insisted Brody as he swung down from his saddle. "Best take a minute and try to figure out what it is before it gets to ailing him too bad."

After speaking soothingly to the bay, Brody knelt down on one knee and got the animal to lift its left front. The boy leaned close, examining.

"What is it?" asked Beartooth, still in his saddle.

"Don't rightly know," Brody answered, still scrutinizing the bottom of the hoof. "Don't see anything yet."

Beartooth dismounted and moved slowly around the rear of the bay, saying, "Let me have a look. Maybe I can spot something."

Brody rose and moved aside. Beartooth sank to one knee and took the raised hoof in his hands. He assumed much the same pose as Brody from a minute earlier, leaning his face close, eyes scouring the inner rim of the horseshoe for any lodged stones or maybe a cut of some kind.

"Whatever's botherin' him sure don't seem to be jumpin' into sight, does it?" Beartooth muttered.

"That's all right, Mr. Beartooth," replied Brody, a faint tightness in his voice that hadn't been there before. "You can quit worrying about that problem and start thinking about a new one."

"How's that?" Beartooth said distractedly, still studying the bottom of the horse's hoof. But when he lifted his face and turned it to look at Brody, he saw very quickly what the new problem was. He didn't understand what it was about, but he had no trouble recognizing the seriousness of it.

Brody Rockwell had backed about four paces away and was holding the Colt drawn from the fancy rig he wore aimed directly at Beartooth's face. It was a big gun for the slender lad, but he held it with a steady hand.

"Is this some kind of joke?" Beartooth said through clenched teeth.

"Not hardly," said Brody, his voice still a little tight, yet as steady as the gun muzzle trained on the former mountain man. "It would be a big mistake on your part to think so."

"Then what the hell is it about?"

"We'll get to that in a minute. But first I want to make sure you don't get no bad ideas about taking me lightly as a threat and trying to turn the tables on me with some foolhardy move. That means you freeze exactly like you are. You can let go of the horse's foot, but be sure to hold your hands out away from your body just the way you've got them." Brody's eyes were by now blazing with an intensity that didn't seem to fit his young face, yet was too strong to disregard. "I don't want to shoot you, but seeing's how I've set this in motion, I won't hesitate if I have to. So happens I'm very good with this gun — my brother taught me, and even he was impressed with how I took to it. I don't fancy myself no fast draw like he thought he was, but I never miss what I aim at . . . and right now that's you, Mr. Beartooth."

Beartooth released his grip on the bay's foot and let it drop back down to the ground. Otherwise he remained perfectly still, kneeling on one knee, his hands extended out before him. His eyes bored into Brody with a hard glare, but he said nothing.

"Now . . . real, real slow, keeping those hands where I can see 'em at all times . . . unbuckle your gun belt and toss it over here toward me," Brody instructed. "After that, the knife . . . I've heard all the stories about how good you're supposed to be with that thing."

Slowly, grudgingly, his mind racing with thoughts of trying something reckless while better sense restrained him in the face of the unwavering gun muzzle, Beartooth complied with the instructions. Once his gun belt and bowie knife had been discarded, he grated, "Now what?"

Reaching into his hip pocket with his free hand, Brody withdrew a set of handcuffs and held them out for Beartooth to see. "Now these. I saw them lying in your washroom earlier, then helped myself to 'em when I went back saying I forgot something. Once you invited yourself to take this ride with me, I figured they'd come in handy." He gave the cuffs a toss so that they hit the ground and skidded close to Beartooth's knee. "I expect you know how they work. So stand up and clamp one bracelet around the bay's front rigging dee and the other one on your right wrist. Reckon you won't be making no sudden moves after that, not if you gotta drag along a horse in order to do it."

"You go to hell, you snot-nosed pup! I ain't gonna put those irons on for nobody," snarled Beartooth.

"Your choice," Brody said coldly. "If you don't cooperate, I'll have to shoot you, then go back to the ranch and put the cuffs on that pretty Miss Victoria instead. That was my original plan, to take her hostage for what I got in mind. But then, like I said before, when you insisted on riding out here with me, I decided you would work just as well."

"You're a cold-blooded little bastard, ain't you?"

"You can call me names all you want, but it don't change nothing," Brody said in a flat tone. "I'm really not out to hurt anybody. But if you force me to, I will."

More than the threat of being shot himself, the potential for harm coming to Victoria drove Beartooth to once again comply with what he was told to do. He rose to his feet and fastened one of the handcuff bracelets around the saddle's front rigging dee and then, grimacing almost as if in physical pain, he clamped the other tight around his right wrist.

Brody's shoulders appeared to sag a bit, as some of the tension eased out of him. But the gun remained steady. "I'm glad you had the good sense not to make me shoot you," he said.

"Don't expect me to return the favor if I ever get the chance," Beartooth responded. "Now, what the hell is this all about?"

"Money. Like I told you right from the get-go. And I don't mean the piddly wage you offered to pay me. I mean more than that — a lot more."

Beartooth continued to glare at him, but said nothing.

"What I've got in mind is simple," Brody went on. "When I ducked back into that washroom before we left, I did something else besides grab those handcuffs. I left a note where one of your vaqueros or somebody will be sure to find it. It's a ransom note with demands for your safe return. I already had it written and in my pocket, I just had to scratch out Miss Victoria's name and replace it with yours. Like I said a minute ago, my original plan was to kidnap her for the ransom. I figured after I'd worked for you for a couple of days and nobody was paying much attention to me, it'd be easy to find a chance to grab her and do what I'm doing now. You sticking your nose in and insisting on riding out with me today just gave me a chance to set things in motion a little quicker."

"Does your ma know about this? Is she part of it?"

"She's part of it. But not in the way you mean — not no part of planning this or knowing anything about what I'm up to." Brody's mouth pulled briefly into a tight, straight line before he continued. "She never did care much about what I was thinking or what my plans might be. Owen was always her favorite. Since he's been gone, everything I told you about how she's been acting all dull and not giving a rip about anything was true. But I aim to *make* her take notice of me and my plans and end up proud of me."

"Yeah, I can see where turnin' outlaw will make her take notice of you," Beartooth said dryly. "But unless she's got the same twisted way of lookin' at things as you seem to, I don't see how she'll find much pride in it."

"Don't you worry about that," Brody snapped. "My ransom demands, see, ain't about money for *me*. Before I turn you loose, I'm gonna want to be shown papers, all legal and binding, that say Ma's farm is paid off clean, with taxes covered for the next five years. And I'll also make sure there's a statement swearing she'll get no blame on account of what I've done."

Beartooth could see a new burst of intensity flaring in the lad's eyes now, but couldn't decide if it was a touch of madness or just desperation to try and please his mother. "Then what?" he demanded. "Even if you get all those things, after this kind of stunt, there's no way in hell anybody's gonna let you just walk away free."

Brody shook his head. "Don't expect 'em to. I'll ride off and see to my own freedom."

"They'll hunt you down. *I'll* hunt you down."

"You can try. There's hundreds of young fellas drifting across the Southwest. I'm betting I got a good chance of blending in somewhere and settling where you or nobody else will ever catch up with me."

"And what about your ma? You're ready to never see her again?" Beartooth asked,

224

trying a different angle.

Brody's gaze turned flinty. "I'll have done right by her. That'll have to do. She never cared that much about me anyway. And I sure ain't gonna miss workin' that blamed farm . . . So, leaving things the way I figure to leave 'em will have to do."

A sudden lifting of wind — dry and warm, like a last gasp of the day coming ahead of the evening coolness that would soon be upon them — swept over the rolling, grassy hills on all sides. It stirred Beartooth's thoughts, made him consider something that, for the past tense moments, had been shoved aside in his mind.

"Now, looky here, boy," he said earnestly. "I'm fixin' to tell you something that you'll likely take as hogwash, some kind of trick I'm lookin' to pull on you. But I'm serious as a gravestone, and you need to pay close attention."

Brody gave him a look. "All that talk leading up to it only makes me more suspicious about whatever it is you're gonna say."

"Reckon in your place, I'd think the same," Beartooth admitted. "But I'm gonna lay it on you anyway. Think about why I was so pushy about ridin' out with you when you were ready to leave the Double M a little while ago. Didn't really make much sense no matter what I claimed, did it? So, here's a reason that *does* make sense, even though I didn't want to say it flat-out on account of I couldn't then — and still can't — be sure."

"Whatever you got to say, I wish you'd just spit it out. We got ground we need to cover before nightfall."

"Okay, here it is: I got reason to suspect that a pack of Apache raiders has showed up in our valley. My two partners went out checkin' for signs, to make sure, before we spread the word and riled everybody up. Since I hadn't heard anything back from 'em yet by the time you were ready to head out, I was concerned about you ridin' alone and maybe fallin' prey to 'em. I was thinkin' about your ma bein' alone at the farm, too. I wanted the chance to get out and look things over, do the best I could to satisfy myself that you two would be safe in case there was something stirrin'."

The flintiness came back into Brody's eyes. "Mister, when you started out by saying I was gonna think you was spewing hogwash, you said it all. Ain't no Apaches around here for a hunnerd miles, ain't been for years."

"Don't be so sure about that, boy. Was a fella saw some things last night that —"

226

"Enough!" Brody cut him off. "I ain't got time to waste on no more hogwash. Like I said, we got ground to cover."

"That's the point I'm tryin' to make," Beartooth told him. "Dusk is one of the favorite times for an Apache to prowl and strike. If we're gallopin' around out here in the wide open and there *are* any bucks in the area, they could swarm us like flies to a spilled jelly jar."

"That's a mighty big 'if' and an even bigger lie you're trying to cloud my thinking with." Brody made a thrusting motion with his Colt. "You're gonna be riding my bay since you're already chained to the saddle, so climb on up. It'll be a mite awkward for you, cuffed the way you are, but you're supposed to be a horseman so you'll manage. Once you're mounted, you'll be bent over kinda uncomfortable-like, but you'll still be able to ride. And the first sign of you trying to take off or pull some other kind of trick, I'll shoot you out of the saddle and you'll be drug by the chain. Keep that in mind."

CHAPTER 24

Sylvester Krause's announcement that his boss had been "murdered dead" sent an excited ripple through all those gathered in the Lone Star Palace Saloon. Before Firestick was able to say anything, somebody else in the crowd hollered, "Was it Indians?"

Krause's already frantic expression twisted with confusion. "Indians? What the hell are you talking about?"

Several of the men closest to Krause all started trying to answer at once, and the result became an indecipherable babble. Firestick bounded from the stage and, with Moosejaw bulling a path ahead of him, quickly closed the distance to Krause. Waving his arms and raising his voice to a level that cut through the babble, the marshal said, "Hold it down! Everybody shut up, damn it, so we can make some sense out of this!"

The other voices dropped to an anxious

murmur.

Firestick fixed his attention strictly on Krause, a wiry man of average size, fortyish, with a sun- and wind-reddened face built around a somewhat bulbous nose and wide mouth. "Start from the beginnin'. What do you mean, Gus Wingate has been murdered?"

The distraught hired man gazed up at him with deep anguish in his eyes. "I don't know how else to say it. He was shot in the head. Killed."

"When?"

"Earlier this afternoon. Maybe about three hours ago. Me and Marsh, that's the other hired man works for Mr. Gus, we was down by the creek clearing and burning brush when we heard a shot up by the house where the boss was working. We didn't think too much of it at the time, though. We figured he was probably plunkin' at some varmint that had come around, a snake or a rat maybe. Or maybe he was tryin' to bag a deer or rabbit for the stew pot."

"You heard just one shot?"

"Uh-huh."

"But you didn't see anything or anybody who might have had something to do with it?"

"No. We was too far away." Krause's

expression turned mournful. "Lord, if we'd had any idea it meant something was wrong . . . especially anything so bad . . ."

"When did you find out what actually happened — what the shot *did* mean?"

"About an hour or so after it happened. We'd finished our burnin' and made sure the fire was stomped out good and cold, then rode on back to the ranch house . . . And there Gus was, layin' in plain sight over by where he'd been digging some postholes for an add-on to one of our cattle pens."

"You said he'd been shot in the head." Firestick frowned. "Was anything . . . else done to him?"

"What kind of question is that? Ain't havin' his brains blowed out bad enough?"

"If it was the work of Apaches, they'd have for sure done some hackin' on the body," said Moosejaw. Then he added, "Of course, they likely wouldn't have killed him so clean to begin with. And they wouldn't have ignored Krause and the other fella, either."

"Apaches!" echoed Krause stridently. "What's with all the Injun talk? What's going on around here?"

"We've got an Apache raidin' party in our valley," Firestick told him. He made a gesture with one hand, adding, "That's what this whole powwow is about."

230

"Jesus! Why didn't we hear about a thing like that?" Krause wanted to know.

"We were plannin' on sendin' out riders to spread the warning right as you showed up."

Krause wagged his head. "Apaches . . . Lord Almighty. How much bad news can be heaped into one day?"

"The day ain't over yet," muttered Moose-jaw.

"And the more time we spend makin' plans and not startin' to set some of 'em in motion, the more we risk lettin' more bad things happen." Firestick took a deep breath, puffed out his cheeks, and expelled it. "Look," he said, addressing mainly his big deputy, "we've decided several of the right steps to take as far as the Apaches. But that don't mean we can let Gus Wingate's killing go without givin' it some attention, too. So I want you to take over here, Moosejaw. Get those riders and wagons sent out. Make sure whoever goes is well armed with plenty of cartridges. Then go to work on fortifyin' some of those weaker spots on the town's perimeter. I shouldn't be gone too long. I'll take Krause with me and give things out at the ranch a good lookin' over, see if I can make any sense out of what happened. Then I'll be back."

"Sounds reasonable," agreed Moosejaw. He looked as if he wanted to say more, but held off even as his wide brow furrowed with deep creases.

"What is it?" said Firestick, knowing his big friend too well to miss or ignore the signs. "What ain't you sayin'?"

"It's Beartooth," Moosejaw replied. "He's out at the Double M with just Miguel and Jesus to side him in case any Apaches pop up out that way. And he ain't even got word yet that me and Boynton turned up certain signs that there *are* Apaches on the prowl."

"You think that ain't weighin' on my mind, too?" Firestick's question was sharp, testy. "But Beartooth knows how to take care of himself — and those around him, too. And he had warnin' about there bein' *suspicions* of Injuns in the area. That's more than most of the rest of the farmers and ranchers in the valley know right now, and it'll be enough for Beartooth to stay sharp. It'll have to be, until the warning riders get word to him just like everybody else. You think it would be fair for us to single him out for a special warning?"

Moosejaw shook his head. "No, I don't reckon."

"He'd be the first one not to want it that way. In fact, he'd be damned mad if he found out we gave him any special treatment . . . So the best thing for it is to get started with those things we've discussed so's he *does* get word as soon as possible."

Moosejaw squared his massive shoulders. "You're right. But will you at least consider takin' more than just Krause with you back to the Wingate place? You could run into trouble, too, you know. And we can't afford for anything to happen to you."

Firestick grinned wryly. "Trust me, I have my own interest in protectin' my ol' hide. But me and Krause will stay sharp. We'll be okay."

Krause failed to look quite so confident.

Cleve Boynton edged forward out of the crowd. "How about I go along? I won't crowd you none, and one extra gun, one extra set of eyes, could come in handy."

"I appreciate the offer, Boynton," Firestick said. "But you need to carry word back to the Box T that what you saw was for certain Indians. And you heard Tolsvord, he'll want every gun he can get to cover his spread."

"The Dunlap brothers and Newt Woolsey can take care of getting word to Boss Tolsvord about the Apaches," Boynton replied. "And, once they get there, the spread will be armed plenty strong. Bein' minus my gun for another night won't hurt 'em that bad. I can always make it out there tomorrow."

"Sounds like a good idea to me," Moosejaw said.

Firestick gave in. "All right. Obliged, Boynton. Go on over to Roeback's livery and saddle yourself a fresh horse. Me and Krause will meet you there."

Chapter 25

"I don't know if this is a good idea or not," Greely Dunlap mumbled uneasily, casting his gaze around the nearly emptied interior of the Lone Star Palace.

Everybody else had boiled out of the place several minutes before, off on some piece of business or other, all related to the news of Apaches in the valley. Greely, his brother Grady, and Newt Woolsey had lagged behind. They'd seated themselves at one of the round-topped card tables in the middle of the room and ordered up the bottle of whiskey, glasses, and three foamy mugs of beer that now sat before them. Gunther, the bald, slow-moving, tight-lipped bartender who'd remained behind to man the stick after Earl Sterling left with the others, had served them with his usual silent efficiency before retreating to a spot behind the far end of the bar.

"It *tastes* to me like a damn good idea,"

responded his brother, Grady, after taking a big gulp from his mug of beer.

"I'll second that," agreed Woolsey as he raised a shot of red-eye, then tossed it down and reached for his own beer to chase it with.

But Greely didn't look convinced. "Oh, of course the drinks taste good. No argument there. But I'm thinkin' we might better have taken a bottle with us and done some nippin' on the trail as we went back to the ranch."

"The ranch will still be there even if we take time to do a little nippin' here before we ride out. And we'll get back to it, don't you worry," Grady assured him. "But sittin' here comfortable-like to do our drinkin' first is a helluva better than doin' it from the back of a horse, you can't deny that."

"Besides," said Woolsey as he poured himself another jolt of whiskey, "everybody and his cousin — the men who are goin' out in wagons, the riders who are gonna spread the warnings, even our pal Boynton — went tearin' out of here, most of 'em to claim horses at the livery. That's where the law put our horses, too, remember. So, if we went rushin' over there right away, we probably couldn't get close to our nags any-way."

"Stinkin' law dogs," grumbled Grady bitterly. "Something else I'd like to take time to do before we leave town is pay me a visit to that hornin'-in damn Firestick." He absently rubbed his badly bruised jaw and swept a thumb gently over the stitches under one eye. "I owe that sumbitch a big dose of payback, and that's for sure."

"Boy, ain't that the truth. We all do. That big bastard near busted my foot the way he hammered down on it. And then flung me across the room like a wadded-up ol' shirt and wrenched hell out of my back — for which that hard slab of a cot in his damn jail cell didn't help any." As he added these lamentations, Woolsey reached around to clamp one hand on the small of his back. "I got some licks of my own I'd like to get in on that high-minded law dog. I get me another chance at his kneecap, he'll be hobblin' around on a crutch when I get done."

Greely took a drink of his beer. "I ain't disputin' we owe some payback to Firestick — not to mention that cardsharp dandy we was bein' cheated by, the fella the marshal took up for against us."

"Hey, that sneaky skunk is still in town. I seen him here at this gatherin' just a little bit ago," piped up Woolsey. "He came slippin' in through the batwings while Firestick was yappin' up on the stage."

"I'd like to get my hands on that weasel," said Grady. "Hell, I figured he'd skedaddled town by now."

Woolsey shook his head. "Nope, he's still around. Matter of fact, I heard some of the other fellas talkin' — I guess that shootin' we heard out in the street earlier this mornin' when we was still in the clink was that dandy lendin' a hand to help cut down a couple hombres who'd come gunnin' for the marshal."

"Oh? He supposed to be some kind of fancy gunslinger, too?"

Greely raised his voice, saying, "Look, doggone it, that's all interestin' as hell, but none of it is enough to change the fact that maybe we ought not be sittin' here frettin' about those things. If there's Apaches out there on the loose, well, that seems like it should be the main concern of everybody in the valley. And you heard Boynton say he was leavin' it up to us to get word back to Tolsvord at the Box T on that. Seems to me the sooner we do our part to help spread the word —"

"Damn it, didn't I say we was gonna get word back to the Box T?" Grady cut in. "Is fifteen minutes or a half hour gonna make that much stinkin' difference?"

"You never know. It could," Greely said stubbornly.

"Well, maybe you oughta go climb on your horse and hightail it back out there on your own then, if you're convinced it's so all-fired important." A scowl gripped Grady's heavy-jowled face. "Besides, I ain't even sold on the notion there *are* any Apaches around."

"I don't know how you figure that," said Greely. "Firestick seemed mighty convinced. So did Moosejaw. They oughta know, bein' experienced Injun fighters the way they are and all."

"Says *them,*" growled Grady sullenly. "I ain't so sure I believe that, neither. They show up here — them two and the third one along with 'em — tellin' stories about their mountain-man days, and everybody automatically swallows it as fact. For all we know, they could be three goober pea growers from Georgia or some such."

"If that's the case," allowed Woolsey, wrinkling his forehead dubiously, "they been foolin' a lot of people for all the time they've been hereabouts. The thing is, if there's even a *chance* of Apaches prowlin' around, Greely makes a good point. Much as I like the thought of layin' for the marshal and that cardslick dandy . . . well, Injuns in the valley would be a lot more important. And you gotta figure the sooner the better when it comes to us lettin' our pals back at the Box T know the threat, even if it's only a possibility."

"Aw, for Christ's sake," grumbled Grady. "Now that you namby-pambys have taken all the damn fun out of havin' a few drinks, what's the use? We might as well go back to the damn ranch! And soon as we get there, I'm warnin' you right now that I'll be on the lookout for a couple of new drinkin' partners. From here on out, you two sorry varmints can start havin' nice, peaceful tea parties together — without me!"

From his hotel room window, Henry Lofton looked down on the flurry of activity taking place all up and down Trail Street. He supposed he should feel some sort of compassion for the innocent, frightened people scurrying back and forth down there with thoughts of Apache atrocities weighing fresh and heavy on their minds.

But he didn't, of course. He'd long ago realized and accepted that lack of emotion in himself, his inability to feel compassion for others. It was what made him so good at his job of hiring out his gun to kill folks —

or, as he preferred to think of it, to *eliminate* those who were a problem to his employers.

Still, he could understand where the thought of Apaches was not a pleasant one for anybody. Including himself. Once he'd finished his business here in Buffalo Peak, he would want to depart as soon as possible. But the prospect of riding out and possibly being unlucky enough to encounter the red devils on his way gave him pause. And the one man — or at least a *key* man — who seemed most capable of dealing with the Apache threat was the person he needed to kill in order to complete his job.

How ironic.

Ironic, too, mused Lofton, was the fact that in all the places throughout the Southwest where he'd traveled to ply his trade, he had never before been anywhere they were having Indian trouble. Not that it was an omission he regretted. He could have gotten along just fine without ever having that particular experience.

What was more, speaking of regrets, his current situation *did* involve one. It could even be called more irony. As someone who seldom met anybody he was inclined to feel friendly toward, Lofton had actually found Marshal Firestick a likable sort, after the big, gregarious lawmen had jumped into the middle of the scrap with the Dunlap brothers and that weaselly little runt, Woolsey. Lofton had genuinely enjoyed talking with the former mountain man and listening to his tales of those free, wild days in the high reaches. When the Widow Rockwell had named Firestick as the second man she wanted Lofton to eliminate, it had been both surprising and a little troubling.

But for the sake of his reputation, Lofton could hardly balk over such a limited acquaintance. And then, having taken the widow's money, there was no choice but to go through with fulfilling his commitment. Earlier today, when it looked like the vengeful uncle with the Winchester stood a good chance of doing the job of killing Firestick, Lofton had intervened out of some cockeyed sense of obligation, as well as a matter of professional pride, not wanting to let somebody else do his work for him. Now the gunman found himself wishing to hell he'd gone ahead and left it up to the uncle.

After the business at the Wingate ranch, Lofton had gotten back into town just in time to be swept up in the gathering at the Lone Star Palace. Once the threat of Apaches had been revealed and then Wingate's hired man showed up, he'd eased out of the throng and returned to his hotel room to contemplate just where he stood and what his options were given this combination of events. He wanted to finish his job here and move on, that much was certain. But he wasn't sure he was in such a hurry to leave that it might mean fighting his way clear of Indians in order to do it. And with all the focus on Firestick now as the leader of taking the fight to the Apaches, at least until the army got here, it was going to be damn hard to get to him anyway. It was beginning to look, Lofton was thinking, as if waiting for the army to show up might be his best bet. Not only would they take much of the attention off of the marshal, but they would also make the way safer for when it came time to leave.

In the meantime, accommodations here at the hotel weren't all that bad. And, with a couple different saloons in town, he shouldn't have too much trouble finding some games of chance with which to pass the time.

Almost omen-like, as if bidden by Lofton's thoughts, his eyes fell on the Dunlap brothers and Woolsey as they emerged from the Lone Star Palace. A knot started to tighten in the gunman's stomach. He'd never had much occasion to go after payback, mainly because he tended to take care of affronts or any harm done him right at the moment such things happened. And he seldom went looking for trouble unless someone was paying him to.

But these three jackasses, whom he'd expected to be gone from town by now after their early release from jail, had been hell-bent on stomping him through the floorboards of the Silver Spur for no valid reason. And they might have, too, if Firestick hadn't stepped in. Yet there they were, sauntering boldly down the boardwalk toward the town livery, loose again after a totally inadequate amount of time behind bars. And this time — due to the Indian threat, he supposed — they were packing guns.

The knot in Lofton's gut grew tighter.

Maybe here was a case where some unfinished business *did* call for a bit of payback.

After all, it wasn't like he didn't have some time to kill . . .

CHAPTER 26

Lyle Marsh, a middle-aged man with a perpetual squint and a faint limp, was busy constructing a casket when Firestick, Cleve Boynton, and Sylvester Krause arrived at the Wingate ranch. Marsh had covered Gus Wingate's body with a canvas tarp, then hauled some boards out of a nearby shed so he could commence sawing and assembling them while still in sight of the canvas-draped form, in case any scavengers came around.

By the time Firestick and the others got there, the hired man had worked up a pretty good sweat. As the horsemen reined up, he stopped his work and moved to stand closer to the body, sleeving away a smear of sawdust that clung to the beads of perspiration dotting his forehead.

"This is a bad thing, Marshal. A real bad thing." He spoke in a mournful tone, gazing up at Firestick.

Regarding him in turn, the marshal saw that, amid the sweat and sawdust covering his face, there were also a couple of unmistakable tear tracks running down the man's cheeks. "It's hard news, Marsh. That's for sure," Firestick said as he swung down from the saddle.

Marsh stood wagging his head. "Gus was a good fella. Everybody said so. I just can't believe anybody'd do him like that."

Having no response for that, Firestick knelt down and peeled back a corner of the tarp. Wingate had fallen straight back and now lay flat on his back, arms flung wide, one leg thrust out straight, the other folded partly under him. The hole in the middle of his forehead was a neat round circle where the bullet had gone in, but the amount of blood and gore spread out on the ground under and around his head gave unsettling testimony that its exit had been far from neat. The victim's eyes were wide open, though dull and lifeless, and the surprised "O" formed by his bloodless lips made almost as perfect a circle as the bullet hole higher up.

Firestick let the tarp drop back into place, straightened up. "Heavy-caliber slug, a .44 or .45, I'd say," he declared. "Looks like it went in at a slight downward angle, so I'd reckon further that somebody on horseback just rode up and shot him."

"I did some lookin' around for tracks before I headed out for town," said Krause. "Trouble is, we all three ride through this area regular-like when we come and go to tend the cattle. And there ain't been no rain to speak of for days. So, track-wise, I couldn't make out a whole lot."

Firestick walked out a ways from the body, his eyes scanning the ground closely. "I can spot a few fresher marks in amongst the others," he said. Then, lifting his face and looking out across the surrounding grassy expanse dotted with clumps of grazing cattle, he added, "I could stick with 'em for a ways. But once they got out there in the high grass, where the cows have trampled . . ."

He let his words trail off. Turning back, his eyes cut toward the main house, and he gestured, saying, "How about the soddy? Anything been disturbed or taken from inside there?"

The two hired hands looked a little startled. Then, after exchanging glances with Marsh, Krause said, "Jeez, Marshal. We never thought to look. You think that's what this was about — a robbery?"

"Usually some kind of reason for shooting

a man. Lookin' to rob something from him is one of the more common ones. Did Wingate keep any money or valuables in the house?"

"Some items of personal value is all. You know, for sentimental reasons. But nothing like you mean. And no big amount of money. Or if he did, he didn't let on about it to us," Marsh said.

"He made regular trips to the bank in town. When it was time to pay us each month or buy something for the ranch, he went to draw out what he needed," added Krause.

Firestick gestured toward the house. "Let's go have a look."

The marshal started toward the soddy, Krause and Marsh on his heels.

"I'll stay out here and look around some more," Boynton called after them.

The inside of the soddy proved to be surprisingly tidy and clean, especially given the kind of structure it was and the fact that there was no woman in residence to look after such things. Thin sheets of linen hung from the ceiling to keep bits of dirt and bugs from dropping onto everything; the earthen floor was packed hard as a rock and well swept; the kitchen area was compactly arranged with no sign of dirty dishes or unwashed cooking pots; and the three bunks lining the walls at the opposite end of the single room were neatly made and covered with colorful blankets.

"Sure ain't no sign of ransackin'," Firestick noted. "Does anything at all look out of place or disturbed in any way?"

Marsh shook his head. "Not that I can see."

"Me neither," Krause agreed.

Firestick's brow creased. "Excuse me for sayin', but this almost looks *too* clean. As if somebody went to a lot of trouble to set everything right after a bad trashin' or some such."

Again Krause and Marsh exchanged looks, their expressions equally puzzled. "This is how Mr. Gus sort of demanded it to look," Krause explained. "He was real fussy about always keepin' the house in good order."

"It was on account of his late wife," Marsh added, pointing to a framed picture of an attractive middle-aged woman that hung over one of the bunks. "He had this thing — a sort of guilt, you might call it — about never bein' able to afford a house better than this soddy when she was alive. He said she worked her fingers to the bone to keep the place a real home, not a hole in the dirt, and he meant to do the same in her memory."

"Of late, the past year or so," said Krause, "he could've afforded to build something better. He even talked about it. But then he always held off. That guilt thing again, like Lyle said, is my guess. Because he was never able to put up anything better for his wife, he somehow didn't think he deserved better for himself."

"Speakin' of how he felt about himself," Firestick said, "I happened to run into him in town last night. I hadn't seen him for a while, but based on the way he looked when I did — and I ain't talkin' about just the fact that he was shit-faced drunk — he didn't look like he'd been treatin' himself too good at all lately. Unshaven, shabby clothes . . . Nothing like the care and attention I see around us here."

"No denyin' he took to drinkin' awful bad and not lookin' after hisself very good these past couple months," said Marsh. "But knowin' how he felt about the house, me'n Sylvester have been makin' sure to keep the things up the way we know he'd want it if . . . well, until he came back around to hisself again."

"Sounds like a mighty complex fella. Not too long ago one of my friends called him tormented," Firestick remarked.

"He was that," Krause said somewhat sadly. "Most everybody else saw him as a decent man, but he was never willin' to look at himself that way because he kept seein' what he reckoned to be shortcomings from the past. And that shootin' business with the Rockwell boy — yeah, that tormented him to no end."

Marsh eyed the marshal directly. "There was some shootin' involved when you saw him again last night, wasn't there?"

"Yeah, there was," Firestick allowed. "But *I* was the one who did the trigger-pullin' before it was done with, not Wingate. He should've had no reason to drag himself any lower over that."

"He did, though," said Krause. "He was frettin' over it at breakfast this morning. Said he was the cause of it all the same."

"Hard to counter a fella who wants that bad to find reasons to beat himself up," said Firestick.

"Maybe so. But those jaspers who started the trouble last night — they claimed to be doin' it over the Rockwell shooting, right? What if the shooter who came around here today had the same reason — they were lookin' to get even with Mr. Gus for one or both of those other shootings?" asked Marsh.

Firestick thumbed back the brim of his hat and sighed. "You know, from what I can tell right now, that's probably as good a motive as we got to go on. Trouble is, anything tied to last night's shootin' I already had to deal with earlier today. And as far as a link to the Rockwell shootin' . . . For starters, I don't think even Rand Wilson, that little varmint who caused the trouble last night, really gave a damn about Owen Rockwell. He was just lookin' for an excuse to skin his shooter and try to make a name for himself as a gunny. So, as for any other connection to the Rockwell shootin', you gotta wonder why it would take so long for anything else to crop up . . ."

"One thing I can tell you is that the Widow Rockwell, Owen's ma, is carryin' around a load of blame and hate for Mr. Gus that would sink a river barge," pointed out Krause.

Firestick twisted his mouth sourly. "Yeah, I know. She's carryin' around a load almost as big for me. But can you really picture the widow or her younger boy comin' out here — again, after all this time — to blast Wingate in the name of revenge?"

Marsh hung his head. "Hell, I don't know.

I guess not. But dang it . . ."

"I reckon word has spread all over by now about Mr. Gus not carryin' a gun anymore. But it would've took a while. Maybe that explains the lag in time for somebody to come after him — until some yellow skunk figured out there wasn't much risk, what with him drunk most of the time and no longer goin' heeled, when it came to confrontin' him head-on," suggested Krause.

"I suppose that could explain part of it." Firestick frowned in thought. Then, fixing his gaze directly on Krause, he said, "But wait a minute. When you was first tellin' me what happened, you said you and Marsh heard a shot, but didn't fetch up here right away because you figured Wingate was probably shootin' at a varmint. If you knew he was no longer packin' a gun, why would you think that?"

Krause's answer was straightforward and simple. "Like any ranch I've ever worked on, Marshal, we keep two or three varmint guns stashed around in different places — sheds and whatnot. You never know in case some kind of mangy critter might pop up and catch you when you're away from your saddle gun or not carryin' your sidearm." He shrugged. "Hearin' Mr. Gus burn a cartridge, even though he'd quit carryin', wouldn't've been all that unusual."

Marsh looked like a pang of pain had passed through him. "For cryin' out loud, Marshal, you ain't suspicionin' that me or Sylvester had anything to do with shootin' Mr. Gus, are you?"

Firestick sighed. "No, not really. Reckon I'm grabbin' at straws on account of I can't make sense of no other reason. That and those damn Apaches also weighin' on my mind."

Marsh's eyes bugged to the size of two boiled eggs. "Apaches?" he echoed in a strangled voice.

"Yeah," Krause muttered offhandedly. "Appears we got an Apache raidin' party somewhere in the valley."

"Well, hell!" Marsh wailed. "Don't you think that's something you ought to have told a fella right off?"

CHAPTER 27

Moosejaw was taking a well-earned breather. He'd spent the day following Apache signs, much of the time with an itch between his shoulders like one of the red heathens was drawing a bead on him with an arrow, then he had ridden hard to bring word back to town. Now, for the past hour or so, he'd been overseeing the preparations Firestick had left him in charge of. Only after the warning riders and the escort wagons had headed out did he relax enough to realize how hungry and exhausted he was.

The hungry part wasn't an especially big deal, since his appetite was seldom fully satisfied, and the exhaustion was the kind that left a body feeling more keyed up and restless than actually being ready to rest.

Which left it to Daisy Rawling, Moosejaw's lady friend, to spot his weariness and insist it receive some attention. Though many, including Daisy herself, might laugh at attaching the term "lady" to anything about her, that's the way Moosejaw saw it, and woe to anybody foolish enough to cross him on the subject.

The way she was fawning over him at the moment, demanding he plop himself down on a sawed log stool positioned near the wide-open front doors of Daisy's blacksmith shop while she fetched him a pair of thick beef sandwiches, a double slice of pie, and a pot of coffee from the Mallory Hotel kitchen only increased the fondness with which he gazed upon her.

"I tell you," Daisy was saying while he chewed hungrily and washed the bites down with gulps of steaming coffee, "if I'd known you was out there chasing after Apaches all day, I would've been worried sick."

"Well, there weren't no chance to tell you before I had to light out," Moosejaw replied. "But now that you say it would've troubled you, I reckon I'm glad that's the way it went. I wouldn't have liked doin' what I was doin', all the while knowin' you was back here frettin' so."

"A gal has a right to fret if she wants to," Daisy said determinedly. "And even though I understand how *you* had no chance to say anything to me on account of how it came up sudden-like and you had to leave out from the ranch . . . well, the same excuse don't hold true for that doggone Firestick. He should have let me know what was going on when he made it into town. Soon as I see him again, I aim to give him a piece of my mind for not doin' so!"

"Aw, come on, Daize," said Moosejaw. "Firestick's got enough on his plate, what with the Apache trouble and now what sounds like a murder havin' took place out at the Wingate ranch. Don't you think he deserves to be cut a little slack? He couldn't have told you too much about what I was up to anyway, not until I reported back what I'd found. Before then, he had to be careful what he said so's not to rile up an Injun scare in case it turned out to be a false alarm."

The fact he was sitting down put the big deputy at eye level with his diminutive gal friend. Diminutive in height, that was; otherwise Daisy was all woman, and then some. Moosejaw's words caused her pretty mouth to press into a tight line as her abundant breasts swelled out against the leather apron she wore. Clamping her fists onto hips that flared full in a pair of dungarees, she looked for a moment like she was ready to argue heatedly against Moosejaw's defense of the marshal. But then her expression shifted, mellowed, and abruptly looked less contentious.

"Well . . . maybe you're right," she allowed somewhat grudgingly. "I guess maybe I do need to cut Firestick some slack. Especially since I sort of let him down, too, earlier this morning."

Moosejaw frowned around a forkful of apple pie that he'd just shoved into his mouth. "How so?"

"When those skunks from the Bar 6 showed up and tried to ambush him," Daisy explained. "I should have made it out onto the street quicker in order to give him a hand against 'em." She jabbed a thumb over her shoulder. "I was back there by the big forge, pounding a wheel rim into shape. The ringin' of my hammer drowned out the sound of gunfire when it first started. By the time I realized what was going on and grabbed up my shotgun to make it out to the street where I could have helped the marshal, it was mostly over. That gambler fella in the gray coat had stepped in and plunked a bullet smack in the noggin of the Winchester shooter."

Moosejaw nodded. "Yeah, I heard about that. Firestick didn't get a chance to go into much detail with me given what little time we had, but it sounded like it was a mighty close call for him."

"He was in a bad way, pinned down behind that water trough like he was," said Daisy. "Another few seconds, though, and I'd've cleared the street of that ambushin' trash. But like I said, the gambler fella beat me to it."

"And don't think I ain't glad he did," Moosejaw declared. "You want to talk about frettin'? How do you think I woulda felt arrivin' back in town to hear that my gal was tradin' lead out in the middle of the street?"

"I hope it would have made you proud. Seems only right that it should," Daisy said, brown eyes flashing. "You know dang well I can take care of myself. What's more, I might've played a part in savin' one of your best pals from getting seriously ventilated."

"I know that. And I *woulda* been proud," Moosejaw said quickly, seeing he had somehow upset her. "It's just that —"

"Never mind," Daisy cut him off. The fire in her eyes died down almost as fast as it had appeared. Her mouth curved into a pleased smile as she added, "It was worth it to hear you say 'my gal' when you referred to me."

Moosejaw blushed. "Heck, Daize, how else would I refer to you? Everybody in town knows how it is between us."

Daisy placed the calloused palm of one of her hands on Moosejaw's cheek. Letting it gently slide off, she said, "I don't give a hang about what everybody else in town thinks they know about us. I just care what you think and say."

The big deputy's face reddened even more, and he hurriedly finished off the last bite of pie. Reaching for his coffee cup to wash it down, he said in a low voice, "You know I ain't much at puttin' things into fancy words. But you also know — or dang sure ought to — how I feel about you . . . us."

Daisy's smile stayed in place. "I know. I do. But hearin' it put in words, even unfancy ones, is kinda nice once in a while, too."

"I'll be sure to keep that in mind," Moosejaw told her. "But it might take gettin' this Apache business out of the way before I can fit in some practice so's I'll be able to do a better job at puttin' the words right."

"I ain't asking for a lot. Just hearing how you feel, however you say it, will be good enough for me."

Moosejaw wagged his head. "No. If it's important to you, then I want to do it proper."

Daisy made no reply to that, just continued to gaze fondly at him.

Draining the last of his coffee, Moosejaw leaned over and placed the emptied cup on the ground beside his foot. Straightening up, he swept his eyes up and down the length of Trail Street as it extended in either direction from the blacksmith shop. Activity on the street was still brisk, yet it appeared decidedly less frantic than it had been earlier when word of Apache presence in the valley first spread. The expressions on the faces of the folks going about their business remained sober, focused, but for the most part there was no sign of fear or panic. These were tough, durable people who'd made it this far on the frequently harsh frontier, and that core of rugged resolve was showing plainly. Looking on, Moosejaw felt a swelling of pride for being part of it.

Then something else that had been nudging at him on and off for a while picked that moment to crowd back into his thoughts. And having Daisy present to bounce it off of was an opportunity too good to pass up.

"Let's go back for a minute to that gambler fella — Lofton his name is, by the way. You had any call to be around him or talk to him much?" Moosejaw said.

Daisy frowned, plainly surprised by the

question. "No, can't say I have. Not hardly at all. What makes you ask?"

"Not really sure," Moosejaw answered, his eyes continuing to scan the street. "It's just that . . . I don't know what, exactly, but doggone it, there's something about him that rankles me some."

"Rankles you how?"

"He just don't . . . There's something phony about him. Leastways that's the feelin' I get. Only I can't put my finger on what it is that gives me that feelin'."

"Firestick don't appear to have no problem with him," Daisy remarked. "In fact, he seems awful chummy with him."

Moosejaw scowled. "I know. That bothers me, too. Firestick is usually mighty sharp at spottin' something false about somebody. He reads people way better than me. Yet he don't see nothing wrong with this fella."

"Well, the gambler *did* save his life. Or mighty close to it. That's gotta count for something in the way of how Firestick looks at him."

Moosejaw wagged his head. "No. The Firestick I know would see right through this jasper's phoniness, no matter what he did or didn't do. Still, he don't seem to. Not in this case."

"Did you talk to him about it?"

"With everything goin' on, I ain't had no chance."

Daisy said, "Well, maybe he *does* feel the same as you, and neither has he —"

"No," Moosejaw cut her off. "I could tell if it was something like that. When it comes to this fella, Firestick genuinely likes him. For some reason he ain't pickin' up on the same false note I am."

They were both quiet for a minute. Then Daisy said, "Maybe your problem is that you're jealous."

Moosejaw gave her a sharp look. "What in blazes is that supposed to mean?"

"Calm down. Don't get your feathers in a ruffle, just hear me out."

"If I do, I hope you start makin' more sense than how you started out."

"Think of it," Daisy went on. "It's always been you, Firestick, and Beartooth. You always took care of one another. Never needed nobody else, right?"

"That's the way it's been for a good long spell, yeah."

"So now, earlier today, when Firestick got himself in a fix, neither you nor Beartooth were there to help him out. So, instead, the gambler — Lofton — stepped in and did what neither of you could . . . See what I mean? Maybe jealousy ain't the right word.

Not all by itself anyway. Maybe it's a combination of jealousy and a little guilt."

"Why should I have any guilt?" Moosejaw wanted to know. "I wasn't shirkin' my duty or anything like that — I was doin' what Firestick sent me to do."

"I'm not sayin' you *should* feel guilty. Or jealous, either one." Daisy gestured with her hands for emphasis. "I'm just . . . well, suggesting what might be behind the way you're looking at Lofton. The human brain is a mighty complicated thing sometimes. Maybe you don't want Lofton to be on the up-and-up because you don't want him — or anybody — horning in on the way you three big oafs look out for each other."

Moosejaw regarded her closely for several seconds, not saying anything. Then, gradually, his mouth fell into a lopsided grin. "You know, speakin' of complicated brains . . . Behind that leather apron and those hammer-swingin' muscles, I think maybe you've got one of those."

Matching his grin, Daisy said, "That don't mean I can't still slap a headlock on you and squeeze until you see things my way. But only if you force me to, that is."

"One of these days," Moosejaw replied, "I may take you up on that. Number one, on account of I think I might like bein' in a headlock put on by you. Number two, on account of I still think there's something phony about that Lofton character, and I intend to keep an eye on him until I know for sure."

Daisy threw up her arms. "You stubborn mule. You're hopeless!"

A further exchange of such endearments was interrupted by a stocky man in matching trousers and vest, no coat or tie, who came hurrying down the street and veered toward the blacksmith shop doorway at the sight of Moosejaw sitting there on his log stool. Hans Greeble, owner and proprietor of Greeble's General Store, was a somber, business-minded fifty-year-old who habitually appeared in need of a shave and a comb to sweep back the limp strands of iron-gray hair that spilled down above his thick black eyebrows. Despite this somewhat disheveled look, he was amiable and fair in his dealings, and his store was one of the foremost places to shop for a wide variety of supplies.

Supplies, it turned out, was exactly what was on his mind.

"I'm glad I caught up with you, Deputy," he said in a rush. "Sorry if I'm barging in, but I just thought of something I think is important for you and the marshal to know."

Moosejaw stood up. "Sure thing, Mr.

Greeble. What's on your mind?"

"Milt Kruger and his freight wagons — the supply train that outfits my store and others in town — he's on his way here now," Greeble reported with an anxious look on his face. "Last word I got, he was planning on heading out from Presidio either yesterday or the day before."

It took only a second for Moosejaw to realize the implication behind the store owner's words. When he did, he adopted an anxious look of his own. "Thunderation! It's about three days from Presidio to here. That means, if Kruger and his wagons started out day before yesterday, they could be rolling across Jacinto Flats by the middle of the day tomorrow."

"Exactly! You can see why I thought it was an important matter to bring to your attention."

Jacinto Flats, as the name indicated, was a long expanse of flat, mostly barren land found just past the eastern edge of the valley, angling in from the south and stretching back for miles. In contrast to the grassy, rolling hills that surrounded Buffalo Peak below the Viejas, the ground running through Jacinto Flats was the remains of an ancient lake bed, empty of decent graze or much of anything besides spine-like upthrusts of rock and a spiderweb of deep ground fissures where the land had split apart during frequent dry spells. It was a great, wide-open stretch for freight wagons to traverse easily, as long as they avoided the fissures. But that meant it was also a wide-open place with little in the way of cover should the Apaches spot and attack the supply train as it was passing through there.

"I'm sorry I didn't think of it sooner," Greeble continued. "But in all the hubbub following the news of the Indian raiders and the preparations that needed to made . . . well, it didn't cross my mind. Not until just now."

"That's all right, Mr. Greeble. The main thing is that you did think of it, while there's still time for us to try and do something about it," Moosejaw told him.

"Do what? What are you thinking?" asked Daisy.

Moosejaw scowled. "Ain't rightly sure. Not yet . . . Dang it, I wish Firestick would get hisself back here."

CHAPTER 28

Brody Rockwell set a hard, steady pace, doubling back to the east and aiming himself and Beartooth on a course that took them above the town of Buffalo Peak and below the Double M Ranch, where they'd started out. With his mount's reins in Brody's grasp as the boy rode in the lead, all Beartooth could manage, his right arm yanked awkwardly cross-body and chained to the saddle, was to grip his saddle horn with his free hand and hold on tight for the ride.

In the distance, but growing closer, loomed the unique shape of Buffalo Hump Butte. As the sun sank lower in the sky behind them, the shadows of the horses and riders were thrown farther and farther out ahead, making squirming, ever-darkening grotesque shapes on the ground. While the face of Buffalo Hump Butte was bathed in bright reddish-orange, on the back side it threw its own still, velvety shadow.

At length, just as the bottom arc of the sun was biting into the western horizon, they reached the base of the butte. Brody reined up and brought them to a halt in among some long fingers of rock that splayed out away from the base. Tumbled boulders, tangled underbrush, and a few stunted trees partially filled some of the gaps between the fingers. A short distance from where Brody stopped, a narrow creek twisted across the ground. It seemed evident that the lad had selected the spot based on having been here before.

"We'll give the horses a chance to cool out before we let 'em drink," he announced as he slipped from his saddle. "Then we'll make camp here tonight. Tomorrow we go higher."

"What do you mean, we go higher?" Beartooth wanted to know.

"Don't know how to say it any plainer. Tomorrow we go up — up to the top," Brody said. "From up there I can see comings and goings for miles in any direction. If your friends try anything sneaky or make an approach other than how I left instructions for them to do, it will go bad for you."

"That's a great idea. You go ahead and plant yourself up there good and high.

That'll leave you trapped to a fare-thee-well," Beartooth urged sarcastically.

"Not as long as I got you under my gun," Brody responded. As if reminded by the words, he drew his Colt and jabbed it casually in Beartooth's direction. "If your friends are foolish enough to try and call my bluff . . . well then, maybe it will go bad for both of us. But no matter, you still won't be around to benefit from it."

"You think you've got it all figured out, don't you?"

"As a matter of fact, yeah, I do. I spent a lot of time thinking it through from every angle."

"How about the Apaches? How do you reckon to play that angle?"

Brody gave a derisive snort. "I don't. Because it's an angle that don't exist." He waggled the gun again. "Climb down out of that saddle. Slow and easy. Time to let the horses drink."

A handful of minutes later, as the horses were slurping noisily from the creek, Beartooth tried again. "I'm tellin' you, kid. Stayin' here tonight — a camp, a campfire, the whole business — could be signin' our death warrants."

Brody shook his head stubbornly. "Your friends won't react that fast to my note. It'll

270

take 'em at least —"

"I'm not talkin' about my friends! I'm talkin' about the damn Apaches, you young fool. If they're out there anywhere close by and they —"

"Now it's *if* they're out there? You're pretty bad at lying, Mr. Beartooth," Brody told him. "Better just give it a rest — your mouth and my ears — because I ain't buying one damn lick of it."

It was Victoria Kingsley who found the note that Brody left.

She'd gone into the lean-to to lay out fresh towels for when the men came in and got washed up for supper. Dusk was descending rapidly, and aromas of the meal she had cooking wafted from the kitchen and all through the house. The delicious smells even reached into the lean-to. Included among them was the sweet scent of the two peach pies Victoria had set out to cool just before heading back with the towels. She smiled to herself as she thought of how pleased Beartooth would be when he discovered she'd made his favorite.

That thought led to her wondering about the neighbor boy, Brody Rockwell, whom Beartooth had hired for some part-time work and who'd joined them for lunch. She hadn't thought to ask if he would also be sitting in on supper. No matter, really; she'd prepared plenty of food. It would simply mean setting another place at the table if necessary.

A moment after resolving that matter in her mind, her eyes fell on the note propped up against the washbasin. It was scrawled with pencil on stiff, coarse paper. Picking it up and holding it over by the window where there was better light, she read:

TO MARSHAL FIRESTICK & EVERYBODY —

I HAVE TOOK MR. BEARTOOTH AS MY HOSTAGE. I WILL HOLD HER HOSTAGE WITHOUT HARM AND RELEASE HER SAFE AS LONG AS MY DEMANDS ARE MET.

I WANT PROOF THAT A CLEAR DEED AND TITLE TO THE FAMILY FARM HAS BEEN GIVEN TO MY MOTHER AND THAT NO ACTION WILL BE TAKEN AGAINST HER FOR WHAT I AM DOING. SHE KNOWS NOTHING ABOUT IT. I WANT THE PAPER PROOF AND $100 IN CASH BROUGHT TO ME BY THE MARSHAL. BRING IT TO BUFFALO HUMP BUTTE NO

LATER THAN DAY AFTER TOMOR-
ROW. I WILL BE WATCHING FROM
UP HIGH SO NO TRICKS.

DO EXACTLY AS I SAY AND I
WILL NOT HARM ANYBODY.

OTHERWISE THERE WILL BE
BLOOD.

— BRODY ROCKWELL

Victoria's hands were trembling and her breathing had quickened by the time she finished reading. Her eyes scanned the words again, hoping that she had somehow misread them the first time, that what she'd seen wasn't real. But it was. Terrifyingly real. What was more, where it now said "Mr. Beartooth," that had been scrawled above the name originally written there but then marked off by having a line drawn through it. The original name had been her own — "Miss Victoria" — thus explaining the subsequent uses of "her" in two places where no correction had been made.

With her heart pounding up in her throat, Victoria rushed from the lean-to. She desperately hoped she would catch sight of Beartooth and find him grinning one of his broad, teasing grins before revealing that this whole thing was some kind of madly inappropriate joke.

She called his name with sinking hope. But he did not answer. She called again, her voice rising shrilly. Still no sign of Beartooth or the boy, Brody, either one.

Miguel and Jesus, wearing questioning expressions, poked their heads out from a door in the livery barn at the far end of the corral.

Victoria started racing toward them, waving the sheet of paper with Brody's message on it.

"Miguel! Jesus! Something dreadful has happened!"

CHAPTER 29

"Shit! I can't see nothing. Somebody get down here and hold a match for me, will you?"

"Oh, for Christ's sake, it ain't that dark yet. If that mare has got a stone or something in her shoe, you oughta be able to see it."

"Well, maybe I oughta — but I can't. Only that still don't change the fact that this nag is steppin' wrong for some reason. I ain't squattin' down here like a toad for my health, you know. Now, are one of you gonna climb down and give me a hand, or not?"

Greely Dunlap frowned down at his older brother. The latter knelt at the right hindquarters of his horse, while Greely and Woolsey remained in their saddles. Neither of the mounted men appeared in any hurry to be accommodating.

"You know," said Greely, "this is one more

reason why we shoulda got started right off, instead of tarryin' at the saloon back there in town. Now, if we turn out to be slowed by a lame horse, we're gonna end up goin' more than halfway home in the dark. I don't like that worth a damn."

"Ain't you a little old to be scared of the dark?" Grady sneered.

"No, but I think we all got cause for concern about what might be *in* the dark."

"Apaches, you mean? Good God, are we back to that again?"

"You can scoff all you want. But me, I don't see no reason not to put stock in what Firestick had to say."

Grady groaned. "Oh, for the love of . . . Okay, if you got so much belief in what the marshal spouted, then how about his claim that Apaches don't like to fight at night? Ain't that enough to ease your worries some?"

"It ain't night yet. It's dusk," Greely said stubbornly. "And that's when he said they like to go on the prowl. We start strikin' matches out here in the middle of nowhere, and those red devils happen to be prowlin' up over the right hill, they could spot us from miles away."

"Okay, that does it. Now you're gettin' me spooked," piped up Woolsey. "One thing's for certain — if any Apaches *are* prowlin' hereabouts, then the longer we sit in one place yappin' about 'em, the more like sittin' ducks we make ourselves. So the only thing for it is to do whatever it takes to get on the move again as soon as we can."

So saying, he swung down from his saddle and went over to Grady. Digging in his pocket for a match, he said, "I'll strike a lucifer for you. Just get ready to use the light quick and find what you're lookin' for."

Sighing heavily, Greely stomped one foot deeper into its stirrup and made his own dismount. "Hold on a damn minute. Let me get over there, too, so's we can crowd in tight and block as much of that light as possible."

Half a minute later, that's exactly what he and Woolsey were doing, huddled shoulder to shoulder and leaned forward so they hovered over Grady and the horse's hoof he had lifted for examination. Woolsey struck his match and held it in close.

"There it is!" Grady exclaimed almost immediately. "Now I see that pesky little rascal."

He opened his jackknife and slipped the blade carefully behind the jagged piece of rock that was wedged partially under the inner rim of his horse's shoe. The mare tried to pull her foot away, but Grady held fast and cooed soothing words to her. Before he started any prying, the match flickered and died out.

"Aw, damn, I almost had it," muttered Grady. "Fire up another one, Woolsey, so I can see to finish this."

"You got your knife right there, why do you need another match?" said Greely. "Just flick that damn stone out of there and be done with it."

Through clenched teeth, Grady said, "Oh yeah, that'd be real smart. I go pokin' and slicin' where I can't see and I'm liable to do more damage than if we'd just left the stone there."

"One more match ain't gonna matter now," said Woolsey, getting more and more fed up with the brothers' bickering. "Greely, lean in here close again . . . Grady, be ready with that knife . . ."

Once more a match flared. With a deft stroke of the knife blade, Grady pried free the bothersome stone and let it fall to the ground with a soft *plop.*

"There. There, old girl, that's better, ain't it?" he said to the horse as he let go of the foot and stood up beside her. He patted the mare's flank and clucked gently. Then, turning his head to address the other two men, he said, "Lemme walk her around some to make sure that took care of her ailment. Then we can be on our way."

"Thank God," grunted Woolsey. "This spot is givin' me the willies. The sooner we put it behind us, the better I'll like it."

Woolsey and Greely returned to their saddles while Grady led his mare around in a tight circle. At first the animal stepped gingerly on the hind leg that had been bothering her. Then, discovering there was no longer any pain when she did so, she quickly began walking strong and steady.

Grady chuckled. "Looks like that did it. She's gonna be fine now."

"Climb back up on that hurricane deck, then, and let's make tracks out of here," Greely told him.

Once Grady had remounted, the three wheeled their horses and again pointed them in the direction they'd been headed before the stop became necessary. But as soon as their mounts were turned, each of the riders spotted something up ahead that made them immediately draw back on their reins.

What they saw was the shape of a lone horseman — unmistakably silhouetted against the murky sky — poised motionless atop a rise about thirty yards from where they now paused three abreast.

"So, what the hell is this?" muttered Greely.

"I ain't sure, but at least it don't look like no Apache," replied Woolsey. Yet the uneasiness that for some reason trickled through him didn't make the assessment nearly as much of a relief as it should have.

"Well, whoever he is, there ain't but one of him," snarled Grady. "And he's planted in our way."

With this, he went ahead and gigged his horse forward. Greely and Woolsey followed suit.

When they'd narrowed the distance to about half of what it originally had been, the still-motionless horseman spoke. He held his head tipped slightly forward as he did so, keeping his face masked in deep shadow under the wide brim of his hat.

"Evening, gents. Finding it a pleasant night for a ride, are you?"

The Box T men once again checked their forward movement.

"We got no complaints," replied Grady amiably. "Don't know if 'pleasant' is a word I'd use, though. And another word I sure as hell wouldn't use is 'smart' — not for a lone rider like you to be out and about under the circumstances."

"Oh? And what circumstances are those?"

"Ain't you heard? Accordin' to some" — Grady cut a sidelong glance toward his younger brother — "a pack of Apaches have crossed the border from down Mexico way and are prowlin' this neck of the woods."

"You say that as if you're not convinced it's really true. Or, if you are, you appear quite willing to brave the risk."

"There's three of us, mister," Woolsey said, stating the obvious. "Even still, we're keepin' our eyes peeled and not lettin' any grass grow under us until we get where we're goin'."

"Always a good idea to be alert and cautious."

"You don't mind my sayin'," spoke up Greely, "there's something about you that seems familiar. You from around here?"

"I'm from a lot of places. But I've been around these parts for a while now and, yes, you should find me familiar."

The stranger lifted his face then, and in the fuzzy light that was no longer day but not yet night, his features were revealed to Greely and the others.

"It's that gambler fella," Woolsey half-whispered.

"The stinkin' cheat," grated Grady.

Henry Lofton smiled coldly. "I'm flattered

you remember me, given the small minds you possess."

Grady stiffened. "Hey, bub, I don't know what you think you're up to, but you'd best watch your mouth. You wanna talk small minds? Seems like you ain't stoppin' to think about there bein' no Marshal Firestick around to back you up this time."

"And we're still chapped from bein' short the money you cheated us out of," added Woolsey. "That startin' to give you a hint you ain't in a very good position with us, you damn fool?"

Lofton continued to smile. "Still banking on your three-to-one odds, eh? See, that's what I mean about small minds. Just like you imagined the three of you against the Apaches would be sufficient."

"You don't need to concern yourself about that," Greely told him. "The unfinished business between us and you — now, there's where you *should* be concerned."

"Oh, I am . . . I'm concerned you yellow curs will turn and flee before we can settle our unfinished business once and for all."

"What the hell are you talkin' about?" Grady growled. "You don't see nobody fleein', do you?"

Lofton gave a faint, almost-imperceptible shake of his head. "Not yet. But what I do

282

see is that this time around, the three of you have been thoughtful enough to strap on some sidearms. The trouble with physical brawling, you see, is that nothing truly permanent is established. Hence, a situation such as we presently have before us. Though blood loss and bruises were inflicted, no one came away truly satisfied the matter was resolved. But had we initially gone ahead and settled our dispute with lead, the results would have been permanent and conclusive. Something I suggest we take the opportunity to achieve now."

As he talked, Lofton's right hand slowly, almost casually, swept back the front of his frock coat, exposing the gleaming .45 holstered on his hip. The eyes of all three Box T riders locked on the gun for a long count before lifting again to meet Lofton's flinty gaze.

Grady licked his lips. "Now, hold on a minute, mister. You're pushin' this awful damn hard."

"Indeed, I am."

"We ain't no gunnies," protested Woolsey. "Sure, we're some rough-and-tumble ol' boys who like to scuffle and raise hell. But we never gunned nor seriously hurt nobody with our hoorahin'."

"If you'd had your way at the Silver Spur,"

Lofton intoned flatly, "the three of you would have stomped me into a broken wreck, maybe left me crippled for the rest of my life. You're dirty liars if you say otherwise."

"You don't know that for a fact," Greely insisted. "You can't say for certain about something that never took place."

"The hell I can't," said Lofton. "I've seen cowardly peckerwoods like you three in every town from Galveston to El Paso."

Grady's mouth curled with a combination of anger and defiance. "To hell with this son of a bitch. He's still only one man and there's three of us. Why are we wastin' time just talkin'?"

"Because," Lofton said, his voice barely above a whisper, "when the talking stops, it'll be time for you to die."

Those ominous words hung in the air for several tense clock ticks. There was no other sound, no movement. It was as if everything froze, still and silent.

And then, with jarring suddenness, all of it erupted into sound and fury.

Lofton never fancied himself a fast gun. But when it was time to use one, he was unhesitant and deadly accurate. That's what most of it came down to, really, even for those renowned as being lightning-fast "shootists." Where most men might pause, blink an eye, perhaps feel a last-second pang of remorse or reluctance, a top gunman would simply draw and go to work.

And that's what Lofton did in this instance. At the first twitch of movement from one of the Box T men, he pulled his .45 and started blasting. Grady took the first slug, high in the chest, about an inch under his Adam's apple. Next, a bullet to Greely's stomach doubled him violently forward in his saddle. Working in descending order of whom he reasoned to pose the biggest threat, Lofton swung his sights last to Woolsey and was surprised to find the little man with his own gun already drawn and starting to aim. The two men fired simultaneously. Lofton's .45 slug slammed hard, knocking Woolsey into a backward somersault off the rump of his horse. Woolsey's bullet, in turn, sliced the air close enough to Lofton's left ear for the hired gun to feel the heat of its passing.

Grady and Woolsey had both hit the ground dead. But Greely, folded nearly in half by the round in his gut, not only managed to stay in his saddle but also to draw his own pistol. He was attempting to aim with a weak, badly trembling arm, when Lofton cut his attention back to the youngest Dunlap brother. Without thinking about it, Lofton recentered the muzzle of his .45 and triggered a fourth and final bullet. Greely pitched from his saddle and hit the ground, now a lifeless lump.

A new kind of quiet, eerie and heavy, settled over the scene. The only sounds were a few soft chuffs from the horses — all of whom had stood obediently still during the brief exchange of gunfire — and the faint clicking noises as Lofton replaced the spent cartridges in his Colt.

When the cylinder was full and the gun returned to its holster, Lofton wheeled his mount and rode off in the direction of town.

CHAPTER 30

Firestick was somewhat surprised at how quiet and calm the town seemed, the streets mostly empty, when he rode back in with Boynton and Gus Wingate's two hired men. It was full dark by now. The four had taken time to finish building a rough casket, dig a grave, and bury Wingate on the crest of the hill next to his wife and daughter. They'd all agreed there was no doubt that's where he would have chosen for his final resting place. It was further agreed that, as soon as it was safe, maybe as soon as tomorrow, somebody would accompany Pastor Bart back to the spot in order to hold a proper burial service.

At the jail, they found Moosejaw standing out front, waiting to greet them. "I was beginnin' to wonder if some of those hair-lifters might've got hold of you out there. Seein's how they didn't, light on down and come inside. We got a pot of coffee and some sandwiches waitin'."

He didn't need to make the offer twice. The riders dismounted, tied their horses, and followed Moosejaw through the door. The "we" he'd referred to turned out to be Sam Duvall and Frank Moorehouse, who was also on hand. He'd come to check on the wounded prisoner and stayed to chew the fat with Moosejaw and Duvall.

"Ah, that's what I like to see — three bushy heads of hair still intact for me to ply my trade on," he remarked now as he helped dispense the sandwiches and coffee.

"You can thank Sam for the fresh pot of coffee. Kate had the grub sent over from the Mallory Hotel kitchen," Moosejaw said. Then, addressing Firestick directly, he added, "She's gonna want to see you the first chance you get."

"Don't worry, I plan on it," Firestick said as he raised a cup of steaming brew to his lips. He took a scalding sip, then: "On the way in, I saw that the town looks settled in pretty snug. You get the weak spots we talked about reinforced?"

Moosejaw nodded. "Done. Got guards posted at the key places, rotating in four-hour shifts. The warnin' riders took off some time ago, and two escort wagons with four heavily armed men in each rolled out shortly after that. With any luck, the riders should make it back before mornin'. Hard to say about the wagons. They might hole up at one of the farms and then wait to come in after daylight."

"All sounds good," Firestick said.

"Moosejaw took over like a regular general. He even had Shield here hopping to orders," spoke up Sam, reaching down to absently pat his dog. "You'd've been right proud of him."

A corner of Firestick's mouth quirked up. "I wouldn't want this to go to his head, but I ain't seen a day since I knowed the big ox when I couldn't be proud of him."

Moosejaw's ruddy cheeks took on spots of deeper color. "Aw, you're just sayin' that because it's true," he said, trying to downplay the praise, even though it was clear he enjoyed it. "But there ain't none of us ready for too much back-pattin' until this whole business is over."

"You ain't wrong there," Firestick agreed. "Speakin' of which — any word yet from either of the forts I sent telegrams to on when we might be gettin' help from one of 'em?"

"Fort Leaton wired that they're sendin' a detachment of forty men, but the wire didn't say how soon they'd get here."

"Well, it's something — knowin' there's soldier boys who'll be showin' up sooner or later." Firestick tried to sound more hopeful than he actually succeeded in doing.

"Yeah, well, we got something else on the way, too, and it ain't necessarily good news," said Moosejaw.

"What's that supposed to mean?" Firestick asked.

Moosejaw explained about the supply train headed their direction, then added, "Right after Greeble told me about it, I sent a telegram off to Presidio to try and find out exactly when they left. Got an answer real quick — it was day before yesterday."

Firestick gritted his teeth. "Damn. Barrin' a breakdown or something, that'll put those wagons smack in the Jacinto Flats by the middle of the day tomorrow."

"That's about what I figured, too."

Moorehouse said, "I can see where that's of concern — for the sake of the supply train, I mean. But keep in mind that Milt Kruger always travels with his wagons heavily guarded."

"That's true enough," Firestick allowed. "But havin' guards who are ready for an attempted ambush by outlaws or the like is one thing. Men who are prepared for Apaches, that's another."

"The first answer that comes to mind," Moosejaw said, "is to send some men out to warn Kruger what he might be rollin' into. And then stick with him to serve as reinforcements the rest of the way in case trouble does hit. The only problem with that goes back to what Earl Sterling pointed out in his saloon earlier — we start sendin' men out here and there and everywhere, then pretty soon we've got things spread mighty thin when it comes to coverin' the town."

"We ain't gonna let that happen," said Firestick. "Like you figured, the warning riders ought to be back by daybreak, and the men who went with the escort wagons not too long after that. That'll give us enough to send out a force to help protect Kruger's wagons."

"What about our plan to circle up into the Viejas and hit the Apaches in their own camp?"

"That might have to wait. First we got to see to the protection of as many people as we can, then we commence our fightin' back."

"What about the murder of Mr. Gus?" asked Krause. "Where does that fit in — the gettin' to the bottom of it, I mean?"

Firestick's forehead creased deeply. "You probably ain't gonna like hearin' this, but

I'm afraid the answer to that is the same — it might have to wait. Naturally me and my deputies will keep our eyes and ears open for anything that might be tied to it. But the safety of a whole bunch of people has to get attention ahead of questions surroundin' what happened to a fella who's already dead. You can understand that, can't you?"

Krause pursed his lips. "I reckon . . . maybe. But a cold-blooded killer on the loose is a danger to other folks, too, ain't he? Leastways until you figure out who he is and why he done what he —"

"Take it easy, pard," Marsh interrupted, placing a hand on Krause's shoulder. "What you're sayin' makes sense, but so does the way the marshal has to look at it from his end. Ain't nobody gonna forget what happened to Mr. Gus. We ain't gonna let 'em. But he's dead — there don't have to be no rush about findin' who did it, not compared to dealin' with the risk that might be out there facin' other folks, includin' women and kids."

Some of the tension visibly lifted from Krause. He dropped his eyes. "Yeah. Yeah, you're right. That's the way Gus would want it, too."

"I ain't gonna forget what happened to Wingate. Not by a bucketful," Firestick promised him. "Me and my men will turn over every rock until we uncover some sign of the snake who done it. You're just gonna have to give us some time, that's all."

"I believe you, Marshal," Krause replied earnestly. "I'll keep my mouth shut and stay out of your way so's you can do your job as you see fit. And when it comes to the Apache trouble, you can count on me and Lyle as two more guns against those devils if and when you need us."

"That's for sure," Marsh added.

Firestick nodded. "That's good to hear. Not that I ever doubted it."

"You two ain't figurin' on goin' back to your ranch tonight, are you?" asked Moosejaw.

Marsh wagged his head. "Much as we hate the thought of leavin' the house and the cattle untended, no, we know better than to reckon just the two of us would have much luck holdin' off an Apache swarm. They'd end up gettin' what they came after, and our scalps to boot."

"It's a tough decision to have to make, but it's the smart one," Moosejaw allowed. "The house can be rebuilt and the cattle herd, too. But bein' dead has a stubborn way of stayin' permanent."

"In the meantime, as long as you're here

in town, do you know where Pastor Bart's church is?" said Firestick.

The two hired hands exchanged looks. "Not exactly," said Krause. "But we'll be able to find it."

"I can show you," spoke up Moorehouse. "I need to get back to my place anyway, and the church is right on the way."

"Obliged," said Krause and Marsh together, heads bobbing.

"After you've stabled your horses, take your bedrolls and report to Pastor Bart," Firestick told them. "He's makin' his church available to all outlyin' folks who come into town for safety. You'll be welcomed and made comfortable there." He cut his eyes to Boynton, adding, "Same goes for you, too, Cleve. I hope you wasn't intendin' to try and make it back to the Box T tonight?"

Boynton grinned crookedly. "No way. I'm flat-out bushed. Matter of fact, walkin' clear down to the church sounds like a powerful hike to me." He jabbed a thumb. "How about I claim one of your empty cell cots and sack out right here tonight?"

Firestick shrugged. "No skin off my nose. Those cots are about as comfortable as a slab of wood, but for stickin' close and helpin' out like you have all day, you've earned the right to claim one if you want."

CHAPTER 31

Firestick was walking down Trail Street, on his way to see Kate at the hotel, when three riders came tearing into town at a hard gallop. He paused, straining in the spotty illumination cast by the street lamps to see who it was. When recognition hit him, he first did a bug-eyed double take and then stepped out into the street to wave them down.

Victoria, Miguel, and Jesus reined up sharply at the sight of him. Firestick felt his mouth pulling into a grimace, knowing that the three of them being away from the Double M this time of night — without Beartooth — did not signal good news.

"Oh, Firestick!" Victoria exclaimed as she swung down from her saddle hurriedly, yet still gracefully. She'd only learned to ride since coming to work at the Double M, but had taken to it like she was born in the saddle.

As soon as her feet touched the ground, she came rushing toward the marshal, waving a sheet of paper. Miguel and Jesus remained mounted, looking on with grim expressions on their dark faces.

"What is it, gal? Where's Beartooth?" Firestick wanted to know.

Shoving the piece of paper out to him, Victoria said, "Everything is explained right here. It's a shocking development!"

Scowling, Firestick stepped deeper into the glow of the nearest street lamp so he could make out the words scrawled on the paper. As he began to read, he was vaguely aware of others — including Kate from the hotel, and Moosejaw from the direction of the jail — filtering into the street around them.

"What's goin' on? What's this all about?" Moosejaw asked of no one and everyone. He had noted the absence of Beartooth, same as Firestick had done, and an expression of considerable concern was etched already on the big man's face.

"It's Beartooth — he's been kidnapped!" Victoria told him, her own features pinched by strain and worry.

A murmur rippled through the gathering crowd.

The words hit Moosejaw like a blow.

"What!? How? By who — the Apaches?"

"No, not Apaches," said Firestick, holding out the sheet of paper to him. "That might lessen the danger he's in by some, but not a helluva lot."

While Moosejaw read Brody Rockwell's message for himself, Firestick swept his eyes over the others crowding around. "Listen, everybody. This is a whole new problem. A serious one. But right at the moment, it ain't one you can be of any help with. You'll hear the details soon enough. In the meantime, where you *can* help — and where you can't afford to let down your guard — is the Injun situation. So, go on back to what you were doin'. Let us handle this, and you keep stayin' sharp and alert for any Apache sign. That's what you can do that'll be in the best interests of everybody."

There was some mumbling and a moment or two of hesitation, then the group began to disperse as instructed.

Firestick's eyes found Kate. "We're gonna need use of your barroom for a little while. Any objection?"

Kate shook her head. "Of course not. Whatever you need."

"Miguel, Jesus, Miss Victoria — let's get in off the street," Firestick said, his voice steady and edged with only a hint of tightness. "Moosejaw, bring that damned paper. We need to lay out a plan for how the hell we're gonna deal with this."

The little bastard was sharp, Beartooth had to give him that. It deeply galled the former mountain man, who'd survived decades of life in the harshest wilderness and countless skirmishes with Injuns and a whole range of fierce critters, to accept that he'd been snared by a still-green-around-the-edges kid who wasn't much older than one of his saddles.

The initial way he'd been caught off guard by Brody, coming so out of the blue and totally unexpected, was one thing; no way he could have been prepared for that. But the rest of it, being saddle-cuffed and all, none of it giving him the slightest opening to turn the tables, that was starting to chafe plenty raw.

Even now, with darkness having fallen and the two of them settled into their night camp, Brody continued to take every precaution — except for the stupid damned fire. If there *were* any Apaches around, not to mention owlhoots of some other stripe who might be out for their own brand of trouble, the flames would give away their position for miles.

But as far as negating any threat from or escape by Beartooth, the intense young man seemed to have everything covered. In addition to keeping his captive chained to a cumbersome saddle, he had tied one of the saddle's stirrups to a thick growth of dried bramble that rattled and crackled like a pan of popping corn if stirred even the slightest bit. This would allow Brody the chance to get some sleep that night, secure in the knowledge that any excessive motion by Beartooth — like trying to rise and carry off the saddle or perhaps use it as a weapon to smash down on the sleeping boy — would rattle the brush and give warning long before any such thing could be accomplished.

"It's amazin' to me," Beartooth told him as they sat chewing jerky and drinking some coffee the boy had made. "I look at you in the light of the campfire, and you still appear the polite, innocent young lad who showed up at our ranch this morning and took lunch with us. But inside your head, you got a mind like a snakes' nest — writhing and poisonous."

"Looks can be deceivin'," Brody replied tonelessly. "Ain't you ever heard that old saying?"

"Plenty of times. Even *thought* I'd run into

some pretty good examples before. But you take the cake."

They sat silently for a time after that. Beartooth continued to study the lad. The way he took periodic sips of his coffee and then shuddered slightly each time at the bitter taste of the strong brew. He was barely off a sugar tit, Beartooth thought. At home, he probably drank nothing stronger than buttermilk or lemonade; if he did have coffee, he likely loaded it with sugar and cream. Wasn't even shaving yet. A jolt of red-eye was apt to knock him out for a week . . .

And yet he'd been slick enough to make Beartooth his captive and keep him that way.

Damn it to hell.

Beartooth calculated the distance from where he sat to the fire, and then how far Brody was beyond that. Too far. If he attempted to jump up, grabbing the saddle and ripping it loose from the bush so he could make a desperation rush at the kid . . . he'd never come close. Not before that Colt centered on him.

The only question, then, would be whether or not Brody would actually shoot. Saying you're willing to do it and then backing it up with a trigger pull against another man, another human being, were two very different things. Not everybody was able to bridge that gap — not without a big gulp of hesitation. Which *might* give enough extra time for a man as cat-quick and experienced as Beartooth to make good on such an attempt . . . leaving whether or not the former mountain man felt ready to take that risk as the real question hanging over the situation.

The answer was no, he didn't. Not yet.

Double-damn it to hell.

Into the silence, Brody abruptly said, "Under the circumstances, this is probably gonna sound kinda ridiculous . . . but I really regret you feeling that way about me — that I'm snake-mean and crazy. Coming from somebody I truly respect . . . well, like I said, I'm sorry to hear it."

Beartooth emitted a dry chuckle. "That's pretty rich. Tellin' a body how much you respect 'em when all the while you've got 'em under the gun and are keepin' 'em chained and tied like a ruttin' hog. Somehow that don't seem like the actions of somebody who don't want to have no hard feelin's against 'em."

"But my reasons for doin' these things don't stem from malice or craziness," Brody insisted. "I explained all that to you. I'm doin' it mainly for my ma. The last thing I want is to have to hurt somebody. And if I was in it strictly for myself, don't you think I'd be asking for a lot more than just a hundred bucks to make my getaway with?"

"A hunnerd bucks, a thousand . . . No amount of money will take you far enough to where me or one of my pals won't catch up with you," Beartooth grated. "And when we do, that's where your regrets will really start."

Brody took another sip of his coffee. Lowering the cup, his young face took on a forlorn look, etched deep by the flickering patterns of light and shadow cast from the flames. "I'm sorry if it has to be that way," he said in a low voice.

"What else could you expect?" Beartooth said harshly. "If you leave me alive, I'll come after you. And what I set out to hunt down, I catch."

Brody turned his head. "You sound like you're *encouraging* me to kill you."

"It wouldn't matter. Came to that, my partners would be the ones to hunt you down. They'd be just that much more driven and relentless. Damn it, you young fool, what I'm tryin' to do is get you to come to your senses and call this whole thing off before it's too late."

"It's already too late." Brody's eyes shone bright, the intensity in them amplified by the reflection from the fire. "I set this ball in motion . . . There ain't no rolling it backward now."

Saetta wore a well-pleased expression as he gazed out on the secluded mountain camp where his braves were once again busily carving and skinning several longhorn carcasses. "More of the White Eyes' cattle, taken with ease. It is good," he declared. "Every sign indicates that our medicine remains strong for the success of this raid."

"Then, while it is so," said Taluma, standing beside him, "we should continue to strike and strike boldly. Do you not agree, my uncle?"

Saetta smiled tolerantly. "Something else that remains strong, I see, is your lust to spill white blood."

"I make no pretense otherwise," admitted Taluma.

"No, you do not. Nor would I want a nephew of mine to put on a false front. Since last we talked of such things, you have held your tongue and followed my commands without question. Yet all the while it was clear, to my eyes, that the thirst was building in you."

"You said the time would come, before

this raid was concluded," Taluma reminded him.

"I also said that what I wanted to accomplish first, was this" — Saetta swept his arm, indicating the activity in the camp — "securing important supplies, starting with enough beef to fill the meat pots of our village for the summer and beyond."

"Are we not well on the way to meeting that goal?"

"Indeed. Before the sun rises, the first of our pack ponies will begin the journey back to our village loaded heavily with meat and hides that our women will be waiting to finish curing and treating."

Taluma held his tongue, yet so eager to hear the rest of what his uncle had planned that tiny muscles were fluttering anxiously under his skin.

"To help their passage," Saetta continued, "those of us who stay behind will divert attention away from them by breaking into smaller groups and making our presence well known to the White Eyes in this valley. Judging by the activity our scouts reported of riders they saw scurrying away from the town at dusk, I believe they may already suspect we are here. After tomorrow, we will leave no question about that in their minds."

Taluma no longer attempted to conceal

his eagerness. He couldn't have, anyway, no matter how hard he tried.

"You, my nephew," said Saetta with great somberness, "will honor me by leading one of the groups. Our scouts are continuing to scour the valley even as we speak. By morning they will have reported back on what appear to be the most promising targets for us to strike. From these, you will have the opportunity to do what you so badly crave — to spill white blood. But remember, the gathering of more supplies — blankets, seed, cartridges, anything of use to our people — remains part of your mission, as well."

Taluma's eyes were bright, almost feverish. "I will remember, my uncle. And I will make you proud."

Saetta nodded. "I know you will. Go now. Rest. Prepare . . . Make sure the pouches of clay and berry juice are ready to be mixed for the paint we will be wearing on our faces."

CHAPTER 32

"So, what time did they ride away from the Double M? Who actually saw them leave?" Firestick wanted to know.

Victoria, Miguel, and Jesus exchanged looks.

Victoria said, "I was in the house. I wasn't aware Beartooth had left the property at all until . . . well, until I came upon *that.*" She tipped her head toward the note that Moosejaw still clenched in his fist. "But somewhere around four or so, I heard someone washing up in the lean-to. I supposed it must be the young lad, Brody, cleaning up before going home."

"*Sí,* that would be about right," agreed Miguel. "That was close to the time Mr. Beartooth and the boy came to the corral to saddle up their horses. Jesus and I were in the barn, working on those new stalls, when Mr. Beartooth stuck in his head and said he was riding out for a while. He said to keep a close eye while he was gone."

"A close eye for what?"

"Earlier in the day," Miguel explained, "he told me of the talk about Apaches possibly being in the area. He told me not to say anything to Jesus or Miss Victoria, not to worry them until we found out for sure."

"And then, when we were getting ready to leave the ranch just a little while ago," said Victoria, "some of the riders you sent out to spread the word came by and confirmed there truly are Indians in the valley."

"But when Beartooth left earlier," said Moosejaw through clenched teeth, "he had no way of knowin' for certain. Which probably explains why he rode off with the boy to begin with — to see that the kid got home safe, just in case."

The five of them — six, counting Kate — had the Mallory Hotel barroom to themselves. Kate had put out a decanter of wine, a bottle of whiskey, and some glasses. Victoria poured herself some of the wine; none of the others had as yet reached for anything.

"Unless the kid already had him under the gun at that point, and was forcin' him to go along," suggested Firestick.

Moosejaw gave a violent shake of his head. "That's the thing I can't wrap my noggin around nohow — Beartooth lettin' a pup of a kid get the drop on him. Injuns, no Injuns, no matter if the kid had guns bristlin' out his ass — pardon my coarse language, ladies — I can't see the Beartooth I know lettin' hisself get snookered so easy."

"Maybe that's exactly why it happened," Firestick said. "Beartooth didn't feel any need to have his guard up, because Brody Rockwell *was* just a pup of a kid."

Moosejaw wagged his head some more. "It's still hard to buy."

"Did the kid even have a gun?" Firestick asked.

"*Sí.* A big shiny one," Jesus answered. "He said it used to belong to his brother."

"It looked almost too big and heavy for the skinny boy to drag around," added Miguel. "He said he wore it to look more like a man so he would have a better chance for Mr. Beartooth to hire him."

"I heard them talking about that, too," said Victoria. "Beartooth was still kidding him a little at lunchtime, saying how they'd reached an agreement it wasn't really necessary to continue wearing a gun in order to do whitewashing."

"That's another thing I don't get," said Moosejaw. "What would make Beartooth take a notion to hire the kid in the first place? We already got plenty of help for what work needs doin' around the ranch, don't we?"

"Sympathy," Victoria was quick to reply. "Beartooth didn't hire the boy because he felt the Double M needed help — he hired him because of Brody's sad tale about him and his mum needing money in order to keep their farm."

Moosejaw snorted. "Now, there's the first thing about this that makes sense, or at least fits the Beartooth I know. Him and that mush heart of his for every sad tale of woe."

"There are worse traits a man could have," Victoria said defensively.

"Margaret Rockwell." Firestick made no attempt to hide the trace of bitterness in his tone when he said the name. "You can bet I aim to have a talk with that old gal about this. I don't care what the note says about her having no knowledge or blame. She raised one lousy son, who hurried himself into an early grave, and now, due to her blindness over how worthless he was and her hatred against all the wrong people for what happened to him, I'm thinkin' she may have poisoned the mind of the boy who left that note. One way or another, she's got some accounting to do."

"If she has any sense," said Moosejaw,

"she ought to be comin' in with the escort wagon that Pete Roeback took out that way. With both of her boys gone, she'd be all alone on that hardscrabble farm. No matter how ornery and spiteful she is, I don't reckon she'd want to leave herself there as Apache bait. Would she?"

Firestick frowned. "Hard to picture it, but when it comes to her, she's the type who'd be hard to make a call on as far as what she'd do in any given situation."

"Reckon we'll know soon enough, when Roeback's wagon gets back."

"But in the meantime, what about Beartooth?" Victoria fought hard to control her voice, but a tremor of anxiety came through nonetheless. "He's somewhere out there under the gun of a highly irrational youth, in the midst of prowling savages that neither of them are fully aware of. You don't propose to leave him in that predicament for the time it may take to arrange meeting his kidnapper's demands, do you?"

Now it was Firestick and Moosejaw who exchanged looks.

To the surprise of the others watching, one corner of Moosejaw's mouth abruptly quirked upward. "Takin' it slow and easy, playin' it safe . . . those ain't exactly our strong suits, are they?"

"No more so than givin' in to demands and threats," said Firestick.

Miguel looked suddenly fretful. "But, *señors* . . . The note warns that the boy will be on a high perch, watching closely. At any sign of trickery, he says there will be blood — Señor Beartooth's blood is who he means, no?"

"That's what he wants us to believe, yeah," Moosejaw said.

"But there's a little thing called timing," added Firestick. "Between when the kid wrote that note and now, unless he grew wings and put 'em to use before sunset, I'm willin' to bet he ain't on his high perch just yet."

"The kid will think he's the one who's got time on his side." The excitement was growing in Moosejaw's voice. It seemed obvious that his and Firestick's thoughts were running on closely parallel tracks. "He's got to know it will take a while to put together the money and paperwork he's askin' for. That's why he stretched things out as far as he did, allowin' until day after tomorrow. But what he ain't takin' into consideration is us not bein' quite so patient, not sittin' around twiddlin' our thumbs and waitin' for him to jerk the strings we dance to."

Kate stepped forward, her pretty brow furrowed. "Wait a minute. You two aren't talking about going out to Buffalo Hump Butte immediately tonight, are you?"

"That's the general idea," Moosejaw declared.

Firestick gave it a beat, expelled some air, then said, "Well, not exactly."

All eyes darted to him.

Moosejaw's mouth gaped open. "Whatya sayin'?"

"I'm sayin' only *one* of us is goin' out there," Firestick responded, squaring his broad shoulders against the fierce scowl his old friend hammered him with. "There's too much else goin' on for both of us to be gone at the same time."

"And I suppose you figure you're the one goin' to the butte?"

"That's the way I see it."

"What if I see it different?"

Firestick held his eyes. "After all our years together, it'd be a hell of a thing for us to butt heads now, with so much on the line. Wouldn't it?"

"That's just the point. For all those years, it's been the three of us stickin' together. Any time one of us got in a tight spot, the other two always —"

Firestick cut him off. "But it's bigger than just the three of us now! Don't you see? This town, the people in it, the folks on the surrounding farms and ranches . . . they're all countin' on us."

"What about Beartooth? Ain't he countin' on us?"

"And we're not leavin' him out. But we can't *both* concentrate on strictly him, not and leave other things lacking."

"The town is buttoned up tight. Guards are posted. Warning riders and escort wagons have all been sent out and should be showin' back up by morning." Moosejaw jutted his chin out defiantly. "What's lacking?"

"The supply train on its way across Jacinto Flats," Firestick was quick to answer. "Without bein' warned and without added guns, if Kruger's wagons get caught by Apaches out there in the open, they'll be massacred to hell and gone."

Moosejaw showed some signs of wavering. The thrust of his chin pulled back slightly. He blinked once.

Seeing this, Firestick pressed his case harder. "Look, you've done a hell of a good job here gettin' the town forted up and ready." That's the whole reason we can both be gone at the same time and leave it in the hands of men like Duvall, Moorehouse, and Roeback when he gets back. But that can't be done until the riders and wagons return so's men can be spared again, this time to accompany you. You and me can both be gone at the same time, but we can't both cover the same place, not with Beartooth bein' held captive at Buffalo Hump Butte and those freight wagons rollin' in clear off to the southeast.

"Your early days with Fremont's army in New Mexico gives you more experience with Injun fightin' out in the open, on the flat. That's what makes you best suited to head up bringin' Kruger in safe. As for me, and I know you'll probably want to argue this, but I move a mite quicker and lighter in the high rocks like the butte is gonna present."

Moosejaw bristled. "Oh, I don't know about that. I say I'm at least as . . ." This time he interrupted his own flow of words and let whatever he was going to say just trail off. He planted another fierce scowl on Firestick.

"It's the most effective way to cover everything we need to cover. And you can see it, too," the marshal stated quietly but firmly. "Ain't like either one of us is drawin' picnic detail."

"But you're not going to the butte alone, are you?" Kate said to him.

"One man movin' quick, quiet, and alone has the best chance to approach the butte unseen and get in position ahead of Beartooth and his kidnapper."

"No use tryin' to argue with him," advised Moosejaw. "He's stubborn as seven mules and can sling words like a gaggle of politicians with fresh-oiled tongues."

"Flattery will get you nowhere," said Firestick, one corner of his mouth lifting in a lopsided grin.

"I'll tell you somewhere I *am* gonna get," Moosejaw snapped back. "When this is all over, you and me are gonna have us a race to the top of Buffalo Hump Butte. We'll settle who moves best on high rocks. And then, once we get to the top, we're gonna commence to arguin' about anything and everything and not come down until we hit a subject where I outargue you right into the dust."

Firestick's grin widened. "I welcome the challenge. Comes to that, it'll mean we must have made it through these pesky other little problems spread before us in the here and now . . . Anything on the other side of that oughta be easy."

CHAPTER 33

Firestick's plan was straightforward and simple. Not to execute maybe, but at least simple in concept. Past experience had instilled in him the belief that overly elaborate schemes only added up to that many more things with the potential to go wrong. In the end, no matter the degree of complexity, what it usually boiled down to were the basics of luck and timing.

Firestick reckoned he had the timing calculated fairly well. When it came to luck — well, that remained to be seen. Which way that fickle force would swing was out of his hands.

For starters, the whole thing hinged on the assumption that Beartooth and his captor had headed directly for Buffalo Hump Butte as soon as the boy had revealed his true intentions and put Beartooth under his gun. Hard as it might be to believe, yet given no indication otherwise, it had to be further assumed that the former mountain man *was* still in the duplicitous pup's custody. The only other explanation for not hearing from him would be that he was dead, a possibility Firestick refused to contemplate.

The mere hint of such a thing, however, did force the marshal to contemplate something else. Something that entered his thoughts jarringly and refused to leave until he spent some time pondering on it. Young, quiet, scrawny Brody Rockwell — lost for so long in the shadow of his rambunctious older brother and then his embittered mother — seemed like such an unlikely villain that it was hard to take him seriously in the role. Making it barely believable he could get the drop on somebody as savvy as Beartooth, let alone picture him as a truly dangerous threat. Which probably explained how he'd caught Beartooth so flat-footed to begin with. So, what if all that outer mildness was only a shell that hid a deeper something that was truly menacing? Menacing enough to harm not only Beartooth, but others, too . . . Others like Gus Wingate.

A link between Wingate's murder and his shooting of Owen Rockwell months back had been gnawing on the edges of Firestick's mind right from the get-go. Hatred for Wingate over Owen's death had certainly existed in Margaret Rockwell, that was well known. But imagining she would ever try to even the score with bullets fired by her own hand was never a serious consideration, especially as time passed.

But who was to say what kind of influence she could have been having on Brody over that same period of time? With his kidnapping demands and threats of "there will be blood" if they weren't met, he had now clearly demonstrated that he wasn't the timid young lad everybody had taken him for. So, what else might he have demonstrated? Could the menacing part of him, which had emerged from behind his timid mask to pull off a kidnapping and write those demands, also be capable of pulling a trigger on the man who'd shot and killed his brother?

It was a question that sank its teeth into Firestick's brain and refused to let go. The timing seemed wrong, considering how — according to the testimony of Victoria and the vaqueros — Brody had been at the Double M during the time Wingate was shot. But had they been watching him that closely? Could they be certain he hadn't slipped away long enough to do the deed and then returned before anybody had missed him? Or could it be possible he had detoured by the Wingate ranch *after* he had Beartooth in custody? Such conjecture seemed far-fetched, but it nevertheless triggered a precautionary insistence that Brody should no longer be thought of as a pup, as the quiet, likable kid everybody had known — or *thought* they had known — before now. From this point on, he had to be considered a dangerous hombre, and maybe even a killer.

Moving on from that unpleasant line of thought, Firestick shifted to doing some reckoning on likely routes for approaching Buffalo Hump Butte. Again keeping it simple, logic said that since Beartooth and Brody had left the Double M headed for the Rockwell farm — which lay to the south — then a course correction with the butte as their new destination meant they would be coming in from the west, passing either above or below the town. This left Firestick's best option for making it to the same place unseen by them to circle wide to the south and east and then cut back from the opposite side.

So, that was how he headed out. Choosing a sturdy, sure-footed black gelding from Roeback's livery and outfitting himself in a dark coat and hat, the marshal spurred south out of town. Before leaving, he provisioned himself with two full canteens of water and a pouch of beef jerky. He also made time for a brief, private embrace with Kate and a bone-crunching handshake with Moosejaw before melting away into the dark.

It was still early enough that the moon hadn't fully risen and the stars weren't yet burning with their full brilliance, but he still had enough light to see across the undulating, mostly treeless terrain. In addition to the water and jerky, he'd also brought along a pair of high-powered binoculars, carefully wrapped and stowed in his saddlebag. Weapon-wise, there was a Winchester Yellowboy riding snug in its saddle scabbard by his right leg, along with plenty of spare cartridges also in his saddlebags. The cartridges were .44 caliber, a match for the long gun as well as the army Colt revolver holstered on his right hip with more of the same filling the loops in the shell belt around his waist. He wasn't lacking for the means to fight a small war, if it came to that.

Still, running all this through his mind as he rode, he couldn't help but feel a pang of regret for one item he didn't have along . . . Ol' Thunder, his prized Hawken rifle resting on hooks above the front door back at the Double M's main house. The Hawken dated back to his early days in the mountains and had served him faithfully over all that time. In a manner of speaking, it was as close a friend as either Moosejaw or Beartooth.

With the availability of new and improved arms following the war — repeating rifles, revolvers, and such — it only made sense for men living in the wild and relying on guns as a major part of their survival to adapt and change with the times. Which Firestick and his pals did — none more so than he himself. Getting used to lever-action repeating rifles was a transition that came almost without effort for all three of them. Somewhat more surprising, however, was the seemingly natural ease with which Firestick took to a revolver, both in speed and accuracy. It was a skill that didn't really play a big part at first, but once they hit Texas — and especially after they pinned on badges — it proved increasingly beneficial.

Nevertheless, Firestick's attachment to his Hawken, Ol' Thunder, stayed strong. Even after he'd begun using a Winchester much of the time while still in the mountains, Ol' Thunder was never very far from his reach. Its range and .50-caliber punch, as a matter of fact, had played a major part in the whole "Firestick" handle that the Indians began calling him by. Though he still kept it meticulously cleaned and oiled and regularly used it for hunting, Ol' Thunder had quickly proven unwieldy and rather impractical for his marshaling duties on the streets of Buffalo Peak. He'd gotten in the habit of leaving it hung over the doorway at the ranch.

Even if he *did* have it along now, he had to admit, carrying it with him for the upcoming ascent of a rugged rock face in the dark would surely add to the chore. On the other hand, he'd seen more than one occasion where a single, well-placed shot from long range — something his Hawken could deliver like no other — made as much or more impact than a whole closer-range volley . . .

At the base of Buffalo Hump Butte, wrapped in his bedroll blankets with his head resting on the saddle he was chained to, Beartooth was surprised to find himself actually relaxing to that point that he was ready to try and catch some sleep. Reasoning it out, he concluded there were a couple of reasons for this.

Number one, he was weary. It had been a

long day full of twists and turns, and he'd learned a long time ago, under situations far more tense than this, that it was never a bad idea to catch some rest whenever possible in order to be ready for whatever might come next.

Number two, odd as it seemed given his predicament, he didn't feel all that threatened by Brody Rockwell. Oh, the kid definitely had a twisted outlook on things, but unless he was backed into some kind of corner where he felt seriously threatened, Beartooth believed his captor genuinely wasn't out to hurt anybody.

What was more, though no such opportunity had presented itself yet, Beartooth couldn't help but think that sooner or later, the kid would slip in some way and give him an opening to turn the tables. And if nothing else, there was always the certainty that Firestick and Moosejaw were even now cooking up something of their own in the way of coming to his rescue.

The thought caused Beartooth's mouth to twist wryly. Not that he wouldn't welcome the sight of those ugly mugs slipping in over the rocks right about now, but what wouldn't be so welcome was the string of horse laughs he'd be getting for the next God only knew how long, due to letting himself get caught the way he had by a green kid.

Of course, he had a ribbing to look forward to, no matter how or when he got out of this fix. Still, it could at least be diminished some if he managed his own escape rather than relying on them. There was a fine kettle of fish to ponder. Would he rather be rescued sooner by his pals — or would he rather it dragged on a bit longer if it meant being able to pull it off by himself?

And then there was the factor that lay outside even the slightest hint of ribbing or horse laughs — the possibility of Apaches being somewhere nearby. In that case, all bets were off. No matter the kid's intentions about not wanting anybody harmed, he could have set them up for slaughter, just as sure as a couple of lambs staked for cougar bait.

Whether or not there actually *were* Chiricahuas on the prowl from below the border, Beartooth had no way of knowing for sure. Last he knew, Moosejaw hadn't got back with definitive word on what he had found. But Boynton had told a pretty convincing tale. And ever since he'd heard it, Beartooth had felt an inclination toward believing him . . .

It was dark now. For the time being, he

and the kid should be safe. Apaches generally didn't attack at night. But the dark didn't stop them from maneuvering, getting in position. Especially not when they had a nice bright campfire to lure them like a beacon to await the predawn half light that was one of their favorite times to strike.

Beartooth cursed under his breath. All of a sudden he no longer felt so relaxed and ready for sleep.

In town, Moosejaw paced. Part of the time he paced back and forth in the jail office; other times, when he realized he was disturbing the slumber of Duvall and Shield, he would go outside and work on wearing a trough in the street out front. Daisy came by and kept him company for a while, but not even her normally soothing presence was enough to put him at ease on this occasion. When it got late and she saw she wasn't accomplishing a whole lot except losing sleep of her own, she kissed him good night and went on home.

Like Beartooth, Moosejaw knew the wisdom in grabbing rest when opportunity presented — particularly given what might lie in store tomorrow, when he took a force of men out to intercept Kruger's freight wagons. But knowing he *should* get some rest and actually being able to do so were two different things. Especially when not all of the warning riders were back in yet.

Four of the six men who'd gone out to spread word about the Apaches had returned. The remaining two, the pair assigned to ride south and east, where some of the bigger ranches were scattered the widest, were still out there somewhere. Once they showed up safe and sound, Moosejaw told himself, then maybe he'd be able to relax a little.

That still left the two escort wagons that had gone out to bring in some of the smaller, more vulnerable outlying families. But it was expected from the get-go that, because they were moving slower and taking on passengers, it would likely be pushing daybreak before they rolled back in. Moosejaw figured he'd settle for what rest he could manage in the interim.

As he paced, these thoughts and more ran through the big deputy's mind. He thought of Firestick and Beartooth, naturally. He reminded himself how tough and competent his pals were, how many close scrapes they'd gotten through together. But there was the kicker, the together part. This time they were scattered, *not* together. He understood, and grudgingly accepted, that was how it had to be — how it had been forced upon them by so many things popping on such a wide canvas, and how times had changed so that their responsibilities were bigger than to just each other. He understood, but that didn't mean he had to like it.

He also understood the responsibility resting on him when it came to getting a timely warning and reinforcements to Kruger and the men traveling with him. Seeing to it the supplies made it through was important to the town — keeping them out of the hands of the Apaches and minimizing the loss of lives potentially hanging in the balance was even more crucial. But the towering former mountain man was resolved to get it done. He knew how many people — Firestick chief among them — were counting on him.

In his room at the Mallory Hotel, Henry Lofton was also struggling with restlessness. Earlier, when Victoria and the others from the Double M got into town, Lofton had been down the street at the Lone Star Palace, trying unsuccessfully to scrounge up a poker game and settling instead for a lengthy, pleasant, mildly flirtatious conversation with Frenchy Fontaine, Earl Sterling's hostess/entertainer, who also wasn't having much luck drawing a crowd.

It was only after Lofton got back to the hotel that he heard about the kidnapping and the role played in it by one Brody Rockwell. That was unsettling enough. Then, when he further learned that Marshal Firestick was heading out to try and rescue his old friend and was already gone from town, it unnerved him even more.

What the hell was going on? How many angles for revenge was Margaret Rockwell simultaneously playing, he couldn't help but wonder. That her youngest son had pulled off this kidnapping without her help or at least knowledge was too much to swallow.

Not that Lofton gave a damn about the two of them taking action to gain a clear deed to their lousy farm. To him, a back-breaking plot of ground hardly seemed worth the effort or risk. But that was their business . . . except for the nagging little detail of the risk now overlapping onto him because he happened to be still in the vicinity and could be linked to the Rockwells via the job he'd hired out to do for the mother. The job that was only half done. And now the part that remained before it could be called finished had been lured away and made even harder to get at. What was more, if Firestick got his hands on the kid, as he'd set out to do — how much would the little brat squeal if he was taken alive?

The safest and smartest thing to do, Lofton told himself, might be to consider this job blown up — through no fault of his own — and make dust the hell out of here at first light. But he couldn't warm to that notion, even if it did have merit. The professional in him didn't like leaving a piece of business unfinished. And however the matter between him and Firestick played out, he now had reason to want to confront the Rockwell woman again — and maybe her son, as well — to demand an accounting for this foolish kidnapping complication.

Plus there were the damn Apaches.

To trade one set of risks for facing the chance of losing his scalp if he got in too big of a hurry to ride away from here was certainly worth some added consideration. Besides, if Lofton recalled correctly from the initial meeting between the marshal and all the townsmen earlier, Margaret Rockwell's name had been mentioned as one of several candidates to be brought to safety by the escort wagons that had been sent out and hadn't returned yet. Based on that, he reasoned he could find a way to meet with her again, once she'd been brought in, and get some answers on the added concerns he now had due to the actions of her son. He had ways of finding out things he wanted to know, and that way he wouldn't have to be worried about looking over his shoulder for stinking Apaches while he was doing it.

Yeah, that would be the best way to relieve his concerns.

Then there'd still be time to take care of the marshal.

CHAPTER 34

By the time Firestick reached the east face of Buffalo Hump Butte, the moon was high and a blanket of brilliantly sparkling stars was spread over the sky. Only a trace of breeze cut the night, leaving what few streaks of thin, horizontal clouds there were to hang essentially motionless.

The marshal appreciated the illumination now, as he faced the wall of creased, weathered rock he was about to ascend. There would still be plenty of deeply shadowed recesses and light-blocking overhangs he'd have to negotiate mostly by feel, meaning he'd take all the lighting, even muted, he could get for as long as it lasted.

Riding in over the final stretch of wideopen grassiness, however, had been a different matter. All during those last few miles, Firestick had felt as exposed as a bug crawling across a slice of bread. Knowing how a dust cloud kicked up by his horse's hooves would capture the moon- and starlight, he'd held the gelding to little more than a brisk walk. The time and distance had passed with agonizing slowness.

In case he'd miscalculated and Brody Rockwell — or, worse yet, the Apaches — were already atop the butte looking down, he could be riding straight into gun sights or an arrow pointed his way. Closely scanning the rim of the butte all during his approach had revealed no movement or any other sign to give evidence of this, but sensing the possibility was a little nerve-grinding all the same.

The highest point of the butte stood about three hundred feet above the prairie from which it rose. It was roughly oval-shaped across the semi-flat top, seventy or so yards at its widest, about fifty at its narrowest. Most of the way around its girth the formation shot straight up, but it was gouged with deep, weatherworn creases and troughs that provided decent purchase for climbing. Here and there were flat, smooth expanses that would be more of a challenge. The western face, where Firestick reckoned Beartooth and his captor would be located, sloped outward for much of the way at a sixty- or seventy-degree angle, making it the easiest face to ascend.

Shortly after settling in the area, Firestick, Beartooth, and Moosejaw had used the western face to climb the butte and take a look out over the valley from its top. This was a common practice for newcomers to the area, almost a rite of passage. Compared to the grand vistas the three former mountain men had been used to seeing on a regular basis back in the Rockies, it had hardly been overwhelming. Nevertheless, for the area, the butte was significant, and checking it out had been worthwhile.

Though he'd had no reason since that original reconnoiter to return and make the climb again, Firestick could still picture things fairly clearly in his mind. Once he reached the top tonight, he knew he would have no trouble finding suitable concealment where he could await the arrival of Beartooth and Brody. Barring something unforeseen, that was pretty much the remainder of his plan from this point. Get to the top first, wait for them to show up, jump the kid, and free Beartooth.

Simplicity.

Some reason to refine this bare-bones scheme might present itself once he was in place. If so, fine. If not, he'd go with the way he had it worked out now.

But first things first. After saddle-stripping

and loosely tying the gelding, so that it could eventually pull away and free itself in the event things went bad, he gave it a good watering from his hat, then made sure there was plenty of graze for it.

Next he outfitted himself: canteen; saddle pouch containing jerky, binoculars, spare cartridges; Winchester fitted with a leather sling. All slung over his shoulders. The high-topped, moccasin-soled buckskin boots he habitually wore in lieu of the standard high-heeled cowboy boots more commonly seen on men in the area fittingly completed his attire.

After crouching completely still and silent for several minutes, attuning himself to the night noises so he would more readily recognize anything out of place, Firestick then straightened and began his climb.

Except for a few spots where the creases in the rock were so deep that any sight of a solid handhold was lost in inky blackness, causing Firestick to reach and grope cautiously until he could be certain he was gripping something solid, the ascent was only moderately difficult. He took his time, careful not only to avoid slipping and falling, but also not to dislodge any loose rocks that would clatter to the bottom. Sound traveled oddly on the high rocks, especially in the still of the night.

It was still early enough in the spring that the air had grown steadily cooler since the setting of the sun. Nevertheless, Firestick had a light sheen of sweat dotting his forehead and temples and dripping under his arms inside his coat by the time he reached the top.

Staying on his belly, he eased up over the rim and edged slowly forward until he reached some loose boulders and a scrim of evergreen brush, which he wormed in behind. He lay there for several moments, breathing shallowly, once again locking all his senses on full alert for any sound, motion, or smell. When he was satisfied it was safe, he rose to a semi-crouch and began to move around. Before doing so, he lifted the canteen and saddle pouch off his back and stored them, along with the sling from the rifle, where he'd been lying. He took the binoculars from the pouch and hung them around his neck by the leather thong attached to them. The rifle he carried lightly in one hand.

Firestick familiarized himself with the center area of the rugged, slightly domed surface. Then he began working his way around the edges, being careful to stay back far enough so he wouldn't be skylined to anyone looking up from below. Visibility was grand in all directions. In the distance, he could see a few winking lights that marked the town of Buffalo Peak.

And then, as he worked his way around the rim above the western face, he caught a faint whiff of wood smoke from down below. The dying wisps of a campfire.

He dropped to his belly again and slipped closer to the edge, choosing a flat, solid slab of rock that wouldn't crumble or release even the tiniest sprinkle of pebbles when he peered over. He laid the Yellowboy down beside him and brought the binoculars up to his eyes. His head moved slowly from right to left, sweeping the magnified viewing field along the out-sloping base . . . until, through a scraggly overhang of gnarled, mostly bare tree branches, he could make out the glow of reddish coals. He held on the sight for a long time, determining there to be no movement, no sound. Just the reddish pinpoints, fading. And the occasional fresh waft of smoke.

Firestick shifted back from the edge and released the breath he hadn't realized he was holding. He felt confident it was Beartooth and Brody down there. It had to be. No Apache would build a fire and let it gradually die out like that. They'd build it, use it, then extinguish it quickly and smokelessly when they were done.

So his quarry was down there, right where he'd calculated. And tomorrow they would be up here, where he'd be waiting for them.

All he had to do now was let it play out. Be patient, not give in to the temptation that was suddenly coursing through him, urging him not to wait, to go ahead and slip on down and get it over with.

But no, he'd resist that. His plan had gotten him this far, by damn. He was going to stick with it.

CHAPTER 35

Moosejaw's intention to finally catch some sleep after the final two warning riders got in didn't pan out. For starters, the pair didn't return alone. Riding with them was Gerald Tolsvord and one of the wranglers from his Box T spread. All four men wore grim expressions and showed signs of having ridden hard. Inasmuch as it was well past midnight and Trail Street was long since empty, they came galloping in full steam and four abreast amid a cloud of dust that boiled from boardwalk to boardwalk.

Moosejaw stood in front of the jail, watching them approach and feeling a knot tightening in his gut, knowing they were bringing some kind of added bad news.

Tolsvord didn't waste any time getting to it. "Where's Marshal Firestick?" he demanded.

Not caring much for the gruffness of his tone, Moosejaw's initial reaction was to want to bark right back. But consideration for the tension showing on the rancher's face and the overall tension gripping the whole valley made him hold his own gruffness in check. Instead he replied evenly, "He's out of town investigatin' a crime."

Tolsvord frowned. "The murder of Gus Wingate? I would have thought he'd be returned from that long before this."

For a moment, Moosejaw felt surprised that Tolsvord would know about the Wingate killing. So many things were happening so fast that it was a little head-spinning to try and keep up with all of them. But then the big deputy remembered that Firestick had headed out to the Wingate spread with Sylvester Krause *before* the warning riders were dispatched. So the riders already knew about the shooting before they took off, making it evident and not surprising that they'd do some talking about that, as well as spreading the news of Apaches.

"Things have been poppin' mighty fast around here," Moosejaw understated. "Wingate's murder and the Apaches are only part of it."

"Yeah, well, keep your tally sheet out," said one of the riders, young Bob Sapp. "Because we came across something more you can add to it."

Moosejaw scowled. "What's that supposed to mean? Quit talkin' in riddles."

Tolsvord's grim expression gave way to one of sadness, maybe even a twinge of pain. "Three of my men — Grady and Greely Dunlap, and Newt Woolsey — have also been murdered," he said dully. "These boys found their bodies, gunned down and shot to pieces, on their way to warn me that the presence of Apaches had been confirmed. I insisted they take me back to the scene on their return."

"The Box T was our last stop, so we figured it was okay to take the time," Sapp added. "Mr. Tolsvord brought along a wagon and a couple of extra men to take the bodies back to the ranch. You and Marshal Firestick said that Apaches don't usually attack at night, so we thought that would be all right, knowin' we'd be comin' here to tell you about it right away and all."

"You think it was Injuns who killed those men?" asked Will Capron, the other rider who'd gone out with Sapp.

Moosejaw gave him a somewhat pitying look before saying, "If it'd been Apaches, son, you wouldn't have to ask that question. You'd have found the bodies in a lot worse shape than just riddled by bullets."

"There might be some comfort in that,

but not a lot," said Tolsvord. "I'll be the first to admit those men didn't have a lot of admirable qualities. But they were still men, damn it. Two of them were blood kin to my wife, and all three rode for my brand. They didn't deserve to be left for coyote pickings." His eyes swept the faces around him. "Apaches . . . Cold-blooded killings . . . What in hell has befallen our valley? What have we done to deserve this?"

"I don't know about 'deserves,' " said Moosejaw, "but I do know it's not over with."

"What else can there be?"

Without wasting words, speaking bluntly, Moosejaw told them the rest. About the kidnapping. About the unsuspecting supply train due in over a wide-open expanse that would make it ripe pickings for the Apaches. Before he was done talking, both Duvall and Boynton emerged from the jail and stood with him. When Boynton heard what had befallen the Box T men he'd sent on ahead, he winced as if struck by a physical blow.

"That's hard news, and I feel awful about it, Mr. Tolsvord," he stated remorsefully. "I had no idea anything like that would happen. I just wanted 'em to get confirmation about the Apaches to you as soon as possible and then be there to help guard the ranch."

"Of course, Cleve. You have no blame in the matter," Tolsvord told him. "If you'd ridden with them, your body might at this very moment be lying out there on the prairie with theirs, and what purpose would that serve?"

"Boynton's a good man. He's been in the thick of things all day, helpin' both me and the marshal," stated Moosejaw.

"I saw where I could do some good around here, and figured one less gun out at the ranch wouldn't make that much difference," Boynton further explained.

Tolsvord made a dismissive gesture with one hand. "I said I understood, Cleve. You're fine. I have no quarrel with your decision. And rest assured we left the ranch well guarded. Some outlying cattle may be at risk, but that can't be helped. In close, everyone's on full alert so that the main house and buildings are well protected."

"I wish I had that strong of an assurance for all the other ranches in the valley," said Moosejaw, heaving a sigh. "But we did everything we could. Now we've got to turn our attention to Kruger's incoming wagons."

"What have you got in mind to do about

that?" Tolsvord wanted to know.

"I figured on leadin' out a well-armed force of men at first light to join up with 'em and see to it they make it in okay."

"What about the army? Aren't they sending anybody?"

"They are. But we ain't for sure when to expect 'em."

"How many men you figuring to lead out?"

"Around ten, is what I've been thinkin'."

"Why wait? Why not head out sooner?" Tolsvord made another gesture, waving his hand skyward. "It's a clear night, visibility is good. We had no trouble riding in, and you've been saying the Apaches aren't likely to attack at night. The sooner you leave, the sooner you make it to Jacinto Flats."

Moosejaw startled to bristle, but once again held himself in check. He sensed the rancher wasn't meaning to find fault with his plan, the way it half-sounded, but rather that he was leading up to something. "I've been holdin' off for the riders and men with the escort wagons to make it back," he explained. "Number one, I wanted to make sure they were accounted for and hadn't run into any trouble. Number two, I didn't want to take another body of men out before they got back in order to keep from leaving the town shorthanded."

"That makes sense. Good thinking." Tolsvord pursed his lips. "But consider this. All the riders now *are* back, and there's six or seven of us standing right here. We only need a few more to make your ten."

"True enough," Moosejaw allowed. "But the wagons still haven't made it, and these two boys have already spent hours ridin' hard. They need food and rest."

"We can go some more. We got plenty left in us, Deputy Moosejaw," Bob Sapp was quick to speak up.

"That's right," seconded Capron. "We'd be honored to ride out with you and help bring in that supply train."

"And I figured all along on being part of it," said Boynton.

Sam Duvall added another voice. "You've done a good job of getting the town all set, Moosejaw. Everybody here knows what they need to do. And me and Moorehouse have already agreed to spearhead things in your absence. What's bein' suggested might not be a bad idea."

Moosejaw's eyes went to the face of each man as he chewed on the notion. Lord knew, he was anxious enough to get the waiting over with and be underway. But at the same time, he didn't want to get caught

344

up in a rush and end up overlooking something.

He'd already been thinking about the men he wanted to take with him. Boynton had been on the list. And Miguel, from the Double M; as well as the late Wingate's hired men, Krause and Marsh. That made five, counting him. Now, plus Sapp, Capron, Tolsvord, and the Box T wrangler who'd ridden in with them. That added up to nine.

As if reading his thoughts, Tolsvord said, "If need be, I can spare another man or two from my ranch. If we go ahead with this, I was going to ask to stop by there anyway. It would only be a short jog out of the way. I had the bodies of the Dunlap brothers and Woolsey sent back discreetly. I owe it to my poor wife to be the one to break the news to her. Two of them were her nephews, after all . . . I promise not to take long, and we might even want to grab some fresh horses while we're there."

Moosejaw once again scanned the faces turned toward him. Then, abruptly, he said, "All right. Let's do it. I've got some men in mind I want rousted up to join us. Then we'll need everybody outfitted with horses, guns, plenty of ammo, some provisions . . . Sam, you go wake Moorehouse, will you, so we can let him know what's goin' on . . ."

CHAPTER 36

It took the better part of an hour before the rest of the men were gathered and everybody was provisioned and ready. As part of this, Moosejaw faced the difficult task of having to turn down the pleas of young Jesus, who desperately wanted to come along. The big deputy finally convinced him that it was equally important that he stay with Miss Victoria and help defend the town.

Two other young men whom Moosejaw wasn't able to dissuade, however, were Sapp and Capron. He finally settled for insisting they at least take time to wolf down a couple of sandwiches and some coffee before riding out again. He enlisted the help of Kate and her hotel kitchen for this. Victoria, who was being put up for the night by Kate, also pitched in. Additionally, they put together a sack of biscuits, some fruit, and coffee beans for the group in general. From his store,

Greeble provided extra cartridges, some bedroll blankets, and a roll of clean linen for bandaging in case of a bloody engagement with the Apaches.

All this preparation roused the attention of a number of citizens apart from those directly involved. Among them was Daisy. She gave Moosejaw a kiss for luck, right in front of everybody, that caused him to blush bright crimson, but at the same time swell with pride and determination to make good on his promise to return safe to her.

And then, just as the men were ready to ride out, a delay — albeit a welcome one — was brought about by the arrival of the first of the escort wagons rolling in sooner than expected. It was the one led by Pete Roeback, and it came loaded with families and a smattering of precious personal belongings. One of the families had contributed a somewhat rickety secondary wagon to help carry the cargo.

This makeshift caravan was promptly directed to the church, where Pastor Bart was waiting to usher the women and children inside and make them as comfortable as possible while the men unloaded and distributed their personal items. Naturally the commotion of getting this done drew the attention of even more citizens, all eager to pitch in and lend a hand.

When Roeback heard about the supply train being on its way in and Moosejaw's plan to take out a force to help keep it safe, he immediately volunteered to join the venture. Once again Moosejaw had to talk somebody out of riding with him, imploring Roeback to stay and help Moorehouse and Duvall keep watch over the town. Reluctantly, the liveryman agreed.

Shortly after that exchange with Roeback, Moosejaw got his men mounted up and at last they rode off into what was left of the night.

Among those who'd been drawn out of their slumber by all the activity in the street was Henry Lofton. He pulled on his clothes and found his way from the hotel to the church. At first not understanding their purpose, he was in time to see Moosejaw and the others ride away.

By joining in to help unload and redistribute items from the wagons, it didn't take long — keeping his ears open and asking a couple of well-placed questions — for the hired gun to catch up on things. Once he came to understand that this was the escort group that should have rounded up the Widow Rockwell from within the territory it set out to cover, Lofton quit giving a damn about what the big deputy and his posse were up to and began searching for the Rockwell woman. Even though the church was noisy and crowded, he was surprised he hadn't noticed her by now.

Finally, after scouring the faces from one side of the room to the other and not spotting the one he was looking for, Lofton pulled aside one of the neighboring farmers who'd come in with the wagons and put it to him direct. "There was a widow lady out there in your neck of the woods who should have come in with this group — do you know where she is?"

"Yeah, I know where she is," came the answer. "She's too damn crazy for her own good, so she's still out there. She refused to come in with us."

"What? Why in hell would she do something like that?"

"You tell me and we'll both know, mister. Other than, like I said, she's plumb crazy. She always was an odd duck, but this takes the prize. Roeback threatened to hogtie her and drag her along by force. She waved a shotgun in his face, swore she'd use it if he tried. Kept sayin' she had a son who hadn't returned home yet and would be expectin' to find her there when he did. Said it wouldn't do for him to find her gone and be left wonderin' what became of her."

"Isn't that the lad who has now kidnapped one of the town deputies?"

"That's what I hear tell. But nobody was aware of that at the time Roeback was arguin' with the widow. She didn't know nothing about it, and none of us knew to try and tell her. Not that I expect it would've made a whole lot of difference. The threat of Apaches didn't budge her any. From what I've seen, once a crazy person gets their twisted-up brain bent in one direction, there ain't no changin' it."

The farmer drifted away, and Lofton was left standing somewhat dumbfounded. Now, what the hell should his next move be? The mental instability of Margaret Rockwell seemed pretty clear-cut. Not to mention the added complication introduced by her son and his kidnapping stunt. That made both of them loose ends that posed a danger to Lofton, because they could be traced back to him.

Any time he hired out to somebody, there was that risk — that his employer could, at some later date, name him as a paid killer. But always before, such a move meant the employer would be equally incriminating himself. But when you threw an obvious strain of craziness into the mix, that changed everything, skewed it all out of balance. And the way Lofton saw it, that was the fix he was on the brink of being sucked into. He had loose ends to worry about in the forms of Margaret Rockwell and her son, and he had unfinished business in the form of Marshal Firestick.

If not for the latter, he might decide to cut his losses and take the chance of trying to ride away from all of it. But with somebody like Firestick, he knew better. The marshal would come after him. And sooner or later, he'd catch up. That would make it merely a matter of delaying the inevitable.

No, Lofton told himself grimly, the best way was to stick around and clean it up right here. Tie off those loose ends, then take care of the unfinished business and have it done with.

"Excuse me . . . Mr. Lofton?"

He came out of his musings to discover Kate Mallory standing beside him. Next to her was an attractive, chestnut-haired woman with striking blue eyes.

"Pardon me for intruding on your thoughts and for eavesdropping a bit prior to that," said Kate, "but I couldn't help but hear you inquiring about Margaret Rockwell."

Lofton's first inclination was to deny the question, claim that the pretty hotel owner must be mistaken about what she'd thought she heard. But it was only a fleeting thought, one too easily disproven and thereby apt to draw all the more suspicion. So, instead, he said, "Yes. Yes, I was startled to hear there was someone out there who'd refused to come in with the wagons."

"Do you know Mrs. Rockwell?" asked the chestnut-haired woman.

Before Lofton could reply, Kate said, "Allow me to make some introductions. Mr. Lofton, this is Victoria Kingsley, the cook and housekeeper for the Double M horse ranch owned by Marshal McQueen and his two friends, Moosejaw and Beartooth. Victoria, this is Henry Lofton. He showed up in our town only a couple of days ago, but in the short time he's been here, he managed to play a very important role by aiding the marshal when he was ambushed yesterday right out on Trail Street."

Lofton pinched the brim of his hat, and Victoria gave an acknowledging nod as she said, "In that case, you must know that all of Buffalo Peak owes you a great debt."

"Actually," replied Lofton, "it was I who was repaying a debt. It so happened that, shortly after I arrived in town, the marshal came to my aid when some saloon rowdies had me cornered and appeared ready to give me a pretty severe beating."

"It sounds as if you've seen our town at its most inhospitable. Trust me, it's not always that way."

"I'm sure it's not. And, even if an opposite opinion had crossed my mind, standing here now in the presence of two such lovely ladies would have permanently erased any doubt."

"Very gallantly spoken," said Victoria. "Which, on the subject of ladies being present — or not, as the case may be — I still find myself curious about your relationship with Mrs. Rockwell."

"You must have heard by now," Kate interjected, addressing Lofton, "how the Widow Rockwell's son, Brody, has kidnapped Deputy Beartooth and left ransom demands in the form of a note. Victoria was the one who found the note and discovered what had taken place."

"Naturally, that raised questions — even suspicions, to be honest — as far as what the boy's mother may or may not know about his actions," explained Victoria. "That's why some of us were so anxious to see her arrive with these wagons, and why I may seem overly persistent when it comes to anything regarding her."

"I understand, of course," said Lofton, inwardly breathing a sigh of relief now that he understood the thrust of the interest from these women. "I'm afraid, however, you're going to be disappointed by what little I have to offer. You see, I only met Mrs. Rockwell very fleetingly. 'Met,' in fact, is probably even too strong a word. It was a very brief encounter."

"Yet it apparently left enough of an impression to cause you to inquire about her here tonight," Veronica pointed out, those blue eyes becoming very penetrating.

Lofton cleared his throat. "Yes. Yes, that's absolutely true, isn't it? I guess, now that I think about it, it was the circumstances under which I encountered the poor woman that caused her to stick in my mind so."

He shifted his gaze to Kate, saying, "You remember when I had tea with you and the marshal in the hotel dining room this morning and told you I'd just come from a brisk walk around the town? Well, it was during that walk that I ran into Mrs. Rockwell — out at the little cemetery on the outskirts of town. For whatever reason, I included a sweep past the cemetery as part of my walk, and she was there putting flowers on some graves. We spoke very briefly, but it was the great, deep sadness in her eyes that really stuck with me. I don't think I've ever seen anyone who looked quite so sad and lonely. Later, when the men were meeting in the saloon and making plans to send escort wagons out to bring in some of the more vulnerable families, I heard her name mentioned. I guess that's why I thought of her again here a little while ago, wondering if she'd made it in safely or not."

"Unfortunately, she didn't," said Victoria with what sounded like a trace of bitterness in her voice.

To which Kate added, "Yeah. Unfortunate as far as having any chance to learn something from her. Maybe even more unfortunate for her most of all, if the Apaches pay her farm a visit."

Once he'd made it through the inquisition from the two women, Lofton slipped outside and leaned against a shadowy corner at the rear of the church. He blocked out the drone of voices and the constant sounds of bodies shuffling and repositioning, and he pulled deep inside himself to do some hard thinking.

Loose ends. Unfinished business. He never left either one behind. Never.

With any luck — which he was damned

well due — either the marshal or the kid, one of them, might get canceled out when Firestick caught up with the kidnapper and his hostage. Most likely, Firestick would be the one to come out on top. And then, figuring the same as those nosy hens from a few minutes ago, he would be coming to find out how much the mother knew.

The mother. The widow.

That was where he could end it all, Lofton told himself. Get to the widow first and wait for the marshal to show up. Tie off the final loose end, finish his business.

Apaches don't attack at night. How many times had he heard those words in the past couple of days? So, he could make it to the Rockwell place yet tonight, before sunrise. After that, what were the odds of the Apaches, even in daylight, choosing that particular farm out of all the others left abandoned by the escort wagons, left full of easy pickings with no resistance for the raiders to face?

Lofton licked his lips. He was a gambler, and he knew how to play the odds.

And the more he thought about it, the more he liked his odds for going out to the Rockwell spread and not leaving until he made sure there were no chips left stacked against him.

Chapter 37

Due to the cold and discomfort and the writhing nest of thoughts filling his mind, Firestick had not rested well through the balance of the night. As the final trace of starlight faded and became the glow of a new day creeping up along the edge of the horizon, he quit trying. He rose from where he'd burrowed in tight to the evergreen scrim and once again stalked the domed top of the butte. He stayed in a low crouch as he moved, carrying the rifle in one hand, eyes sweeping in all directions.

Twice he paused on the flat slab of rock directly above the campsite he'd previously spotted, and peered at length over the rim. No sign of anything stirring down there yet at this early hour. No longer any hint of campfire coals or lingering scent of smoke.

At least the moving around warmed him some. He couldn't help thinking how good a cup of hot coffee would taste right about now, but then he quickly willed away such pointless conjecture. He was hours away from any such comfort. But that was all right. Before then, he intended to have Brody Rockwell under his gun, and that would be comfort enough to last a good long while.

It was as these thoughts were trickling through his mind that he noticed movement up in the Vieja foothills. He dropped quickly to his belly and wormed close to the north rim of the butte, sliding into the notch where a tall, flat-topped boulder had split apart. He brought his binoculars to his eyes. The sun wasn't up yet, so he didn't have to worry about a reflective glint.

For several seconds, the magnified view picked up nothing but barren, broken rock. Firestick lowered the binoculars and scanned again with his naked eyes. Nothing that way, either. What the hell? *Something* had been moving up there.

He raised the binoculars again. There they were!

A column of mounted Apaches, riding single file, came up out of where they'd been temporarily concealed by a shallow gully in the broken jumble of rocks. At their head rode a thick-chested, middle-aged warrior holding a Henry repeating rifle. Streaks of war paint colored the bronze skin of his cheeks beneath fiercely intent dark eyes. All the braves riding behind him also had painted faces and carried rifles. Some had bows slung over their shoulders, as well.

Firestick counted as more and more of the column poured up out of the gully. Twelve riders in all, leading five heavily laden pack ponies, angling toward the southeast, where the Mexican border reached up the closest.

The marshal did some fast reasoning, and it wasn't long before he thought he had it calculated pretty close as to what was taking place here. This wasn't all of the pack ponies, not even half. Based on the tracks Moosejaw had first investigated, he'd estimated about twelve of the twenty-five or -six ponies that originally came into the valley showed too light to be carrying riders. That meant six or seven more were still up in the mountain camp, undoubtedly being watched over by a couple of braves who'd stayed behind. These first five, loaded with bulging bundles of cowhide-wrapped beef, were being sent back early to deliver the half-cured meat to the women of the tribe so they could finish processing and storing it.

Not all of the warriors currently riding

with the pack animals would stick with them all the way to the border, Firestick knew. Only one or two would go all the way to their home village. The rest would be peeling off once they'd made sure the precious supplies were well on their way. They would then continue raiding for a wider range of supplies than just meat, and given how their faces were painted, they no longer meant to do so on the sly — they were bent on making their presence fully known and spilling plenty of white blood by way of leaving a calling card.

Firestick eased back in the notch and wiped at the binocular imprints around his eyes.

Actually seeing the Apaches painted up and on the move was a bit unnerving, but it didn't really change anything as far as the preparations he, Moosejaw, and the others had in place. Firestick had every confidence and expectation that his towering friend had his part under control. The only question was, when had the warning riders and escort wagons made it back to town, so that Moosejaw would be free to ride out with his force of men and go to the aid of the freight wagons on their way from Presidio?

If they hadn't left already or were just leaving about now, there was the chance they could cross paths with the painted column on its way down out of the mountains. But again, if it came to that, Firestick had confidence in Moosejaw being up to the challenge. From the minute he led his men out of town, he would be scouring the ground and the horizon for signs of trouble, and there was nobody sharper at spotting any hint of danger.

Apart from those riding with the pack ponies, the Apaches no doubt had one or two scouts fanned out ahead and to either side of the column's planned route. If, in fact, it looked like the two groups were on a course to intersect, they'd recognize it as soon as or sooner than Moosejaw. Then it would become a matter of whether or not the Apaches wanted to make a fight of it right then and there — or if they'd try to avoid conflict until they got the pack ponies farther on their way, and choose a later time to start staging the kind of hit-and-run attacks they were masters at.

Gritting his teeth, Firestick decided there really wasn't much question. Unless they were forced into it, the Apaches would almost certainly hold off for the chance to employ their hit-and-run tactics later. Which, if and when it came to that, would likely take a harder toll on Moosejaw's group.

Bitter as it was to contemplate, Firestick also knew that was part of the risk the townsmen had assumed when they'd agreed to ride out for the sake of saving Kruger's supply train from a possible massacre. Furthermore, the marshal reminded himself with a ragged sigh, he was in no position to do a damn thing to change any of it. The die was cast. All he could do was see to the successful completion of his own task, and then hope that maybe — *maybe* — there'd be a chance for him and Beartooth to ride like hell and perhaps be in time to give Moosejaw a hand.

These thoughts had barely crossed his mind when — almost as if summoned by them — a faint scent reached Firestick's nostrils. It took him a moment to recognize it — not because it was difficult to place, but more like because there was something inside him that fought against the timing of what it was . . . wood smoke.

That empty-headed fool of a kidnapper down at the base of the western face was starting a morning campfire!

CHAPTER 38

"I'm getting pretty doggone sick of hearing about your imaginary Indians," lamented Brody Rockwell as he fed some larger pieces of the gnarled tree branches he'd previously broken up into the hungrily licking flames. The branches crackled and gave off a twisting plume of smoke.

"If you're trying to distract me or scare me or whatever you think you're up to," he went on, scowling at Beartooth on the other side of the fire, "you ought to be able to tell by now that it ain't working. So, why don't you let up — or at least change your tune to some other line of hogwash."

"Yeah, you'd know about hogwash, wouldn't you? I'm beginnin' to think that's about all you got between your ears," Beartooth grumbled in response. "I've stayed alive for as many years as I have by never failin' to take precautions and by not bein' blind to good advice when I got it. You might want to keep that in mind."

"I might," Brody allowed. "But then, on the other hand, I'd also have to take to mind how all your precautions and whatnot didn't do you a whole lot of good when it came to me, did it?"

"Go ahead and gloat, you snot-nose," grated Beartooth. "You might think you got me in a fix right at the moment. But that don't mean I won't figure a way out — unless, that is, your stubbornness serves us on a platter to the Apaches. Then there may not be a way out for either of us."

"I told you to shut up about that. I'm tired of it," snapped Brody. "The only fix I see myself in is wakin' up cold to the bone. I aim to take care of that real quick by stokin' up this fire and boilin' a pot of coffee, so's I'll get warm on the outside and inside both. You quit ranklin' me with that Indian talk, I'll share with you. Otherwise you can dang well wait for the sun to get around to warmin' you."

Several miles to the south, at the Box T Ranch headquarters, while Gerald Tolsvord was belatedly breaking the news to his wife about the deaths of her nephews, Moosejaw was overseeing the changeover to fresh horses for his men. An additional Box T wrangler was also enlisted to join their force, making it ten in all.

As the men cinched up their saddles, topped off their canteens, and checked the action of their weapons, Moosejaw stood leaning against a corral post, gazing narrow-eyed off to the east, the direction they would soon be heading. Where the first sliver of sunlight was getting ready to poke above the horizon. Where the Jacinto Flats lay in the distance, and where they hoped to reach Kruger's supply wagons . . . before the Apaches got to them.

Margaret Rockwell opened her eyes to the stab of brilliant sunlight slicing through chinks in the shutter over the east window of her kitchen. She raised her head from where it had been resting on her arms folded atop the kitchen table, the position in which she'd fallen asleep at some point during the night. She sat up straight in her wooden chair, one of three pulled up around the table. The candle that had been burning in the middle of the table before she'd drifted off was now only a hollow ring of dried wax with a blackened curl of burnt-out wick in its center.

Margaret stifled a yawn with the back of one hand, then rocked her head from side to side, working out the stiffness in her neck, coming the rest of the way awake. And then the thoughts flooded in, reminding her what she was doing at the kitchen table, why she had fallen asleep in this manner rather than in her bed. She emitted a low groan. Amid the rush of thoughts and memories, she realized something more, became aware of things not being where they belonged — like the fourth chair at the table and the shotgun she had laid at her elbow before falling asleep.

With a sharp intake of breath, Margaret stood up and turned in a somewhat unsteady half circle as her eyes swept the interior of the small, tidy cabin. Her gaze came to rest on the man sitting in a wooden chair — the fourth missing from the table — over by the front door. The man sat with the chair turned backwards, his arms across the top of the backrest. He was smiling. Margaret's shotgun leaned against the wall beside and slightly behind him.

"You!"

"None other," drawled Henry Lofton, keeping his smile in place.

"What's the meaning of this? What right have you to barge uninvited into my home while I was sleeping? And I will have the return of my shotgun, if you please!"

Lofton wagged his head. "No, I don't please. Leastways not just yet, not until you and me get some things straightened out between us."

"The only matter that exists between us is already straight." Margaret's nostrils flared. "Or rather, it *should* be — if you were a man who lived up to his reputation and the bargains he makes."

Lofton stood up. "You let me worry about my reputation, lady. Which is exactly why I'm here."

"Your job is only half-done. You have no business being anywhere else except on the trail of that worthless Marshal McQueen. Whose life you not only have failed to take, but from what I understand, you actually went to the trouble of saving! Is that a new reputation you're working on — becoming a life*saver* instead of a life-*taker*?"

"Before I'm through here," said Lofton, taking a step toward her, "you got a real good chance of finding out firsthand how I go about doing my job. That includes taking the lives I'm hired to take, as well as those of any double-crossers or interfering fools who try to get in my way."

"You're not making any sense. The only interference you've met is from your own clumsy choices. And certainly no one is double-crossing you."

"Oh no?" sneered Lofton. "Then what do you call that cute little kidnapping stunt your son, Brody, is in the middle of right this very minute with the marshal's partner, the one they call Beartooth?"

Alarm streaked across Margaret's face. "What about Brody? What are you saying? I've been worried sick about where he is, why he didn't come home all night!"

Lofton halted in his advance on the woman. He regarded her closely. If she was putting on an act, she was doing a damned convincing job of it.

Margaret didn't wait for him. She closed the distance between them and clutched his shirtfront in her fists. "What do you know about Brody? Tell me, damn you!"

Lofton pried her off him, firmly but not too roughly. He walked her backward to the chair where she had been to begin with. "Here. Sit down. I'll tell you what I know. After that, you're gonna have to make me believe you had no part in any of it."

CHAPTER 39

Atop Buffalo Hump Butte, Firestick had positioned himself at a point on the rim where he could keep an eye on the column of Apaches off to the north and at the same time look down on the campsite he assumed to be occupied by Beartooth and his captor. Brody was likely responsible for the fire. Beartooth had never received word for certain that it was Apaches whom Cleve Boynton had spotted, but just being aware of that possibility would have caused him to play it cautious and refrain from a fire.

Either way, the hoof was now in the milk pail and the spoil was accomplished. How the two parties had been positioned to begin with, the Apaches would have passed unseen by the men at the bottom of the western face, and the way the latter were snugged down in between those splayed-out fingers of rock, their presence would never have been noticed by the raiders . . . if not for the damn campfire and the smoke it was giving off.

Since the sun was up now, Firestick had to be careful about using his binoculars so as not to give away his own presence from any reflected glare. Folding down the wide brim of his hat, making a kind of cone, he used this shadowy recess to keep the lenses unexposed yet focused on the Apaches, wanting to closely track their reaction when they inevitably saw the smoke.

He didn't have to wait long.

Spotting the gray wisps reaching up into the sky, the chief at the head of the column signaled a halt. A moment later, he motioned up the rider next in line — a younger buck bearing a strong facial resemblance, possibly a son or blood relative of some kind. The two palavered briefly. Then the chief held up four fingers before closing three and using the final extended one to point in the direction of the butte and the smoke rising from alongside it. His meaning was plain enough. Four braves were being sent to investigate the source of the smoke. Considering they were painted for war, however, that investigation was understood to mean more than just taking a look-see . . .

Firestick muttered a curse through

clenched teeth. He kept his high-powered glasses trained on the four braves as they peeled away from the others and heeled their ponies hard for the butte. He could see the eagerness on their faces, but he could also see they were going to be smart about their approach. They were keeping to the north, aiming to come in around the curvature of the butte so they'd remain unseen by those at the fire. When they were in close, they'd dismount and then begin to work in closer still on foot. Slowly, silently, they'd glide over the rocks — a couple of them likely going high, the other two staying at ground level, using the underbrush and outward-sloping base of the west face for cover, until they were practically on top of the unsuspecting pair.

Firestick swung his glasses back to the distant column. They were on the move again, the chief obviously having confidence in the braves he'd sent out to take care of the job they were assigned.

That was one slim piece of luck. It would take several minutes for the approaching braves to reach the butte and then begin working their way closer to the camp. By then, the column would have moved on quite a distance. That gave Firestick the amount of time he needed to do some maneuvering of his own. His task had suddenly multiplied. Now he not only had to rescue Beartooth, but he also had to keep him — along with himself — out of the hands of the Apaches.

Returning to the evergreen scrim where he'd left his canteen and saddle pouch, Firestick took a minute to catch his breath and drink deeply from the canteen. Discarding his binoculars, he stuffed an extra box of cartridges into each coat pocket. Then it was back to the western rim.

As he moved into position there, he found himself wishing once again he had his Hawken rifle along. The Yellowboy was a fine weapon, and its multiple-shot capability provided an edge of its own, but the added reach and punch of Ol' Thunder had advantages, too. He could stay up on the rim and, from any one of a dozen different spots, knock down two or three of the advancing braves before they even knew where he was shooting from.

The trouble with that, though, was that he'd be too far away to do Beartooth any good if even one brave made it through. Not to mention the question of how Brody Rockwell might react, realizing that somebody else shooting at the Apaches almost certainly meant that somebody was there to try and relieve him of his captive.

No, there weren't any two ways about it. In order to do the most good, Firestick had to get down there closer to the camp.

The killdeer is a medium-sized bird common to many places in North America, including the Rocky Mountains through late spring and early fall. Its orange rump, white belly, and distinctive black rings high on the chests of both males and females make them readily identifiable. This is also true of the distinctive sound they make — *"k'deer"* — from which their name was derived.

As much or more than almost any other bird, the killdeer uses sound very effectively. They call out frequently, and one of their most profound habits is to use a "distress call" as a form of defense for the nests of their young. They combine this call with a very convincing "broken wing act," in which they flop around on the ground as if they have an injured wing and cannot fly. Predators see this and follow the injured bird, getting ready to pounce. Then, when the killdeer has sufficiently distracted the would-be predator and lured it far enough away from the nest, it will suddenly "heal" itself and fly to safety.

During their time in the mountains,

Firestick, Beartooth, and Moosejaw had taken a particular interest in killdeers and were especially impressed by their cleverness. From this, they'd each developed the ability to closely mimic the call of these birds, then they'd built that into a form of communication among themselves for situations in which a spoken word might not only be inadvisable, but could prove fatal. More than once, they'd used this vocabulary of birdcalls to warn or otherwise signal each other in order to extract themselves out of close calls when they'd suddenly found Indians thick and tight on all sides.

It had been years since any of the former mountain men had used their "killdeer talk," but it was the kind of thing that, once practiced and ingrained, they never forgot or mistook for anything else. So, that morning, when Beartooth first heard *"k'deer . . . k'deer"* as he was lifting his coffee cup to his lips, he knew instantly who it was and what it meant.

"I'm close by," Firestick was informing him.

Beartooth finished taking his drink of coffee, outwardly showing no change.

Then the next call came: *"K'deer . . . k'deer . . . k'deer."*

"Danger . . . Get ready."

Setting his coffee cup on the ground

374

beside his foot, yet not looking around, Beartooth said in a low, calm voice, "Brody?"

"Whatya want?"

"You got your gun belt on?"

"You dang betcha I do."

"How about my guns — the Winchester from my saddle boot and my revolver. They close by to where you are?"

"Yeah, they're right here beside me. All you gotta do is turn around and look for yourself. Why all the questions, anyway?"

"Oh, let's just say I got a feelin' is all . . . Be sure to keep 'em close, you hear?"

CHAPTER 40

Firestick had descended to a spot less than thirty feet above the campsite. Looking down through the bare, gnarled branches that overhung the gap where Brody and Beartooth were snugged in between fingers of weather-pitted rock, he could just make out the crackling fire and the two forms on either side of it. He could also see that Beartooth was handcuffed to a saddle, a fact the marshal would have to take into consideration when deciding his next move.

The way down the western slope so far had been almost ridiculously easy. He'd followed a trough-like crease in the rocks that was well worn from frequent use by visitors seeking the least-challenging way to the top. In addition to being easy to negotiate, the trough was worn so deep for most of the way that Firestick was able to remain virtually invisible by staying crouched low within it.

Trouble was, he'd worked so hard at keeping himself undetected that, in the process, he'd lost track of two of the approaching Apaches. The pair who had stayed at ground level, he continued to catch sporadic glimpses of as they closed in, gliding smoothly, cautiously over rocks and through underbrush. The ones who'd gone up higher — possibly to a level equal with where he was now, maybe above him — were a question mark.

Having covertly signaled his chained partner, the marshal rapidly descended another dozen feet. His idea was to position himself where the overhang of gnarled branches presented an opening of some kind, through which he could drop his Colt down to Beartooth. An instant after that, he would launch himself down onto Brody and disarm the kidnapping little weasel before he could retaliate in any way. Then, together, he and Beartooth would deal with the Apaches.

It almost worked out that way.

It would have gone a hell of a lot smoother if, only ten seconds before Firestick was ready to put his plan into action, an Apache brave hadn't raised up about twenty yards from where the marshal was still half-crouched in the trough. The Apache had a

Winchester braced against one shoulder and was aiming down through the overhanging branches, drawing a bead on Beartooth.

Firestick reacted without hesitation. He adjusted his grip on the .44 he'd been holding loosely, getting ready to toss it down, then swung the muzzle to center it on the rifle-wielding Apache and triggered a round through the brave's rib cage. The Indian spasmed and jerked the rifle's trigger before he pitched away and went toppling limply down off his perch. The weapon's sharp *crack!* filled the air.

Firestick wasted no time changing his grip on the Colt as he rose up in the trough, extended his arm, and shouted, "Beartooth! Pistol comin' down!" even as he released the gun.

He didn't wait to check the accuracy of his toss. He couldn't afford to. Twisting his body as he lunged the rest of the way up out of the trough, gripping the Yellowboy in his left hand, he threw himself forward and down and went crashing heavily through branches and bramble and into the campsite below on the side opposite Beartooth. A startled, slowly reacting Brody Rockwell partly broke his fall, but he nevertheless hit the ground with a jolt that knocked much of the wind out of him.

The crack of more rifle reports and the whistle-slap of slugs tearing through the brush and whining off rock forced him to keep in motion and work past the jarring effects of his hard landing. He scrambled to his feet, pushing off the battered shape of Brody, who'd been driven to his hands and knees, arms trembling as he, too, tried to push himself up. Firestick spared him further effort by slapping the flat of his rifle butt against the side of the lad's head, knocking him out cold.

More bullets sizzled into the campsite. Firestick dropped to his belly and wormed in behind Brody's saddle. As he was doing this, he heard closer gunfire — a double report from his own pistol sounding on the other side of the fire. Mixed with the two shots was the metallic ring of a chain being blasted apart. An instant later, Beartooth came clambering over the saddle and dropped in beside him. He was fisting Firestick's .44, and a broken chain was dangling from the handcuff clamped to his right wrist.

"Mornin'," Firestick drawled. "I see you got the gift I sent you."

"Yeah. Not to sound ungrateful, but it's only got three pills left in it. Don't know exactly what this little set-to is about, but

I'm thinkin' I could use a little more fire-power."

Firestick jabbed a thumb over his shoulder. "Right behind me I saw your own gear — gun belt and rifle — when I dropped in. Help yourself. Then you can give me my gun back."

Beartooth shifted backward, reached over, and retrieved his weapons. Moving up beside Firestick again, buckling on his sidearm and checking the action of his rifle, he said, "What's the story on the kid? You didn't kill him, did you?"

"Not yet. Just put him to sleep for a while is all."

The incoming rounds had stopped pouring in. The only sound was the snap of the twigs in the fire.

"Okay. What about the rest of this, then?" asked Beartooth. "Apaches?"

"You guessed it."

"Wasn't hard. Boynton had me pretty well convinced right from the get-go, and I've had an itch between my shoulder blades ever since. Especially with that damn kid paradin' me around out in the open and stokin' up campfires every chance he got." Having plucked cartridges from Firestick's shell belt and used them to replace the spent rounds in the "borrowed" Colt,

Beartooth handed the .44 back to him, adding, "How many we talkin' about?"

"A dozen or so in all. Four — well, three now — in this particular bunch that was takin' an interest in you and your young friend."

"They've stopped shootin'. You reckon that means they're gonna give up and go away to pout now that you showed up and crashed the party?"

Firestick made a sour face as he holstered his Colt. "You ever know an Apache to give up that easy? Especially after I beat one of 'em at his own game of sneak and shoot and blew him clean out of his moccasins?"

"Be nice to think. But, no," said Beartooth, "I don't reckon they'll make it that easy. Besides these three, what about the rest of the dozen? What are they up to?"

"Unless I miss my guess, or unless they got lookouts scoutin' for 'em who ain't very good at their jobs, I'm thinkin' they're headed to introduce themselves to some supply wagons on the way in from Presidio."

Beartooth scowled. "And you're wastin' your time pullin' my fat out of the fire here?"

"Pullin' your fat out of the fire is sort of a bad habit of mine," Firestick said dryly.

"Aw, come on," Beartooth protested. "This little spot of trouble with a wet-behind-the-ears kid? You should've known I had a plan. Matter of fact, in another couple minutes, I'd've been out of this fix, slick as could be."

"Well, hell. Too bad I *didn't* know. I could have saved myself a cold, uncomfortable damn night up on top of this rock."

"So, I hope you're at least gonna tell me that Moosejaw or somebody is on the way to protect those wagons."

"Consider yourself told. We finish cleanin' up this swarm of mosquitoes here, I thought maybe me and you could mosey along and give him a hand."

Beartooth grunted. "Now, I see. The real reason you came after me was so's you could drag me along to help you two pull a bigger ball of fat out of a bigger fire."

"You're kinda hung up on fat," said Firestick, raising his head cautiously and taking a quick scan, high and low, out ahead of them. "But if we don't quit lyin' here just chewin' it, those Apaches are gonna find a way to slip up and have our scalps for breakfast."

"Don't think I'd care much for that. You got some kind of idea?"

"Well, seein's how a couple of 'em are comin' in down low, this ain't an especially bad spot. One of us could edge back a little deeper in this notch, pull both of these saddles up in front of him, fort-like, and wait for them to make a move. They gotta show themselves to get in. When they do, be a good position from which to greet 'em with some lead . . . The only problem that'd leave is the brave workin' his way in somewhere up higher. He reaches a position to shoot down on this spot, like that other rascal was fixin' to do, it would be bad news."

"So, one of us needs to scoot out of here and deal with him on higher ground."

"You volunteerin'?"

"Reckon you've done your share of crawlin' around on this ol' rock already. Besides, I got a hankerin' to stretch my legs some. Cover me while I clear out of here?"

"What do you think? I didn't go to all the trouble of savin' you from this pipsqueak just to turn you over to an Apache carvin' knife."

"Now, don't start in with that again, damn it. I told you how I was stringin' that kid along and how any minute I was ready to —"

"Never mind that right now," Firestick cut him off. "Just get a move on!"

Turning away from Beartooth, the marshal drew his Colt, raised up suddenly, and fanned off half a dozen rounds, randomly spraying a wide sweep of rocks and brush in the near distance, emptying the cylinder before dropping back down. Return fire immediately slashed the air above his head. Looking around as his hands automatically began reloading the Colt, he saw no sign of Beartooth. He bared his teeth in a humorless smile.

Moving with catlike grace and speed, Beartooth scrambled up inside the deep trough for a ways, then abruptly pulled himself out and bellied in behind a low spine of jagged rock running along one edge of the depression. Bullets had skimmed below his heels as he sprang out of the campsite, but he couldn't be sure if they'd been aimed at him or if they were just part of a wild volley in response to Firestick's cover fire. Either way, they hadn't scored a hit, and he felt confident he was secure for the moment. With luck, they hadn't seen his departure at all — or at least hadn't seen him skin out of the crease to take up this current position.

Now he had to make it count for something. Keep on the move; stay undetected. Until he spotted and gained an advantage over the Apache who was somewhere up in these high rocks with him.

Beartooth's mouth curved in a cold, wolfish smile, not unlike the one Firestick had displayed down below.

Up in the high reaches again. Playing a deadly game of cat and mouse with Indians out for blood. Just like the old days . . . Damned if it didn't feel pretty good!

CHAPTER 41

In the campsite, Firestick quickly dragged the two saddles — the one he'd originally ducked behind, plus the one Beartooth had been chained to — in closer around him. He piled them together to form a short but solid barricade, then dragged the limp body of the still-unconscious Brody behind it with him. As an afterthought, he kicked out with his foot, toeing dirt onto the fire, smothering most of it and creating a temporary smoke screen of sorts.

Then he waited, eyes constantly moving, ears on high alert for the faintest hint of any sound that didn't belong. A couple of times, he swept his eyes upward along the butte face over his head. Not surprisingly, he saw no sign of Beartooth or the third Indian. But that gave him no particular cause for concern — he had full confidence in his old friend being able to hold his own.

Generally speaking, Apaches were notorious for their patience. In this instance, though, Firestick had a hunch it wasn't going to come down to that. For one thing, the four braves who'd peeled off from the rest of the column had all looked young and eager. Warriors hungry to spill the white man's blood and likely getting their first chance to do so. He was counting on such an attitude to crowd their patience.

Plus he had quickly and easily cut down one of their number. That would sting their pride, make them angry — and anger was always a hard counterpoint to patience. What was more, knowing that the warriors in the column they'd left behind were on their way to stage more and possibly bigger raids would make the temptation to rejoin them for greater glory an even stronger draw to the young bucks. All the more reason for them to want to get this business with a mere two or three White Eyes over with as soon as possible.

Getting this over with quickly rated pretty high for Firestick, too, and he had little doubt Beartooth felt any different.

Toward that end, the two Apaches maneuvering at ground level suddenly took a stab at testing Firestick's defense, and at the same time trying for some quick results. Out near the ends of the splayed fingers of rock, they burst simultaneously up from the brush and loose rubble, about a dozen feet apart from one another, and poured a rapid-fire barrage of lead in on him. While one of them kept firing, the second one broke into a run, yipping shrilly, and advanced several lunging steps closer, before darting again to cover in the face of the marshal's return fire.

It was an exercise meant to startle and unnerve as much as anything, and against someone less savvy in the ways of Indian fighting than their target on this occasion, it might have succeeded to some degree.

For Firestick, it only served to prove that his saddle barricade did an effective job of turning aside bullets, and that his guess about the young braves being a mite over-anxious appeared to be on the money.

As the marshal replaced spent shells in his rifle, Brody Rockwell stirred on the ground beside him. Placing a hand to one side of his head, the kid emitted a series of groans, each one progressively louder.

When he tried to sit up, Firestick told him, "Best lie still and be quiet, bub. You don't, either I'll give you another rap on the head or one of those Apaches out there will do worse by plantin' a bullet in it."

"Ain't you ever gonna lay off the dang

Apaches? How many times I gotta tell you that —" Raised on one elbow, squinting fiercely at the marshal, the kid abruptly stopped in mid-sentence. He squinted even harder, as if he couldn't see clearly or as if what he was seeing he couldn't believe. "Wait a minute! You ain't . . . Who in blazes are you?"

"Look a little closer. I didn't hit you that hard."

"Marshal Firestick!" Brody blurted. "What are you doing here?"

"It didn't occur to you when you kidnapped one of my deputies that I might take an interest?"

"But I never . . ." Brody looked around, his bewilderment only increasing. "Where's Mr. Beartooth?"

"Don't worry, he ain't far. He's workin' on keepin' some of those Injuns off our back."

"You mean there really *are* Indians?"

Firestick jabbed a finger, pointing. "The bullet holes in these saddlebags didn't get there by themselves."

"My God . . . I didn't think . . ."

"No, you *didn't* think, you squirrel-brained little jackass," growled Firestick. "If you had, none of us would be in this fix. Leastways not this particular one."

A moment later, as if to emphasize exactly what *this fix* was, the Apaches cut loose with another tactic. Once again, they rose up in unison and began pouring rapid-fire shots at the pair hunkered deep in the notch. At the height of this, the one farthest out broke away from the rubble he'd been shooting from behind and attempted to race across the opening between the fingers of rock, seeking to gain fresh cover on the other side.

"Oh, no, you don't, you son of a bitch!" roared Firestick, leaning forward across the saddle barricade and triggering his Yellowboy as fast as he could lever in fresh rounds.

Bullets singed the air all about the running Apache. A couple kicked up geysers of dust in front of him. Finally, a slug caught a piece of his pumping forearm and spun him partially around. Halted, then turned back the way he'd started from, the Apache flung himself headlong into a diving roll and regained cover amid the rubble he'd first sprung out of. He did this with more bullets pursuing him, whining and punching into the rocks. Yet none, miraculously, scored another hit.

Once the runner had been halted and turned back, the Apache providing cover fire stopped shooting and dropped from sight. A sudden silence gripped the scene, the only movement coming from the layers of powder smoke curling lazily in the air.

Firestick dropped low behind the saddle barricade once more and began reloading the Yellowboy. As he did this, his gaze came to rest on young Brody, who lay on his belly, one arm extended around the end of the saddles, gripping a Colt in his fist. A faint wisp of smoke rose up from the gun's muzzle, and it suddenly hit the marshal — although, peripherally, he'd had a vague awareness while it was happening — that the kid hadn't hesitated to join the fight against the Apaches.

"Jesus!" Brody said now, his face still so close to the ground that the breath expelled by the exclamation caused some dust to puff up. "That happened so fast! I . . . I . . ."

"You acted like a man and helped turn the attack," Firestick finished for him. "Had that brave made it to the other side and gotten into those rocks over there, he'd've been in position to work around on that side — while the other one did the same from where he's at — and they'd've closed on us like pincers. That would have put us in a lot sorrier shape."

Brody continued to seem a little stunned, either from the sudden burst of gunplay or perhaps still from the wallop to the head.

Maybe a little of both. He said, "Will they be back? Will they try something more?"

"You can bet on it."

"But the one who was running — it looked like he got hit."

"One of us got a piece of his arm, yeah. But not enough to finish him." Firestick grimaced. "You could put bullets in both legs and one arm of an Apache, and he'd use the one good arm he had left to drag himself over the ground to keep comin' after you."

Brody swallowed. "You say that almost as if . . . well, as if you *like* Apaches."

"Don't kid yourself. Admire 'em in some ways. Respect 'em, I reckon you could say. But like 'em? Not hardly." Firestick shrugged. "Mainly, I know 'em as enemies. And that means knowin' never to sell 'em short."

"I hope I'll never need to, not after this. But I'll be sure to remember what you said."

"Uh-huh. Well then, while you're digestin' that, let me give you a couple more pieces of advice you can chew on."

"Such as?"

"Number one, after you're done usin' your gun, always be sure to reload right away." Firestick gestured toward the Colt still in Brody's fist. "We've been palaverin' for a couple minutes now, and you ain't done a lick toward replacin' the spent shells in that thing. Do you even know how many rounds you fired, how many live ones you got left?"

Brody cut his eyes down to his gun. "No, I guess I don't."

"Well, in this particular case it don't really matter."

"Why not? Why'd you bother telling me then, if —"

Suddenly Firestick's .44 was in his fist, and it was aimed at Brody. "It don't matter," he said, "on account of I'll be relievin' you of that hogleg. Hand it over."

Without waiting, Firestick reached out and plucked the Colt from Brody's hand. He shoved it into his waistband, all the while keeping his own Colt trained steady on the young man. "Don't know how long it'll be before you're free to ever carry a gun again," he said, "but what I told you will still have worth if and when the time comes. In the meantime, here's another piece of advice: You're under arrest, so don't get no dumb ideas."

Forty feet above the campsite, Beartooth crouched motionless. Only his eyes moved.

From this vantage point, he'd seen the attempt by the Apaches down below to try and gain an advantage over Firestick by splitting apart to form a two-pronged threat on his position. He hadn't been able to see Firestick during the exchange that ensued, but that didn't matter, as long as the marshal was able to lay down enough firepower to turn back the Indian runner.

It had been mighty close, though, and it had been difficult for Beartooth to restrain himself from joining in when it looked like the brave had stood a chance of making it across. The only thing that held Beartooth back was knowing that if he opened up, it would expose him to the third Apache up in the higher rocks. Had that exposure resulted in him being picked off, not only would it have been bad for him, but it would have left Firestick in perhaps even greater jeopardy.

Thankfully, none of that transpired.

So the situation wasn't any worse, but neither was it any better. Except for the evidence of one thing: Wherever the third brave was, he wasn't in a position to have a clear view of Firestick. Not yet. If he was, the exchange that had just taken place would have given him the perfect chance to try for a shot. If he knew Beartooth was up in the higher elevations with him, which was uncertain, he would have faced the same issue of revealing himself. But if Firestick had been a clear target for him, Beartooth felt confident the brave would have taken the risk. That was the Apache way.

What it was going to come down to, then, was that sooner or later one of the men higher up on the butte face was going to make the mistake of exposing his position. And when he did, the other was going to be ready to make him pay.

CHAPTER 42

"Even though I helped fight off those
Indians, you're still gonna take away my gun
and put me under arrest?" Brody Rockwell
sounded surprised and genuinely hurt.

"You pitched in against those Apaches
because you were thinkin' of your own
hide," said Firestick. "Don't mean I ain't
grateful for the help, though. But it also
don't mean I'm willin' to forget you're a
kidnapper who, up until a few minutes ago,
had one of my best friends in chains."

"So, does that mean you're gonna chain
me now?" Brody asked, his eyes darting to
the cuffs hanging on Firestick's belt.

"Not necessarily. Long as you're gun-
stripped and I can keep you in plain sight, I
don't reckon I have to be in a big hurry
about it," Firestick told him. "But if you try
something stupid, I won't hesitate to change
my mind. No matter how squirrel-brained
you are, I gotta think you're smarter than to

risk bein' on your own against those cherry-cows."

"You ain't wrong about that. I should have paid more attention to Mr. Beartooth all along."

"What you should have done most of all was not turn into a damn kidnapper," Firestick growled. "What the hell's wrong with you, anyway?"

Brody averted his eyes. "You don't know the whole story. I . . . I had my reasons."

"What about Gus Wingate? You know anything about who had reason for gunnin' him down in cold blood?"

Now the kid's eyes lifted and went wide above a sagging mouth. "What? What are you saying?"

"Don't know how to tell it any plainer. Surely you know who Wingate is, right? Your neighbor, the fella who shot and killed your brother a couple months back . . . Well, some time yesterday afternoon, somebody returned the favor by plantin' a slug right in the middle of his forehead." Firestick was being purposely blunt and harsh in order to try and jolt the most honest reaction he could get out of Brody. From what he was seeing so far, the news was exactly that — a jarring surprise to the boy.

"Mr. Wingate . . . Good Lord. Who'd want

to do a thing like that?"

"You tell me and we'll both know. He wasn't robbed, none of his cattle were stolen, and it wasn't Apaches." Firestick's gaze bored harder into Brody. "Kinda narrows it down to somebody with reason to dislike the man. Maybe even downright hate him. The way you might hate a fella who did serious harm to kin of yours, like a son or a brother, for instance."

Brody's eyes bugged wider still. "You can't mean me! I'd never do something like that. I never held a grudge against Wingate. I knew better than anybody how my brother could get under a body's skin, so I believed you — my brother kept pestering him until Wingate had no choice but to draw against him out of self-defense."

"Come on, Brody," Firestick said through clenched teeth. "It sure as hell is no secret that your mother had a grudge against Wingate. She hated his guts every minute of every day. You expect me to believe you lived in that house with her and none of that hate for your brother's killer ever rubbed off on you? Next you'll be tryin' to get me to believe she's truly in the dark about this whole kidnappin' stunt of yours, too."

"She is!" Brody insisted. "She knows nothing about this. Just like I know nothing about what happened to poor Mr. Wingate."

"Well, hell then. Maybe there's the answer to all of it." Firestick made a gesture with one hand. "While you was out learnin' the kidnapper trade, maybe your ma's hatred for Wingate pushed her to the point that she decided to take matters in her own hands, so she hauled off and went into the killin' business."

"That's crazy talk! You can't possibly believe what you're saying." The boy's shrill voice cut through the air like a knife.

And then, an instant later, something else cut through the air — a flaming arrow! The missile came in a shallow arc, originating from the outlying pile of broken rocks behind which the wounded Apache runner had ducked only minutes earlier. It didn't reach the saddle barricade or the White Eyes behind it. It wasn't intended to. Instead, it fell about six yards short, and the fiery tip sank into a tangle of dried brush growing along one side of the notch. The bristly kindling burst instantly into flames.

A moment later, a second arrow arced in and sank into a similar tangle of brush on the opposite side of the notch. Once more a hungrily licking fire blossomed and began to spread.

"They're trying to burn us out!" hollered Brody.

"Tryin' and doin' is two different things," Firestick shouted back as he rose up behind the saddles like he'd done before, slamming the Yellowboy to his shoulder.

"Give me my gun," pleaded Brody.

"No. You concentrate on that fire burnin' closest on your side. Start flingin' dirt on it!"

The dry, flaming brush was crackling and hissing now, like the gnashing of sizzling teeth. Smoke began pouring up and swirling.

Firestick saw what the plan was. Obscured by the smoke and flames, one of the Apaches was going to make another attempt to race to the other side of the gap out near the ends of the splayed rock fingers. After that, even if the White Eyes managed to beat back the flames, it would be just a matter of time before they found themselves trapped instead by a crossfire of lead and arrows.

But a sword could cut two ways, Firestick reminded himself. If the boiling smoke blotted the Apaches from his sight, then that meant he was also blocked from theirs. As long as he stayed behind the saddles, that was.

"Keep flingin' that dirt, boy!" he ordered

as he lunged to his feet and sprang forward over the saddles.

"What?" gasped Brody. "Where are you . . ." But he was talking to nothing. Firestick had disappeared between the walls of flame and into the swirling smoke.

Overhead, the first billowing clouds had nearly reached Beartooth. He, too, recognized what the Apaches were up to, and this time he was poised to do whatever was necessary to prevent it. He couldn't do anything from where he was to help fight the fire, but he could, by damn, do something to ruin the plan of using its diversion to corner his pal in a box there'd be no way out of.

Emerging on the other side of the smoke wall, Firestick saw that he was just in time to stop the rest of what the Apaches had in mind. For this second attempt, it was the nearer of the pair who was making the run for the other side of the gap. If Firestick wasn't mistaken, this also looked like the young warrior who'd been summoned by the chief of the column and sent to lead this undertaking. Not that it made any real difference, but if it *was* the same brave, and if the facial resemblance between him and the chief whom Firestick had noted through his binoculars meant kinship, then the marshal couldn't help but find some added satisfaction in this particular confrontation.

Firing from the hip, levering and triggering the Yellowboy as he ran, Firestick's bullets hammered solidly into the running Apache. He stopped short, his body jerking from the impact of each slug. His left foot kicked in an awkward, pawing step as he turned a quarter of the way around, before being knocked away and down, dropping heavily to the ground.

Firestick halted his own forward rush and dropped to one knee. Bringing the rifle to his shoulder, he swung its muzzle quickly toward the pile of rubble farther out, bringing it to bear on the approximate spot where he'd seen the other Apache rise up and shoot the first of the fire arrows. Luck remained with him. The target he was seeking was still there, in plain sight, risen again to full height, now with a rifle once more in his grasp rather than a bow. But one of the hands gripping the rifle was doing so awkwardly, crimson tracks spiderwebbing down over the wrist from the earlier wound to that arm. This damage, and the brave's apparent stunned surprise at seeing Firestick burst out of the smoke like he had, combined to make his reaction shaky and slow. Fatally slow.

Firestick fired a single shot that sent a bullet punching through the brave's throat. The rifle the man was trying to raise slipped from his dead grasp, and he crumpled to the ground on top of it.

With the two Apaches down, Firestick's thoughts jumped immediately back to the fire. He shoved to his feet and wheeled about.

That move, that sudden turn, very likely saved his life. In the midst of it, as he came around, he heard the wind-rip of a bullet passing less than an inch from his head — right where the *middle* of his head had been a split second before. A moment later came the *boom* of a rifle report.

Firestick's eyes cut upward to the butte face just as a second rifle spoke. Watching, the marshal saw an Apache spasm within a shallow rock seam where the bullet from the latest shot found him. In seeming slow motion, the Henry repeater the brave had been holding slipped from his grasp, and then he tipped rigidly forward, falling out of the seam and turning end over end through the air, until he smashed with a sickening sound onto the jagged rocks below.

Swinging his gaze sharply to a different

spot in the higher rocks, Firestick could see Beartooth leaning out from another weather-scooped depression, beginning to lower the Winchester he'd been pointing at the fallen Apache. A haze of smoke from below was drifting up over him. But when he turned his head and grinned down at Firestick, the grin shone through clear and bright.

CHAPTER 43

"I'd have nailed that red devil sooner if I wasn't distracted by those other two tryin' to close the gap on you," Beartooth was explaining. "Then, when you took the crazy notion to bust through the smoke and charge out into full view of everybody, that tipped things a whole different way. I never got a glimpse of that higher-up varmint until then, when he leaned out to take a potshot at you."

Firestick rubbed the back of his neck. "Yeah, and a mighty close potshot it was. Wasn't sorry to see you stop him permanent-like from makin' another try."

"All I heard was a bunch of shooting. But with the fire and all the smoke, I couldn't tell who was doing what," lamented Brody Rockwell.

"That's okay, kid, you did your part," Beartooth told him. "You saved our saddles and kept the fire from spreadin' a lot worse

405

than it would have otherwise."

It had taken all three of them to put the fire out completely, but it was true that Brody had held the flames largely at bay until Beartooth and Firestick were able to join in and help smother them. In addition to that, the combination of the fire and the shooting was enough to spook the horses Beartooth and Brody had ridden in on, causing them to pull their picket pins and require some chasing and coaxing before they could be rounded up again. The trio had only just completed that chore and were still catching their collective breath from it.

"When we put those saddles to use now that we've recaptured these cayuses of yours," Firestick said with a weary sigh, "I've got some gear up top to reclaim, and then we'll have to go around to the other side where I left my horse."

"You should have told me you had some stuff up there when I was already partway up," Beartooth replied.

"In case you forgot, I was a little busy concentratin' on other things."

Brody said, "If you two old — er, I mean, since it's understandable if you fellas have had your fill of climbing up and down this ol' butte, I could go up and fetch whatever's up there. I could bring it down on the other side, where Marshal Firestick's horse is."

"You hear that, Firestick — we got us a volunteer," said Beartooth.

"I heard him," Firestick grunted. "But there's just one little problem."

"What's that?"

"He was a prisoner before he was a volunteer. I don't make it a policy," explained the marshal, "to send my prisoners on convenient little errands on which they might have the chance to skedaddle away."

"Aw, come on," protested Brody. "Where would I skedaddle to? I wouldn't even have a horse."

"He's got a point," said Beartooth.

"So do I," argued Firestick. He scowled fiercely at his old friend. "Jesus Christ, you of all people ought to understand. Are you forgettin' he kidnapped you? That he's been wavin' a gun under your nose and had you in handcuffs until just a little while ago?"

Beartooth absently rubbed the raw skin around his wrist where the cuff had been clamped before being unlocked and removed after the fire was put out. "No, I ain't likely to forget that," he muttered. "Still, I don't think he's a bad kid. Not really. He maybe got a little mixed up in his thinkin', but —"

"Look out!" Brody suddenly exclaimed.

The three of them were standing once again near the inner point of the scorched, smoky notch, having returned there to get the saddles and other gear after catching up with the spooked horses. The way they were positioned while talking had Firestick and Beartooth with their backs to the butte while Brody was facing them, his back to the sprawled dead bodies of the two Apaches out in the wider gap. It was this positioning that allowed Brody to see what neither of the two former mountain men could — the bruised, scraped, bloody Apache rising up out of some broken boulders several yards to one side of the smoldering notch. His battered face was twisted with a savage grimace, and in his hands he was somewhat shakily lifting a Winchester rifle.

As he emitted his warning shout, Brody's hand streaked out and grabbed from Firestick's waistband the Colt the marshal had stuck there earlier after confiscating it from the lad. Gripping the heavy weapon securely, Brody swung it clear of Firestick and then leaned forward, extending his gun hand in a thrusting motion. The Colt roared, spewing flame and lead. The Apache who had appeared so ghostlike proved to be very much a flesh-and-blood apparition as the bullet slammed him backward, exiting from between his shoulder blades in a spray of gore and gristle that painted the rocks behind him.

Firestick and Beartooth wheeled around, simultaneously drawing their own guns, to see what Brody was shooting at. A moment later, all three were scrambling over broken boulders to reach the body for further examination.

"He must be the sniper you shot off the ledge," Firestick said to Beartooth after they were standing over the crumpled form. "Looks like neither your bullet nor the fall were enough to finish him off."

"I don't think so," countered Beartooth. "For one thing, the varmint I shot had on a blue shirt. Plus, I hit him up in the side of the neck. This one's wearin' a yellow shirt, or leastways it was before it got dyed blood-red. And he's been hit most recent in the chest by Brody, but before that in the rib area."

Firestick gave a low whistle. "I'll be damned. This is the one I shot just before I tossed you my gun and flung myself into the camp. I shot him through the ribs, and he wouldn't have had as far to fall."

"You mean he's been crawling around down here in these rocks all this time?"

asked Brody.

"Looks like," allowed Firestick. "Probably knocked him out for a while. Then, when he came around, he must've known he was dyin' but wanted one more chance to try and still take some White Eyes with him." He regarded Brody. "Remember how I told you an Apache would drag himself along on a bloody stump to keep comin' after something or somebody he wanted to kill? Well, there's your proof."

Beartooth said, "And this one might very well have scored one more kill before he departed for the Happy Huntin' Ground, too . . . if not for the sharp eye and quick actions of Brody."

"Reckon he might have at that," agreed Firestick. Then, feeling the eyes of both Beartooth and Brody boring into him, he set his jaw firmly and returned their looks. "But that don't change nothing, if that's what you two are givin' me the stink eye about. One good deed don't automatically wipe the slate clean of everything that came before."

"I count more than one deed," said Beartooth. "The kid fought his ass off to hold back that fire. And, before that, he helped you drive back those two Apaches out yonder the first time they tried to bridge that gap."

"Both times he was lookin' out for his own hide. Ain't nothing special about that."

"What about this time?" Beartooth insisted. "He likely saved one of us — not him — a bullet in the back. If he was the no-good you figure him to be, he could have just jumped out of the way and said nothing, allowed that Apache a clean shot. Instead, he jumped in the thick of it."

Ignoring his friend, Firestick held out his hand to Brody, saying, "I'll have that hogleg back again, kid."

Brody, who was still holding his Colt even though Firestick and Beartooth had holstered theirs, hesitated. "What if I decide to give it to you business end first?" he said. "Since you got your mind so all-fired made up that's the way I am, what have I got to lose?"

"That's no good, Brody. That's not the way," Beartooth was quick to tell him. "You try that, you'll have me against you, too. But if you show some sense, there's only so much anybody can do if I refuse to press charges against you."

"Don't do his thinkin' for him. Let's see what kind of decisions he makes on his own," said Firestick. "Besides, there's things you don't know about yet, Beartooth. Like the cold-blooded murder of Gus Wingate, for instance. We've just seen a good example of how quick mild-mannered young Brody can be with a gun — don't it make you wonder, at least a little bit, if Wingate might have got a private showing ahead of us?"

"That's not true!" Brody protested. "I already told you. I never went near Mr. Wingate!"

Firestick said, "That'd probably be more convincin' if you wasn't pokin' a gun in my face while sayin' it."

Several tense clock ticks went by. Brody's nostrils flared, and his breath came in rapid, short gusts. Then, abruptly, his shoulders sagged and so did the gun muzzle. "Go ahead, take it," he said in a low voice. "I could never use it on the likes of you."

Now it was Firestick who hesitated. The hand he'd been holding out to take the gun lowered and came to rest at his side. "On second thought," he said, "you keep it."

Brody's eyes widened. Hopeful, but confused.

Before he could say anything, Firestick continued, "There are still Apaches in this valley. We have reason to believe their main force is headed to intercept a train of freight wagons comin' in from the east. We have friends on the way to try and prevent that, but they could always use more guns to help get the job done. I figure we've already lost enough time with this speck of business here. If we're gonna do our friends any good, we'd best not lose any more."

"Hold on a minute," said Beartooth, frowning. "You really think it's a good idea to drag this young fella into something like that?"

"Will you make up your damn mind?" Firestick growled. "You ready to put some trust in him or not?"

"It ain't a matter of trust. It's a matter of how fair it'd be to expect that much out of him."

"I got no problem with pitching in," said Brody. "I *want* to help out. I want the chance to prove myself some more, so I can . . . well, maybe not wipe that slate all the way clean, but at least rub off part of the dirt."

"Here's the thing for both of you to understand," Firestick said. "We get that wagon train through and those cherry-cows run off, we'll be takin' this up again. It ain't over. I ain't sayin' Brody's free to go; I ain't condemnin' him. Under different circumstances I'd throw him in the clink until I had a chance to sort things out. But I can't afford the time to haul him back to town to lock him up, and I ain't about to turn him loose and then have to hunt him down again. So he goes with us, where I can keep an eye on him and maybe get some good out of him in the process. Clear?"

Beartooth and Brody both nodded, said nothing.

"All right, then. Get saddled up. I'll reclaim my stuff off the top and meet you on the other side, where I left my horse."

Firestick started up the face of the butte but stopped after a few feet. Looking back over his shoulder, he said, "Kid."

Brody looked up. "Sir?"

Firestick pointed. "I warned you once about checking the loads in your gun after you use it. Don't forget. We get in the thick of some more Apaches, you're gonna want to make sure you got a full wheel."

CHAPTER 44

Saetta felt more uneasy than he should have.

After all, by any measure, the morning was going well. The first group of the pack ponies, heavily laden with life-sustaining meat wrapped in useful hides, was safely on its way to the border, and then on to the mountain village of his people. And now, just recently, two of his outlying scouts had brought news of several freight wagons they'd sighted heading into the valley from the east. Though the exact contents of these wagons could not be certain, if it was any kind of standard haul, it would be precious cargo, indeed. A wide variety and plentiful quantities of all the goods it might take the looting of a dozen or more ranch houses to yield. All in one place, all accessible to a single bold strike.

It was almost too good to be true. Even the happenstance of the scouts venturing in that direction, away from the rich grassland

415

where the big cattle herds and larger ranch headquarters were to be found, seemed a fateful stroke of luck. They'd done so after their curiosity was roused by spotting a group of men headed that way, into barren flatland, for no apparent reason. After following at a distance, they had then seen the men linking up with the wagon train.

Was it this very thing, Saetta wondered, that was bothering him? The fact that too much good fortune seemed to be coming too easily?

Of course, the wagons would be well guarded, especially now that they had been joined by the added men — most likely for that very reason. So there would be a cost to taking them. That part would not be easy. But no Apache was ever unprepared or unwilling to pay that kind of price.

What was truly bothering Saetta, as he knew and grudgingly admitted down deep, came from the fact that Taluma had not yet returned after being dispatched to investigate the smoke seen back at Buffalo Hump Butte. If whatever he'd encountered there had gone well, he should have been back by now. The fact that he wasn't . . .

The uncle in Saetta wanted to send some braves back to find out what had befallen his nephew and the others. But the chief in him knew this was neither wise nor what was best for the good of the overall mission. If they were going to attack the wagons, he had no men to spare, especially considering the report he'd been given about the reinforcements just added.

The Apaches' lot had long been to fight superior odds. Including the scouts who had reported in, Saetta now had nine warriors. Against nearly twice that many, if the scouts' count was accurate. Saetta was willing to risk those odds, but no worse. To hold off or to turn away altogether from such a rich potential prize would cause him to lose face in the eyes of his warriors. They would know he was being overly cautious because of his nephew.

Saetta could feel the eyes of his warriors on him now, as he struggled with his uneasiness. *A chief must be strong and decisive,* he told himself. Then, looking to the north, where the upthrust of Buffalo Hump Butte had long since faded from view behind them, he added, *And a young brave must rise or fall on the merits of his fate and his own skills.*

Turning back to his warriors, meeting their eyes with flinty resolve in his own, Saetta raised his rifle and thrust it suddenly toward the east, toward the barren flats and the unseen wagons he knew to be rolling across them.

Kate Mallory and Victoria Kingsley sat over cups of tea at a table in the hotel dining room. The clock on the flower-patterned wall had just chimed ten times. Outside, sun-washed Trail Street showed a moderate amount of activity, but nothing like a typical mid-morning in Buffalo Peak. Earlier, the dining room had seen a handful of breakfast customers, but now the women had it to themselves.

"This is delicious tea," Victoria was saying. "I hope you didn't go to unnecessary trouble just for me."

"It surely was no trouble. We commonly serve tea here. I myself often have some, because, as you noted, our cook, Marilu, does such an excellent job of brewing it." Kate smiled. "I must admit, though, that because you're English, I made the assumption, without really asking, that it would be your preference."

"I certainly don't mind," Victoria assured her. "But ironically enough, after living and working out at the Double M for so long, I've grown rather fond of strong coffee, and I seldom bother with tea for myself."

Kate rolled her eyes. "Yes, I know from

their visits here how the Double M men like their strong coffee. But I sincerely hope they're not browbeating you into making too many sacrifices away from your own tastes."

"Firestick, Beartooth, and Moosejaw?" Victoria arched a finely penciled brow. "I'm sure you know better than that. Despite their colorful names and loud, rugged ways, they are three truly gentle men. Some of the finest I've ever had the pleasure of being around."

"You're right. I'm not surprised to hear that." Kate took a sip of her tea. "It's just that you seem so ladylike and refined and we see so little of you here in town, well, there's a certain amount of curiosity about you and how you've adjusted to conditions out there."

"Curiosity . . . as in gossip, you mean?"

Spots of color appeared on Kate's cheeks. Her pretty mouth twisted ruefully. "Yes, I guess that's the word. Damn it. And I must have sounded like the queen of nosy tongue-waggers for blurting it out that way. I'm sorry, that's not at all the way I meant it."

"No, of course you didn't." A tolerant smile touched Victoria's lips. "I'd be surprised if there *wasn't* gossip about me. And I fully understand that I don't help by not coming into town very often and therefore probably seeming rather aloof. But the simple answer is that I don't need to come here very often, because Firestick and the others do such a marvelous job of providing everything I want or need. All I have to do is make the most minor mention of anything in the way of food stock or perhaps some fixing up needed around the house, and practically before I can turn around it's taken care of."

"That sounds about a million miles removed from the way many so-called men of the house behave. Including my late father," mused Kate. "Don't get me wrong, my mother loved him madly — as did I — but Pops was the world's worst procrastinator when it came to chores around the house. It drove my mother mad. But then, magically, when they opened this hotel, he turned the complete opposite and demonstrated no end to handyman skills and the willingness to promptly get them done. I sometimes think the influenza that claimed Mom caught her in a weakened state because she was still reeling from the sudden change in Pops. Then, after she was gone, he quit caring about everything . . . even sticking around himself."

Kate abruptly leaned back in her chair and

expelled a quick burst of air. "Whew! Listen to me prattle off in a direction appropriate to nothing we were talking about. I beg your pardon."

"Not at all," Victoria said softly. "The subject of loss and absent loved ones isn't far from anyone's thoughts in this valley today. Not under the circumstances. Thankfully, there are no reports yet of the Apaches actually claiming any lives. Yet with so many men out on the hunt to confront them — or be otherwise placed in danger — a fear for that kind of loss can't help but be in the hearts of those left waiting."

Kate regarded her more closely. "You are a very wise and deeply caring person. I hope, going forward from this — and I refuse to believe in anything but a positive outcome — that we make it a point to see more of each other and get to know one another better."

"I do, too," said Victoria earnestly. She paused to display another smile, this one with a trace of uncharacteristic impishness. "Although I suspect I already have a substantial head start on knowing a good deal about you, from hearing Firestick bring your name up so often."

Kate arched a brow. "I may regret asking . . . but would you care to expound on that?"

Before Victoria could respond, the bell over the front door of the adjoining hotel lobby sounded as someone came in. A moment later, that someone passed on through into the dining room. It was Daisy Rawling. Her blond hair was pushed up under a slouch hat, there was a smudge of soot on the end of her nose, and she was wearing a pair of men's bib overalls over her abundant curves. The contrast in her attire compared to the more feminine apparel of the other two ladies did not seem to give her the slightest pause.

"What have we got here, gals? A meeting of the Female Lonely Hearts Club?" she greeted. "Mind if I sit in?"

"Of course you're welcome to join us, Daisy," said Kate, albeit taken slightly aback.

Daisy pulled out a chair and plopped down. No sooner had she done so than Marilu appeared.

Marilu's face immediately broke into a wide, warm smile. "Miss Daisy! Land's sake, it's good to see you! You ain't stopped by for breakfast in ages. I hope that's what you're here for, ain't it? We ain't had enough eatin' customers so far today to amount to a hill of beans. I'm anxious to flex my cookin' muscles and make somebody a serious meal."

"I'm sure sorry to disappoint you, Marilu," Daisy said. "But I'm afraid I ain't in no mood to call on your hankerin' to cook. Not today. With my man — not to mention all the others — off chasing those blasted Apaches, I reckon I'm off my feed with a touch of worry."

"Can I get you something? Coffee maybe?" said Marilu.

Daisy shrugged. "Yeah, sure. Always room for coffee." She paused, looking thoughtful, then cut her eyes over to Kate. "Is the bar open?"

"Why . . . sure. If need be."

"Good. You hear that, Marilu? Pass that cup of coffee through the barroom on your way back and introduce it to a shot of Mr. Bourbon. Will you do that, please?"

Marilu chuckled. "I sure will, Miss Daisy. How about you other two ladies? More tea, long as I'm fetchin'?"

"That would be fine, Marilu," said Kate.

The chuckle became a girlish little giggle. "Want me to introduce your tea to Mr. Bourbon, too?"

"No, I don't think that's necessary," Kate assured her.

With that settled, Daisy shifted forward in her chair, resting her elbows on the tabletop, and said to Victoria, "Speaking of introductions, although we've sort of met in passing a time or two, I don't think we've ever really been properly introduced." Daisy thrust out her hand. "I'm Daisy Rawling. Pleased to meet you."

"I'm Victoria Kingsley. And it's a pleasure to meet you, as well," said Victoria, shaking hands and smiling.

"I suppose you know that Moosejaw is my fella," Daisy said, settling back in her chair again. "He's the big lug who shoulda got around to introducin' us sooner. Though the chance for that ain't come around real often, I reckon, on account of I don't get out your way much and you never make it into town very often."

"We were just discussing that," Kate mentioned.

Daisy nodded. "I figured as much. That's why I called us the Female Lonely Hearts Club."

"I wondered about that," said Victoria. "I wasn't sure of your meaning."

Daisy's eyebrows lifted. "Well, it's plain enough, ain't it? We're three lonely hearts pinin' for our Double M men, who are out courtin' danger. Right? I mean, I got my ties to Moosejaw. And everybody knows that Kate here and Firestick are sweet on each other. That only leaves the feelings between you and Beartooth, Victoria — for which, according to the hints I get from readin' between the lines, maybe ain't fully sprouted yet but are planted and takin' root all the same."

"They are?" said Victoria, the words coming out with a bit of an unladylike squeak.

"They ain't?" countered Daisy.

Looking flustered but struggling not to be, Victoria said, "Well, I must say it comes as news to me that . . . I mean, I certainly never thought . . . well, perhaps 'never' is too strong a word, but . . . that is to say, while I do get on very well with Beartooth, any feelings between us are . . . are . . ."

Kate saved her by saying, "Are your business, frankly. And if you don't feel comfortable speaking about them, you needn't explain any further."

"Of course not," Daisy quickly agreed. "And if I spoke out of turn and embarrassed you, I'm sorry. Me and my big yap do that sometimes. Too dang often, I'm afraid."

"You're fine. You meant no harm," Victoria said, looking relieved to get off the subject.

"At least one place I don't have to worry

about speakin' out of turn is when it comes to my big lug and me," said Daisy. "And you can bet there are some changes comin' there."

"Oh? How so?" asked Victoria.

"Why, mainly that it's just a matter of time before I steal him away from you. Maybe it ain't sunk through that thick skull of his yet," said Daisy, her voice taking on a hushed, conspiratorial tone, "but one of these days Moosejaw and me are gonna be hitched."

"Really? When did he pop the question?" Kate wanted to know.

"Aw, he ain't got around to that yet," Daisy said dismissively. "But that don't mean it ain't gonna happen. In the meantime, Victoria, I just wanted to take this chance to thank you for takin' such good care of him — along with the other fellas — until I go ahead and lay full-time claim on him."

Victoria gave a little laugh. "Well, you surely are welcome, Daisy. Moosejaw is a fine, er, 'fella,' and I'm certain he will be in good hands when you take charge of caring for him."

"That's sure my aim," said Daisy solemnly. "All the big lunkhead's gotta do is make it back to me in one piece. Hell, as far as that goes, the Apaches could even slice him up some, and there'd still be more man left than you'd find in most."

"If you're going to kill me, I wish you'd go ahead and get it over with," Margaret Rockwell said tonelessly. "With all that's come to light, if you've been telling me the truth, it's the least I deserve."

"What would I have to gain by lying to you?" Lofton responded. "Nobody wanted the business between us to be done more than I did. And if your crazy kid hadn't scattered the deck by pulling that stupid damn kidnapping stunt, it would have been. Marshal Firestick would have stuck around town instead of traipsing off after his snatched deputy, I would have planted a slug in him, and it would have been over. I'd be long gone from here by now."

"You had your chance to kill the marshal — or at least *allow* him to be killed — long before you ever heard about the kidnapping. What's your excuse for not doing it then?"

"I had my reasons. I don't owe you no explanations about that or anything else. All I owe you is one death. And, before we're through, you might end up getting the bonus of a couple more."

Margaret's shoulders sagged. She could

do little else, tied to the kitchen chair the way she was, her arms pulled painfully behind her back and lashed securely at the elbows and wrists. "If you mean me, then go ahead. I welcome it. I deserve it. And anything you do to the marshal, I'm beyond caring. But my son, Brody . . . for the love of God, not him."

"I think you and me are a long ways past readin' God into anything we do or don't do," sneered Lofton.

"But Brody isn't! He's an innocent boy."

"He's a kidnapper. Hell, maybe even a killer, for all we know, if he spotted Firestick coming after him and made good on the threats in his ransom note."

Margaret shook her head determinedly. "No! He'd never do anything like that. It isn't in him . . . He's a gentle soul who never would have been driven to do what he did if I'd paid proper attention to him instead of getting so blindly caught up with hate and revenge. Whatever he's done, whatever happens to him . . . I see now it's all my fault. It all comes back to me."

"That's exactly what I'm counting on, Mother Dear . . . all of it coming right back here to you." Lofton bared his teeth in a nasty smile. "Whether he brings the boy back alive or not, Firestick's going to follow the string right here to confront you, not believing — just like I didn't, and still don't — that innocent little Brody dreamed up that kidnapping all on his own. And when the noble marshal gets here, he's going to find me waiting to tie off my loose ends and finish the last of my business."

CHAPTER 45

"If they're out there," Milt Kruger was saying, "I'm blamed if I can see how they're gonna catch us off guard anywhere in this stretch. It's as flat and edge-burnt as an overcooked pancake. Where they gonna hide?"

Riding beside Kruger at the head of three heavily loaded freight wagons, Moosejaw said, "You'd be surprised at how little concealment an Apache needs to make hisself dang near invisible."

The wagons were less than halfway into the Jacinto Flats. Overhead, the sun was nearing its noon peak, making the day hot and on its way to getting hotter. The chalky dust of the ancient lake bed, without the slightest breeze to stir it but lifted by the hooves of the mules and horses as they plodded steadily along, was already depositing a thin layer on the clothes and sweaty faces of the men who, along with Moosejaw, had joined the train just a couple hours earlier. The slow *clop* of hooves on the hard ground, along with the creak of saddle leather and the groan of wagon frames, made a monotonous drone of sound that hung in the air like it was wrapped in the dust.

"We're gonna have to stop for a nooning along here pretty soon," announced Kruger. He was a stocky man of about fifty, not overly tall, with a barrel chest and forearms revealed by the rolled-up sleeves of his shirt to be nearly as thick as some men's thighs. A bowler hat was cocked jauntily atop a headful of bristly pale hair, and an unlit cigar stub poked out one corner of his mouth.

"It ain't gonna get no cooler, and the mules will need water, rest, and a feedbag," the teamster continued. Then, with a lopsided grin, he added, "I ain't above pushin' my men harder than they like, but my darlin' mules I do not abuse."

"I won't fault you for that. I've seen plenty of men who can't hold a candle to a good mule," Moosejaw said wryly. "Besides, I rode my men hard to make it out here and join you as soon as we could. Them and their horses could use a breather, too."

"You bet. It's a fine lot they look, worthy

of bein' treated well. And volunteers to a man, eh? Puttin' themselves through this for the sake of seein' to the safety of me and mine. When we get to town, I'll be after standin' each of 'em a stout drink."

"They'll appreciate it. I'll see to it they do."

"By the way — and meanin' no disrespect to you, you tall mountain who I would not want to offend or angrify in any way — why was it you said neither the marshal nor your other deputy friend is joinin' us?" asked Kruger.

"Actually, I never said." Moosejaw shrugged. "But now that you and your men have been warned and we're on our way with everybody's eyes peeled, there ain't no reason not to get into it some. You see, in addition to the Injun trouble, we've had us a flare-up of other crimes and problems in and around town. Some murders, a kidnappin' — all comin' kinda jammed together."

"Saints a'mighty! I can see where that'd be spreadin' you badge-toters kinda thin in order to try and cover it all."

"Exactly. Since I had some experience fightin' flatland Injuns in the past," Moosejaw explained, "me and Firestick figured I was best suited to give you and your men a helpin' hand in case those Apaches try to spring on you out here."

"But how would they even know we're comin' in?"

"That's a good question. It don't seem likely they would. They've been holed up in the Vieja Mountains to the north of the valley and the town. We know they came in with plenty of pack ponies, so that means, more than just a killin' raid, they're out to take supplies back to their people. They've hit some cattle herds already." Moosejaw paused, his expression darkening, jaw muscles tightening visibly. "Just a matter of time, though, before they start hittin' ranches and farmhouses for other kinds of goods, and the lives of folks who get caught in their way will only slow 'em down so much."

"Red devils!" Kruger hissed.

"You can see why we took a hard interest as soon as we thought about you and your wagons comin' in," Moosejaw said. "Even though it seems unlikely they'd be sniffin' out this far, they *do* have outlyin' scouts on the lookout for the most prime targets to hit. If — somehow, some way, for whatever reason — one of those scouts did venture far enough to catch sight of this train . . . well, you can imagine what a prize it would represent."

"No, I'd rather not imagine it," Kruger said through clenched teeth. "I have guards on my wagons, as you can see. As I always do. A deterrent to owlhoots out for easy pickings. With the trusted men I have riding shotgun — honest, loyal men, most of 'em havin' been with me a long time — word has spread by now that there are no easy pickings from a Kruger freight haul . . . But men who are trained and prepared to hold off an Apache attack? That's a different matter."

"Pretty much what we figured. That's why we're here," stated Moosejaw. "Don't misunderstand — most of the men I brought with me ain't trained Injun fighters neither. Especially not against Apaches. Not too many around who are. But these are tough, determined men who've got a town and a valley to protect. You can bet they're prepared to do what it takes."

Kruger met the big deputy's eyes and held them fast. "Nobody could ask for more. Whether we encounter Apaches or not, I'm grateful beyond words."

A total of eight men were originally accompanying the freight haul. Two rode each wagon — a driver and a shotgun guard —

434

with Kruger riding out ahead and another horseman bringing up the rear. Once Moosejaw and his men joined up, the big deputy dispersed two riders to each of the wagons, one on either side, two more back on the drag, and an additional one, Miguel Santros, riding farther ahead on point while Moosejaw fell in beside Kruger.

When Kruger signaled a halt, Moosejaw kept half of his men mounted and on watch while the teamsters tended first to their mules and then themselves, crawling under the wagons for a few minutes of shade. The townsmen saw similarly to their mounts and then also availed themselves of some shade until Moosejaw signaled a switch with those who'd initially stayed in their saddles. Moosejaw and Kruger remained mounted the whole time, drinking from their canteens, chewing some jerky, eyes scanning in long, slow sweeps.

"Once we start up again," said Kruger, "we'll stick with it steady until we make it to town. Barring any trouble, we should arrive by evening."

Moosejaw grinned. "Get ready for some whoopin' and hollerin' when we roll in. Folks'll be mighty glad to see we made it."

"That's fine by me," Kruger said. "I'll be glad we made it, too. Hell, I very likely may join in on some whoopin' right along with 'em."

Cleve Boynton came walking up, leading his horse.

"Why don't you find some shade while you got the chance, Cleve?" Moosejaw asked him.

The Box T man shrugged. "The sun don't bother me much. Plus, I reckon I'm feelin' a mite too restless to relax anyway. If it's all the same to you, I think I'll spell Miguel awhile and take a turn on point. Maybe go out a distance farther. The way ahead looks a little rougher. Still flat, but with a lot of cracks in the dry ground and a few stands of low rock."

"Fella's got a good eye," Kruger remarked. "He's right, this stretch comin' up does have a lot of split ground — fissures, they call 'em. I usually ride out a ways farther through here myself. Lookin' to make sure none of those cracks have grown or reached into our regular path so's we don't end up droppin' a wheel into one of 'em and risk bustin' an axle."

"Definitely sounds like something to avoid," agreed Moosejaw. "Go ahead, Cleve. Spell Miguel if you've a mind to. Don't venture too far ahead, though. Look sharp."

"We'll be startin' up again shortly and

comin' along behind," Kruger said.

Boynton nodded. "I'll signal if I see anything."

"Well, that tears it," grated Beartooth, glaring down at the ground from the back of his horse.

"No mistakin' it," Firestick agreed, studying the same markings.

"Tears what? No mistaking what?" Brody Rockwell wanted to know, as he also concentrated on where the two men seemed to be looking, but without being able to tell what it was they saw.

"Tracks. Ground sign, boy," Beartooth said tersely. "No time to teach you now, but when you know how to read 'em, they tell a story plain as day."

"It's the story we wasn't hopin' for, even though we half-expected it," added Firestick. Then, reading the questions remaining in Brody's eyes, he explained a bit more. "Ten riders on shod horses, coming from the direction of town, passed through here earlier. They went on east, toward the old lake bed. Later, the string of Apaches we been followin' — the ones those four from back at the butte branched away from — came along and also spotted their tracks. A lone rider, a scout most likely, showed up here, too. They palavered. The pack ponies that were part of this bunch we been followin' continued south toward the border. The rest of 'em headed east, on the trail of those shod horses goin' into the Flats."

Brody said, "And those are the men from town, going out to help guard the freight wagons on their way in?"

"Gotta be."

"But the Apaches are going after them anyway?"

"Don't know how, but somehow they appear to have sniffed out those wagons comin' in. You damn betcha those cherrycows want those," Beartooth said.

"But we're going to help stop 'em. Right?" asked Brody.

"You damn betcha," Beartooth said again.

CHAPTER 46

Cleve Boynton, riding about forty yards ahead of the others, was the first victim. Seemingly out of nowhere, a rifle shot split the shimmering air and the Box T man pitched from his saddle.

Watching from back at the head of the wagons, Moosejaw had time only to hiss a curse through gritted teeth before hell broke loose all around him.

From the emptiness that stretched in every direction, rising up from within the twisting ground fissures that ran close along either side of where the wagons were passing, Saetta's warriors shed the layers of dirt they had covered themselves with and lifted their rifles to aim with deadly accuracy. They first took down the lead mules, bullets splitting skulls and smashing brains. As the stricken beasts began to drop, the wagons ground to a halt, and the other animals in harness, now trapped with the stink of blood and death filling their nostrils, screamed in panic.

Next, men and their mounts began falling victim to the volleys that followed. In the shock and confusion that resulted from this savage attack, seconds passed before any return fire was loosed. It took that long before most of the men fully understood what was happening. One second they had been surrounded by flat nothingness and then — as if the very earth had come alive — they were being riddled to pieces.

"Under the wagons! Take cover under the wagons!" Moosejaw shouted as he wheeled his mount sharply. But before the animal could complete its turn, a pair of slugs pounded into its mighty throat. It staggered sideways and started to go down. Moosejaw barely had time to kick his feet out of the stirrups and throw himself free before the horse crashed to the ground. On hands and knees, with bullets whining overhead and tearing gouges in the ground at his heels, the big deputy scrambled forward and flopped between the bodies of the fallen mules who'd been the front pair pulling the lead wagon. The massive carcasses gave solid cover on both sides even to his wide-shouldered frame. Slugs thumped loudly into meat and muscle but were stopped short of coming through.

A moment later, Kruger came clambering in behind him just as Moosejaw raised his Schofield revolver and fired .45-caliber rounds into the brains of the second pair of pullers who were still in harness behind the fallen ones, rearing wildly and threatening to stomp him with their frantically kicking feet.

"My God! My God, my beautiful mules!" Kruger exclaimed, almost sobbing.

"I'm sorry you had to see that," Moosejaw said as he twisted around and started triggering more rounds from the Schofield — his only weapon since he'd been unable to grab his Winchester from its saddle scabbard when the horse went down — at their attackers. The latter had begun ducking in and out of the fissures now, shifting their positions. "But these mules are still serving you in death, just like when they were alive. In fact, they might prove to be the only things able to keep *us* alive before we're done."

Moosejaw heard more shots ringing out from the wagons, and from the corner of his eye he could see men doing as he'd instructed and scrambling underneath them for cover. "Spread the word down the line," he hollered. "Tell the men to crowd under

441

the axles so they've got cover from the wheels on either side . . . Tell 'em they can use dead mules for cover, too . . . Or horses, or even the bodies of already dead men!"

"That's the devil's talk! That's inhumane!" Kruger protested.

"It's called survival, Mr. Kruger. Trust me, the dead won't mind a few more bullet holes in 'em," Moosejaw told him. Then, baring his teeth in a humorless grin, he added, "Tell you what. If I go down, you got my my permission to use my body — I'd make a nice big chunk of cover."

Firestick raised his hand to signal a halt. He, Beartooth, and Brody were riding three abreast, though spaced at wide intervals to minimize a combined, larger dust cloud that would have been produced by their rapid pace across the dry, desolate land.

Drawing back on his reins, Firestick cocked his head to one side and adopted the pose of someone listening intently.

"What is it? Why'd you stop?" Beartooth called over.

Firestick didn't answer right away. When he did, he narrowed his eyes, peering ahead, and said, "There. Can't you hear that?"

Beartooth frowned. "No, I can't say as I . . . Wait a minute. Yeah, now I do."

"So do I," said Brody. "It sounds like shooting, away in the distance."

"Sounds like it because that's what it is," said Beartooth. He, too, stared intently out ahead. "I can hear it, but blamed if I can see any sign of the ruckus, not even across these damn barren flats."

Firestick produced the binoculars from his saddle pouch and brought them to his eyes. After several beats he lowered them.

"See anything?" Beartooth said.

"No. Nothing clear. Pickin' up too much heat shimmer in the air."

"But there's only one thing it can be. Right?" said Brody. "So we've got to go ahead and move up closer. It's what we came here for, ain't it?"

Beartooth cast a sidelong glance at Firestick. "Kid sounds awful eager for another skirmish with the Apaches. Kinda makes you question the sense in him — and the sense in us for bringin' him along, don't it?"

"Well, *ain't it* what we came here for?" said Brody.

"Good sense aside, he ain't wrong. It is what we came for." Firestick's jaw muscles clenched visibly. "Come on, let's get a little closer."

■ ■ ■ ■

The Apaches had ceased the punishing volleys for now and had dropped back unseen
into their concealment. This left the men of
the wagon train to swelter and sweat in their
own pockets of desperate cover, nerves
scraped raw by the carnage around them
and the sporadic incoming rifle shots mixed
with an occasional arrow that had an even
more unnerving psychological effect.

"What are the red bastards doing?" rasped
Kruger, jammed in next to Moosejaw between the mule bodies. "Why don't they
show themselves — come out and fight?"

"They *are* fightin'," said Moosejaw.
"They're doin' it the Apache way, that's all."

"Well, it's a helluva bloody way if you ask
me."

"Yeah, that it is," allowed Moosejaw. "But
don't mean it ain't effective. Like I said, it's
the Apache way. They'll string a piece of a
man's gut out for him to see. Then they'll
leave it for a while in order to give him a
good chance to think about the really nasty
thing they're fixin' to do next."

By passing word up and down the line,
Moosejaw had been able to determine by
this point that six of their number had been

killed. Four more were wounded, two seriously. All of the mules were dead, and the horses that had been carrying riders were either dead or scattered. The sparse bit of good news was that each man still in fighting condition had a fair amount of ammunition and — save for Moosejaw and Kruger — a canteen at his disposal.

It wasn't much, but it was enough to carry them through the balance of the day, anyway. Time and again, Moosejaw had stressed conservation when it came to burning up cartridges.

The thing he hadn't said, at least so far, was the part about each man saving a bullet for himself.

"So, what are they likely to do next?" Kruger asked hoarsely.

"Probably not a whole lot different than they're doin' right now. Leastways not until nightfall," Moosejaw replied. "They'll keep plinkin' at us as long as they got light, hopin' to pick off a couple more."

"Then what happens after it gets dark? I think I heard somewhere that Apaches don't fight at night."

A corner of Moosejaw's mouth quirked upward. "Yeah, I hear that a lot myself. But the true way it goes is that Apaches don't *like* to fight at night. Don't mean they never do. And I got a hunch this is shapin' up to be one of those exceptions."

"Jesus. That's a helluva thing to contemplate. Those silent devils slipping through the night . . . My God, we couldn't see them in the daylight!"

"Don't go to pieces on me now, Kruger," Moosejaw said sternly. "If we got any chance at all, it's gonna come from keepin' cool heads. Especially me and you — these other men are lookin' to us for a way to make it through."

"Yeah, yeah, I know that," Kruger said, his breath coming in rapid bursts. "But what chance *do* we have, realistically?"

Moosejaw scanned their surroundings with narrowed eyes. "We're still alive, damn it. As long as a body has breath in him and weapons at hand, he's always got a chance."

As flat as the ancient lake bed appeared to be, it nevertheless still had a certain amount of undulation to it. From the crest of a long, very gradually rising slope that reached an elevation eight or ten feet higher than most of the surrounding terrain, Firestick again put the binoculars to his eyes and focused them out ahead. The wagons and their plight came into view with all the clarity the marshal needed to cause his mouth to twist into a bleak grimace.

"How bad is it?" Beartooth wanted to know.

Firestick handed him the glasses. "Not good. See for yourself. They got 'em pinned down. Looks like the cherry-cows caught 'em by surprise and did a pretty good job of choppin' 'em to pieces before they ever knew what hit 'em."

"Son of a bitch," Beartooth hissed. "I see how they did it. They're usin' those cracks in the ground that run all over — slitherin' around in 'em like damn worms or snakes or some such."

"Snakes that have a little added distance to their bite on account of bein' able to use bullets and arrows," said Firestick. "A mighty dangerous kind."

Beartooth held the binoculars out to Brody. "Take a look, kid. But brace yourself. That dustup back at the butte was one thing. What you're gonna be lookin' at here is Apaches at work on a bigger and worse scale — and this still ain't as bad as they can get."

Brody took the binoculars and looked through them. He swallowed hard a couple times before lowering them. When he did, his face was a shade paler, but his expression was no less determined. "We still gotta

447

do what we came here for. More than ever, we gotta do something to help those men."

Beartooth took the glasses back and returned them to Firestick. "Kid called it right. He's a mite short on details, though. You got any ideas?"

Firestick passed the back of one hand across his dry lips. "Those worms might be usin' cracks in the ground pretty effectively right at the moment," he said. "But they didn't get here by crawlin' all this way on their bellies. Somewhere nearby are their horses."

"Horses?" echoed Beartooth.

"That's right," Firestick said. "Those soldier boys from Fort Leaton sure as hell ain't gonna make it in time to do us any good. But that don't mean a good old-fashioned cavalry charge wouldn't still be just the ticket for bustin' apart that upper hand those Apaches think they're holdin'. So, what's the key ingredient to a cavalry charge?"

"A cavalry unit," answered Beartooth, scowling because he still didn't see where the marshal was headed. But then, abruptly, his eyebrows lifted and a sparkle came to his eyes. "But on second thought, a cavalry unit don't go nowhere without . . ."

"Horses!" Brody finished for him.

"Now you're gettin' the idea," said Firestick. "Come on, unit . . . Let's go find some nags to carry us into battle."

CHAPTER 47

They found the Apache ponies in a wind
scour, a shallow depression scooped out by
swirling winds over many years, located
about half a mile from where the wagons
were pinned down. Nine ponies, hobbled
securely but with no guards, because the
chief had needed all his braves for the attack on the White Eyes.

Leaning on his saddle horn, eyeing the
pack, Firestick said, "Well, there's our
cavalry charge. We fancy ourselves horse
wranglers, now's the chance for us to prove
it. I say we unhobble these rascals and head
'em straight for the wagons. Once there, we
split 'em and herd 'em in tight along either
side, right over those cracks in the ground.
With a little luck, that oughta flush out the
Injuns hidin' there, or at least give cover to
the men in the wagons so they can rush out
and join us in takin' the fight to the
Apaches."

"Long as they don't mistake who we are and aim their fight at us, too," remarked Beartooth.

Firestick shrugged. "It's the best I can come up with. Once we cut these critters loose, there ain't gonna be no turnin' back. If you got a better idea, now's the time to spill it."

"Never said I didn't like the idea. Just meant to point out I hope those fellas in the wagons catch on quick to what we're up to." Beartooth grinned recklessly. "Besides, I always wondered what it would be like to be a soldier boy. I ain't about to pass up the chance to play one. Hell, I figure if we're representin' a whole cavalry unit, then I oughta rank at least a captain."

"In that case, Captain," said Firestick, "how about whippin' your troops into action and let's get this charge underway."

Moosejaw was the first one to hear the low rumble of the approaching horses. At first it sounded like thunder, but given the clear sky overhead, that didn't make any sense. Then he saw the boiling dust cloud getting nearer, and within it the hazy shapes of the racing animals. Next he heard the yips and hollers of the men driving them.

"What the hell!" muttered Kruger next to

451

him. "Is that more of the devils showing up?"

Moosejaw hadn't fully grasped what was happening, but somehow he sensed it wasn't necessarily a dire development. "I don't think so," he said guardedly. "In fact . . ." His words trailed off as his ears identified a familiar tone to some of the yips and hollers. Next, fleetingly, through the dust haze, he was able to spot a couple of broadshouldered outlines belonging to the riders those sounds issued from. Complete recognition, hard as it was to believe, hit him a moment later.

"Send the word up the line to get ready," he shouted in an excited voice to the men under the front wagon. "Those Apaches are about to be scrambled out of their hidey-holes here in a minute. When they are, we go out and take 'em!"

Which was exactly how it played out.

When the pony herd drew within a few yards of the wagons, Firestick and his "cavalry unit" split them according to plan, driving them into two hard-charging lines along either side, thundering over the fissures and humps of earth that concealed the Apaches. The latter — partly to avoid being trampled and partly to try and capture what they recognized as their own fleeing ponies — sprang from hiding, exposing themselves. At this, the men from the freight train poured out from under wagons or from behind dead mules and horses and rushed to engage them. The battle that ensued was short-lived and fierce. Curses were hurled, and the roar of rifles and revolvers filled the air, interspersed with the tattoo of pounding hooves. This time it was the Apaches who were surprised and rattled and the white men who seized the moment with savage resolve.

It was over almost before the dust from the stampeding horses had settled. The nine Apaches lay dead. A couple of additional wounds were suffered by the men from the wagons, but none life-threatening, and no additional lives were lost.

Firestick and Beartooth rode at a trot back to the lead wagon, where Moosejaw stood waiting for them. His face was streaked by sweat and powder smoke.

The big deputy squinted up at his two longtime comrades. "Not to sound ungrateful," he said, "but it sure took you fellas long enough to get here."

Leaning on his saddle horn, Firestick replied, "We don't get out this way very often, so we couldn't help but stop and admire the scenery now and then along the way."

"And then we made the mistake of lookin' through the binoculars and spottin' your ugly mug," added Beartooth. "Since that pretty much ruined the rest of the scenery, we figured we might as well come on ahead and drag your overwide ass out of this latest fix you got yourself into."

CHAPTER 48

At first light the next morning, a rescue party from Buffalo Peak arrived at the stranded wagons. Prominent among them was Frank Moorehouse, primed to act in his role as a doctor. Prominent, too, were a dozen workhorses brought to hitch up in place of the fallen mules. While Beartooth and Moosejaw had stayed behind to help with the burying of the dead, the care of the wounded, and the dragging away of animal carcasses, Firestick and Brody had made the trip back to town to arrange sending out the assistance.

Somewhat surprisingly, however, neither the marshal nor the boy returned with the rescuers. This stemmed primarily from Brody learning about his mother's refusal to leave her farm when Roeback and his group had gone out to round up her and the other outlying families. Although there was every reason to believe the Apache

455

trouble was now quelled, more than twenty-four hours had passed since anyone last saw the widow — enough to raise considerable concern in her son's mind about her safety.

This dovetailed with another report received by Firestick regarding the gambler, Henry Lofton, who'd gone missing from town at a time when it seemed mighty curious for anyone who knew about the Apache threat to head out alone into the valley. This came on the heels, the marshal was additionally told by Kate and Victoria, of Lofton asking a lot of questions about Margaret Rockwell not coming in with the rest of the outliers. The consensus was that he may have taken it upon himself to go look after the widow, even though the excuse he offered for having any interest in her at all seemed awfully tenuous.

Brody's pleas alone likely would have been enough for Firestick to accompany him in going to check on his mother. After all, he owed the boy at least that much for the strong accounting he'd shown during the Indian skirmishes. But in spite of that, there also were still some questions in the marshal's mind about what part the mother might have played in her son's kidnapping plot — not to mention if she was in some way behind the gunning down of Gus

Wingate. And now he had to wonder about the curious connection to Lofton, the alleged gambler . . .

In the early light, the Rockwell farmhouse, which Firestick had visited only a very few times, looked shabbier and somehow more ominous than he remembered. The surrounding fields looked badly in need of tending, as did the smattering of livestock — a few pigs and chickens — that were in view.

Brody seemed not to notice any of this as he rode directly to the hitchrail in front of the house and lighted from his saddle.

"Take it easy, boy," Firestick said to him. "We'll go in together."

But Brody didn't wait. Starting toward the house, he called ahead, "Mother? Mother! Are you in there?"

In response, the front door opened. And then, quickly stepping into view, there stood a smiling Henry Lofton. He held a double-barreled shotgun aimed casually from the hip, its twin muzzles trained steadily on the new arrivals.

"Welcome home, sonny boy," Lofton said calmly. "Your dear mother has been worried sick about you."

Brody stopped short, his body going rigid.

Then, when Firestick sensed that the coiled spring he'd become was ready to lunge forward again, he clapped a hand on the kid's shoulder and held him fast.

"That's smart thinkin', Marshal. You hold that tiger real still and both of you keep your hands well away from your guns," cautioned Lofton. "Any more sudden moves from either of you, I cut loose with both barrels of this gut shredder Mother Dear was kind enough to loan me. The two of you would be turned into a pile of mangled meat that nobody would ever be able to sort out."

From inside, a quavering woman's voice wailed, "Do what he says, Brody! Don't test him — he's insane!"

Lofton's smile widened. "Ain't it pure heartwarming how a mother's protective instincts will shine through . . . even in a homicidal bitch like the grief-stricken Widow Rockwell in there."

"If you've harmed her, I'll see you dead," Brody promised in a hoarse whisper.

"That's highly unlikely," responded Lofton. "In case you ain't got it through your thick skull yet, I'm the one holding the upper hand here, boy. The best you're going to get out of this — if you watch your mouth and do exactly as I say — is seeing dear Mom one more time before I send the both of you to join your brother and pa."

"If that's your hole card, then why not go ahead and play it? Why drag it out?" said Firestick.

Lofton regarded him with narrowed eyes. "That's a mighty strange request — a man asking for his death to be hurried up. The only time I've ever heard of anything like that is from someone wanting to be spared torture from Indians or some such. Speaking of which, can I assume that your presence here signals that the hostile Apaches have now been dealt with?"

Firestick glared at him, said nothing.

"Very well, I'll take that as a yes. I knew right from the first you had sand, Marshal, and I'm sure the good townsfolk are rightfully pleased and proud of you. But I hope your past successes don't have you standing there with something percolating inside that head of yours that makes you think you can bull your way through a shotgun blast."

"Why not try me and find out?" Firestick prodded. "You got no reason to hesitate, no matter how messy it's gonna be. You should be used to it. After all, that's what you do, ain't it? Kill? Kill for hire?"

"You're a little late figuring that out. Aren't you . . . *pal?*" Lofton snickered. "I suckered you in that first day we met. You told me your life story and were practically ready to adopt me, right along with those other two ruffians who fell down out of the mountains with you. To tell the truth, I took a liking to you, too. It actually bothered me a little when I found out you were on the list the bloodthirsty widow had hired me to get rid of. To the point I actually intervened and saved your life that day out in the street."

"Pardon me for no longer feelin' particularly grateful for that."

Lofton shrugged. "No matter. Guess I resented somebody else horning in on my job. But even while I was taking aim at that other fellow, I knew it was just a matter of time before I'd end up with you in my gun sights."

"Me and Gus Wingate. We were the ones on your list, I take it?"

"Now you're catching on."

"In town, I heard about the three Box T wranglers who also got gunned down — the same three we tangled with that first day in the Silver Spur. Was that you, too? Something just to keep your trigger finger limbered up?"

"They were no-account pigs," Lofton snarled. "Too gutless to be packing iron on that first occasion, but that wouldn't have stopped them from stomping my insides out if they'd had their way. I would have gotten around to killing them right there in the saloon if you hadn't shown up." He tossed a disdainful shrug. "I saw my chance a little later, and decided to make them pay for putting their grubby paws on me. They were no loss to the world, and you damn well know it. Hell, I ought to get some kind of civic medal."

"I don't care about any of that. I want to see my mother," Brody demanded.

"That brings up my last question," said Firestick, keeping his eyes trained on Lofton. "Why stage all this — why add the boy and his mother to your list? She paid you, didn't she? Do you always kill your clients after you've done the job they hired you for? All you have to do is finish me off and you'd be square."

"Answer's simple," Lofton told him. "She's too crazy to leave behind as a loose end that could tie me to two killings, one of them a lawman. It's true I've got a reputation in certain circles as a hired killer. There's even a few law dogs who know — or suspect — that about me. But they can't prove anything, because my clients never talk. If they did, they'd be incriminating themselves right along with me. But somebody who hires me to do a pair of killings and at the same time sends her son out to stage a kidnapping that can't help but complicate everything into a big tangle . . . That made her somebody too insane to trust not to talk in case she tried to make some deals when everything started falling apart on her."

"My mother had nothing to do with my kidnapping plans," Brody protested. "She knew nothing about it!"

"Sure. And I'm just supposed to take your word for that?" Lofton arched a brow at Brody. "Nice try, kid, but you're wasting your breath."

"So, by getting rid of us three, you figure you've got it all covered?"

"Not pretty, but it will have to do. There may be some more suspicions tied to my name, but nothing anybody can prove. Hell, nobody will ever be able to say for certain that I was ever even here."

"Except for one thing," Firestick said.

"Oh? And what's that?"

"The dead body you're gonna leave behind when you make me kill you because you're too stupid and stubborn to give yourself up for arrest."

Lofton emitted a nasty laugh. "You're half-right. I sure as hell don't intend to let you arrest me."

"I'll give you one more chance. A three-count. Then I'm gonna draw my Colt and kill you."

"That's going to be mighty hard to do when I pull these triggers at the first sign of a muscle twitch from you and you are instantly blown to pieces. I checked the loads in this scattergun. Ten-gauge. That's a mighty tough way to go, and you'll be sentencing the boy to the same."

Firestick bared his teeth in a thin, cold smile. "Oh yeah. I forgot to mention how that shotgun you got on loan is gonna do part of my work for me. You see, you might've checked the loads, but you should have checked the whole thing a lot closer. Then you would have seen what I'm lookin' at from this end — how somebody at some point rested that shotgun muzzle-down on a patch of wet ground and left those muzzles plugged tight with mud that's since dried. You pull those triggers in that condition, the only one who's gonna get blasted is you, from the blowback you'll set off. And, just to make sure, I'll be plantin' a couple .44s in you before you hit the ground."

"I've got to hand it to you, mountain man," Lofton said, his smirk returning. "That's a very original bluff. Way better than trying to convince me somebody is sneaking up behind me or some piece of hogwash like that. But it's hogwash all the same, and we both know it. What's more, you've gone and worn out my patience."

Firestick's head tipped in a barely perceptible nod. "Fair enough. You've gone and used up that three-count I gave you."

Shoving Brody aside, Firestick's right hand streaked for the Colt holstered on his hip. In that same instant, true to his word, Lofton pulled both triggers of the ten-gauge. The powerful gun roared, belching smoke and flame, and the ends of its twin barrels parted and peeled back like the petals of a flower bursting open all at once. The blowback screamed in reverse down the barrels, shattering Lofton's trigger hand and ripping open three-quarters of his midsection. He was driven backward, slamming hard against one side of the door frame. In the fraction of a second he seemed to hang there, two .44 slugs from Firestick's Colt pounded into his chest, spinning him and then pitching him face-first onto the floor inside the house.

CHAPTER 49

It took a while, but in the days and weeks that followed, things around Buffalo Peak returned to a semblance of normalcy. There was a good deal to grieve and be sad over, but there was also the sense of knowing that matters could have turned out worse than they did. Mostly, the tough frontier spirit that had brought the folks of the valley this far and sustained them through numerous past hardships took hold once more and began pulling them forward yet again.

The cavalry detachment from Fort Leaton showed up late on the evening after the freight wagons had been retrieved and Firestick returned to town with the body of Henry Lofton over his saddle and Margaret Rockwell in handcuffs. Under the command of a fresh-faced captain named Smith, the troopers spent a handful of days scouring the Vieja Mountains looking for the Apaches who'd stayed behind with the remaining pack ponies. No sign of them was found, and the soldiers, deeming the Indian threat nullified, eventually went back to the fort.

For her part in the murder of Gus Wingate, the Widow Rockwell was held in the Buffalo Peak Jail until a U.S. marshal out of Presidio arrived to take her back to be tried and sentenced there. Brody accepted this, yet nevertheless he stood by her side throughout.

As far as Brody's own crime of kidnapping — since Beartooth refused to press charges against him and Firestick was swayed by the way the lad had fought courageously against the Apaches, not to mention the fact that he might have saved the lives of one or both lawmen at the butte — he faced no consequences. In fact, the money his mother had paid Lofton was returned to him, and it was enough to cover the overdue taxes on the farm. By throwing in with his new neighbors, Lyle Marsh and Sylvester Krause, Gus Wingate's loyal hired hands who were in line to take over Gus's ranch by default, a partnership was formed that had the potential for someday becoming one of the biggest spreads around.

Both Milt Kruger and Gerald Tolsvord, who already had one of the bigger spreads in the valley, suffered painful losses of men, though three of them were at the hand of Lofton, not the Apaches. Despite this, nobody had any doubt that the Box T would endure. And although Kruger swore he'd spearheaded his last wagon train, in less than six months he was out hauling freight again.

Frank Moorehouse did a yeoman's job of treating and following up on the healing of the wounded.

Pastor Bart was kept busy conducting a number of sad funeral services, and he did a fine, soothing job on each one.

And Sam Duvall and his dog, Shield, finally got a reprieve from what had turned out to be extended jailer duty when the U.S. marshal out of Presidio took both Margaret Rockwell and Whitey Chapman, the Bar 6 wrangler who'd participated in the ambush attempt on Firestick, off of his hands.

For the three former mountain men who wore badges for the town, the peaceful aftermath, in the short term, started to show alarming signs of becoming boring. This subject fell under discussion one evening when all three of them were taking a leisurely dinner in the Mallory Hotel dining room. The fact that they were in the company of Kate, Daisy, and Victoria quickly turned their mournfully stated longing for action into something of a spirited exchange.

Daisy started it off, demanding of Moose-jaw, "You want action, you big lunkhead? How about you marry me, the way we've been discussin'? I'll see that you get all the doggone action you can handle!"

Moosejaw was clearly taken aback. "Marriage? I don't remember us discussin' nothing about marriage."

"Well, we *should* be, you big lug. That's my whole point. If us gals waited for you men to get around to poppin' the question, nothing would ever get done, and all of creation might come to a screechin' halt."

Now Moosejaw's expression turned a little desperate, and his eyes swept over the others around the table with a *somebody please help me out, here* look.

"Well, I don't know if marriage is the answer for all of creation," Kate offered, taking a middle-of-the-road approach, "but I'm sure it would be bound to have advantages over shoot-outs or Indian fighting or the like."

"Or being kidnapped," added Victoria.

Beartooth looked at her. "Were you worried about me when you found out I was kidnapped?"

"Why, certainly," she replied. "If you recall, I was the original choice to be taken, according to the ransom note. Would you not have been worried about me?"

"Well, of course! You're a lady. Something like that would've just naturally been harder on you."

"Because ladies are all supposed to be delicate flowers, you mean?" challenged Victoria. "But apart from that sort of drivel, one thing I can assure you is that no lady would sit around afterward and mope about *not* experiencing such an adventure again."

Beartooth frowned. " 'Drivel'? 'Mope'? Those are kinda harsh words, ain't they?"

"See how they're needlin' each other?" said Daisy. "That comes from both of 'em havin' feelings for one another but bein' too stubborn to admit it. That's why you and me don't needle each other, Moosejaw, on account of we're right out in the open with our feelings."

"That might be okay for us, Daize," said Moosejaw a bit uneasily. "But you oughtn't be so freewheelin' about goin' around tryin' to lasso other folks together. I'm sure they can work a thing like that out for themselves."

"Maybe so. But it never hurts to give some things a nudge once in a while, either," Daisy insisted. "Look at the marshal and Miss Kate. No sooner had you three landed in town than anybody with a brain could see the two of them start makin' moon eyes at each other right off. But they dawdled and dawdled about it, just like this other pair, until I gave 'em a nudge and got 'em to finally start showin' some real interest."

"You did?" said Kate.

"Moon eyes?" said Firestick.

Ignoring them, Daisy went on, "In fact, the only one sittin' at this table who *didn't* get bit by the dawdle bug was me. The first time I laid eyes on my Moosejaw here, I knew he was the one for me, and I didn't hold back."

"No, that wouldn't be you, Daisy," allowed Beartooth.

"Which is why I ain't holdin' back on this marriage business, neither," Daisy said, turning her attention back to Moosejaw. "When it comes to wedding vows bein' spouted by anybody in this group, they dang well better come from me and you first, you big lug. You got that?"

"Wedding vows?" echoed Firestick.

Kate gave him a sharp look. "Is that such a horrid thought?"

Firestick found himself groping for the right response. "Well, no . . . Not for some people, I mean . . . That is to say . . ."

Beartooth stood up suddenly. "Listen! Did

you hear that?"

"Hear what?" said Firestick and Moose-jaw in unison.

"I heard what might have been a gun-shot . . . from way down the street."

"We'd better go check," said Firestick, rising also.

"Can't take no chances," agreed Moose-jaw as he, too, stood up.

The three men headed for the door. Over his shoulder, Firestick said, "You ladies stay here. Don't come near the doorway!"

A moment later the lawmen were gone.

The three ladies sat looking a little stunned by the rapid abandonment.

Until Victoria said, "Is it just me, or did anyone else fail to hear anything remotely sounding like a gunshot?"

"I certainly didn't," said Kate, scowling.

"Don't worry, gals," said Daisy matter-of-factly. "Those three scoundrels ain't runnin' *toward* the sound of gunfire. They're runnin' *away* from the sound of wedding bells. Thanks to me and my big yap. But they'll be back. And when they get here, we'll have to cut 'em some slack . . . After all, they can't help it if they're only men."

That final statement hung in the air for a moment. And then they all broke into a round of hearty laughter.

ABOUT THE AUTHORS

William W. Johnstone has written nearly three hundred novels of western adventure, military action, chilling suspense, and survival. His bestselling books include *The Family Jensen; The Mountain Man; Flintlock; MacCallister; Savage Texas; Luke Jensen, Bounty Hunter;* and the thrillers *Black Friday, The Doomsday Bunker,* and *Trigger Warning.*

J. A. Johnstone learned to write from the master himself, Uncle William W. Johnstone, with whom J. A. has co-written numerous bestselling series including The Mountain Man; Those Jensen Boys; and Preacher, The First Mountain Man.